Prai[illegible]

Once Upon a [illegible]

"Charming[illegible] rs, realistic relationshi[illegible] create a pleasant anc[illegible]

—[illegible]*ers Weekly*

"Writing this [illegible] and lively deserves to be savored. Highly recommended."

—*Library Journal* Starred Review

"Burrowes creates a powerful story replete with heartfelt emotion and rich characterization."

—*RT Book Reviews* Top Pick of the Month, 4.5 Stars

"Warmth, sensuality, and humor infuse Burrowes's writing, and fans of Suzanne Enoch and Sarah MacLean should enjoy this series."

—*Booklist*

"Grace Burrowes weaves her magic with words… a memorable love story—excellent and exquisite."

—*Long and Short Reviews*, A Best Book

"Beautiful scenery, a well-knitted family, a hint of mystery, and a love story that will wind itself around your heart. This author has a way of luring you away for a few hours of utter bliss."

—*BookLoons*

"Once again, Grace Burrowes captivated me with a wonderful story and a tender romance featuring a thoroughly engaging central couple."

—*All About Romance*

"Very few authors can build chemistry like Grace Burrowes. I loved everything about this book."

—*Books Like Breathing*

The Bridegroom Wore Plaid

A *Publishers Weekly* Best Book of the Year

"Historical details enrich Burrowes's intimate and erotic story, but the real stars are her vibrant characters and her masterful ear for dialogue. Burrowes is superb at creating connections that feel honest and real."

—*Publishers Weekly* Starred Review

"Charming… As always, Burrowes creates a character-driven novel… The slowly simmering sensuality and the strong bonds of family hold readers' interest and hearts."

—*RT Book Reviews*, 4 Stars

"This delightful Scottish Victorian romance… will engage readers with emotion and sensuality… Burrowes has a talent for filling traditional romance situations with depth and the unexpected."

—*Booklist*

"The shining, exquisite jewels of the story are the love scenes that range from frolicking fun to the soul-mate, magical, joyous love… a rich, emotion-filled tale to be enjoyed more than once."

—*Long and Short Reviews*

"Deliciously sensual, intricately plotted, and filled with a cast of appealing characters… pure pleasure."

—*Library Journal*

"A classic Grace Burrowes character-driven romance… A gently sensual romance that will remind historical romance fans why this genre never loses its appeal."

—*The Romance Reviews*

"The most fascinating facet of this book was the intense character study… It's difficult to pick this up and read it without being able to identify closely with one or more of the characters."

—*Minding Spot*

"A delicious Highland romp… A witty, sensual Victorian Scottish historical romance that will capture your imagination."

—*Romance Junkies*

"Grace Burrowes has done it again with this marvelous tale of unleashed passion and suspense… a brilliant start to a delightful series."

—*Dark Divas Reviews*

Also by Grace Burrowes

The Windhams

The Heir
The Soldier
The Virtuoso
Lady Sophie's Christmas Wish
Lady Maggie's Secret Scandal
Lady Louisa's Christmas Knight
Lady Eve's Indiscretion
Lady Jenny's Christmas Portrait
The Courtship (novella)
The Duke and His Duchess (novella)
Morgan and Archer (novella)

The MacGregors

The Bridegroom Wore Plaid
Once Upon a Tartan
Mary Fran and Matthew (novella)

The Lonely Lords

Darius
Nicholas
Ethan
Beckman
Gabriel
Gareth
Andrew
Douglas
David

The MacGregor's Lady

GRACE BURROWES

Published by Sourcebooks Casablanca, an imprint of Sourcebooks, Inc.
P. O. Box 4410, Naperville, Illinois 60567-4410
(630) 961-3900
Fax: (630) 961-2168
www.sourcebooks.com

Printed and bound in Canada.
MBP 10 9 8 7 6 5 4 3 2 1

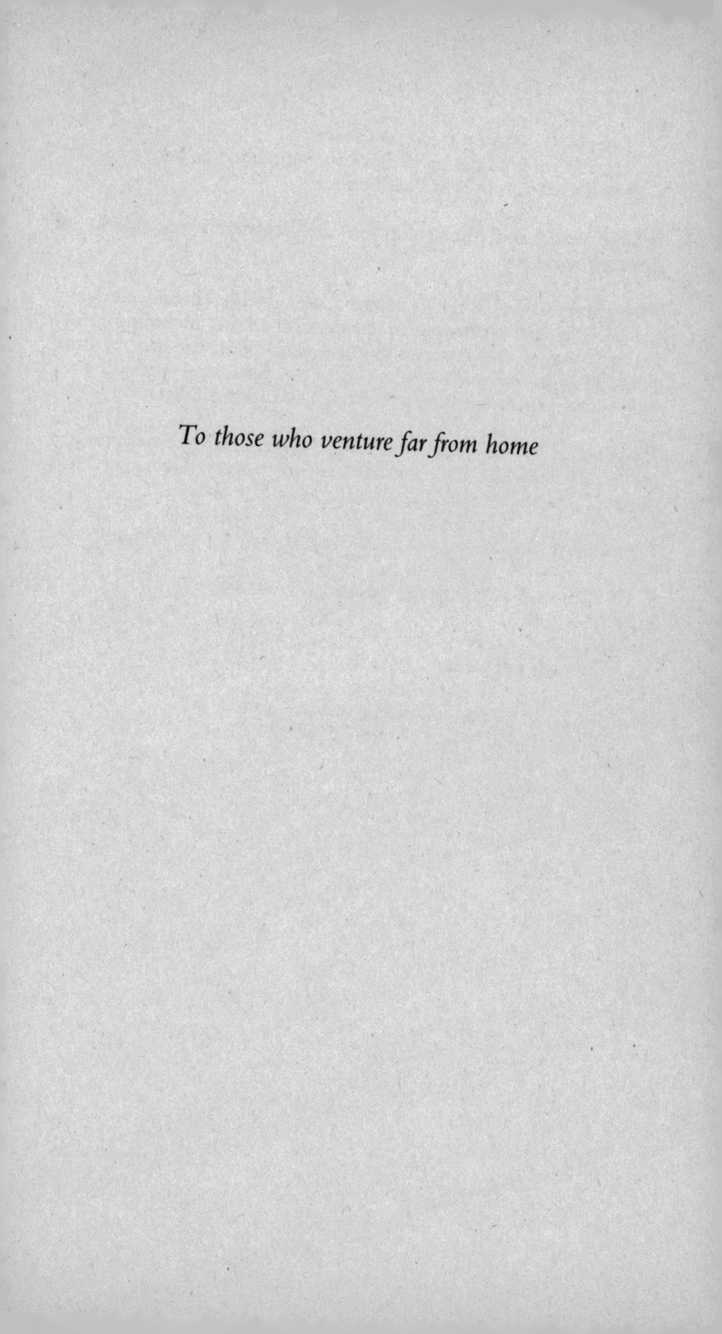

To those who venture far from home

One

ASHER MACGREGOR, NINTH EARL OF BALFOUR, HAD crossed the Atlantic five times in his thirty-some years on earth, each passage worse than the last, each leaving him a little more symbolically at sea.

And yet, he'd learned a few things in his wanderings. Though the *Harrow* had made port yesterday afternoon, her captain would wait until morning to come into Edinburgh's harbor, so he might get a day's work from his crew before they went ashore to drink and whore away their pay.

Giving Asher one more night to avoid his fate.

Asher also knew that after a winter Atlantic crossing, Miss Hannah Cooper and her aunt, Miss Enid Cooper, would be weary travelers. They had no notion the aging Baron Fenimore was using them to punish his nephew for being… what?

Being alive, very likely.

Asher climbed from the traveling coach at the docks, the heavy vehicle being the only one in his Edinburgh mews suited to dealing with muddy, slushy streets and heavy loads of baggage.

"Stay with the horses," Asher admonished the coachy and both footmen. The docks were safe enough by daylight—for docks, and particularly for a man with some height, muscle, and frontier fighting skills. Asher knew which quay would be unloading the *Harrow*'s cargoes and debarking its passengers, but the whole situation brought back memories.

Memories of being eleven years old, on just such a cold, blustery morning, on just these docks, and only servants to fetch him to the family he'd never met.

Memories of landing back on Canadian shores as a twenty-year-old, hoping for some sense of homecoming, of welcome, only to realize he wouldn't *even* be met by servants.

And two more returns to Scotland, both solitary, one at age twenty-two, and the most recent—the hardest one—less than six months past, both with a disappointing sense of bowing to an empty fate.

A lonely fate.

Dockside, a tender shipped oars and lowered a gangplank as the passengers and a small crowd on the wharf cheered. Families were reunited, travelers tried to adjust to walking on land, and one old gent creaked to his knees and kissed terra firma on the weathered and chilly wooden cheek of the wharf.

A total of six women debarked. Two were clearly of the lower orders, the younger showing sufficient symptoms of scoliosis to ensure a crabbed old age. They bustled away in the direction of a waiting mule cart, a sturdy yeoman at the reins.

Two were just as clearly wellborn, or at least well off, though the younger of this pair suffered acute strabismus. They climbed into a black-lacquered coach-and-four, two liveried footmen behind.

Leaving…

His guests. Plain but not too plain in their attire, the older one taking a bench while the younger one stood by like a protective hound, scanning the wharf for either danger or welcome. The young lady suffered neither a hunched back nor a squint, though she was afflicted with red hair.

Nearly the same shade of red hair as Asher's sister, Mary Frances.

The older woman patted the bench; the younger shook her head. Her bonnet ribbons weren't tied in a fetching, off-center bow, a sign she either wasn't seeking the approval of fashionable Society or wasn't native to Great Britain.

The younger Miss Cooper looked chilly, wary, and alone, and though she was a burden Asher had done nothing to merit, neither did she deserve to stand watch in the bitter shore breeze, courting an inflammation of the lungs.

"Ladies, I hesitate to be so bold, but if you're Miss Hannah Cooper and Miss Enid Cooper, I'm Balfour, your escort."

"Mr. Balfour." Miss Hannah bobbed a stiff curtsy, one hand braced on the back of the bench. "Pleased to make your acquaintance."

"Lord Balfour." Miss Cooper held out a hand. "Forgive my niece her form of address. We discussed it endlessly on the crossing, but we are weary and forgetful."

"And likely chilled," Asher said, bowing over the

older woman's gloved fingers. "The rest of your bags will be sent on to the town house. If I might take you to the coach?"

The aunt kept her hand in his and rose with his assistance. The young lady merely watched while Asher tucked the aunt's hand over his arm and gave a few instructions to the stevedores. He did not linger over civilities, knowing Miss Hannah's impassivity could mask fatigue, bewilderment, homesickness, and other emotions common to the weary traveler in a strange land.

"This way, ladies."

At first he thought Miss Hannah was having difficulty walking on land. After days at sea, it could be like that. The ceaseless, nauseating movement became normal, and then concentration was needed to adjust to stillness.

"How was your crossing?"

"Truly, truly unpleasant, my lord," the elder Miss Cooper said. "I dread the return trip already." She chattered on about the food, the crowding, the rough crew, the cold, the endless stench of the sea, and all manner of discomfort, and occasionally, she'd stumble a little, lean on Asher for a moment, then resume both her walking and her complaining.

When she at one point turned her face up to his with the apparent intent of batting her eyes—Uncle Fenimore must truly have taken Asher into dislike—Asher noted that the aunt's pupils were a trifle enlarged.

"Though I must say"—she paused for breath as they neared the coach—"it is exceedingly good to hear the

Queen's English spoken with the Queen's accent and intonation. It has been twenty years, you know, since such a sound graced my ears. Twenty years."

Of course he did not know, nor did he care. Miss Cooper shook her head at the sorrow of it all, and Asher glanced over his shoulder to see how this dirge was striking the niece. The poor girl had doubtless endured an ocean of such woes, for a woman dependent upon the poppy was usually a self-absorbed creature indeed.

Miss Hannah's expression was unreadable, and her remarkably ugly brown bonnet had remained on her head, despite the limp ribbons and a brisk breeze. She trundled along unevenly behind them like a servant, but her head was up and her gaze was darting all over the passing scene, like a small child on her first trip to the trading post. A coil of russet hair tried to escape the bonnet's confines near her left ear.

"This is the Balfour coach," Asher said. He handed in the older woman, then extended a hand to the niece. She glanced around one more time as if reluctant to part with the scenery—Edinburgh was a lively and beautiful city, after all—then darted into the coach after barely touching her fingers to his.

He climbed in, predictably tipping the coach with his considerable weight. When the thing righted itself—an earl's coach must be well appointed and well sprung, regardless of the expense—Asher thumped the roof with a gloved fist.

Miss Enid pulled the shade closed on her coach window, no doubt because her eyes were offended by the Scottish winter sunshine.

"Tell me, my lord, will we pass an apothecary on the way to our accommodations?"

"We shall. Edinburgh has shops aplenty, including apothecaries, though the town house is quite commodious. If you need a common medicinal, we likely have it on hand."

"I've the very worst head. Didn't I tell you, Hannah, my head would plague me terribly? A touch of the poppy might provide a little ease."

"I'm sure we can accommodate you." As much as old Fenimore grumbled about aches and pains, there was bound to be an entire pantry of nostrums and patent remedies somewhere in the house Fenimore had used as freely as if he owned it. "What about you, Miss Hannah? Has your health suffered as a result of a winter crossing?"

She was peering out the window and trying not to get caught at it. Asher didn't smile, but something of his amusement must have shown in his eyes, because she shifted her gaze to meet his, like a cannon swiveling to sight on an approaching target.

"I am in good health, thank you."

The tones were clipped, the vowels flattened, and the sound was music to Asher's cold ears. Her accent might strike some as uneducated, but it would never sound slow-witted. That accent connoted a wily mental agility, and he hadn't heard it in too long.

"Boston, if I do not mistake your accent?"

The aunt waved a hand. "Oh, the accent! There's nothing to be done, I'm afraid. She's had the best tutors, the best dancing masters, the best instructors of deportment and elocution, but none of them made any headway against that accent."

This use of the third person on a fellow occupant of the same coach, even a large coach, had the effect of compressing Miss Hannah's lips and turning her gun sights back to the streets. When she shifted her gaze, the fugitive coil of hair escaped the bonnet altogether to lie in coppery glory against her neck.

Edinburgh was a bustling place year-round. Its better neighborhoods—some of them less than fifty years old—did not empty out in summer, nor did the city limit its social activities to a mere three months in spring. Asher had enjoyed his visits here, as much as he enjoyed any city, and he rather liked Miss Hannah's curiosity about it. As the horses trotted off in the direction of the New Town, he recounted various anecdotes about the place, suspecting his guests were too tired to manage much conversation.

And all the while he talked, he watched Miss Hannah Lynn Cooper as surreptitiously as close quarters would allow.

She was a disaster of the first water in terms of fashion—something he also had to like about her. The bonnet, with its wrinkled ribbons, peculiar brown flowers, and slightly bent brim was only the beginning. Her index finger poked out of her glove. The seam wasn't frayed, the end of the finger hadn't been obviously darned, the glove was simply shot, and stained across the knuckles to boot.

Her cape was stained as well, especially around the hem. Her attire was adorned with salt, mostly, which could have been brushed off had she cared to apply a deal of effort. The aunt's clothing was in much better repair, her hems tidy, her gloves pristine and whole.

Perhaps the aunt had been waiting for landfall to take the girl in hand?

Asher wished her the joy of such an undertaking, for no amount of finery would help with the proud tilt of Miss Hannah Lynn Cooper's nose or the determined jut of her chin. Her mouth was wide, and her lips were generous. She compressed them constantly, as if to hide this backhanded gift from the Almighty.

And to go with such a definite nose and chin, the Deity had also bestowed on the woman large, agate eyes with long, velvety lashes. The eyebrows were bold slashes in dark auburn, a dramatic contrast to pale skin and coppery hair. Such features would have been handsome on a man, but on a woman they were… discordant. Arresting and attractive but not precisely pleasing.

Not boring or insipid, either.

In any case, Miss Hannah Cooper was going to be a royal project to launch socially. He'd been hoping for a giggling little heiress he could drive about in the park a few times, the kind of harmless female who'd be overcome with mortification when she misstepped. This one…

Asher prosed on about the city's history, but in the back of his mind, he had to wonder if Miss Hannah Cooper would have been more comfortable marching about the wilds of Canada than taking on the challenge of a London social Season. Northern winters were cold, but the lack of welcome in a London ballroom for those who were different, foreign, and strange could be by far colder.

Hannah had been desperate to write to Gran, but three attempts at correspondence lay crumpled in the bottom of the library waste bin, rather like Hannah's spirits.

The first letter had degenerated into a description of their host, the Earl of Balfour. Or Asher, Mr. Lord Balfour. Or whatever. Aunt had waited until after Hannah had met the fellow to pass along a whole taxonomy of ways to refer to a titled gentleman, depending on social standing and the situation.

The Englishmen favored by Step-papa were blond, skinny, pale, blue-eyed, and possessed of narrow chests. They spoke in haughty accents and weren't the least concerned about surrendering rights to their monarch, be it a king who had lost his reason or a queen rumored to be more comfortable with German than English.

Balfour was neither blond nor skinny nor narrow-chested. He was quite tall, and as muscular and rangy as any backwoodsman. He did not declaim his pronouncements, but rather, his speech had a growl to it, as if he were part bear.

When that observation had found its way onto the page, Hannah had started over.

The second draft had made a valiant attempt to compare Boston's docks with those of Edinburgh, but had then doubled back to observe that Hannah had never seen such a dramatic countenance done in such a dark palette as she had beheld on Balfour. She'd put the pen down before prosing on about his nose. No Englishman ever sported such a noble feature, or at least not the Englishmen whom Step-papa forever paraded through the parlor.

The third draft had nearly admitted that she'd wanted to hate everything about this journey, and yet, in his hospitality, and in his failure to measure *down* to Hannah's expectations, Balfour and his household hinted that instead of banishment, a sojourn in Britain might have a bit of respite about it too.

Rather than admit that in writing—even to Gran—that draft had followed its predecessors into the waste bin. What Hannah could convey was that Aunt had not fared well on the crossing. Confined and bored on the ship, Enid had been prone to frequent megrims and bellyaches and to absorbing her every waking hour with supervision of the care of her wardrobe.

Leaving Hannah no time to see to her own—not that she'd be trying to impress anybody with her wardrobe, her fashion sense, or her eligibility for the state of holy matrimony.

Her mission was, in fact, the very opposite.

Hannah eventually sanded and sealed a short note confirming their safe arrival, but how was one to post it?

Were she in Boston, she'd know such a simple thing as how to post a letter, where to fetch more tincture of opium for her aunt, what money was needful for which purchases.

"Excuse me." The earl paused in the open doorway, then walked into the room. He had a sauntering quality to his gait, as if his hips were loose joints, his spine supple like a cat's, and his time entirely his own. Even his walk lacked the military bearing of the Englishmen whom Hannah had met.

Which was both subtly unnerving and… attractive.

"I'm finished with your desk, sir." *My lord* was probably the preferred form of address—though perhaps not preferred by him. "I've a letter to post to my grandmother, if you'll tell me how to accomplish such a thing?"

"You have to give me permission to sit." He did not smile, but something in his eyes suggested he was amused.

"You're not a child to need an adult's permission." Though even as a boy, those green eyes of his would have been arresting.

"I'm a gentleman, and you're a lady, so I do need your permission." He gestured to a chair on the other side of a desk. "May I?"

"Of course."

"How are you faring here?"

He crossed an ankle over his knee and sat back, his big body filling the chair with long limbs and excellent tailoring.

"Your household has done a great deal to make us comfortable and welcome, for which you have my thanks." His maids, in particular, had Hannah's gratitude, for much of Aunt's carping and fretting had landed on their uncomplaining shoulders.

"Is there anything you need?" His gaze no longer reflected amusement. The question was polite, but the man was studying her, and Hannah bristled at his scrutiny. She'd come here to get away from the looks, the whispers, the gossip.

"I need to post my letter. When do we depart for London?"

He picked up an old-fashioned quill pen, making

his hands look curiously elegant, as if he might render art with them, or music or delicate surgeries.

"Give me your letter, Miss Hannah. I maintain business interests in Boston and correspond frequently with my offices there. As for London, we'll give Miss Enid Cooper another week or so to recuperate, and if the weather is promising, strike out for London then." He paused, and the humor was again lurking in his eyes. "If that suits?"

She left off studying his hands, hands that sported neither a wedding ring nor a signet ring. What exactly was he asking?

"I am appreciative of your generosity, but I was not requesting that you mail my letter for me. I was asking how one goes about mailing a letter, any letter, bound for Boston." Hannah disliked revealing her ignorance to Balfour, but if she was to go on with him as she intended, then his role was to show her how to manage for herself rather than to make her dependent upon him for something as simple as mailing letters.

He laughed, a low, warm sound that crinkled his eyes and had him uncrossing his legs to sit forward.

"Put up your guns, Boston. I know what it is to be a stranger in a strange land. I'll walk you to the nearest posting inn and show you how we shuffle our mail around here. If you still want to wait for the HMS Next-to-Sail, you are welcome to, but I can assure you my ships will see your correspondence delivered sooner by a margin of days if not weeks."

"Your ships?" *Plural.* Hannah made a surreptitious inspection of the library, seeing with new eyes hundreds of books, a dozen fragrant beeswax candles in addition to gas lamps, and thick, spotless Turkey carpets.

"When one is in trade with the New World, one should be in control of the means of distribution as well as the products, though you aren't to mention to a soul that you know I've mercantile interests. Shall we find that posting inn?" He rose, something that apparently did not require her permission, and came around the desk to take her hand.

"I can stand without assistance," she said, getting to her feet. "But thank you, some fresh air would be appreciated."

"We should tell your aunt we're leaving the premises."

This was perhaps another rule, or his idea of what manners required. "She's resting." Aunt was sleeping off her latest headache remedy.

His earlship peered down at her—he was even taller up close—but Hannah did not return his gaze lest she see contempt—or worse, pity—in his eyes.

"We'll leave a note, then. Fetch your cape and bonnet while I write the note."

How easily he gave orders. Too easily, but Hannah wanted to be out of this quiet, cozy house of stout gray granite, and into the sunshine and fresh air. She met him in the vestibule, her half boots snugly laced, her gloves clutched in her hand.

"Perhaps you'll want to wear your bonnet," he said as a footman swung a greatcoat over his shoulders. Hannah counted multiple capes, which made wide shoulders even more impressive. Though how such a robust fellow tolerated being fussed was what Gran would call a fair puzzlement.

The bonnet had spontaneously migrated from whatever dark closet it deserved to rot in to the sideboard in the house's entryway. "Why would I want to be seen in such an ugly thing?"

"I don't know. Why would you?"

Propriety alone required a bonnet for most occasions, but she wouldn't concede that, not when the only bonnet she'd packed was a milliner's abomination. And yet, when they gained the street, she wished she had worn her ugly bonnet.

They'd had a dusting of snow the night before, though the sun had come out and the eaves were dripping. Just as in Boston, the new snow and the sunshine created a winter brightness more piercing than the summer sun.

"A gentleman would not comment on this," her escort said as he tucked her hand over his arm, "but I notice you limp."

That arm was not a mere courtesy, as it might have been from Hannah's beaus in Boston, but rather, a masculine bulwark against losses of balance of the physical kind.

"A blind man could tell I limp from the cadence of my steps. You needn't apologize." The only people in Boston solicitous of Hannah's limp were fellows equally solicitous of her unmarried state and private fortune, but the earl could not know that.

Silence stretched, while they meandered along walks shoveled clean of snow. Hannah knew she limped, but she forgot she knew most of the time. She forgot the ache in her hip that went with it, and forgot all the times her stepfather had told her to stand up straight lest her shoulders become as crooked as her leg.

"Does it pain you?" This handsome, wealthy man was to be Hannah's escort for the next several months, for reasons she could not fathom. His tone was pleasant, his arm a sturdy support, and his question unexpectedly genuine.

Her reply was unexpectedly honest as a result. "It rarely hurts. Not unless I overdo."

"We will have to see you do not overdo, then. Shall we sit? The sun is lovely, and the less time I spend cooped up behind stone walls, the happier I am."

With that startling little revelation, he directed her to a bench in a widening in the walkway. Somebody had dusted the thing free of snow early enough that it was dry, or perhaps the February sun was that strong here in Edinburgh.

He seated her, then took a seat beside her—without asking permission. "Why are you in Great Britain, Miss Hannah Cooper?"

She'd wanted to resent Balfour, whose job it was to deliver her to London, like a federal marshal might deliver a felon for trial. And yet, she shared with the earl an appreciation for the out-of-doors, for plain speaking, and for a sunny bench. Hannah shouldn't derive a sense of kinship with Balfour on such meager footing, and yet, she did.

"I am to find a husband," she said, reciting the litany that had been shouted at her. "I am an American heiress and only a little long in the tooth, and it shouldn't be too hard to find a willing baronet's son or an aging knight."

"I see."

"What do you see?"

"You are a mendacious American heiress." The amusement was back, and maybe a hint of approval.

"And you are an overly observant English gentleman."

Another silence, while Hannah studied her bare hands and tried not to smile. Her escort wore soft kidskin gloves likely made to fit his big hands. Those gloves would feel heavenly next to the skin. Supple, warm, soft… she'd bet his were even lined with silk.

"I am not your enemy, Boston, and I am not English." His tone was gentle, but not apologetic.

"You are the instrument of my enemy, though. You are to squire me about the ballrooms and so forth, and quietly let it be known I come with a fat dowry."

He eyed her sidewise while Hannah pretended not to notice that the brilliant winter sun turned his dark hair nearly auburn.

"You honestly don't want to find yourself some minor title and swan about on his arm for the next several decades? Have a few babies to show off to your friends and relations while casually flashing a vulgar diamond or two at them as well?"

"I have never swanned in my life and I hope to die without the experience befalling me."

Swan, indeed. But the babies… Oh, damn him for mentioning the babies.

"I see."

"What do you think you see?"

"I see why the ugly bonnet," he said, rising. "Come, the posting inn is several blocks off, and I promised to show you how we go about our mails here. We should stop at a grog shop too, so you can see how we do our toddies and rum buns."

That was all he said, no lecture, no lambasting her for her unnatural inclinations, her ingratitude. The lack of resistance made Hannah uncertain, like the bright sunshine, and she leaned on him a little with the disorientation of his response. Perhaps he simply didn't care what she was about—he'd get to fritter away his spring in any case, and she really didn't intend to be a bother to him.

Not much of one, anyway.

As they walked the streets of the neighborhood, Hannah found differences between Edinburgh and Boston in the details, like tea with scones instead of bread and butter, and gas lamps taller than those at home. And were she home, she'd be accompanied by a maid and not this great, strapping man in his beautiful, warm clothing.

He walked slowly, as if he had all the time in the world, as if he hadn't seen these streets over and over in all seasons.

"You are being patient with me," Hannah said.

"I am avoiding the mountain of paperwork waiting for me back in the library. It's a pleasure to share a pint of grog with somebody who hasn't had the experience—also a bit naughty. Ladies do not usually partake of strong spirits, but cold weather provides the exception to the rule, and we're not as mindful of strictest propriety here in the North. And truly, our rum buns are not to be missed."

"A bit naughty" sounded *fun* when rendered in

those soft, dark tones, as if the earl were as much in need of a treat as Hannah might be.

Or in need of a friend with whom to enjoy a bite of forbidden bun?

Two

To Hannah's eye, the posting inn was similar to the posting inns in Boston, except it was three stories of stone, not two, the common was larger, and the stables huge, complete with fenced paddocks and enormous, steaming muck pits in the yard beside the establishment itself.

Once Hannah's note to Gran had been posted, the earl escorted Hannah to a low-ceilinged, half-timbered establishment midway between the house and the posting inn. The place boasted a few customers; one held up his pipe and nodded to her escort.

"Morning to ye."

"Will." The earl nodded but kept Hannah moving toward the rear of the common where high-backed settles faced small tables. Every wood surface in the place was dark with age, from the floors to the timbers to the tables and settles. The room was long and narrow, so the windows at the front afforded scant light, and the few lit sconces added little to it.

"It's like a cave," she said, peering around. Though Edinburgh's New Town boasted hundreds of gas lamps, gas lighting either hadn't found this enclave or was disdained in favor of ambience.

"So a patron might forget the passage of time," the earl replied. He lifted Hannah's cape from her shoulders and hung it on a hook, then hung his own coat on top of hers.

The scent of the place was intriguing—yeasty, like an alehouse might be back home, and with the same cooking odors emanating from the kitchens, but the smell had something woolly about it, too.

"Do you come here often?"

"I do. The town house is too quiet, and they let me sit here as long as I need to. I bring my paperwork, they keep the toddies or teapots coming, and a few rum buns later, I've made some progress."

To Hannah's surprise, he seated himself directly beside her, but then, there were no chairs facing the settles, so where else would he have sat?

"If you're not here to find a husband, why am I to haul you to Town for the Season, Miss Cooper?"

"You aren't going to give this up, are you?"

"I can think of a dozen places I would rather be than London in springtime, mincing around the ballrooms and formal parlors."

Hannah was heartened at the misery in his tone. "I can think of two-dozen places I'd rather be, and not a one of them would be on your list, I assure you." For his list would be in Britain, while hers would be an ocean away.

"Where would you be, Hannah Cooper, if you had your choice?"

"Home, with my grandmother." A pang of something rose up in her middle, not homesickness for the house she lived in, but a wretched, desolate longing for her grandmother's love.

"It passes." He patted her hand, his fingers stroking over her knuckles. His hand was warm, and she wished he'd do it again.

That little unexpected caress and thoughts of her grandmother had Hannah speaking aloud sentiments that could not interest the earl. "Gran is very old, and she hasn't had an easy life. I do not appreciate being made to perform in this husband-hunting farce. She isn't going to live forever."

"Is she in good health?"

"She is."

"She'll probably live another few months then. Ah, our libation arrives."

A serving maid unloaded two mugs and a plate of buns from a tray. The scents were heavenly. Rum, butter, cinnamon, clove, nutmeg…

"A toast." The earl tapped his mug against hers. "To safe journeys and worthy destinations." His comment about her grandmother had sounded offhand, a little callous, but his toast took the sting from it.

"Safe journeys," Hannah echoed. "Worthy destinations."

"Go slowly," he cautioned, taking a sip of his drink.

Rum was a sailor's drink, but Hannah was lulled into a false sense of pleasurable anticipation by the lovely bouquet of spicy, buttery scents filling her nose an instant before the spirits hit her tongue.

Those spirits bloomed, they blessed, and they burned all the way down.

She took a slightly larger sip and set the mug on the table.

"You don't approve of a lady taking spirits?" her companion asked.

Was he *teasing* her? "I shouldn't, but I approve of the medicinal tot to ward off the chill at least. New England winters are serious weather, and this is a lovely concoction."

"I'll make sure you have the recipe to take home with you. Try a bun."

He talked of his first experience of rum, on his initial crossing. The sailors had gotten him drunk with it and dared him to climb to the crow's nest. He'd made it, then fallen asleep, which meant he had to be roped down before the captain got wind of the day's mischief.

"You might have died, trying to get down."

"I might, but I didn't, and it makes an adequate tale to share over a toddy, but Miss Hannah?"

"Earl?" She was not going to my-lord him, and a troop of redcoats would likely appear posthaste if she referred to him as Mr. Earl.

"My job this spring is to see to it you snare a husband, will you, nil you." He took another sip of his drink then set the mug down beside hers.

"And if I don't want a husband?"

"My uncle Fenimore has set me this task as a sort of penance for spending nearly seven years away from my post in Scotland, or perhaps because he owes your stepfather and hates any sort of indebtedness. And yet, I owe my uncle only so much duty. I'd need a damned good reason to go to all the bother of trotting around the social Season merely for the sake of wasting your papa's money—pardon my language."

"My money," she corrected him, and his language was nothing compared to what Step-papa could unloose. "I'm an heiress, recall. My real father left me quite well off, and if I can manage to stay unwed another two years, the funds all become mine."

She should not have told a stranger such a thing, but this stranger had understood why she needed to see her letter to Gran mailed herself, and this stranger was likely the only earl in captivity who loathed fashionable ballrooms as much as Hannah did.

"You can't trust yourself to find a man who'll take good care of both you and your money?"

His question was reasonable, and yet, Hannah hadn't heard it before.

"I notice you haven't any Mrs. Earl."

"Point for the lady," he said, lips quirking. "I'm to hunt one up this spring, but alas, I've no more heart for the quest than you do."

"So what's your damned good reason for braving the ballrooms?" She took another sip of the lovely concoction, though the company was a bit lovely too. "Why squire me about and appear to look over the possibilities when you're not going to make any offers?"

"Perhaps I'll be proven wrong. Perhaps some enterprising little filly will snare me and lead me off to be put in double harness."

"As if you're a coach horse? Strong, sound of wind and limb, but not elegant enough for a hack or nimble enough for work over fences?"

He ran his finger in a slow circle around the rim of his mug. "An excellent question. Rum tends to bring out the imponderables. No doubt the Greeks invented it, and by rights the drink ought to be dubbed the Progenitor of Philosophy." He fell silent for a moment, as if considering this profundity. "We seem to be contemplating similar exercises in futility for the coming Season."

"Your secret is safe with me, sir."

She reached for another bun just as he did, and their hands bumped.

"After you, miss."

She took up a bun, broke it in half, and passed him the larger portion. "You're supposed to say my secret is safe with you."

"Bun-swearing," he said, regarding his pastry. "A kind of alimentary fealty my mother's family would have understood all too well, except you aren't making any secret of your shameless intentions. You're going to waste a great deal of good coin on dresses and dancing slippers, spend many nights out until dawn, leading the unsuspecting swains around by their noses, then laugh them to scorn and catch the next ship for Boston. Not very sporting of you."

And yet, he sounded more impressed than envious.

"Not very sporting of my stepfather to send me away from everything and everyone I love to cross the Atlantic in winter, now was it?"

Hannah wished dear Step-papa might see the scowl her words provoked from the earl. "Not sporting at all, but you're here. Why not make the best of it?"

"What best is there to make of it?" she said, dipping her bun in her drink. "I cannot marry here, else I'll have to spend the rest of my days an ocean away from everybody and everything I hold dear."

"England isn't such a bad place." He studied his drink, as if he were repeating a litany that had never been convincing. "England is pretty, in truth, and there's a lot of variety on one island. I thought I'd go mad missing Canada, but I knew by my first winter in Great Britain there were compensations for leaving Canada. By the second winter, I was mostly complaining about going home to reassure myself I had a home."

Canada? What was a Scottish peer doing wandering around Canada, and what had compelled him to return home?

"You're saying I could learn to like it here." She could certainly learn to like rum buns dipped in grog, and Scottish earls who commiserated with American heiresses. "Eventually, perhaps I could, but I cannot leave my grandmother to fight all the battles with Step-papa. If he had his way, he'd leave her in the servants' parlor, swilling tea and knitting."

"You're protective of this grandmother, which speaks well of you." He broke another bun in half, this time giving her the larger share. "Is she growing vague?"

"Hardly." Hannah nibbled the bun, finding the earl's approval as sweet as the icing. To air her situation like this was a relief of some sort—one she hoped she would not regret. "Gran is old, and she has no one else. She was my father's mother, and she's all I have left of him."

"That doesn't rule out finding a husband who would settle with you in Boston." Balfour spoke gently, as if Hannah might not have reasoned her way to this solution on her own.

"Oh, of course. Some knight twice my age is going to give up all his comforts and honors to brave New England winters and never see his cronies again?"

"It is possible. Many people have found worthy spouses in unlikely locations." His pronouncement had the ring of a tired admonition, not a declaration of unflagging optimism.

"Eat your bun," Hannah said, passing him his uneaten sweet. "Anything is possible, sir. You could find the bride of your dreams in an unlikely location as well."

He said nothing, but gobbled up the rest of his rum bun in about two bites, then rose and held out his hand.

Hannah regarded the large palm, the elegant fingers, the perfectly rounded clean fingernails, the slight callus on the fourth finger from years of holding snaffle reins. Perhaps not strictly gentlemanly hands, but they suited Balfour.

She gave him her hand, and he drew her to her feet.

Still holding her hand, he looked down at her, his expression serious. This close, Hannah caught his contribution to the ambient scents, a clean, bracing male fragrance that put her in mind of spices and sea breezes.

"I will make a promise with you, Hannah Lynn Cooper. I will make a good-faith effort to find a bride, if you will make a good-faith effort to find a husband."

She considered his hand, wrapped around hers. His skin was darker than hers, as if he had Mediterranean blood.

"I can make that promise." If good faith was merely

the absence of bad faith. "I am not optimistic that I will be successful finding a spouse."

He brought her fingers to his lips, and brushed her a kiss that was mostly air plus a touch of warmth and gallantry. When he had given her back her hand, he plucked his coat from the hook, then shuffled the wraps so he could settle her cape around her shoulders first. He shrugged into his coat but didn't button it.

"The rum has warmed me up," he said, winging an arm. "If I am not mistaken, we're due for a thaw, and we'll have nothing but sunshine and mud for the rest of this week, followed of course, by the inevitable blizzard."

He sounded like a Yankee farmer, daring the weather to try to trick him with its inconveniences.

Hannah needed his arm, between the wet cobblestones, her limp, and the rum. He was utterly solid, his pace was sedate, and given the way his coat had hung over hers, his scent was wafting into her nose. Cinnamon, clove, nutmeg, a little ginger, and a dash of sea travel.

His scent reminded her of the rum buns, but in the privacy of her thoughts, Hannah admitted the earl's fragrance was the more attractive.

Asher had caught the lady, though only barely. That was the good news, but the bad news…

Damn and blast if the old man hadn't given Asher an impossible task. Bad enough Asher was to go bride hunting, bad enough he had to drag this red-haired American rebel-spinster-heiress around with him, bad enough she would limp onto the dance floor if she could even dance, worse yet he *liked* the infernal woman, but now he'd nearly dropped her on a patch of ice, and her locomotion was further jeopardized.

"She was bobbing along beside me, enjoying the air, and then she hit a patch of wet ice, and down she went," Asher told the aunt. Miss Hannah had nearly taken him with her, too, so frantically had she struggled to maintain her balance.

The aunt shrugged as she took a sip of her wine. "She falls occasionally. When she was younger, my brother ordered that all of Hannah's clothes be in plain dark colors so the mud wouldn't show. Fortunately, she has gained some poise."

"She doesn't wear dark colors exclusively now, I hope? Here the darker colors are mostly for married women, widows, older companions, and so forth." And the darkest colors were for mourning, to which Miss Hannah might well consider herself entitled.

"You will have to take this up with her." Miss Cooper gestured with her glass of claret, spilling a drop on the pristine tablecloth. "Do you know what a pleasure it is to have Continental wines of an evening? Back home, they are a rare and expensive treat."

"I'm glad you're enjoying yourself." If chronic mild inebriation could be called enjoying oneself. "Assuming your niece recovers adequately, by the end of next week I'd like to depart for London, where the selection of all manner of delicacies will be superior."

"We are in your hands, my lord. My brother told

me to show you every respect, so I must trust your judgment in all matters."

She batted her lashes, and Asher felt a lick of dyspepsia to think the woman might be flirting with him.

"Madam, if you will excuse me, rather than chase you to the parlor for your tea, I'll leave you the table so you might linger over your wine and cheese."

He bowed and left the dining parlor at a swift walk, knowing he was being rude. Let her have her Continental wines, and he'd have his guilty conscience. It was a companion of long standing, not quite an old friend, but the next best thing—a familiar enemy.

Asher found Miss Hannah in her sitting room, her foot propped under a blanket while she reclined on a chaise near the fire. He knocked on the slightly open door, then let himself in, leaving the door ajar as a nod to propriety.

"Good evening, Miss Cooper. How can you read with the lamps turned so low?" And why would she be reading, when she might have turned to any one of her aunt's various patent remedies instead?

"When I started to read it was quite light," she said, putting down a bound version of *David Copperfield*.

"You have bellpulls in America." He fingered the strip of tasseled brocade dangling above her. "Why not have a maid turn up the lamps, refresh your tea, and generally cosset you?"

"Cosset?" She gave him a thin-lipped look, as if this was one of those words that meant something altogether less savory on this side of the Atlantic. Woe unto the London swains who merited that look from her.

"So you neither swan nor permit cosseting," he concluded, moving around the room to turn up the lamps. "Are you comfortable enough? The physician said you could have some laudanum."

Her expression grew, if anything, more severe.

"This is growing to be a long list, Hannah Cooper." He sat on the raised hearth at her side. "No cosseting, no swanning, no laudanum. One wonders what you do for recreation." Though given her aunt's proclivities, he could understand that last prohibition.

"I love to read." She traced a finger over the gilt lettering of the book's title, gently, as if poor Trot's peregrinations through life's vicissitudes comforted her.

"You're going to love to shop, too," Asher said. "Your aunt abdicated decision-making authority in this sphere to me at dinner, so be warned."

She closed the book with a snap, a peacock feather marking her place. "I most assuredly do not love to shop, not for clothing, if that's what you're implying."

He rose and shifted the fireplace screen, then pokered some air into the coals and layered wood and coal on the blaze.

"We don't burn as much coal in Boston," his guest observed. "It has a distinctive aroma."

Coal smoke purely stank, and in Asher's experience, aggravated the lungs. The longhouse had been full of smoke too, though, and that had resulted in all manner of consumptive ailments.

"I prefer wood smoke myself." And starry nights, too. Since returning to Scotland this time, he'd even lain awake, missing the howling of the wolves.

Asher repositioned the screen and resumed his

perch on the hearth. "England has more coal than trees, or it soon will, so needs must. Let's make a list of things you're going to fight me on, shall we?"

"A list?" She caressed the *o* in Copperfield, drawing attention to pale hands, the backs of which sported a deal of fetching, unfashionable freckles.

"Clothing being foremost. Shoes, gloves, hats being assumed additions. Did anyone bring you a tray?"

"I had some cheese toast—a wonderful cheddar with caraway in the bread."

She had hearty appetites, apparently, and her tastes were not too refined—this was more evidence of impending social disaster, but Asher liked her for it.

"I prefer rye bread to the standard brown bread, myself. But back to our list. Under present circumstances, I blush to inquire, but do you dance?"

A look crossed her features, so fleeting he would have missed it, except he was studying the exact arch and swoop of her dark eyebrows.

"I do not."

But she wanted to. That's what that look was about, *longing*. Miss Hannah Lynn Cooper wasn't entirely resigned to her unswanning, I-love-to-read spinsterhood. She longed to dance.

"Let's have a look at your foot." Asher shifted to sit near her legs on the chaise. He was presuming, flirting with naughtiness, even, but he needed to offer her a good distraction for the ensuing topic.

"That is not necessary." She drew back against the chaise as if a malodorous cat had appropriated a place at her feet. "The physician said it should heal nicely in a few days."

"He said we're to keep you off your feet for a few days, at least." Asher drew back the blanket, revealing a slender, elegant foot. "He said it's fortunate I carried you back to the house, or your injury might have been even worse for trying to put weight on it all that distance."

As if Asher would ever again allow any woman to risk harm to her person when he was in a position to prevent it.

And how Hannah Cooper had suffered to be in his arms, remaining stiff and silent until pain alone had inspired her to hold onto him. Asher still hadn't sorted out his feelings regarding those few blocks, the last woman he'd carried in the same manner being Monique. By the time he'd reached the house, Miss Cooper's arms had been around his neck, and her face turned to his shoulder.

While his remorse had weighed more than she had.

"This is a minor bruise," he said, drawing his finger over the faint purpling around the base of her tibia. "You do not strike me as a lady to dramatize her injuries."

She wouldn't *admit* her injuries, if she could help it.

"Do the gentlemen here often use a lady's indispositions to fondle her person?" Her tone was wonderfully dry, her accent amplifying the effect. He sensed she was not offended by his presumption, so much as she was uncertain.

"When the gentleman is thoroughly schooled as a physician, he might use his knowledge the better to care for his injured guest." God help the woman if her definition of fondling was so *pedestrian*. "You kept the ice on it?"

"No, I danced a few jigs," she said, running a finger over the edge of the peacock feather protruding from the book. "I should not have imbibed the rum, so if you're blaming yourself, you can stop. You never said you were a doctor."

His admission had been more careful than that—and he *wasn't* a doctor, not any longer. "What had a tot of rum to do with this?" He traced the bruise, a distortion of an otherwise perfect, graceful foot.

"My gait is unsteady enough, and I knew well the condition of the walks. Rum wasn't going to help me stay on my feet."

Her second toe was longer than her first, as Monique's had been, but Miss Cooper had higher arches. Asher stuffed that thought away, unfairly annoyed with his guest for inspiring it. "So you blame yourself for a little slip, deny yourself adequate lights to read by, and forgo a decent dinner? Will that be punishment enough?"

He closed his hand around her foot, for it was cold and wanted comforting—her foot, that is.

"You are blaming yourself, aren't you, Balfour? This is a duty visit, or do I mistake the matter?"

He slipped a second hand under her ankle and held her foot with both hands. The bones were all where they should be, the tendons in their assigned locations. Nothing about her foot was distorted or misshapen, save for the unfortunate bruise.

All in all, an elegant, functional foot.

"I was your escort, my job by definition to shield you from harm, and I suspect the problem is not with your foot at all, but with your *os coxae* or lumbar vertebrae—your hips or lower spine."

She frowned at her foot as it lay in his grasp, but did not draw it back. "Possibly both, but consider this: had I landed on my backside or my hip, the damage would likely have been much worse. In answer to your earlier question, I do not dance. I do not dare."

Miss Cooper hated making that admission. Asher kept hold of her chilly foot. "For fear you'll fall?"

"Yes, and lest you think the humiliation alone deters me, there is also the risk of further injury. I fell while skating as a child, and the bones didn't knit correctly, hence the limp. The physicians assure me I am as sturdy as the next young lady, but I dread having two misshapen limbs."

She hadn't any misshapen limbs that he could see. He shifted his grip on her foot. "You are too cold."

He hadn't meant the comment to refer to anything other than her foot, but she drew in a swift breath, as if he might have intentionally offended with the deeper meaning. Whatever else was true, Boston society had not been entirely kind to Miss Cooper—or to Asher, at first.

"You've built up the fire," she said. "Thank you."

He set her foot back down on its pillow, her gratitude as chilly as her injured appendage. He reached past her, which had the bothersome result of her flinching away from him, and took a folded afghan from behind her head.

He stood to drape the blanket over one side of the hearth screen. "Shall I send your aunt to you?"

"Why would you do that?"

She was rattled. Direct she might be, but Hannah Cooper wouldn't offer such a graceless retort unless she were unnerved. "To play cards with you? To talk? To read to you?"

"Recall, please, that I just spent weeks in close quarters with my aunt."

Tonight, she had an answer for everything, did Boston. A prickly, off-putting, almost rude answer. Had Asher never felt out of place himself, never struggled with homesickness or a weariness of spirit as wide as an entire ocean, never longed for one place on earth where he could feel safe and included, he might have obliged the woman with the solitude she thought she wanted.

But the terrain Miss Hannah Cooper traversed was all too familiar to him, so Asher took the warmed afghan from the hearth screen, tucked it gently around the lady's foot, then picked up her book from its place at her side, passed her the peacock feather, and began to read from the top of the page.

Everything about the blasted man was beautiful.

Blasted. Less than a week in Scotland, and Hannah was appropriating the local vocabulary, and with just provocation.

Balfour's features were beautiful, far more dramatically so than the typical blond, bland exponent of English aristocracy. His brows were definite, dark, and a trifle swooped at the edges, but they also had a mink-soft look to them, as if a lady might enjoy tracing her finger along their arch. Repeatedly. Both at the same time, and the pads of her thumbs, too.

Hannah was fascinated with his nose, as well, by the nobility of it, the way it finished off a face that belonged on some Highland leader of old.

His hands had been gentle and warm on her foot. His touch had held no presumption, only comfort and strength. And what strength he had, lifting her against his chest as if she weighed nothing. He'd gotten them back to the house at a far more brisk pace than he'd set with Hannah gawking and tottering at his side. She'd been reluctant to lift her nose from his collar, so lovely was the spicy scent of him up close.

His voice was every bit as enticing and dark as the rest of him, and Hannah was tempted to close her eyes and let that voice seduce her to sleep. It could, his words were that powerful, that beautiful in the ear.

The only saving mercy from Hannah's perspective was that if she worked at it diligently, she might resent the man in possession of all these lovely attributes. He gave orders, and worse, he apparently *took* orders that included herding her through the ordeal of a social Season. She gained some consolation from the idea that he was herding himself right along with her, though of course he would be snatched up in the first week.

And Aunt wasn't going to interfere, which was a relief. Worse than Hannah's limp would be the immediate perception that her only relation was dependent on tinctures and medicinal tots from day to day.

"You're falling asleep."

Hannah opened her eyes slowly. "I'm enjoying the story, thank you. If you'd like to leave, I'm sure a maid will be along shortly."

"Of course." He put the book aside and tugged on the bellpull. "*Now* a maid will be along shortly. Let's get you to bed, shall we?"

Before Hannah could protest, he'd scooped her up against his chest. Without winter clothes between them, the embrace was more intimate than it had been earlier in the day.

"Arms around my neck, Boston. We can't court further mishap with you already injured."

She complied, feeling the heat of him and that wonderfully spicy scent wrapping around her.

"I can't believe you agreed to my request without making some tart protest," he said as he crossed the room with her. "I'm heartened is what I am. Cheered even."

"Cheeky is what you are, isn't that the English word?" she said as they moved into the bedroom.

"For God's sake, why wasn't the fire lit?"

He lowered her to the bed and saw to the oversight, pumping the daylights out of a set of bellows to get a roaring blaze going.

"Here." He lifted her up and sat her in a rocking chair near the fire.

"I am not a piece of masonry, to be hoisted about without my permission."

"I'm running the warmer over your sheets, Boston. Perhaps you'd rather get into a cold bed in a cold room and try to manage on your own?"

Must he sound so amused? *Must* he be so thoughtful? "The maid can see to my sheets."

"Now that somebody has considerately rung for a maid."

He disappeared into the other room and came back with the afghan. The afghan he'd warmed and wrapped around her foot with such care and comfort

Hannah had been hard put not to melt. It almost, not quite but almost, had served as consolation for the loss of his warm hands wrapped around that same foot.

"Up you go." He lifted her again, and she participated to the extent her arms were around his neck. He set her down on the bed and delivered another magnificent scowl.

"You do that so well, sir."

"Hoist you about?"

That too. "Frown, express displeasure, disapproval." She shifted on the mattress, because it was cold. Blasted cold.

"I don't want to leave you until the maid comes along," he said, hands on hips. "And I don't think for a minute a nibble of cheese toast was an adequate meal."

"So I should have supper in bed?"

She was hungry, but God was in charity with her, for her stomach didn't rumble very loudly.

"You should be spanked soundly," he said on a sigh.

Step-papa would certainly have agreed.

The maid appeared in the doorway, a hefty young woman with a clean, full-length apron to her credit and her cap neatly tied.

"You'll get Miss Hannah tucked in, please," the earl said. "And mind her foot is injured, and her sheets cold. In future, her bedroom fire is to be lit when we get up from table, the same as every other bedroom."

The maid bobbed a curtsy. "Of course, milord."

He left on that grouchy little scold, and Hannah felt abruptly both the fatigue of a long day and a mild throbbing in her right *os whatever.*

He'd been right about that too: she'd barely twisted her ankle, but the wrench to her hip and back had been as significant as the injury to her dignity.

"I can stand beside the bed while you use the warmer," Hannah said. "The room really is a little chilly."

"It is," the maid said, "and I do apologize, mum, but your aunt is still in the dining room, enjoying an aperitif, and we typically don't see to the bedrooms until the ladies have arisen from the table. Saves on coin that way. Shall I braid your hair?"

As the room gradually became more comfortable, they managed Hannah's hair. The maid was running the warmer over the sheets again when another maid appeared, tray in hand.

"His lordship says you missed supper," the second maid explained. "He said you wasn't to get cranky and peckish."

Hot chocolate sprinkled with cinnamon sat near a pair of rum buns.

If reading Dickens to her hadn't won a bit of her heart, the offerings on the tray surely did.

Hannah propped up her pillows and lay back on her warmed sheets. She took a nibble of delicious rum bun, wrapped her hands around the mug of hot chocolate, and wondered if all the titled, handsome gentlemen she'd meet here would be possessed of such good manners.

And such warm hands.

Three

"A BLOODY DAMNED BIT OF SNOW ISN'T GOING TO KEEP me from leaving the house."

Asher directed his foul language at no one in particular, for at this time of the morning the study was empty of living creatures save himself and a large black-and-orange house cat curled up on a hassock near the fire.

The specter of Uncle Fen's disapproving presence hung close by though, as close as Asher's elbow, where the baron's latest epistle sat on the massive desk, its meek appearance belying its vituperative content.

"You will make all haste for London, the ladies being your responsibility to see suitably housed, attired, and introduced."

The last word was the stinging tail of the lash: *introduced*… As if Asher himself had more than nominal and begrudging entrée among the baron's titled peers and cronies. Asher and the Cooper women would be the socially blind leading the blind.

Or the lame. After two days in bed, Miss Hannah Cooper was much recovered from her injury, recovered enough he need not haul her about in his arms.

Asher was not recovered. Not from the sight of her helpless and in pain, not from the sense of having failed in so simple a task as escorting a lady, and not—God help him—from the realization that holding a woman's foot could be intensely erotic when it wasn't supposed to be.

He knew about women's feet—phalanges and metatarsals, *peroneous tertius*, *brevis*, and *longus*—but he also knew about women purely in the sense a man appreciates the Creator's more refined effort. Knew about their ears and napes and fingers and bellies, and all the luscious parts of them that could be turned to the service of their arousal and Asher's pleasure. Yes, feet could be erotic, but they were supposed to mind their mundane business until Asher recruited them for the business of seduction.

Not even seduction, for he'd never had to seduce a woman, not since he'd turned fifteen and the ladies had started seducing him.

But here he was, haunted by the feel of a lady's foot, soft and cool against the callused palms of his hands. He'd long since accepted that grief did not permanently inoculate a man against arousal, but this, this fascination for a woman who wanted no part of England, Scotland, and the fellows to be found there—

"Bah!"

The cat opened unblinking green eyes.

"I'm to haul them to London, weather be damned, and believe me, cat, the weather will be evil. Every God's blessed aspect of this misadventure will bend to the baron's need to see his heir suffering and miserable."

The cat squeezed her eyes closed in a display of feline indifference.

"Maybe I should make you come with us."

More indifference, reminding Asher of the elders among whom he'd been raised. They weren't indifferent, though, so much as stoic. Anybody who could withstand sixty Canadian winters with nothing but a longhouse and a meager fire between them and the elements had stoicism running in their veins.

And those were his people too.

Asher leafed through the rest of the mail delivered that morning. One thin missive had crossed the Atlantic mere days after its intended recipient: Hannah Cooper had a letter from home, something bound to raise her spirits. Asher hooked his spectacles back around his ears and peered at the letter.

Many people still didn't bother with the expense of an envelope, but Hannah came from money, from people with pretensions to class in so far as the United States boasted of same. Still, the man penning this letter hadn't bothered to limit his sentiments to the inside of the folded paper, but rather, had scratched his message so the last of it could be read on the outside.

"You have disgraced your family, and the only solution remaining is to situate you where you might never again bring shame down upon my house, where you are firmly established as some other man's problem. This is your last chance, Stepdaughter. I suggest you make the most of it."

What had Hannah Cooper done to invite such an admonition? Smiled at some beamish farm boy? Leaned a little too closely on a widower's arm?

Cheered too loudly at a race meet? He could not see the woman now contentedly reading one floor above him disgracing herself in any meaningful sense.

Even if she did have the most erotically appealing feet it had ever been Asher's torment to hold.

He stuffed that thought back into the dark closet from whence it had escaped, and took the little epistle to Miss Cooper's sitting room.

She looked up at him, setting *Copperfield* face down in her lap. "To what do I owe the pleasure, sir?"

She had her feet up on a hassock, and an afghan swaddling both legs. Asher had the sense she'd taken to the comfort like the feline in his study, instinctively seeking warmth and ease to save against the times when there would be none.

"I bring you an epistle from home," he said, making no move to pass her the letter. "Have you enough light to read it?"

"If it's from Grandmother, she doesn't write cursive, so yes, I have adequate light."

He settled on the hearth, blocking some of that light.

"I gather it isn't from your grandmother." He passed her the letter and watched the eager light in her eyes wink out like a snuffed candle.

"Step-papa, then." She took the letter and slit it open, glancing at the contents. "A little sermon, lest I forget his many attempts to guide me into the arms of the suitors of his choice."

"You're finicky. Somehow, one might guess this about you." And she was bitterly disappointed not to hear from this old granny of hers.

"I'm female. We're given to odd notions." She set

the letter aside unread—Asher suspected the missive would shortly end up in the fire—and made as if to resume disporting with Master Copperfield.

"Odd notions such as?"

She returned the book to her lap and gazed past him, into the fire. "I would like to be held in affection by my spouse, not merely tolerated for my fortune, for one thing."

"Affection doesn't strike me as too odd a notion." Though affection for her? A fellow would have to scale the battlements of her disappointment and self-sufficiency, bare his soul, and place his heart entirely in her hands.

But what a lucky fellow he'd be, if she surrendered her heart in return.

"I would like my spouse to take me to wife whether I've a great fortune or only a modest dowry."

"Many men marry women with modest dowries." Many men with modest expectations, or personal fortunes of their own. Perhaps those were in short supply in Boston.

"Men generally only marry women of modest means when the fellow's heart is engaged."

"Affection and means of his own, then," Asher said, and he wanted to add some deprecating little aside, except Boston wasn't being unreasonable at all. Affection in a marriage would be… wonderful.

It had been wonderful.

"Does that smile suggest you are laughing at me, sir?"

"Was I smiling? I thought I was agreeing with you. Is your stepfather so easily disappointed that your modest requirements foiled his ambitions for you?"

"He presented me several choices, all of them beholden to him or deeply indebted to him or even in his employ. I considered each man and declined them one by one. He presented more, and more, until I realized he wasn't going to stop."

"What did you do?" Because clearly, she'd taken control of the situation somehow.

She used her peacock-feather bookmark to stroke her chin, the gesture distracting as hell. "I rejected those too."

"You'll have a whole crop of dandies to choose from when we reach London," he said. Miss Hannah Cooper wasn't being honest with him, not about her romantic past, in any case. "You will consider them too, I hope, and find at least one worthy of your hand."

"What of you? Will you be considering the crop of ladies available to become Mrs. Lord Balfour?"

"Lady Balfour," he corrected her, though he knew she was being Colonial on purpose, as he had often been Scottish on purpose, or even Mohawk. "And yes, I am specifically charged with that happy task."

"You're laughing at me again." She picked up her book and ran her finger halfway down the page. "Not well done of you."

He had to smile. Her choice of expression was British, the rebuke all the more effective for her crisp accent.

"Perhaps I'm laughing at myself. If you could spare me a few more minutes of your busy day?"

She did not put her book down but turned to gaze out the window. "It's pouring snow out there, and you have a wonderful library. Forgive me for appreciating it—at your invitation."

"Despite the snow, I am also charged with getting you and your aunt safely to London post-haste. My uncle the baron has suggested we depart several days hence."

This time she batted her nose with the peacock feather, and Archer had to study the frigid weather lest he snatch the feather from her. "Aunt is not one to put up with discomforts silently."

Unlike Miss Hannah Cooper, who had not once complained about her disability, nor had she complained about her stepfather, exactly. She'd answer Asher's questions, albeit only up to a point.

"If we can't take an express train, we'll go in easy stages. The inns along the main routes boast decent accommodations, so your aunt should have no cause for complaint."

"She will complain, though. Aunt has prodigious ability when it comes to manufacturing complaints."

She studied her infernal feather, while Asher caught the ghost of a smile tilting her lips up.

A smile?

"You want us delayed," he said. "You're enjoying this storm, looking forward to the lousy roads, the delayed trains, hoping they mean you miss the start of the Season."

"They can't possibly," she said. "It's barely March. The Season won't start until the second week of April this year."

"But you'll need a wardrobe." He rose from the hearth to pace. "You'll need mounts for riding in the park and driving at the fashionable hour. You'll need calling cards printed up, and stationery for accepting or declining invitations. You'll need to hire ladies' maids for you and your aunt."

And every one of those needs, Asher would have to see to.

He stopped and speared her with a look. "You plan on fighting me every step of the way, don't you? You won't like the clothing made to order for you. You won't choose a maid until the very last minute. Your schedule won't allow you to try out the horses I select for you, and it will all be in aid of thwarting a stepfather who has tried hard to see you well situated."

And while Asher might commend the lady's fighting spirit—he *did* commend her fighting spirit—he did not at all appreciate that she'd be making a hash of his efforts to endure a Season of Polite Society at the same time.

His brothers Ian, Connor, and Gilgallon, and his sister Mary Fran had all acquired English connections, and to the extent that Asher owed his family, good impressions in London were devoutly to be wished.

Miss Cooper rose as well, shedding her blankets to face him as he glared down at her.

"Were I to engage in such antics, sir, it would be in aid of maintaining my freedom. My stepfather didn't try hard to see *me* situated, he tried hard to see *my fortune* situated under his fat, greedy thumb. I read the proposed settlements, and my prospective husbands were not to have control of my money. He controls *me* now, and he wants to control my money when I marry. He went to great lengths in the attempt. I'm prepared to go to greater lengths to see him thwarted."

She believed what she was saying; Asher concluded that much from the fire in her eyes. "Is he wasting your fortune?"

"He can't." She turned away and went to the window, her limp barely noticeable. "Papa, my real papa, set it up so there are trustees, but they lose authority when I marry or turn six-and-twenty. Papa intended my husband to take over management of my funds, but the marriage settlements simply turn the husband's authority over to Step-papa. He's greedy, not stupid."

"Or he's prudent."

"If he's so prudent, why doesn't he find me a fellow who isn't beholden to anyone? A man who's made his own fortune and will understand how to make the best use of mine? A man who will put that money in trust for our children, for our daughters especially?"

They were good questions, questions the lady's mother should have been asking the stepfather at least. One of Asher's first tasks upon returning to Scotland had been to read Mary Fran's settlement with her English baron. Fortunately, Ian, who'd held the earldom at the time, was a canny negotiator, and Mary Fran and little Fiona were well set up.

"Your stepfather is an ocean away," Asher said. "Nobody can make you marry a man against your will."

"No, they can't. It has already been attempted." Her spine was ramrod straight at this disclosure.

"Did you cry off?"

She nodded once, back still turned.

Oh, Miss Cooper. "You left him literally at the altar?"

"Not alone." She turned to face Asher, arms

crossed over her chest. "When the minister asked if I took that man, I answered as loudly as I could in the negative, before the entire congregation. I said he was my stepfather's choice, not mine, and if Step-papa was so in love with the man, then Step-papa could marry him, for I wanted no part of him. None."

She was in utter, jaw-clenched earnest, and she'd humiliated both her stepfather and her intended as publicly as she possibly could.

"I see." He *saw* she was expecting him to lecture or rebuke or perhaps—worse than either—to laugh. How he wished Mary Fran had exercised the same determination where her late first husband had been concerned. "Then you realize you can enjoy spring in Town, enjoy leading the callow swains around by their noses, enjoy all the female fripperies of fashionable Society, and leave a trail of broken hearts when you return to the wilds of Boston."

"Boston hasn't any wilds, though Massachusetts does."

Half the Irish who'd survived the famine had ended up in Boston, and more than a few stray Highlanders too, making the place wild enough. Asher chose not to share that opinion.

"Boston has you," he said, a reluctant smile blossoming. "That should suffice to introduce a complement of savagery to the place."

"Yes." Her chin came up, and she presented him a dazzling, toothy smile. "It most certainly should."

Aunt Enid entertained herself with a number of games, one of which Hannah had dubbed "if only." The object of "if only" was to remind Hannah obliquely, and with the very best intentions, of course, of what lay in wait at home should Hannah fail to snabble an English husband. Aunt had started the present round as the coach had pulled out of the mews in Edinburgh to take them to the Waverly station. Snow made the going difficult, and as the morning became colder and more grim, the game wore on.

"If only you hadn't made such a public scene with young Mr. Widmore. He was in expectation of a barony, you know."

"He was a third son sent to America to escape some scandal with a female, and he was entirely Step-papa's creature. He deserved what befell him." Hannah turned her face to the window, where the bleak expanse of the North Sea lay visible in the distance.

"No man deserves to be treated that way by a woman he has offered for."

"He's not a man," Hannah said. "He's an errand boy seeking to be richly rewarded for doing Step-papa's bidding. I think it's going to snow again."

"If only you weren't so stubborn, Hannah. My brother tries merely to see to your welfare."

"If it snows enough, we'll be stranded at some inn. That would serve nicely, because I brought some of Lord Balfour's books along. He has the nicest selection of novels."

"Novels, bah. If only you were more given to the pursuits of a normal girl, Hannah. You'd be content to do embroidery and read improving pamphlets."

Hannah let that pass, for she'd never been exactly sure how much of the Widmore debacle Aunt understood. They didn't discuss it, and Aunt Enid brought it up only when she was running perilously low on sermon topics or wandering mentally after a surfeit of some tonic or nostrum.

"If the trains aren't running, do you suppose his lordship will force us to travel in this wretched weather?" Enid asked.

Now that was a first, for Aunt to criticize anything remotely British, and they hadn't even boarded their southbound train.

"I suspect, one way or another, we'll start our journey as long as we have light," Hannah said. In truth, the traveling coach was a great, lumbering conveyance, but it was well sprung and cozy enough. They'd brought hot bricks for the floor and hot water bottles for the ladies' muffs, and because they would stop to change horses every twelve to fifteen miles, the interior would stay fairly comfortable.

If stuffy.

"Dear, can you reach my traveling bag?"

"You just had a dose of your tincture, Aunt, right before we left the house."

"But I have the most awful head, Hannah. If only you understood such pain, not that I'd wish it on my worst enemy."

"You need to be using less, Aunt, not more. How will you keep up with the social calendar I'm expected to maintain if you're sleeping off your headache remedies until midday every day?"

"Hannah, one does sleep until midday when the Season is at its height. One dances until dawn, then sleeps until noon, and barely has time for a few morning calls before going out again in the evening. It's marvelous!"

As if Hannah would be dancing.

Black-gloved knuckles rapped on the window beside Hannah's face. She swung the glass down, a lovely blast of chilly air hitting her.

"We'll be going overland for the first part of the journey," his lordship informed her. He was mounted on a black horse that looked big enough to pull a plow, the beast's trot churning snow up with every step. Despite the cold, the earl didn't wear a hat. He had a woolen scarf about his neck, the pattern a bright red and dark green plaid with a thin white strip mixed in.

Beside Hannah, Enid squeaked, "But that's—we cannot—my lord, you must understand that is not to be borne."

"There's a breakdown on the tracks south of the city. We'll pick up the train in Bairk," the earl said. "And we'll have to move smartly if we're to make that distance by nightfall." He sent Hannah a look, one that warned her delays would not be tolerated and complaints were futile.

"But an entire day in this stuffy old—"

Hannah closed the window before Enid could finish her first volley of protest.

"I did not see a town named Bairk on the map," Hannah said. "Perhaps it isn't so very far."

"Ber-wick, you foolish girl. Berwick-on-Tweed. It's nearly sixty miles!" From Enid's tone, this might as well have been halfway to the North Pole.

"If we change teams regularly, and the roads are well traveled, we could easily be there by nightfall, as the earl suggested." Provided Hannah did not first do away with her aunt and force the coach to stop so she might dispose of the remains.

They had changed teams twice when the great, lumbering coach went swaying off to the side of the road. Something snapped loudly underneath, and the conveyance swung wildly, bumping along the snowy ground for a good twenty yards before coming to a canted halt.

"Oh, my! My goodness! Dearest, my remedies, please. The headache and the nerve tonic both."

"Ladies!" The earl's voice cut through Aunt's ranting. "Is everyone of a piece in there?"

His voice came from above, from the road, and Hannah felt an undignified spike of relief to know he was about and uninjured.

"We're fine," she said, unlatching the window and lowering it. "A little tossed about, but well enough. What happened?"

"Snapped a wheel," he said. "Probably hit a rock hidden by the snow, and it will take some work to repair it. You're likely as warm as you can be in there, so sit tight until we get the team unhitched."

Except unhitching the team took a good deal of time and cursing and rocking the vehicle about. The wheelers grew frantic when the leaders were walked off and the weight of the coach had to be balanced by only two horses. Hannah could hear Balfour's voice as he crooned to the horses, a soothing patter that belied the rising wind and dropping temperatures.

"This is awful," Aunt pronounced. "Just awful, Hannah. If only we hadn't arrived in the depths of winter."

"We've arrived to take advantage of the social Season, Aunt, but had Step-papa considered our welfare, he might have bought us passage to London itself and allowed us a departure when spring was advanced."

For once, Aunt had no reproof to make.

"Ladies?" Balfour, up on his enormous horse, spoke near the window. "We're going to have to get you out of there now. The wheelers won't be content to hold the thing when the leaders are gone, and it will be dark sooner than is convenient."

"Gone?" Aunt Enid seized on the word. "Where are they going? Where are we going?"

"The coach can't go anywhere," Balfour said. "But we're only about five miles from the last coaching inn. I propose to send the coachy back with the leaders for another conveyance. One of you can ride the second leader, and the groom will take the wheelers."

"You go, Aunt."

"We have four horses, though," Aunt Enid said. "Five, if you count your mount, my lord. Why not put Hannah on one of the wheelers, or take her up with you?"

"The wheelers are green," Balfour said. "In this footing, they aren't safe for a lady to ride bareback astride, nor is it safe to ask a horse to carry a double burden."

Aunt's eyebrows rose. "Astride?" And then those same brows came crashing down. "That will leave you and Hannah..." Her voice trailed off, and Hannah saw the befuddled workings of her Aunt's mind follow the situation to its conclusion. "It will be for only an hour or two, won't it, dear? You'll be all right?"

So much for the selfless devotion of a doting aunt. "I've

dressed very warmly," Hannah said. "I'm sure we'll be fine."

The coachy came up astride one of the sturdy beasts who normally pulled the carriage, the groom behind him on one curvetting wheeler while the other danced nervously on the end of its reins.

"We'll have somebody back here for you before dark," the coachman said. "Moonrise at the latest."

Except a lowering layer of clouds would obscure any moonrise.

"We'll manage," Balfour said, glancing at the sky. "Best hurry. There's snow waiting to come down."

"Aye." The coachy moved the horse along. Getting Aunt Enid situated aboard the second leader took a preventive tot of her nerve tonic and a great deal of patience on the part of both men and beasts. The coachman took the lead, letting both wheelers come behind him, with Aunt Enid bringing up the rear on the second leader.

"Isn't it a shame the roads are so miserably inadequate to the challenge of keeping travelers from the ditch?" Enid's voice trailed away in the bitter breeze as the horses trudged off in the direction of the last coaching inn.

"'Isn't It A Shame' is her second-favorite game," Hannah said. "Right after 'If Only.'"

"If only I hadn't forced you out of Edinburgh so early in the season?" Balfour asked. He sounded genuinely displeased with himself.

"She's happy, Lord Balfour. Not a solid week on British soil and already I'm compromised."

"Compro—" His dark eyebrows nearly met, so

thunderous was his scowl. "They should be back in less than two hours. You're not compromised."

"If Aunt loses track of her discretion in some remedy-induced fog, I am compromised, and so are you."

His gaze went to the horses making slow progress toward the horizon. "Then you'd best make sure she understands that I am a gentleman and you are a lady. We behave as such under all circumstances."

"If you say so." The landscape was bleak, the prospect of relying on Aunt's discretion bleaker. "Is it too much to hope we could build a fire while we're behaving so prettily?"

"Not a bad idea," Balfour conceded. "I don't like the look of that sky."

He did more than build a fire. He used the lap robes and horse blankets to fashion a sort of lean-to over cut saplings—aspen poles, he'd called them, with an oilskin for their roof anchored by a thatch of Scots pine—while he set Hannah to collecting rocks from the wagon ruts to line a fire pit. He put the fire at the edge of their lean-to, and made them a floor layered with an oilskin, followed by more wool lap robes and horse blankets.

"By now, you're probably longing for the necessary," he said, kneeling in the snow to survey the little fire.

"Blunt speech, my lord."

"I do believe that's the first time you've my-lorded me."

"The topic seemed to call for it. What next?" She was hungry and thirsty both, but despite the lowering sky, their isolation, and the occasional flurry, not the least bit afraid.

"Here." He passed a sizable pocket flask to her. "I understand you don't object to the occasional tot to ward off a chill."

She tipped the flask to her mouth, his body heat having made the metal unexpectedly warm against her lips. "My thanks."

"Next, we wait, though I advise you to first heed nature's call, otherwise you're going to get all cozy in the blankets there, and have to get up and face the cold."

"You think we can stay cozy?"

"I know we can," he said, taking a nip of the flask before slipping it into the folds of his greatcoat.

"Aren't you worried about your horse?"

"He won't go far, and he'll come when I call him. For privacy, I suggest you avail yourself of those bushes, and I'll take the opposite side. These are spindle bushes, so don't touch. The berries are poisonous."

Hannah considered making some sort of protest, but none came to mind on the topic before her—even poisonous bushes could provide privacy—so she slogged through the snow in the indicated direction.

"Do we have to worry about wolves?" she asked as she made her way around the stand of bushes. They were tall enough, but devoid of leaves. She could see Balfour's shape moving through them thirty feet away. He turned his back to her, and she had to admit it was… comforting, to know he was there, to know he could sort the poisonous flora from its useful or innocuous kin.

"No wolves, not since my grandfather's time. Wild dogs might roam on the heath, but they'll be closer to town in this weather. You all right?"

"Dandy," she said, gathering her skirts up in one

hand and fishing for the slit in her drawers with the other. Her gloved fingers brushed against her intimate flesh, bringing a profound and novel chill with them.

Scotland was turning out to be more of an adventure than she'd foreseen.

"You about done?"

"In a minute."

She turned her back to the bushes as he had, tended to business much to the relief of her innards, and sacrificed a handkerchief in the interests of hygiene. She kicked snow over the handkerchief, wondering if Balfour had done the same, and if wild dogs could scent it through the snow.

"Come along." He came around the stand of bushes, the snow not slowing him down one bit. "These flurries are soon going to thicken into something serious, unless I miss my guess."

How and when he'd found time to set snares, Hannah did not know. A hare and a fat grouse were roasting on spits over the fire an hour later, the aroma enough to turn Hannah herself into a wild dog. He basted the meat in some spirits taken from the boot of the coach, and used a knife to slice Hannah generous servings of both hare and fowl. Bread and butter were produced from the coachy's stash.

"I cannot recall enjoying a meal this much in ages," she said. "It's like a picnic, only better."

He gave her an odd look over the last of his bread and butter. "A bit cold for a picnic."

"And getting a bit dark." Everything here was a bit, a trifle, a touch. Hannah sat on the blankets under the lean-to, as the flurries thickened into *a bit* of real snow. "Will your little structure keep us dry?"

"If you don't poke at it, it should. And it will be warmer here than in the coach, provided the wind doesn't shift."

"What has that to do with anything?"

She'd had a few more medicinal tots of his whiskey, and it was to them Hannah attributed an incongruous, rosy sense of well-being.

"We don't want the smoke joining us under here," he said. "If we have to move the tent, or the fire, we'll be less comfortable. More bread?"

"Couldn't hold another bite."

"Then we'll save it for morning."

"Morning?" A trickle of cold seeped past Hannah's rosy glow. "We can't be here much longer. It's one thing to manage two hours in broad daylight on the plain, Mr. Lordship, but quite another to spend a night unchaperoned under the same, somewhat flimsy roof. I'll have you—"

He reached over from his side of the lean-to and put a bare finger on her lips. His hands weren't even cool.

"I do know," he said. "But attempting to walk back to the inn now would be folly. The wind has drifted snow over the horses' trail, darkness is falling, and the temperature is dropping. Then too, the snow has started."

"Oh."

Something in what he said wanted arguing with, but Hannah was unable to get her mind wrapped around it. For her to navigate five miles of slippery terrain was not well-advised, though he'd mercifully left her limitations off his list of reasons. She had no doubt were he not burdened with her, he could have marched back to the inn without breaking a sweat.

His lordship was a good man. A gentleman. A pity his ilk did not abound in Boston.

"Shall I escort you to the bushes again before we lose the light entirely?"

And he was a blunt man—a trait of which she had to approve, for he was essentially offering to escort her to the privy. Good heavens. What did one say? Hannah lifted her face to the sky, to the flakes drifting down from the heavens in a thickening swirl of small, frigid kisses to her nose, eyelashes, cheeks, and chin.

"Yes."

Four

The lady was half-tipsy, or perhaps a quarter. Asher usually avoided tipsy women, but Hannah Cooper wasn't silly or giddy with it. She was more like a man who'd imbibed a wee dram at the end of a taxing day: relaxed, her sense of humor closer to the surface, her dignity not quite so tiresomely evident.

The liquor was the simplest explanation for the lady eating up her dinner with her bare fingers, wiping her mouth on her scarf, and thanking him kindly for the most crude fare.

She'd drunk from his flask without comment too, and set about gathering rocks and kindling without grumbling. He'd tossed the tasks at her mostly to give her something to grouch about and to keep her moving, but she was singularly lacking in biting retorts.

She came around from her side of the bushes and took his arm as if they were bosom bows.

"It gets like this in Boston," she said. "So cold your lungs shiver with each breath."

"So cold," he took up the conversation, "you don't

dare breathe through your nose, for the thing freezes together on you."

"Yes!" She beamed at him. "That cold. Do you suppose we'll freeze to death in our sleep?"

"Tonight? Of course not. This isn't dangerously cold by my standards. It's merely inconvenient."

"And compromising," she added, her tone dismissive. "I've been compromised before. Will you read to me?"

"Read to you?"

"You did earlier this week. The Walter Scott, I think."

"You're reading Scott now." He'd thought she'd been asleep as soon as he'd started reading. She'd certainly acted asleep. "I can read to you for a bit."

When they were back on their blankets under the lean-to, and Asher had arranged the tarps to keep the snow off the fire, he took up the book, lit a coach lamp, and began to read, slowly, because his glasses were in his breast pocket, and he wasn't about to wrestle them onto his nose before company. For almost an hour, he regaled Hannah with the deeds of old Ivanhoe—an idiot, by Asher's standards—while she sighed and watched the fire beside him.

"Nobody's coming for us tonight, are they?"

"They'd be fools to try. Had the wind not come up, there would have been a broken track to follow, but that's not the case now."

"Time for bed?"

She sounded wistful, as if she were longing for a nice, cozy four-poster after somebody had made good use of the warming pan.

"Time for bed. Give me your cloaks."

"I beg your pardon?" Not so tipsy now—not tipsy at all.

"If we're not to freeze, and we're not, then I need your cloaks. We sleep together, like kittens, and use both our coats as extra blankets."

"You are a very large kitten, Mr. Balfour."

"Call me Asher."

"Is that yet another title? I can't keep them straight as it is. Lord This and Lord That, it's quite confusing."

"Asher is my name, Asher MacGregor."

"If you say so." She untied a cloak and passed it over to him. "Both of them?"

"Please. We'll be warmer this way." He unbuttoned his coat as her second cloak landed in his lap.

"Now what?" Her teeth were chattering.

"Under the blankets," he said, holding up the top several. "You'll be between two lap robes and have several thicknesses above and below you."

"How c-c-cozy."

She curled up on her side in a ball. Asher arranged himself behind her, so she was between him and the fire, then spread their respective outer garments on top of the blankets.

"Asher?"

He scooted down into the blankets and drew them up over her shoulders, spooning his body around hers.

"Mister Balfour Asher Lordship MacGregor? What are you doing?"

"Keeping us both warm." He tucked her close under the blankets, wrapping an arm around her waist and threading another under her neck so she could use his biceps as a pillow. "Now go to sleep. It's the best way to get through a truly miserable winter, endorsed by no less beast than the great white bears of the North. I should know."

After a few minutes, her teeth stopped chattering, while Asher thought back to all the nights he'd spent in the longhouses, shivering his way to sleep to the sound of incessant coughing and the thick scent of bitter smoke.

Nobody in the longhouses had ever smelled quite this good, though, or cuddled this agreeably. Canadian winters might have worn an entirely different face if they had.

He woke several times in the night, cozy and warm, the fragrance of Miss Hannah Cooper's hair tickling his nose. She smelled incongruously of flowers and lavender.

Were their situation not so dire, his unruly body would no doubt be getting *ideas*. To Asher's relief, cuddling, while comfortable and even comforting, did not engender overwhelming sexual cravings.

Evidence that even his long-deprived intimate parts comprehended the folly of entertaining notions about a woman determined to return to her side of the ocean without a husband, fiancé, or similar inconvenience.

"Beastly damned weather, Laird."

Maxwell Lockhart Fenimore was laird of nothing more than a constant bellyache, sore joints, and a lot of bleating sheep, but Evan Draper was a loyal retainer and of mature years himself—also stubborn as hell.

"It's merely cold and snow, Draper. This is

Scotland, and we excel at cold and snow. Did Balfour get under way, or is he still fussing about in Edinburgh?" Though thank God the boy was fussing about on Scottish soil at long last.

"They left the town house for the train station early this morning," Draper reported. "Shall I build up the fire, sir?"

Fenimore's study was a veritable camphor-scented inferno, and yet, the ache in his joints was unrelenting. "You'll provoke my cough if you add coal to that fire. Tell me about the Americans."

"Perhaps your cough might benefit from a wee dram, Laird." Meaning Draper was in want of a wee dram or three, but then, the man had spent much of his day braving the elements, and everybody benefited from an occasional tot.

"Help yourself to the decanters, you reiving ingrate." Had Fenimore been a few years younger, he would have risen to pour the man a drink himself. Instead he twitched at the tartan over his knees and silently cursed old age.

"Don't mind if I do. The American girl limps. The aunt tipples or uses the poppy. I chatted up the maids, and they don't have much good to say about the aunt." Draper tossed back a shot of whiskey and patted the decanter as if it were a pretty girl's bum.

"Draper, have you gone daft?"

"Oh, aye, years ago. It's that cold, too, and the drink is that good. Balfour's being a conscientious host."

"He'd better be."

Without permission, Draper poured himself a second drink and ambled over to the hearth with it.

He turned his backside to the fire, not out of any manners, of course, but because a roaring blaze felt ever so good toasting that part of a fellow's anatomy. "The American girl sasses Balfour, according to the maids. He seems to like it."

This was good news. "You call that a report?"

"She slipped on the ice, and he carried her nigh five blocks in his arms, all romantic-like. The maids were fair swoonin' over it."

Draper's grizzled face split into a beatific smile, one the occasional maid found passably tolerable. There was no accounting for the queer starts of females, though Fenimore suspected cold weather might be a factor. A fellow of Draper's hulking dimensions would give off significant heat.

"Balfour was a physician before he started running from his birthright. I take it he dealt with any twisted ankles, megrims, or sprains the American came up with?"

Draper peered into his drink. "He read to her."

Outside the wind moaned as only a Scottish winter wind could, but inside, Fenimore felt a spark of hope. "Balfour has years of medical education, the woman's worth a bloody fortune, and *he read to her*?"

Half of Draper's whiskey disappeared. "Aye, when they wasn't arguin'. Even the housekeeper found it quite touchin'."

The Edinburgh housekeeper, one Bessie Flaherty, had been old when Roman legions had marched past Arthur's Seat.

"Draper, I do not pay you to decimate my stores of whiskey. You will keep track of Balfour and his charge, and report back to me regularly. Now get out." Though Draper was too honest a man for the rest of the scheme Fenimore intended to put into play. For those machinations, a more dastardly relation would have to serve.

"I'm leaving, Laird." In no particular hurry, Draper set his half-full glass within Fenimore's reach, tossed more coal on the fire, and tugged at the plaid over Fenimore's knees. "And Mrs. Flaherty sends you her regards. I left a jar of her special liniment in the pantry."

That liniment was magic, and yet, if Fenimore had asked for it, the damned woman would have said she had none to spare. "Be gone, Draper, and send my quack to me—with the liniment."

"Oh, aye, mustn't forget the liniment. Sweet dreams, Laird."

Draper toddled off, a good, loyal man with friendly blue eyes, and an incongruous talent for flirting up the maids. And Draper knew what mattered, too, for he'd noted that Balfour had read to the American girl.

Fenimore's gaze went to the portrait hanging over the hearth. A pretty red-haired lass in the Clan MacGregor formal attire held pride of place there, though her dress was at least half a century out of date.

Fenimore lifted Draper's neglected drink—an indulgence for which the snippy little physician would offer a grand scold, if he learned of it—and saluted the lady in the painting.

"I used to read to you, my dear, and you sassed me regularly. Look how well that turned out."

Hannah awoke to the certain knowledge that she was safe. Without being able to articulate how, she knew she was for once beyond the reach of her step-papa and his schemes, she was beyond the whispers and gossip, and she was completely, utterly safe.

The feeling was novel and precious, carrying with it more relief than she'd thought herself capable of. Great, swooning buckets of relief, mental and physical, that made her want to both weep and smile.

And she would have to relieve herself soon too, but not just yet.

She was content instead to drowse in a cocoon of warmth and good scents. Cinnamon, nutmeg, clove… a soothing blend of fragrances wrapped all around her, along with a vague memory of being cuddled and comforted in the night.

"You're awake?"

She felt the words as much as heard them, for she was intimately aligned with Lord Balfour.

He'd asked her to call him something else; she forgot exactly what.

"I'm awake, and it is morning."

"You sleep very soundly, Hannah Cooper. A blessing, considering. And only a few more inches of snow fell during the night."

"Another blessing, of course."

Neither of them moved.

"It's warm in here," Hannah said.

"Verra cozy."

He shifted a little, so Hannah became aware she was resting her cheek against his arm. Had she done that all night?

"It's warm in here," she said again, "and it is decidedly not warm out there. Has the fire gone out?"

"There should still be some coals, and we've bread and cheese to break our fast."

"And then what?"

"And then we wait for help to find us. Your aunt will no doubt raise Cain to see us rescued immediately."

That thought was enough to inspire Hannah to scoot away from him, but not quite enough to get her out into the frigid air.

"My aunt will have dosed herself with her nerve tonics and headache remedies and possets and whatnot until she slept like the dead," Hannah said. "She believes it her fashionable obligation to sleep until noon."

"While you're out on the moor with a winter storm looming?"

Hannah didn't need to look at him; the pity was palpable in his voice.

"Aunt is too… distracted by her petty ills to understand that her own brother expected her to cross the Atlantic in winter, Mister… Lord…" She stopped, and wished it might resume snowing again in earnest. "What was I to call you?"

"Asher," he said, rummaging around among their covers. "Asher MacGregor, ergo, Asher to my friends."

"Are we friends, then?" She hoped they were, because as her mind stirred from its mental blankets, a snippet of memory assailed her. At some point in the odd and cozy night, Balfour had kissed her hair, right above her ear. Not a flirtatious or even naughty kiss, but rather an "I'm here, don't worry" kiss.

He likely hadn't even been awake, which was a profound mercy.

Hannah scooted some more, so she could rest back on her elbows and see her companion. She wished she had not.

His dark hair was disheveled, and it was longish hair, brushing his shoulders. Its disarray made her want to… to sift her fingers through it until it was in some kind of order. And his chin and cheeks were dark with the hint of a beard, though the darkness suited him. And his eyes…

"You do not have polite eyes, Mr. Asher."

"Just Asher will do, and what I have are tired eyes. Sleeping on the ground, even with the pleasure of present company, was not entirely restful. Shall we tend to business now, or procrastinate another five minutes in hopes of an early spring?"

"Where are my cloaks?" Her voice was crisp, and her movements were crisp as she fastened the frogs, and her manner was brisk, but inside, where even *Asher's* dark eyes couldn't see, Hannah was mourning the loss of her little cocoon of blankets and the rare sense of well-being she'd experienced there.

And she'd been right: stranded on the snowy plain—moor, they called it here—curled up under the blankets with the Earl of Balfour, she had been safe. Perhaps *insultingly* safe.

She slogged through the snow to her side of the bushes, sacrificed yet another handkerchief, and didn't even take note of the cold air on her delicate parts. When she rejoined Balfour, he was carrying an armload of dead wood.

"I never did ask how you got the fire going in the first place. Do all English gentlemen travel with a flint and steel?"

"This one does—this Scottish gentleman," he said. "And with some medical supplies, and a hatchet, as well as spare leather, two knives, wool blankets, a compass… what?"

"In *England*?" She took the wood from his grasp, though he made her wrestle for it. "The beating heart of civilization, and you equip yourself as if you were striking out like President Jefferson's explorers?"

"We're still very much in Scotland. Which way is north, Hannah Cooper?"

She surveyed the vast stretches of white all around them, fairly certain she knew in which direction they had come, though the road meandered, so that told her little. She spotted stray clumps of trees—Balfour would know the species and all of its potential uses—some of them fairly sizable, but the landscape was bleak, and the sky even bleaker.

Hannah couldn't reckon their direction by the morning sun, hiding as it was above a cottony batting of clouds.

She couldn't reckon by anything.

"I don't know which way is north." Though she knew in which direction warmth lay.

"And there are landmarks here," he said. "In some places, the moors and dales sport no vegetation higher than your knee, and they go on and on for miles. People die on the moors, people born and raised in the North, people who know better."

He fell silent, as if he'd known somebody who'd

died for lack of a compass. Maybe several somebodies, in the middle of a winter storm.

"Feed a little at a time to the coals," he said, gesturing to the wood with a bare hand. "Too much, and you'll smother the flame."

"I understand how to coax a fire from coals." The words might have been full of innuendo, with any other man, in any other situation.

"Then I'm going to scout the surrounds and retrieve a few more things from the coach, maybe scare up Dusty."

"Who is Dusty?"

"Destrier. My horse. He'll be hiding on the lee side of some thick patch of fir trees, if he didn't find himself a cozy shed and some hay to poach."

He departed, and Hannah bent to her task, thinking over his list. A hatchet was a New World tool—or weapon—and not something one typically found in English arsenals. He'd recognized her accent, too, and been quite at home camping on this moor. He'd kept her warm and well fed, not simply alive.

Warm and comfortable.

Comforted, too, in some regard, and even a bit kissed, unless she'd dreamed that small gesture.

She peered around the end of their little lean-to, searching the area for Lord Balfour.

He was nowhere to be seen.

His tracks led off around where she imagined the road would curve, but the only sound was the chill sweep of the wind across the frozen white ground.

She fed the fire very, very carefully.

"Tiberius, I have the best news!"

Tiberius Flynn, Earl of Spathfoy, accepted a kiss from his wife, though the dear woman was lying through her pretty white teeth. She waved a single sheet of fine stationery he recognized all too easily.

"When are they coming? Be honest, Hester, for only family could put that sparkle in your eye so early in the day."

Her smile faltered then turned mischievous. "You are trying to act peevish, which you do very well, sir, but I know you are always happy to see our family."

Her family, whose visits made Hester happy, so Spathfoy tolerated them as best he could.

Spathfoy led his countess to the saddle room, the coziest and most private location in his London mews, because a woman in her condition ought not to be out in the elements without her husband's protective presence.

Then too, a lady in her condition was given to frequent and unpredictable bouts of kissing, which a husband also tolerated as best he could.

"I have never met a woman so eager to call cousins-by-marriage her family. And no, I have not taken to reading your correspondence. Mama wrote to you, but Joan wrote to me."

The marchioness was nothing if not a reliable correspondent, while Tiberius's sister Joan was a reliable correspondent too—and an effective spy. In claiming the hand of his countess, Spathfoy had unwittingly blundered into the outer reaches of Clan MacGregor, for Hester's brother had married Mary Fran MacGregor, and Hester's cousin had married Ian MacGregor, both siblings to the present laird.

Hence the need for Mama's helpful and informative letters, and Joan's watchful eye.

Hester scooted onto a trunk as Spathfoy closed the saddle-room door. "If Asher brings that American woman south, then I cannot but hope the rest of the family will follow."

Spathfoy contained his joy at such a prospect; indeed he did. "My love, you do realize that my mother, among others, would thus expect me to maintain surveillance over the hulking, kilted lot of MacGregor brothers?"

"There are only four, Tiberius, and you are adorable in your kilt."

He kissed her, lest she elaborate on how adorable he was when they were some distance from the house.

"Besides," Hester went on as Spathfoy shifted to nuzzling her ear, "Ian, Connor, and Gilgallon are all quite civilized now that they're married."

"They're not civilized. They're besotted. This is an entirely different matter, particularly among the Scots, and means they can be trusted only when in the company of their ladies." Much like Spathfoy himself, come to that.

The specific nature of the sigh Hester feathered across her husband's neck suggested a trip back to the house—to the bedroom on the second floor—might be a prudent course. Spathfoy was ever the servant of his countess, especially when her delicate condition had imbued her with all the shyness of a pillaging Roman legion.

"Asher has been back from Canada only a short while, Tiberius. We must help him feel welcome, for he is not married, and his siblings are all quite preoccupied starting families. I have explained this to you."

She kissed his chin, like a tutor might pat a slow pupil on the head.

Balfour wasn't married *yet.* The poor bastard was wealthy, titled, and had a "curious past." This was the reason Spathfoy's mother had sent out her warnings and Joan had monitored the situation as well. For all Balfour could track wolves and hunt bears, he'd be no match for the predators in the London ballrooms.

"Dear Asher has brought protection in the form of that heiress," Spathfoy said, which was quite shrewd of him, "though you and Mama are right: in the interests of protecting their older brother, Ian, Connor, Gilgallon, and Mary Fran will all likely come south. I thought perhaps you and I might spend a few weeks in France."

Hester smacked his arm, which bore the impact of a hummingbird wing brushing past a rose petal. "You are such a tease, Tiberius. I love your sense of humor."

And Spathfoy loved his countess, so he did not make plans for a few weeks of Paris in springtime. He did, however, escort his wife back to the house.

And up to the second floor.

"You took us in a couple of hours before sunset," Asher said.

The man before him lowered bushy eyebrows and extracted a cold pipe from between crooked teeth. "Did we now?"

Asher fished out his wallet and unfolded a wad of pound notes.

"You did. You were kind enough to give the lady your own bed, and you gave me the run of your hay mow and your spare blankets—after feeding us both a substantial dinner."

The man eyed the pound notes. "A substantial dinner?"

"Your missus lent the lady a dressing gown." Several of the notes changed hands.

"We had a fine stew last night," the fellow allowed. "Plenty to go around."

"Plenty," Asher agreed, passing a couple more notes over. "Lamb stew, if I recall, and lots of bread and butter."

"That's a tricky curve there on t'other side o' them trees." The notes disappeared into the farmer's jacket pocket. "Missus was glad for the company."

"I'll fetch the lady then."

"Missus will get the kettle on."

And because Asher knew the fundamental character of the Scottish crofter, he also knew the man hadn't asked for their names on purpose, and wouldn't.

The fewer lies the better when a fellow was being paid for his mendacity.

Failing to scout the terrain in the last of yesterday's fading light had been an oversight no self-respecting frontiersman would have committed. Last evening, keeping Miss Hannah Cooper from panicking, keeping her busy and warm and well fed, had seemed more important than observing the commonsense safety protocol of setting up a new camp.

And so they'd spent the night together, not merely under the same flimsy roof, but wrapped in the same blankets, cloaks, and robes. In sleep, she'd trusted him, burrowing into his greater warmth like a kitten under the covers. And there she'd stayed, barely moving through the night, content in his arms.

It should have been a simple matter of keeping warm, and on one level it had been.

On another level, though, Asher had enjoyed their proximity, enjoyed the scent and feel of her in a way he didn't examine too closely. His pleasure had had to do with keeping her safe, with avoiding the guilt of causing her discomfort or risk. He'd loved Monique dearly, and he was already carrying around enough guilt for a lifetime.

"I've fetched the bread and cheese," Miss Cooper said when he approached the fire. Even when she'd been half seas over, she had not invited him to use more familiar address. "I think the air is warmer than yesterday."

"Which suggests it might snow again," he said. "We're going to have to break camp."

"Break camp? And wait in the coach? It's at a rather precarious angle."

For an instant Asher considered not telling her about the farmhouse just out of sight around that bend. Consequences would arise, serious consequences for both of them if he held his silence. What made him speak was an instinctive repugnance for manipulating the lady's circumstances, even for her own good—perhaps especially for her own good.

And yet, she needed a husband, he needed a wife, and they could both be spared the farce and folderol of a London Season.

"We'll be sheltering at a smallholding around that

turn and through some trees. It ought to be the first place anyone from the village looks for us."

"A smallholding?"

"If we break camp quickly, we can credibly claim we spent the night there, but not if it looks like we stayed here for any length of time."

"I… see."

Her thoughtful expression said she saw what his lies would gain her, and she assented. She rose from the fire, which was blazing merrily, and began to kick snow into it without another word.

And a faint, lingering, what-if in Asher's mind was snuffed out as effectively as the fire, leaving him in an unaccountably surly mood. They folded blankets with equal dispatch and stuffed them back into the boot of the coach. Asher tossed the saplings into the ditch, and except for the way the snow had been trampled all around, there was shortly no evidence of any overnight camping.

Nor of any near-compromises, nor any ill-advised proposals of marriage that might have followed.

They were lucky. They were sitting around a cozy kitchen table, swilling tea and munching on brown bread and butter when a sleigh pulled up in the barnyard, Asher's coachy at the reins. A short while later, Asher handed Miss Cooper into the sleigh, tied Dusty behind, and climbed in after her.

He was all the way back to the village before he swiped a glove over his mouth and found a memory swamping him in the frigid air.

Hannah Cooper had slept soundly, but not soundlessly. She had stirred shortly after dropping off, making the kind of noises that signaled a troubling dream. Half-asleep himself, Asher had kissed her hair, the way he'd once kissed any random, available part of Monique when she'd had the same sorts of dreams—her hair, her ear, her shoulder, it mattered not which part. Not the kiss of a lover, but the kiss of a husband and protector, for comfort—his and hers.

He begrudged Hannah Cooper that kiss, half-stolen as it was from his past. And yet, what he'd felt when Hannah had kicked the snow over the fire was not relief that she'd accommodate a handy subterfuge, but rather, anger that she should so easily reject him as a potential mate, without question, without pause, without thanks, without anything—when in the care of any other man, she might well have perished from the cold.

Five

"Well, if you are sure you were not compromised...?" Aunt Enid sighed gustily, her tweezered eyebrows raised in hope. Hannah kept silent, though this was not the first portentous pause in the conversation. "Then we must consider your misadventure merely that. Lord Balfour holds an earldom, though, my dear, and in case I didn't mention it, earls fall only below marquesses and dukes in the order of precedence."

"You did mention that, Aunt."

Hannah tried to focus on her embroidery—her borrowed novels were still in the coach—but making a tidy series of satin stitches was difficult when her mind kept wandering to the bone-deep warmth she'd enjoyed cuddled up with Lord Balfour. The whiskey had something to do with it, but whiskey alone didn't explain the sense of safety, the comfort she'd felt in Balfour's arms.

"What do you suppose Lord Balfour is about?" Enid asked, eyeing her own hoop of fabric.

"I expect he's seeing to the repair of the coach wheel."

"One would think the household of an earl would at least boast safe conveyances."

"The moors boast rocks," Hannah said, stabbing her needle up through the middle of a French knot.

Enid put down her hoop and studied Hannah by the meager light of the fire burning in the raised hearth of their little parlor.

"If you had been compromised... I'm not saying you were, but *if* you had been, you'd be a countess and wealthy. Your step-papa told me in no uncertain terms we were to be escorted about London by an eligible fellow with a substantial fortune. Some old cousin of a cousin owed him a favor, Hannah. My brother does not squander the favors he's owed."

He squandered the happiness of all in his ambit instead.

"I'm wealthy now, Aunt, and a titled husband will take over my fortune every bit as readily as a plain mister."

Though for all her wealth, Hannah had felt a greater sense of well-being out on the moors with Balfour than she'd ever felt in Boston's finest neighborhood. Did the man have to be so clever at avoiding social ruin?

Not that Hannah would have married him, of course.

Enid put aside her hoop, her expression as animated as if a new patent remedy were under discussion. "My dear, you forget your pin money. The pin money will be spelled out in the settlements, all completely legal, and your pin money will be yours to spend as you wish."

They'd had this discussion on board ship at least a dozen times.

"I believe I'll step out for a bit of air."

Before Enid could flutter in protest or assign Hannah a half-dozen errands to tend to first, Hannah was out of the parlor and on her way upstairs to their rooms. Thank a merciful God, the inn was as Lord Balfour had suggested, commodious and clean. Hannah shared a small suite with Enid; Balfour's room was across the hall.

The day had become brilliantly sunny, and the eaves were again dripping. By night, all would freeze, which meant moving around in the milder air held even greater appeal.

The village of Steeth was an old market town, complete with a common, a church, and the usual variety of shops. Hannah walked a shoveled path encircling the common, and as she came back toward the inn, saw their traveling coach in the yard on the same side as a smithy's shop.

Men loitered about, two holding horses, while boys scampered around underfoot. A wainwright inspected the coach wheels, peering into the undercarriage and trading insults with the blacksmith.

Except it wasn't the smith. The man emerging from the gloom of the smithy, standing there without his shirt, naked to the waist and bulging with muscles was none other than Lord Balfour.

God in heaven, no wonder he'd been able to keep the chill off her. Hannah scooted around to watch as Balfour braced the coach, then hoisted it so the wainwright—no delicate flower himself—could wrestle the wheel back onto the axle. The two men continued taunting each other, with Balfour's tone—*and his physique*—suggesting he could hold up a wagon all day if need be.

And all the while, his chest, arms, and back bunched and rippled with his every breath.

She'd seen men without their shirts, even seen fit young men laboring without their shirts, but this… *Steam* rose off Balfour's shoulders, as if he were some magnificent Vulcan come to the shires for his own entertainment. He hadn't yet shaved, and his countenance was darker than ever. The skin of his arms, belly, and chest had the same sun-bronzed hue as his face, and when he smiled at her, his teeth fairly gleamed…

She'd been found out.

Caught gawking like a schoolgirl. Hannah turned without acknowledging Lord Balfour or his smile. The Englishmen she'd met in her father's parlor would have expired of mortification if she'd seen them without their shirts as others looked on.

Nor would she have wanted to see them.

How long she churned around the little common she could not have said, but at some point, she became aware that she was sharing the path.

"Just think," Balfour said. "All that vulgar muscle could have become your sentence for life had I not prevailed on the goodwife in the dale and her spouse."

He wouldn't be a sentence; he'd be a citadel. "And I haven't thanked you yet." She did thank heavens, though, that he was once again properly clad, right down to his many-caped coat.

"You're thanking me for coming across a convenient way to avoid a marriage between us?"

"I do thank you for that," she said, "but compared to preserving my life when the elements were threatening a dire fate, preserving me from scandal comes a distant second."

"So you would not have married me had we been found out on the moor cuddled up in our bide-a-wee?"

Hannah couldn't read his expression. She would not have married him—earls needed to stick close to their earldoms, even a Boston heiress grasped that much—but, wonder of wonders, she would have been tempted.

Hannah liked Balfour, she respected him, and—most curious of all—she trusted him. "I think it more the case we would not have married each other."

"Despite the display you came upon in the smithy's yard, I am a gentleman, Miss Cooper. I would have had no choice."

"I know." And that had bothered her most as the sleigh had taken them back to town.

"What do you think you know?"

"You didn't enact that little charade in the dale to protect my good name or to preserve my marital options this spring. You did it to preserve your own."

She dropped his arm—when had she taken his arm?—and tried to make a dignified retreat, but he kept up with her easily.

"This bothers you?" His tone was jaunty, and yet the topic mattered to him, or he wouldn't have raised it. "It bothers you somebody might want the same freedoms you seek to appropriate for yourself?"

They were in view of the smithy again, with its complement of men passing the time of day with one another. Hannah had never thought of a smithy as a dark, mysterious place before, never had the urge to linger where she could watch one from the shadows.

If Hannah claimed the right to remain unfettered by marriage, she had to accord Balfour the same latitude. She also accorded him a bit of honesty. "I am not used to being rejected."

The words had come straight from her brain to her mouth, the insight striking her even as she spoke. She was used to being marginalized, not *quite* rejected, but tethered to the fringes of acceptability by a stout rope of inherited fortune—or had she simply decided she preferred to dwell there?

Balfour—he'd given her permission to call him Asher—picked up her hand and tucked it around his forearm. A forearm she could now visualize thick with muscle, dusted with the same dark hair as he had in such abundance on his head. That hair was downy soft. She'd felt it against her cheek the night before as he'd drawn her body close to his.

"Ah," said his lordship, but it was a teasing "ah," not an insulting one.

"Ah, what?"

"I wasn't rejecting you, Miss Cooper, I was protecting your dreams. Don't pull away, if you please. The last thing we need is for you to do yourself another injury and delay us yet more on our way to London."

In his words, in his jocular discussion of reasons not to marry each other, Balfour did Hannah's heart an injury—a small injury. She kept silent, took a firm hold of his arm, and walked more quickly in the direction of the inn.

Miss Cooper flinched at his reference to her clumsiness, and Asher had to stifle an apology. He hadn't meant to be scathing, but the woman was as uncomfortable being beholden to another as... Asher was himself.

"How long will we tarry here in Steeth?" she asked.

"Anxious to take London by storm?"

"Anxious, yes."

She was looking about her with the same honest curiosity she'd shown upon landing in Edinburgh, though Asher suspected she'd allowed another small truth to slip past her full, unsmiling lips.

"Are you truly fretting over what most young ladies consider the dream of a lifetime?" He subtly checked their pace, which the lady had increased to something between headlong and unseemly. Another fall on the ice would not do, but neither was he in a hurry to return her to her aunt's dubious company.

"A London Season with all the trimmings is the dream of a lifetime? Consider, Lord Balfour, much of the Season transpires in ballrooms, and I do not dance."

He'd asked her to call him Asher, but now, when they'd narrowly escaped a forced betrothal, she exhibited a fine command of proper address. "There are always musicales."

"I do not perform reliably or sing worth the name."

His brother Gil was the family charmer, while Con

was a font of common sense. Ian, however, was the family lawyer, and from him, Asher had learned to hear the difference between "I *do not* perform reliably" and "I *cannot* perform reliably."

Miss Cooper, Miss Cooper. For a lady who limped, she was adept at kicking snow over open flames. "What about Venetian breakfasts?"

"Where the primary fare is gossip, in which I do not indulge."

"I believe we've had this discussion, but we must add swanning to the list, and I forget what else." He was being nasty, and it was unlike him. "My apologies, Miss Cooper. I am not enjoying the delay any more than you are."

"You enjoyed repairing the wagon."

He saw no spite in her expression. Perhaps a little female curiosity, such as he'd seen when she caught him sweating off his stint at the forge, or maybe longing, because physical brawn was denied to genteel ladies.

"I enjoy being able to fix what's amiss." This was something about the practice of medicine—when it went well—that he missed. "I like being able to address my situation myself, though I know this is a lamentable tendency in a man headed for an earldom rife with servants and toadies."

"I don't hear you lamenting."

"Like you, I have a list of behaviors in which I do not indulge. Shall we return you to the inn?"

She glanced again toward the smithy. The place was nothing special, a typical village blacksmith's shop, where by the nature of the work, men congregated and passed the time of day while horses were shod or tools were repaired. The forge kept the interior blisteringly hot even on bitter days.

She'd seen him with his shirt off. It hit him low in the gut that she'd seen not just his ungentlemanly muscles, but also his un-English complexion. His un-Scottish complexion, in fact. She was an intelligent woman; she'd realize he wasn't suffering from excessive sun on his entire body in March.

"The inn is comfortable, as you promised us," she said, "but you haven't answered my question, Lord Balfour. How long will we tarry? My aunt's company in close quarters is not easy to bear, though she means well and tries hard."

"Playing If-Only and Isn't-It-a-Shame until you've lost your reason?" Aunt Enid and Uncle Fen would have much in common.

"She tries to be helpful, my lord."

Would he be so charitable toward his uncle? "We'll leave at first light, and the journey from here is easier, because we're close to the coast where the water moderates the worst of the weather. We'll hop the train in Berwick and be in Town in no time."

She put her hand back on his arm, but lightly, just for show, which along with Miss Cooper's my-lording, depressed Asher's mood yet further.

"You might as well see the sights while we're waiting for our wardrobes to be made ready." Enid paused while winding soft ivory yarn into a ball. "That cat's stare is the most unnerving thing. I don't believe I've seen an animal with two different colored eyes like that."

"Several of them live in Lord Balfour's stables," Hannah said as the white cat near the hearth took a bath. The animal boasted one blue eye and one green eye, and both were beautiful, though the whole was disconcerting. "Several in the mews, I mean. Balfour says there's a mama cat who has one or so per litter."

Not Asher, for Hannah was determined to avoid familiarities with the man—further familiarities, rather.

"Well, why isn't this one in the mews, then? And how can you have an objection to seeing the Tower, the Menagerie, the churches, and cathedrals? This is your heritage too, you know. Your family isn't all Colonial savages and backwoodsmen."

"I'm aware of my heritage." Which included a backwoodsman or two, but the only savage Hannah knew was her step-papa. "Why don't you accompany Lord Balfour, and I'll remain here?"

The London town house sported a small library, which boasted more medical treatises and novels than the northern collection had. Hannah looked forward to becoming well acquainted with its offerings, and to neglecting her embroidery shamelessly.

"For you to remain home will not do, Hannah. The Season starts in only a few weeks, and you won't have time for sightseeing. Besides, your restlessness is irksome. You will go, and I will stay home, for I feel a megrim coming on and must away to my bed."

Aunt was becoming a sot. Even now, a tisane that was more brandy than tea sat at her elbow. "This is your second megrim this week."

"It's the weight of expectation regarding your Season, and all the shopping yet to do." Aunt put the back of her hand to her forehead, as if feeling for a fever, and Hannah knew she'd just been trounced.

Though Aunt had a point. Being confined in Balfour's London town house for the past three days was taking a toll. Even if it meant putting up with his company, Hannah would feel better for getting out of the house and away from her aunt.

"Miss Enid isn't coming with us?" Balfour asked when Hannah met him at the foot of the stairs.

"A megrim stalks her."

He picked up the cat that had followed Hannah from the parlor, and the beast began purring and rubbing its cheek against Balfour's chest. "Have you considered taking all of her patent remedies and nostrums in hand? Somebody should. It's easy to misjudge when you're using so many at once, and half of them are more poison than medication."

This was a physician trying to masquerade as the polite host, for which Hannah had to respect him.

"She is to be taking me in hand," Hannah said as Balfour gently scratched the cat under the chin, "though you have a point. My grandmother warned me on the same issue before we set sail."

"The grandmother to whom you've written so regularly?"

Had he no older relatives in whom to confide his troubles, to whom he might turn for consolation and counsel? Hannah stifled an urge to pluck the cat from his arms, the beast was making such a racket.

"She's my only paternal relation. What sights are we to see today, that I might write her of those as well?"

He put the cat down, carefully, not the casual tossing aside a saucy cat might merit from time to time.

"We'll start with whatever you please, Hannah Cooper, and I'll be in your debt, because you've given me an excuse to get out of this house."

He settled her cloak around her shoulders and began to talk of the various churches and monuments they might visit. The weather was moderating—Balfour said that was in part because they had come almost due south from Scotland—and a weak sun was trying to melt the last of the city's snow.

He handed Hannah up into a phaeton, the height giving her a fine view of their surroundings, the brisk air chilling her cheeks between stops. A tiger rode up behind and held the horses while Balfour escorted Hannah from one amazingly ancient house of worship to another.

He spoke of the coronations held, the kings buried, the foul and wondrous deeds done at each location, until Hannah could almost believe his duties were not an imposition, but rather, his opportunity to boast about England's capital city. He fell silent when they saw the lions in the menagerie, inspiring Hannah to suggest they repair to a tea shop rather than visit the rest of the caged animals.

"One feels sorry," she said when Balfour had placed their order. "One feels sorry for the lions, that is. Were they less magnificent, they'd be free to chase the gazelles all the livelong day. But they are wonderful, and so we must cage them up and make them pathetic."

He paused in the arrangement of their outerwear

on a hook. "They're merely beasts. Rather odoriferous beasts, in their current confines."

"They are not merely beasts."

He settled beside her, much as he'd done in the grog shop in Edinburgh, while Hannah tried to find words to reach him. They were not merely beasts, any more than he was just any old earl. "They are lions, made for swift and merciless pursuit of prey, hot, lazy afternoons sleeping off full bellies, and magnificent lives as lions where God intended lions to thrive. We make them something else entirely when we bring them here, pretending because they don't die that we've provided adequately for them."

The quality of his frown changed, his mink-brown brows rising in thought, putting Hannah in mind of otters and how joyously they played in the wild.

"Are you a lion, then, Miss Cooper, captured and brought to civilization from your natural surrounds, here to be caged and kept alive for the enjoyment of your captors?"

She studied him for a long moment then studied him further as their tray arrived. Was *he* a lion? He'd grown noticeably quieter since they'd arrived in the malodorous environs of London.

"You weren't like this that night outside Steeth. You've misplaced your manners, Lord Balfour."

He pushed the cream and sugar at her, letting her fix her cup first then tending to his own. "My manners aren't what's gone missing," he said, stirring his tea.

Hannah sipped in silence, knowing it was a good, strong cup of tea, served piping hot, with rich cream and generously sugared. And yet it tasted off. Balfour's ill humor was that powerful.

His silence spread like gloom over the table, and Hannah spoke to combat it more than to be polite.

"You're right in some ways. I am a Colonial by your standards, and that means I'm closer to the lions. We have them in America, mountain lions with no great ruff, but enormous teeth and claws. When I visited my cousins north of Harrisburg, I heard them. Lions don't roar in the New World, they scream."

He tapped his spoon against his teacup. The porcelain looked tiny in his hand, the teacup absurdly decorated in blue pastel birds and delicate yellow flowers. She plowed on because he said nothing, but stared at his tea.

"I see the pelts baled up on the wharves. I see the men who spend winters hunting the furs. As a young man, my father was one of those men, and he talked to me of his trapping. He routinely braved conditions like those we faced in Steeth. He went months without hearing another human voice, Lord Balfour. He heard the wolves howling, the lions screaming, the woodpeckers searching for their dinners. He heard the snow melting and the ice cracking as the lakes and ponds thawed. You wouldn't expect such a man, so full of life and courage, to enjoy being caged up and gawked at like those poor lions, would you?"

The look he gave her was so piercing, it was as if he didn't see her physical form, but some other manifestation of her. Her words maybe, or her soul.

"Your tea will get cold, Miss Cooper." He set his cup down, having finished the contents in a single swallow.

"You think I'm daft," she said, dutifully taking a taste. "I shall certainly go daft if I have to prance around from now until July, pretending I haven't a thought in my head. What's in this tea? I like it."

"Lavender. I enjoy it for a change from time to time, but we can try a different flavor of tea at each shop."

Where had Asher MacGregor gone? For surely, only the platitudinous Lord Balfour had sat down to tea. "So there's to be more tramping about, cooing at lions?"

"You didn't see anything today that you'll write to your grandmother about?"

Hannah accorded him points for not coming back with a biting rejoinder. "Oh, I'll write to her. I'll tell her you can barely see the sun for all the coal smoke here, and the air stinks of it incessantly, which probably accounts for Aunt's many megrims. I will tell her they've had grand churches here for nigh seven hundred years, and yet the Christian charity is so lacking, people probably froze to death on those church steps this very winter. I'll tell her the wealth of the British empire has long since been acknowledged as coming from her colonies, and yet those colonies still—even decades after the American example—have no representation in the most civilized government in the world."

"Is that all?"

A lift of his eyebrow and a particular heat in his gaze suggested her verbal rebellion had distracted him from his melancholy, so she forged ahead.

"Your Prince Consort has made a life's work of bettering the condition of working men, and yet they despise him for his efforts. Your queen leads her empire but has increasingly little to do with the government thereof. This is an improvement, however, over a king who was mad and a regent who built palaces while his former soldiers starved in the streets. The Americas are better off without you English."

"You are a very opinionated lady," he said, rising. "One might say you're even rude—though I do not—but you are wrong: I am not English. My title is Scottish, and my patrilineage is exclusively Scottish."

This seemed to matter to him, though Hannah was more concerned with the topic under discussion. "I see with my own eyes what's before me." She rose as well, and turned her back to him so he might settle her cloak on her shoulders. "I cannot afford to doubt my own eyes, Lord Balfour. I should go mad if I did."

She wasn't sure, but she thought he might have given her shoulders a smooth pat—a caress?—as she fastened the frogs at her throat. When she turned sharply to look at him, his expression was as severe as ever.

How she missed the man she'd eaten roast hare with outside Steeth, the man she'd cuddled with.

He tossed some coins on the table and held out his arm. "Come, we'll lose the light, and the streets get icy when darkness falls."

Something about their exchange had stifled his running commentary on the wonders of London, and Hannah missed his voice. Missed having at least that much of him attending her.

"I'm not like a lion," she said as they approached his phaeton. "I won't bite everybody who tries to extend me kindness."

"Won't you?"

Was that humor in his eyes? "You're the one who was so accommodating when a freezing night loomed, and has become such a pestilential *lord* now."

And then, when he should have handed her up—always a tricky undertaking, and one Balfour monitored closely—he surprised the daylights out of her.

"I'm sorry for that, for being such a pestilential lord. Perhaps you were a more accommodating guest out on the moor, or more… something." An apology and a backhanded sort of admission, while he kept Hannah's hand grasped in his own.

"I was half-tipsy. I can hardly be expected to observe all the finer points of etiquette with a man who escorts me to the bushes." With the only man to *ever* escort her to the bushes.

"You weren't going to go alone, and you won't go alone into the ballrooms, Boston."

And with those few words, Hannah again felt the sort of warmth she'd experienced on the wintry moor, a sense of safety and well-being, of resting in good hands.

"Neither will I let you face those ballrooms alone, Asher MacGregor. You'd get to pacing and flicking your tail, and then whatever would I do for an escort?"

Hannah clambered up into the carriage as the horse stomped a big back hoof in the mucky slush. Nimble as a cat, Balfour dodged back in time to preserve his boots from the worst of what might have befallen them.

Six

"You will see Balfour compromised with the Cooper girl if it's the last useful thing you do."

Despite the conviction in his words, old Fenimore was ill. Malcolm Macallan could smell it on him, the way a child called down from the schoolroom could smell an upcoming beating on the fumes of his father's breath. "Why would I treat family so shabbily, Uncle?"

"I am not your uncle, and you will do as I say or the sum advanced to you each quarter will disappear like that." Fenimore snapped bony, liver-spotted fingers, his signet ring loose above swollen joints.

Malcolm paced around the study, which was heated to stifling—appropriately enough—and rife with the smell of camphor and decrepitude. He paused before an arrangement of decanters on the sideboard and began lifting the stoppers, sniffing them one by one to chase the scent of decline from his nose. "Your remittance was late last quarter, my lord. Time to get a solicitor whose education started before the turn of the century."

They were cousins at two removes, but for all the affection between them, it might have been twenty.

"Perhaps the remittance was late because you've been tarrying on English soil too long. The likes of you belong in the sewers of Paris. In my day, your kind were hung by the neck as a public spectacle."

Where Malcolm belonged was Greece, Denmark, or somewhere a fellow wasn't defined solely by the nature of the orifices he'd penetrated with his erect cock as a schoolboy.

"I like Asher. What has he done to deserve marriage to a Colonial who likely squints and trots around with a pet squirrel on her shoulder?"

The old man had to work to suppress a smile at that description. "He has deserted his responsibility for years on end, left his family to weather the results of the famine without his title to aid them, allowed his only niece to be all but snatched into the hands of the Marquess of Quinworth, and reduced his brother Ian to assuming the title and taking in paying guests—for the love of God—before Ian would apply for funds from the earldom's trusts."

Malcolm chose a gentle whiskey, one aged in barrels that hadn't been very heavily treated with peat smoke, or perhaps not peated at all. Even in their distilling, the MacGregors took odd starts as often as hares on the heath changed direction.

"You're saying Asher has been independent and proud. Terrible shortcomings in a Scottish laird." Malcolm saluted Fenimore with his drink to add a further dash of sand in the old man's gears.

"He's neglected every one of his duties, and by

God, he will not neglect them any longer. The American will understand a heathen like Balfour. She'll put up with his uncouth manners and bring a sizable dowry to the bargain. She's used goods, and a title, even a Scottish title, is far more than she ought to expect. The two of them deserve each other."

Trust the old man to know everybody's business, even as he was being measured for his shroud, and trust him too, to judge all in his ambit and pass sentence on them as well.

Malcolm wanted no part of Fenimore's game, and yet… a man had to eat. Even frittering his life away in Paris, a man had to eat, and so did his dependents.

"If I'm to do the pretty on the London social stage this spring, I will need a house, a wardrobe, a coach-and-pair as well as a riding horse. I might very well have to pursue the lovebirds to the house parties and perhaps even into the fall Season. The paltry sum you send to ensure I remain at a safe distance from home is not adequate for the scheme you set me to now, Fenimore."

The baron twitched the afghan over his knees—the MacGregor plaid, though the MacGregors wanted no part of him—licked old, colorless lips, and stared at the fire. "You are unnatural in so many ways."

The accusation hardly qualified as an insult, except for the quiet despair with which Fenimore spoke. Malcolm took a sip of lovely libation and struggled against something close to pity—guilt, perhaps? Not for seizing an advantage with the old man, but for taking advantage of Asher MacGregor's bad fortune.

"I am the only family you have left who doesn't curse your very name," Malcolm said. "Babies are being born up at Balfour, you know. Ian, Connor, Gilgallon, and Mary Fran are all happily married and having fat, healthy Scottish babies, given wonderfully Scottish names, swaddled in clan plaids and sent to sleep with the old songs. My cousins don't invite you up there, don't mention you might like to bide with them while the Queen is larking about Deeside with her royal consort."

"That is none of your affair. How much, Malcolm?"

Bless the old boy's fixity of purpose. "I want more than a season of finery in which to advance your schemes. I want security in my old age, something you've enjoyed for an obscenely long time."

Fenimore couldn't help how old he'd become, but he definitely deserved to be twitted for living off his deceased wife's wealth in such a miserly fashion.

Malcolm compared the overstuffed elegance of the Fenimore study with his garret in Paris, a cramped, noisome space alternately freezing and sweltering by seasons, a place holding few meaningful memories and too many bottles of wine when a man needed decent whiskey in his veins.

The baron batted a gnarled hand in the direction of the bellpull. "Ring for Draper. He's not yet departed for points south."

Malcolm obliged. Yes, it was a petty command, and yes, the baron could easily have reached the bellpull in a few steps, but Draper's presence would signify an intent to be bound by any terms struck.

Then too, as Malcolm studied Fenimore's increasingly frail form he had to allow that maybe the baron wasn't *unwilling* to get up and ring for his man of business, perhaps he was *unable*.

The trip to the Royal Menagerie shifted something in Asher's regard for Miss Hannah. The first time he'd seen the Menagerie, he'd been an adolescent. He'd pleaded a sudden, pressing need for the jakes, and as soon as he'd had some privacy, he'd given in to tears. He'd never quite known why, and it hardly mattered now. Taking Miss Cooper to see the lions hadn't been the least bit gracious on his part; it had been… a test.

Rude, presuming, and not at all kind.

Maybe she'd sensed that, and maybe she'd wanted to cry a little too, for the lions, which was to say, she'd passed the test. He didn't know whether to be pleased or disappointed, for himself, for her… none of it made much sense.

In any case, the tenor of his sightseeing trips with Miss Hannah moderated, and the weather followed suit, shifting from bitter to brisk, however temporarily.

She liked the parks most of all, and was content to stroll the walks on his arm, saying nothing for long stretches as she bobbed along beside him. She also liked to browse the shops, though not for herself. She was forever sending little gifts—ribbons, trinkets, scented gloves, sketches—home to her grandmother, and she'd occasionally ask him questions about this birdsong or that flower.

"Do all Englishmen know their flora and fauna as well as you do?"

"I can't answer for them one way or another. I haven't a drop of English blood in my veins."

She referred to him as English to tease him, or to ensure he paid attention.

Paying attention to Hannah Cooper was becoming all too easy, even when she merely occupied the place beside him on a quiet bench. Hyde Park was never entirely deserted, but in late morning, the nannies had taken their charges back to the nurseries, the shop girls weren't yet taking their nooning, and the fashionable crowd was still abed.

"Is that why you don't sound English?"

"I sound English compared to you." When he was sober and could ape the accents he'd heard at university, he sounded much more English than she. Ian, next in line of Asher's siblings, had found that university accent uproarious until he'd acquired one of his own.

Miss Cooper scuffed a half boot over the dirt beneath their bench and tried unsuccessfully to hide a smile. She liked being from Boston, however many and varied her other dislikes might be. "You don't sound American, Asher MacGregor, but then one hardly knows what an American accent might be. We're so lately full of Irish and Scots. Before that it was French, Dutch, and English. We've many Africans as well."

"Slaves." He didn't miss that aspect of the New World at all.

"Not in Boston." Her spine straightened, and lest he be treated to an abolitionist homily, Asher gestured to a bed of tulips several yards up the walk. A few early stalwarts suggested the entire bed would be a bright, bobbing yellow in a few weeks' time.

"I am hopelessly in love."

She left off scuffing her boot. "I *beg* your pardon?"

He was bad to tease her like that, though she was a woman much in need of teasing. "That's what an English gentleman would know about yellow tulips, that they stand for the sentiment 'I am hopelessly in love.'"

"I've heard of this symbolic bouquet nonsense, though if you ask me, a yellow tulip ought to be simply a yellow tulip."

That was her common sense talking, trying to deliver a little homily of its own. Asher leaned a touch closer, so he could catch a whiff of her scent. She used lavender soap, as most of his household did, but twining through that came a hint of something sweet and clovery.

"I declare my love for you."

"Sir, you will not… Oh."

He'd done something no English and few Scots would have dared attempt in Hyde Park in broad daylight: he'd plucked the first red tulip to bloom from a tightly planted drift.

And his crime—surely the English would have made appropriating a single, temporary bloom a crime—was worth the risk, because for the first time in his experience, Miss Hannah Lynn Cooper, late of Boston and points north, was blushing and *bashful*.

She didn't turn as red as the tulip, but she colored up nicely and ducked her face to stick her nose in the flower. This was foolishness—tulips bore hardly any scent—and it resulted in a smudge of orange-yellow powder on the end of Miss Hannah's nose.

"A proper Englishman would be glancing nervously about at the trees right now." Asher withdrew his handkerchief. "He might be twitching his nose, making discreet signals that you've become unpresentable."

"Unpresent—" She didn't rear back when Asher dusted off her nose. She frowned though. "Am I presentable now?"

"We're working on it. A few more trips to the modiste, several more to the milliner, and my hopes might be rewarded."

Abruptly the frown became a scowl. "And here you were doing so well, Balfour. But no, you must ruin a perfectly lovely spring day with talk of the coming debacle."

Her nose, once again free of unintended cosmetics, was aimed toward the sky. He liked that nose. In its angle and dimensions, that nose spoke of confidence and honesty. A nose such as hers might be coaxed to do some nuzzling in the right company on a cold night—provided such company did not start prosing on about marriage and dowries first.

"A suitable engagement would hardly be a debacle, Miss Hannah. You have an unnatural aversion to marriage and family if you believe that. It can be wonderful, to have a family."

He hadn't meant to say the last part, and she was regarding him again in that studying way of hers, suggesting she knew he'd revealed more than he'd planned to. "You have a family, I take it," she said. "Where are they if they're so wonderful?"

The pain of her question was spectacular, all the more so for being unexpected. The ache hit Asher bodily, constricted his airways and coiled in his gut, and then ricocheted around in his mind, leaving a trail of guilt, loss, and rage.

"I've sent for some of them. By the time the Season

starts, I expect two or three of my siblings will come down from Aberdeenshire for the express purpose of helping me fire you off."

He didn't deserve their aid—Ian in particular had already served well above and beyond the call of duty—and neither did Hannah deserve his foul mood, but of all the things he might have been prepared for her to ask, the whereabouts of his family was not among them.

"I have half brothers," she said as she twirled the red tulip between gloved fingers. "They are spoiled rotten, and I love them. I want a home of my own and babies as much as the next woman, but I already have a family. Tossing aside the family I have for the family I dream of having hardly washes."

She was in spectacular form today, casually pummeling every bruise on Asher's soul, and without even knowing the havoc she wrought.

He forced himself to focus on the plain sense of her words. "You refer to your not-quite-sainted grandmother, whom you must protect at all costs. An Englishman might not bow as easily to your stepfather's schemes, or the right Englishman would have wealth of his own." So would a Scotsman, for that matter, but Ian, Gilgallon, and Connor were happily married.

Miss Hannah sat forward and braced herself on the bench with both hands, hunching her shoulders in an unladylike attitude. "My grandmother depends on me, and I owe her. When Papa died, Mama would have let all the help go, taken to her bed, and remained there all her days. Grandmother stepped in and maintained order, even though my mother treated her miserably.

When Mama married my stepfather, it was my grandmother who alerted Papa's lawyers to the need to see to my fortune."

"She sounds very devoted." Also meddlesome, and not even an impoverished Englishman wanted to marry into meddlesome female relations.

"She is mine to love now, so this foolishness of a marriage in England will not do."

Hannah Cooper was living up to her nose, demonstrating a determination that boded ill for the coming social Season, and she intended to have her debacle on Asher's watch. Because that would not do either—for his sake as well as hers—Asher tried for some honesty.

"If you do not take, if you are shunned or ridiculed because you engage in outlandish behavior, word will reach my uncle and very likely your parents as well."

"My stepfather is not my parent."

"Nonetheless, he's in a position to make you miserable." Just as old Uncle Fen would make Asher miserable.

She said nothing for a time, confirming Asher's sense the damned stepfather had made Hannah miserable already.

"Shall we go, sir? Aunt will be rising from her nap, and it looks to be threatening snow or sleet."

She didn't get to her feet. Already, she'd absorbed enough English etiquette to resort to the weather for a change of subject and to wait for his assistance before she rose—or maybe her hip was paining her from all their tramping around.

"Your aunt will likely sleep through dinner again." Enid slept most of the time, in fact, which was the reason—*most* of the reason—Asher had sent for reinforcements. A chaperone asleep at the switch was no sort of chaperone at all, and servants would hardly keep such a development to themselves.

He rose and extended a hand down to her. "Come, it does look like the weather might turn nasty."

As they made their way back toward Park Lane, Asher casually noted each species of bird, tree, and flower around them. In the Canadian wilderness, such knowledge could spell the difference between a full belly and an empty one, between life and death.

And yet, here he was, far from the wilderness, in a land where a man learned of flowers only so he might speak symbolically through them in courtship, and the women—the *ladies*—understood such sentiments easily.

Ian MacGregor, heir to the Earl of Balfour, loved his brothers and loved them dearly. This was likely why he also wanted to bash their idiot heads together regularly.

"Asher is laird, head of this family, and holds the title—if he summons us, we go." At Ian's opening salvo, Connor and Gilgallon exchanged younger-brother looks that presaged mutiny, or at least a long, tiresome spate of arguing.

"I agree with Ian." Their sister, Mary Fran, spoke up from the love seat she shared with her husband, Matthew. They held hands, their laced fingers resting on Matthew's thigh, Mary Fran's lap being rather less in evidence than it had been several months ago. "I'd quite honestly like to spend time around our brother," Mary Fran said. "He holed up at Balfour for most of the winter, like some sort of monk. If we avoid him, he might as well still be trapping bears or whatever he was so happy doing in Canada."

He hadn't been trapping bears—or not merely trapping bears. Ian knew that much.

"I'll pour." Ian's wife, Augusta, left his side to tend to the hospitality, though adding whiskey to his brothers' tempers wasn't necessarily wise.

Gilgallon, the most charming but also the most hotheaded, led the charge. "Asher disappears for so long he's declared legally dead, then pops up last autumn with almost no warning. Royal decrees are issued, he snatches the earldom back from you, and then at the first sign of spring, he's off to frolic in London?"

Augusta served the first drink to Gilgallon's blond, English wife, Genie, the second to Con's beloved, petite Julia. Genie passed the drink to Gil without taking a sip, which was interesting—and might explain why Gil would rather linger in the North, glued to Genie's side, even with spring approaching.

"A London Season is hardly a frolic," Genie said, English refinement echoing in every syllable. "A newly minted earl with a mysterious past will be mobbed, and he won't know what's about to hit him."

Connor, the most quiet and blunt of the siblings, spoke as Julia took a delicate sip of her drink. "Asher is no stranger to a dangerous wilderness. I'm saying he might not want us Trooping the Colours in full regalia. He wired Ian. Let Ian scout the situation. The rest of us can get down there on a week's notice or so."

"Spathfoy and Hester have been biding in the

South since autumn," Ian said, because the family now included Augusta's cousin Hester and her English earl. "Asher's invitation was to his entire family, and I agree with him. We haven't all been under the same roof since Grandfather's funeral."

A man who'd impersonated the head of the family for a few years could pull rank like that. Mention of their departed grandfather had Gil downing his whiskey and Connor reaching for Julia's hand.

"If Asher has been racketing about the Canadian mountains these past years, then he's going to be a curiosity among the English," Mary Fran said. "We can't leave him on his own any longer, not if he's asking for our help."

Another silence descended, this one thoughtful.

"We needed his help," Gil said, his tone more bewildered than angry. "For years, we needed his help, and he let us think he was dead."

"The family has his help now," Ian said. "His shipping venture is thriving, and I get the sense that's not his only commercial success. Every MacGregor on two continents can apply to Asher for assistance now."

"I wouldn't mind seeing Town in spring," Julia volunteered. "Winter takes so long to give up its grip this far north. Then too, some shopping might be in order..."

She let the suggestion hang, but Ian felt the other women catching the notion like hounds grabbing the scent of the fox.

"I'll no be squirin' ye around the damned shops," Connor muttered.

Julia patted his hand and kissed his cheek. "I do so love to show you off in your kilt, Husband."

Connor's mouth, usually so grim and unsmiling, turned up in an indulgent grin.

And that settled it. Without shouting, without breaking furniture, without negotiating, they were all going south—and without forcing Ian to reveal confidences he'd promised Asher never to divulge.

Whenever Balfour came upon Hannah, her emotions went in two directions: first, she resented his intrusion, and it *always* felt like an intrusion. She'd look up to find him lounging in a doorway, his expression impassive, arms crossed while he studied her in handsome and inscrutable silence.

She never knew how long he'd been lurking, poaching on her privacy while he quietly regarded her.

After she wrestled that resentment under control, she'd then have to tuck Grandmother's letter away—she read it very frequently—which created a second resentment, like an echo. The letter was her only link with home, her only link with what mattered most to her in life, though that was not Balfour's fault.

And pulling against those resentments, like some great beast of burden, came the memories of feeling safe and warm in Balfour's embrace, of accepting a single flower from him as he teased her in the park, of his resolutely downward gaze as they discussed caged lions.

"You are hell-bent on ruining your eyes, Miss Hannah." Balfour ambled into the parlor and turned up the lamp. "Are you ready to go in to dinner?"

He didn't ask about Aunt Enid, which was considerate of him. "I am."

She folded the letter, rose, and crossed to the rack of cue sticks on the opposite wall. When Balfour extended a hand down to her, she took it, noting as she always did the slight rasp of his calluses against her fingers and palm.

Progress down the stairs was slow.

"Your hip is paining you. It hurts worse on the days when we walk in the park, doesn't it?"

Her hip was killing her. "Or perhaps on the days when it snows, or the days when I get out of bed." Or the days when she contemplated what would happen when she arrived back in Boston without a husband.

He tucked her hand over his arm. "Would you rather take a tray in your room?" Dark eyes regarded her not with impatience, which would have been welcome, but with honest concern.

"I am being difficult. I do apologize."

"Your grandmother has written only the once. You miss her, and you worry for her."

This was Balfour's attempt at consideration, cataloging the aches and pains about which Hannah could do nothing, and yet, his honesty was a comfort too.

"Grandmama can only print—her eyesight is very poor—and she doesn't want to spend postage on an exchange of gossip."

Balfour paused with her while a footman opened the dining-room door. "Is that an exact quote from her letter?"

"Close enough."

"Elders seem to share a number of characteristics,

regardless of culture. I can recall being told in the longhouse that talk would not see the firewood gathered."

The comment was an extraordinary observation in any context, also the most personal disclosure he'd offered her.

"The longhouse?" She expected his expression to shutter as it so often did, or a humorous light to come into his dark eyes while he deftly turned the subject back onto her. Instead he ushered her through to the dining room, a warm, candlelit space fragrant with the scent of beef roasted to a turn.

"I have boyhood recollections, the same as any other man, though mine are of the Canadian wilderness. It's beautiful there, but… absolutely uncompromising. Maybe a little like you."

An attempt to tease, but as with so many of Balfour's sallies, a compliment lurked at the edge of the observation. "How old were you when you left?"

"Eleven summers." He paused by Hannah's chair, set to the right of his. "Eleven years old."

He seated her without saying more, but then he surprised her. "Your turn to say the blessing, Miss Hannah."

Her turn? He'd said a perfunctory word or two over the food at every evening meal, and she'd seen him close his eyes for a moment before tucking into his food on other occasions. Unlike many men of Hannah's acquaintance, he wasn't heedless of his spirituality.

Neither was she. Hannah spread her napkin on her lap and cast around for inspiration. None arrived, the habit in Boston being for Step-papa to blather on until the soup was cold. Hannah bowed her head and thought of bread and butter consumed under a lean-to.

"For what we are about to receive, for safe havens, and for loved ones even when we can't be with them, we are grateful. Amen."

He quietly echoed her amen, and the ordeal of yet another meal in the Earl of Balfour's handsome, charming, and all too perceptive company began.

Seven

Asher had the knack of putting his guest off merely by drawing breath, which was fortunate.

He was coming to like looking at Hannah Lynn Cooper too much, to enjoy watching the way lamplight played with the red-and-gold highlights in her hair. He liked to feel her hand slipping into his, liked to think she appreciated that he would not let her fall.

He liked to ponder the quality of her silences as she ambled through the park with him, liked to provoke her into smiling despite herself.

"Might I have the butter, Miss Hannah?"

She put the little silver dish by his elbow. "You always start your meal with buttered bread."

He hadn't realized that about himself. "A man can do without some thin soup, while bread and butter will sustain life. Wine, Miss Hannah?"

"Please."

"You're learning to drink it, I gather."

"I'm learning that water in London is not like water at home. I can see why tea is the mandatory beverage here."

Ale was probably consumed in greater quantity than tea. He didn't point that out because she was about to make another blunt pronouncement. "And why is tea mandatory?"

"Because the water in London is undrinkable in its plain state."

True enough. "You must not say as much in public."

She sat back and remained silent while the soup course was removed. Asher waved the footmen off, as he usually did. The meal was sitting on the table in plain sight in chafing dishes, and he and his guest were more than capable of feeding themselves.

"I will not embarrass you, sir." Her admission was grudging, offered more in hope than confidence, though her manners were impeccable.

"You will not cause embarrassment purposely, and yet I suspect you will not take, though it won't be entirely your doing, and I doubt it will matter to you. I like this about you, Hannah Cooper, even as I wish you might accept the smoother path of compromise and accommodation. I'm hoping I don't embarrass you either."

Because compromise and accommodation also weren't in his nature.

She stopped mid-reach toward her wine. "Does this have to do with that comment about the longhouse?"

Upon consideration, he found that yes, it did. "I am not the ideal escort for a young lady seeking to make a fine impression on Polite Society. I suspect my uncle offered my services as a way to punish me more than a way to see you effectively introduced."

"I'm a punishment?"

"Don't sound so pleased."

She smiled, a gorgeous, mischievous grin that suggested if she'd wanted to, if she'd had the least inclination, she'd do well enough among the London bachelors. "Tell me about the longhouse and why you are such a sorry excuse for an escort."

"I wouldn't go quite that far. I am an earl, I'll have you know." Though this was the first instance he could recall having a use for the title.

"Where I come from, your title is not considered an attribute you've earned, and you view it in the very same light. Now, *tell me about the longhouse*."

Much to his surprise, over the rest of the meal, he told her. He told her about interminable bitter winters spent in snug proximity to people who'd known him since birth. He talked about the beauty of the wilderness, the scope of the knowledge a fellow needed to survive there, and the curiosity and dread he'd felt entering the trading post as a boy of eight.

What surprised him was how easily the happy memories came, how easily and how plentifully. He did not speak about the coughing, about the remorselessness of disease under such circumstances—especially not about that—about the starvation in early spring.

Not even Ian had asked him for this recitation; nor would Asher have welcomed his brother's inquiries.

Hannah Cooper listened, asking questions when he occasionally fell silent.

What tribe were his mother's people from?

How long had he lived with his grandparents after her death?

How long had he lived at the trading post after his grandmother's death?

What was it like crossing the Atlantic at the age of eleven?

How did a boy of eight reconcile a life in the wilds with life among his father's people?

"Not well, not easily. The minister who took me in was kind, but at the trading post, they wore too many clothes in summer, they used too many utensils to consume their food, they tried to go about in winter as if it weren't murderously cold, when what was wanted were long, long stories told by the fire. My mother's tribe included people who could recite our entire history from memory, an undertaking that goes on for *nine days*, and yet it wasn't until I got to Scotland that I heard some decent tales told in English."

"From?"

"My father's father. My father died immediately after learning of my existence and sending for me."

She patted his hand. Not a surreptitious little gesture, but a firm squeeze of his hand followed by a soft, warm pass of her fingers over his knuckles.

Gestures of comfort had been rare and few in his life, at least his life among his father's people. They were a ridiculous bunch, making war on one another without ceasing, though they shared the same God, lived side by side, and aped one another's fashions. And yet, Scots, English, Welsh, Irish, and even Americans had a pecking order as well-defined as chickens confined in the same malodorous coop.

He brought Hannah's hand to his lips in a traditional gesture he approved of but had seldom used.

"It's late, and I've talked enough. Shall I see you to your rooms?"

"Please. I also want to check on Aunt Enid. She barely stirred when I asked if she was coming down for tea."

Asher appropriated a candle, the sconces having been turned down for the night, and led Miss Hannah through the darkened house. Perhaps it was his imagination, but he thought she leaned on his arm more heavily and took longer to navigate the steps.

"You might try a tot of laudanum," he suggested as they approached her door. "Just because your aunt has made a crutch of her patent remedies doesn't mean you would fall into the same trap."

Even soothed with a glass or two of wine, Miss Cooper ought to have fired off a tart retort, ought to have pinned his ears back for his presumption—she'd made a point of refusing laudanum more than once. They couldn't very well part on the cozy, almost friendly terms on which they'd passed the meal, could they?

"I've already fallen into the patent-remedy trap, or nearly so. I believe my stepfather was ready to snap it closed on me."

He stopped outside her door. By the light of a sconce at the end of the hall, she looked tired and wan, but not defeated. Never defeated. "Did this come about because of your hip?"

She wrinkled her nose. "Because of my stupidity. When I was twenty, I had one of those nasty falls, and the physician prescribed bed rest. My stepfather suggested some elixir for the pain because, when I took it, I was far more biddable. Grandmother figured out what he was up to—as I was only twenty, he could still try to marry me off—and had a stern talk with my physicians, my mother, and my maid. I've avoided even strong spirits ever since—at least until I became acquainted with the local version of grog."

No wonder she was loyal to the old woman, and no wonder she viewed a London Season as a mere inconvenience. She knew what it was to fight for her freedom, and she was fighting still.

And yet she had offered him a respite from some adult version of homesickness.

He set the candle down, leaned in, and pressed his lips to her cheek. He lingered only long enough to catch her lavender-and-clover scent before he stepped back. "It will be an honor to escort you about Mayfair this spring, Miss Hannah Cooper, and I was wrong when I predicted that you would not take. You will be, as they say, all the rage."

He bowed and withdrew before he could say anything more foolish than that—before he could *do* anything more foolish—and left her standing outside her bedroom, illuminated by the light of a single candle.

The Earl of Balfour kissed gently, sweetly, at complete variance with his hard, dark eyes, his blade of a nose, and his odd, growling accent. Hannah took the memory of the earl's good-night kiss with her into her bed and woke with it the next morning.

She'd liked his kiss. Not one scintilla of disrespect had marred the gesture, nothing presuming. He smelled good, like Christmas and sweet spices, and he'd kept his hands to himself, touching her only with his lips.

That such a large man could be delicate was breathtaking.

Also deceptive.

"Turn loose of my shoe, sir, or I shall scream." Hannah used the same tone she regularly applied to her younger brothers, though it apparently had no effect on full-grown earls.

"It's just a dancing slipper." He gave the shoe in her hand a hard tug, though not hard enough to wrest it from her grasp. "You have at least twelve pairs. Go ahead and scream. Perhaps it will motivate your aunt to leave her bed for a change."

No, it wouldn't—and how lowering was that?

"I will not allow you to visit your fool scheme on my hapless apparel, my lord."

This gave him pause in the tug-of-war going on between them. "You almost never call me 'my lord.'" As he made this observation, he seemed to grow larger. He used the shoe to step closer to Hannah, so close she could see his eyes were not in fact black, they were a dark, gold-flecked brown.

And bore no hint of compromise.

A startled gasp came from the doorway as a maid bearing a tea tray came to an abrupt halt, eyes wide.

"Leave us," the earl barked. The maid set the tray on the low table before the settee, dipped a curtsy, and departed.

The dancing slipper was of that pale shade of pink referred to as Maiden's Blush. Hannah could not envision an occasion when she'd be caught dead in such a color, but her newly acquired collection included Spring Dew (green), Moondust (ivory), Spanish Pewter (gray), and assorted other impracticalities.

The earl leaned closer, nose to nose with Hannah. "I would verra much like a cup of tea." He turned up Scottish when intent on a goal.

"Unless you're going to drink it out of this dancing slipper, then you'd best let me have my shoe back."

He turned loose of the slipper, but for a long moment did not step back.

A visual contest of wills ensued, two people locked in mutual, unblinking glowers, even as Hannah knew she was being ridiculous. She forgot she could not back down, and instead took note of the contrasts in the earl's morning attire. His shirt was snow white, his cravat dark blue silk, his morning coat a darker blue, and his shirt studs and sleeve buttons gold. His waistcoat was of yet another shade of blue embroidered in a paisley pattern with gold threads.

With his dark complexion, the ensemble was quietly elegant and… lovely.

And again, his scent—nutmeg, clove, cinnamon—stronger than it had been the previous evening. With something like amazement, Hannah watched her own hand reach up and free a fold of his cravat from the lapel of his coat. She eased one finger between soft layers of fabric, tugged silk from linen and wool, then smoothed her palm over the center of his chest.

He moved back slowly, as if he'd spotted a predator across a clearing in the woods and was avoiding the snap of even a single twig.

"Shall you pour, Miss Hannah?"

He sounded damnably composed, while for Hannah, something wild and fluttery paced the confines of her belly. "Of course."

Balfour waited for her to take a seat, then waited for her to gesture him into the place beside her on the settee, though of all the men he was—lord, Highlander, frontiersman—the earl was the least in evidence.

"You steal my shoes then stand on ceremony, sir?"

"You call me 'my lord' only when you're trying to distract me?"

She did not reach for the teapot. Bad enough when he was being obstinate; now he must turn up teasing.

"Your eyes change color with your mood, Balfour. Did you know that?"

"I suspect it's true of most people, and I apologize for troubling you over your dancing slipper."

To distract *herself*, Hannah began the ritual of the tea service. "My shoes are now safe from your larceny?"

His gaze was on her hands as she added cream and sugar to his Darjeeling then stirred for him, removed the spoon, and passed him his cup and saucer.

"Your hands are cold, Hannah Lynn Cooper. This room is cold, in fact."

He hadn't answered her question. "Do not think of closing that door, sir."

He was already on his feet, closing the door and then poking up the fire to a roaring blaze. "Fat lot of good propriety will do you when you're expiring of lung fever under my roof. And no, your shoes are not safe from me. You were supposed to be visiting with your aunt as you do every morning first thing, and I intended to relieve you of only the one pair."

He stood with the brass-and-iron poker in his hand, though a claymore would have been appropriate to his posture, too.

"I doubt my slippers would fit you, sir, and Maiden's Blush is hardly your color."

He set the poker back in its stand and began a perambulation of Hannah's room, turning quickly enough that Hannah suspected he might have been hiding a smile. He did not blend with these fussy, overstuffed surrounds, and yet she liked the look of him sniffing at the sage sachets hanging from her curtains and fingering the brushes on her vanity.

"We really ought not to be alone in here together." And Hannah really did not practice hypocrisy very convincingly, for this was the man in whose arms she'd spent a lovely, cozy night.

"Then agree to give me one of your dancing slippers—a right one."

Hannah took a sip of tea, then realized she'd drunk from the only cup she'd poured—his. He'd watched her do it, too, the wretch. His smile said as much.

"You'll ruin my slipper. Waste not; want not."

"Such a Yankee. Are you going to tell me Maiden's Blush is your favorite color?"

She had to get him out of her room, and not because propriety required it. "I'm telling you every scheme, exercise, and magic potion has been unavailing where my *disability* is concerned."

"So you've let somebody put a lift on your heel before?"

Because he was watching her, even as he brought a bowl of potpourri to his nose, he likely saw her hesitate as much as heard it.

"You have not allowed this previously." He set the dish down and stirred the contents with his third finger before rejoining her on the settee. "Why not?"

Arguing was not evicting him from her room. "Nobody thought of it."

He sat forward, straining the seams on his coat, making the settee creak softly. "You do not have pain in your foot, your knee, or your leg, as far as I can tell. If the difficulty is in your back and hip, then it's possible your right leg is simply shorter than the left. Your fall might not have had much to do with it, other than rendering you weaker for a time as a result of inactivity, which exposed the underlying condition."

While he spoke, he poured a second cup of tea, added cream and sugar, then passed it to Hannah.

She took it, being sure their fingers did not brush again. "You should not be discussing my person in such terms." Not in England, in any case.

"Shall I send for a physician to discuss your own *limbs* with you? Another physician? An old fellow who smells of mildew and lemon drops, who'll no doubt want to examine your *person*?"

"Thank you, no. Aunt Enid would get wind of it, and the letters would be flying, and thank you, no." She took a sip of tea, finding it both soothing and bracing, and cradled the cup in her hands rather than set it on its saucer.

"So you'll let me try, Hannah? If it doesn't work, then there's no harm done, except to ensure you'll never encase your dainty feet in Maiden's Blush."

Hannah, not Miss Cooper, or even Miss Hannah. Maiden's Blush, indeed. "I could not be so blessed."

And the idea of him seeing her shoes—she ordered them by color—was vaguely disquieting, but that he might have seen her collection of stockings went beyond intolerable. "If this scheme works, Balfour, then you'll expect me to dance."

He sat back, again making the settee creak. "If this scheme works, then maybe you won't be in as much pain. Maybe you'll *want* to dance."

Oh, drat him. Drat him and blast him. *Damn* him, in fact. She hid behind another sip of her tea.

"That's the problem, isn't it?" He spoke softly, pushing a lock of hair back behind her ear. "You cannot bear another disappointment. You long to dance, but you've given up."

"*Given up?*" If he'd knocked her to the floor, he could not have been more ruthless, and the gentleness in his touch made his words that much more difficult. "*Given up*, because I don't seek to bedazzle some spotty young fool on the dance floor? Given up, when all I want is to look after my grandmother and have the benefit of an inheritance left to me by my father?"

She set her teacup down with a bang and marched across the room to put space between her and the presuming, too insightful earl. "If I had given up, my lord, then I'd be married to Jeremy Widmore, carrying my second child by now, and likely sporting bruises in all manner of private places. If I had given up, I'd be in my bed, praying that my husband would content himself with his mistresses and gambling, while I watched the funds my children needed frittered away for Widmore's pleasure or my stepfather's."

She whirled in a flurry of skirts and speared the earl

with a glare. "If I had given up, I'd be envying Aunt Enid her laudanum addiction, for that's what it is. *She* has given up, but as long as my grandmother draws breath, I cannot, I shall not, I…"

Could not breathe.

He was beside her in an instant. "Sit." He did not scoop her up against his chest as he had so easily in Edinburgh, but his arm was around her waist, conducting her to the bed, the nearest piece of furniture that would hold both of their weights. "Head down, breathe slowly."

His hand on her nape had her bending forward. "Don't move."

She didn't. Even in the short stays she refused to lace too tightly, it was easier to breathe like this. "God in heaven, what is that for?"

He held a short, wicked-looking knife. The handle was bone with some scrimshaw design etched on it, and the blade positively gleamed.

"I'm going to cut you out of your goddamned stays."

Hannah bounced away from him, which was difficult given how high the bed was. "That will not be necessary."

The knife disappeared, up his sleeve, into his boot, into some sort of sheath affixed somewhere on his person—Hannah knew not which.

"Tell me about Widmore, Hannah."

She'd started out the day as Miss Hannah, Miss Hannah Lynn Cooper who'd enjoyed the most innocent good-night kiss last night. This morning she was Hannah, her name spoken in a low, harsh rasp, and she was about to be laid bare by a knife-wielding Red Indian Scottish Earl Physician.

Despite all inclination to the contrary, she talked. "Widmore was the last threat, the one I'm fairly certain step-papa manufactured to inspire me to acquiesce to this trip."

Balfour reached out with the same hand that had gripped her slipper so tightly, the same hand he'd used to fix her tea and brandish that knife, and brushed his thumb over her cheek. Hannah didn't realize what he was about until he tasted the pad of his thumb then produced a handkerchief.

The wild and fluttery sensation in her stomach leapt higher at the sight of him tasting her tears.

She took the little cotton square from his hand lest he wipe her face for her.

"Go on, lass."

As if she hadn't already explained, as if Balfour knew in his bones there was more to the tale.

"He was not honorable."

A calculating coldness came into Balfour's eyes, one that gratified Hannah even as it took her aback. "I have many connections on the American seaboard, Hannah Cooper. I can make sure this Widmore never has an opportunity to be dishonorable with a young lady again."

The image of the knife flashed in Hannah's mind, and just then, she was glad this earl was, among other things, also part savage. She adored him for it, in fact, and wished she were part savage too.

"His sins will catch up with him."

If anything, this tired pronouncement made the chill in the earl's eyes deepen. "I'd rather you allow *me* to catch up with him, Hannah Cooper, me and my knife and a quiet, dark alley. If the knife won't do, there are herbs that can make a man wish he were dead and leave him—"

Hannah put a finger to his lips and barely, barely resisted the urge to run that finger over his eyebrows.

"That won't be necessary. When I return to Boston, having failed so spectacularly in London, Widmore will have reason to gloat, and that will be his revenge upon me. He'll trouble me no more."

Balfour grabbed Hannah's hand and kept it in his grasp, and abruptly, Hannah's problem was not tight stays or a soaring temper.

"You could marry me, Hannah Cooper. If I'm to do my part for the earldom—and I shall—then I must marry. As my countess, you'd suffer no more Widmores bothering you, no more dodging your stepfather's schemes, no more fretting over the fate of your fortune, and we could easily see your grandmother comfortably settled."

He was talking himself into this rash offer, grabbing for reasons in support of it only as he glowered at his would-be intended and kept her hand captured in his own.

And Hannah loved him for it—purely, unabashedly loved him for his protectiveness and for the simple, honest workings of his honor. Her regard echoed the way old Sir Walter's characters became impassioned in their high-flown romances, and would give her something to dream about when she was old.

As old as the grandmother, upon whom, Hannah would never turn her back.

Hannah touched her fingers to his lips. "Asher,

please don't. My grandmother is very old, and I would not abandon her to the tender mercies of strangers. As long as she must bide in America, my stepfather could find a way to hurt me through her. He's a vengeful man, is Step-papa."

Very vengeful. The temptation to blurt out just how vengeful was nigh overwhelming, but that admission would provoke Asher into a renewed proposal—of marriage or murder; they were equally endearing offers.

"So bring your grandmother here, Hannah. We'll keep her in toasted bricks and possets and teach her to cheat at whist. We'll give her great-grandchildren to tell her stories to."

This was such a low, unforeseen blow, that Hannah wrapped her arms around her middle and leaned into the man beside her. "You must not say such things. Enid barely survived this crossing, and Grandmama is increasingly frail."

His arm came around her, a welcome support that shifted to an embrace. His chin rested on her temple, and memories of a frigid night in a warm embrace swamped Hannah's reason.

"Among my people, both my father's people and my mother's, the safety of a guest is a host's sacred responsibility. I need a countess. You need to be free of your family's scheming. We'd find our way well enough, Hannah."

For mere instants, she let herself consider the bounty he laid at her feet. Asher MacGregor was wealthy, and in their short acquaintance, Hannah had found him honorable as well.

He was also practical, not easily shocked, no slave to

fashionable Society's dictates, and while not precisely handsome, his looks appealed to her strongly.

Then too, he made her feel safe, his scent was lovely, and he'd never once offered her a hint of disrespect.

"Finding their way" with him would not be a matter of furtive couplings three Sundays a month in the dark. He would not take a mistress without giving Hannah children as well, and he would never publicly shame his countess.

Before the list of his positive attributes could grow any longer, Hannah reminded them both why no such list would ever be long enough. "You are an earl. Your responsibilities lie here. My responsibilities lie in Boston. My grandmother buried her son there, and that means a great deal to her. She also feels a duty to mitigate the worst of my stepfather's decisions affecting my mother and younger brothers."

A large, warm male hand came up to cradle Hannah's jaw, a caress that brought equal parts comfort and despair.

"She could live another ten years, Hannah, the only years when you might bear children. Will you martyr yourself to her cause so she can martyr herself to your mother's?"

Plain, accurate speaking.

"If I must," Hannah said, making no move to sit back. Her grandmother hugged her from time to time, in private, but nobody held her. Her brothers jostled against her getting into or out of coaches, Aunt Enid leaned on her—but an embrace like this, one that offered warmth and comfort, was more dear than rubies.

"You do not argue with me, Balfour. Have your manners asserted themselves belatedly?"

His hand stroked over her hair, wracking Hannah's composure sorely. "I abandoned my family when the famine had decimated our resources. I had reasons, or so I told myself, and my brothers did not argue with me, but then I did not return to Scotland, and one year turned into five, and then it became prudent for me—in my narrow view of things—for Ian to take on the title. I was declared dead—I let my brothers and my sister think I was dead—rather than come home and see to my Scottish family."

Within the circle of his embrace, Hannah sat back—and even that much was monumentally difficult. She took his point. "I cannot stay here, and you cannot leave your responsibilities behind to bide in Boston."

And yet in the space of a few moments, it had become much harder for Hannah to contemplate that journey back across the Atlantic. Lest the return trip to Boston become impossible, Hannah rose and crossed to the wardrobe, extracting the pink slipper custom-made for her right foot. She brought it to him and put it into his hands.

"If you'll excuse me, my lord, I have to check on Aunt Enid."

His arguments had all apparently been silenced, and while that was a relief—the idea of becoming his countess was extravagant, generous, and ridiculous—it was also a profound grief.

He stuffed the slipper in his pocket, paused by the door, offered her a silent bow, and withdrew.

When the door clicked shut softly behind him, Hannah did not square her shoulders and cross the hallway to offer her aunt mendacious good cheer and false subservience. Hannah instead plunked herself down on the settee, helped herself to a sip of the earl's cooling tea, and assumed his place on the sofa.

She took out the handkerchief he'd given her and permitted herself a few minutes of honest, bitter tears.

Asher made it no farther than the hallway, where he had to stop and lean his back against the paneled wall—only to hear Hannah weeping.

Red Indians were accused of having a cold demeanor, one roused only by the primitive emotions of lust and anger. The same could probably be said of the English, though they'd likely piss themselves before they admitted to lust in decent company.

Stoicism was not a lack of feeling, but an ability to control expression of that feeling. One learned stoicism in the cramped, smoky confines of a longhouse. One learned depths of reserve and patience, with oneself and others. The alternative was to brave brutal winters alone, facing impossible survival odds.

Monique had understood this, or at least accepted that it was so when Asher had explained it to her. Asher missed her with a jagged ache, missed the sound of her laughter and the way she'd been able to steady him with a look, with a touch. He missed the privilege of comforting her with his body and with his simple presence.

He was not in love with Hannah Cooper, and she was not in love with him. His offer of marriage had been impulsive and pragmatic, and her rejection of it should not have stung, particularly when she was right: he was bound to Scotland, while her obligations were in Boston.

And yet, Asher did not leave his place outside her door until the sound of her weeping had ceased.

Eight

"It's this wretched weather." Enid took a sip of her tea then set the cup down on the tray in her lap. "If only it would warm up. And that bitter wind… all the flowers will be ruined."

Like my sanity. Hannah pretended to measure out a dose of Enid's most recent pet remedy but counted out only one-third of the prescribed number of drops. "We get cold snaps like this in Boston, too, Aunt, and the Holland bulbs were just making a start. They won't be daunted by a dusting or two of snow."

"I do hope we don't get a late spring. Ball gowns and mud are not a pretty combination. You can put that right in my tea, dear."

Hannah upended the spoon into Enid's tea, stirring a few times for good measure. "I really wish you'd try to put these medicines aside, Aunt. You need some fresh air and activity."

"Activity?" Enid downed her doctored tea like a stevedore with his ale. "Activity is not at all fashionable, not unless it involves shopping."

Hannah went to the window, but a layer of ice had

formed on the outside of the pane, making the view into the back gardens distorted. An inch of wet snow covered the struggling daffodils and tulips. Even to shop, Aunt was not likely to brave such weather.

"Her Majesty endorses walking, and she and the Prince take their children out of doors regularly."

Enid settled back against her pillows. "Since when does an American look to British royalty for guidance on child-rearing?"

"She's the mother of seven, and she hasn't lost a child yet." Seven, so far, and an eighth likely on the way.

Enid sniffed and drew the covers up. "She also chooses to spend her holidays in the wilds of Scotland, and if that isn't peculiar, I don't know what is. Our host is her neighbor, you know, or his lands march with hers at Balmoral. That's how the English say it: the lands march."

Hannah turned and braced her hips against the windowsill. Her backside ached, but from inactivity rather than overuse. "When were you going to tell me that I'm being introduced to Society by a Canadian earl?"

"There is no such thing. Would you mind closing the draperies, Hannah? The light is most cruel."

The light was honest, revealing what Hannah had suspected: Aunt colored her hair, and having been unable to see to this subterfuge for the past month at least, her dark locks were showing gray at the roots.

Hannah closed the drapes. "Lord Balfour was raised by his mother's people in the Canadian wilderness. When his grandmother died, he was taken to the trading post, and there put into the care of an Anglican priest who set about notifying the earl's father of his existence. It was the same priest who'd married the earl's parents and said the blessing over his mother's grave, otherwise the earl would likely never have been sent to Scotland."

"Balfour was the best your parents could do, Hannah. We will contrive, somehow, to find you a suitable match despite the earl's unfortunate history. You mustn't speak of it, mustn't let on that you know he was raised as a savage. He was probably taught how to scalp people. I shall have nightmares if we don't change the subject immediately."

Because the danger of being scalped right here in fashionable Mayfair was so very great. "Shall we play cards, Aunt? Or the earl has taught me backgammon. I could show you how it's played."

Enid let out a great sigh and closed her eyes. "Leave me. My head will soon be pounding if I cannot find rest. Thank God for modern medicine."

Thank God, indeed. Hannah left the room on swift, silent feet, and was closing the door in similar fashion when the earl spoke from immediately behind her.

"Let me guess: she's at death's door, though she ate a hearty enough spread with her tea, and we must put straw in the street because the noise is intolerable."

Balfour was attired in, of all things, a kilt. A beautiful swath of rich, patterned wool that swung about his knees, hugged his hips, and would have flirted with gross immodesty in a high wind, but for the pouch resting against his thighs. "I beg your pardon?"

Were she more honest, she'd beg to sketch him in that kilt.

"Laying down straw is the old-fashioned signal that

there's illness in a house, and it does dampen the street noise. You and I are escaping, Miss Hannah." His dark eyes held mischief, not merely teasing.

"I wasn't aware we were imprisoned." Mendacity was becoming a habit.

"Come along." He took her by the hand and started off down the corridor, leaving Hannah no choice but to follow. "We are not imprisoned, but I've had some ideas, and I want to try them out."

Hannah made no reply, for it seemed to her that a man in a kilt could move more swiftly, with more purpose to his gait than the same man in morning attire. Then too, his knees were disturbingly in evidence, as was the occasional flash of strong, male thigh.

"You'll need a cloak of some sort," the earl observed as he hauled Hannah toward the back of the house. He paused before the service door and plucked Hannah's old brown velvet cloak from a hook. "This will do."

Before she could protest—perhaps a kilt robbed a man of social niceties in addition to exposing his knees—Balfour had her cloak settled around her shoulders and was fastening the frogs. The brush of his warm fingers beneath Hannah's chin was almost as unsettling as the sight of his bare… limbs.

"We've not far to go." He shrugged into a wool coat and snagged two pairs of ice skates from the last hook in the hallway.

"We're going skating?"

He ushered her through the door and wrapped her arm over his. "Observant, you Americans." He gave her hand a condescending little pat and swept onward through the back gardens. "Sometimes, in the middle of winter, when it was as cold as the ninth circle of hell, we'd scare up a hunting party just to have an excuse to move around. It didn't matter if we found any game or not, we just... even the Prince Consort is known to play shinny hockey. You're familiar with the malaise of remaining cooped up for too long."

Intimately. "I am, but surely the ice won't be solid..." The idea of landing smack on her backside on *ice*... Hannah stopped walking and unlooped her arm from Balfour's. "This is not well-advised, sir."

"Shall I return you to your aunt's lively company, then, Miss Hannah?" He advanced on her, kilt flapping against his knees, the devil in his dark eyes. "Shall I settle you in with yet another novel by old Sir Walter, perhaps inflict yet another round of Tennyson on you? Maybe Dickens is more to your taste?"

"Dickens is mean. Like you."

That stopped him just as he was nose to nose with Hannah there in the mews for anybody to see. In the frigid air, over the scent of the stables a dozen yards upwind, Hannah caught a whiff of the earl's fragrance. Clean, spicy, bracing.

"Explain yourself, woman."

"Dickens holds up his own society in the worst possible light. He ridicules everybody and calls it humor."

The earl braced his fists on his hips, the ice skates bumping against a chest that might have been made of granite. "God bless us, every one? Tiny Tim getting his operation so he can walk without a crutch? That's ridicule?"

Without a crutch? "Wretched, vile… Damn you, I cannot go skating."

He studied her for a long moment, dark eyes speculative, mouth unmoving, a tower of masculine stubbornness in the bitter air. A loose strand of Hannah's hair whipped against her mouth, but she would not drop his gaze and turn for the wind to loosen it.

Balfour's bare hand—why had he no gloves on?—brushed at her cheek. "It's all right to be scared, Boston. You think I'm not dreading the coming ordeal, too? I'm going to land on my backside more often than Dickens could imagine at his most ironic. Come along."

This time he didn't lace their arms; he took Hannah's hand in his.

"What do you mean, you're dreading the coming ordeal?"

"Not this little outing—I was skating almost before I could walk—but this London Season. I spent much of the winter relearning dances I'd gained only a nodding acquaintance with as a lad. Not the sword dances, not the dances of my mother's people, but these stilted, measured, one-two-three inanities. I acquainted myself with what wine goes with which dish, with the damned order of precedence. If I'd been smart…"

He was leading Hannah through a series of backyards, gates, and hedges, until they'd come to a small, fenced square.

"If you'd been smart?"

This earl, the one who wore a kilt and knew the way between the marked streets, was an interesting man, a man whom Hannah did not understand exactly, but she couldn't ascribe meanness to him, either.

He took a key from the pouch that hung from his waist and offered Hannah a crooked smile. "If I had been smart, I would have hired myself what they call a finishing governess here. A gray-haired old field marshal of the ballrooms, a lady who would brook no nonsense and tie me to a posture board for hours." He unlocked the gate and stuffed the key back in the pouch, then led Hannah into a tree-lined patch of snow-dusted grass. High hedges sheltered the square from any passing viewers, and in the middle of the grass sat a small pond with a bench on its bank.

A small frozen pond.

"Perhaps I'll watch, Balfour, while you demonstrate your skill."

"Perhaps I'll carry you bodily to the center of the pond and leave you there."

A lick of true unease uncurled in Hannah's belly. "I'd crawl to the bank."

"For God's sake, Boston, can't you trust me the least little bit? I'll not let you fall, lass."

He motioned for her to sit, and with a sense of unreality, Hannah did. When he called her Boston, his voice held a gentleness that caressed and reassured even as it unnerved—and his tone held exasperation too, as endearing as the gentleness.

"I've modified the right skate, you see." He unknotted the ties of the skates as he knelt beside Hannah. "It's an experiment, a chance for you to get used to the notion of a lift. You won't have to try walking with it, but you can put weight on that side and test it out."

He began strapping the skate to Hannah's half boot. She tucked her skirts away as he did, for it seemed… it appeared…

She was going to go skating, and he'd been right: she was afraid.

The earl finished with Hannah's skates and shifted to sit beside her while he strapped on his own skates. "These are probably the largest skates in the whole of Victoria's realm. Shall I test the ice?"

Reprieve. "Yes, please. Test it thoroughly."

Part of her hoped it would crack and he'd get soaked and they could call off his blighted experiment, but another part of her—the part whom everyone expected to limp through the remaining decades of her life—watched him with interest.

He got to the ice in a few steps and stood in his skates, taller than ever, while the breeze whipped at his kilt. His first circuit of the pond was unremarkable, a wagon-wheel pattern that tested the ice at the perimeter and then in the middle. The way the wind occasionally flapped his plaid back against his thighs tested Hannah's composure.

Such muscle, such strength, such oblivion to the risk of exposure.

"It's solid," he called out, "not a crack to be heard."

Boston had its share of winter weather, being a northern seaport. It had ponds, and children and even courting couples who skated on the ponds, but never in years and years of observing had Hannah seen anybody perform on skates as the earl could.

He built up speed in circuits of the perimeter, crossing his front foot over the back in an accelerating tempo; then somehow he was spinning rapidly in place, like a human top. He could ease out of his spins into slower loops then take off in the opposite direction. He finished with a small turning leap, landing easily then coming to a scraping stop right before Hannah's bench.

"It's solid," he said again, grinning even as his chest worked to drag in air. "Come out on the ice and see for yourself, Boston." He extended his long arm, his bare hand reaching for Hannah.

She put her gloved fingers in his, rose, and tottered down the bank.

The ice did not crack, and the earl did not drop her hand.

"Have you skated much, Hannah?"

Good. He would call her Hannah on this outing. She needed him to call her Hannah so she could call him Asher. "As a child, but not since I fell."

"We all fall, but I'll not let you fall today—unless it's to land on a nice, soft earl."

He would be about as soft as the oak bench Hannah had just left. "How do we do this?"

He moved around, shifting as easily on the ice as if he were barefoot in soft spring grass. "We begin in the traditional English manner, with a promenade."

"A *slow* promenade."

He grinned at her, slipped one arm around her waist, and clasped her left hand in his left. "On three."

Hannah gave him credit for not moving until the count of three, she gave him credit for sliding along with her at a pace more funereal than decorous, and she gave him credit for being solid and warm and—

Some unevenness of the ice, a protruding leaf, some infernal thing had Hannah's skates shooting in opposite directions. In one moment, she went from being a statue moved by the earl's impulsion to a panic in progress.

"I've got you, Boston. I've got you."

He growled it in her ear, his hold on her implacable. He had her. He would not let her fall.

"Try again," Hannah said. "I'll pay more attention." To her feet rather than her escort.

He organized them again in promenade position and started Hannah on another slow glide. "I caught you admiring my sporran, you know."

"What's a sporran?"

"My purse. I made this one when I first got to Scotland, leatherwork being something I'd been learning since infancy. Let's turn a bit, shall we?"

He moved her in a slow arc, then a wide figure eight. "How's the lift working?"

"It's different. I can tell it's there." It wasn't entirely comfortable, either. "I feel taller." Straighter, but she wasn't going to admit that.

"You'll probably ache some from the unaccustomed arrangement of the joints."

"I ache from the accustomed arrangements. Tell me about your family."

⁂

Hannah clung to Asher's hand, and yet her voice was admirably steady. A man who didn't have his arm around her waist or his hand laced with hers wouldn't know she was scared.

Nor would he be able to catch the scent of lavender that clung to her person.

"I have three younger brothers, Ian, Gilgallon, and Connor. Mary Fran is the baby of the family, but call her that, and she'll skelp your bum but good."

"Skelp?"

"Paddle, spank. Try moving your right foot, just a wee push..."

She gave the smallest, nearly ineffective push with her skate and Asher let the momentum pick up their pace minutely.

"Do your brothers wish you'd stayed in Canada?"

"I haven't asked them. They gathered willingly enough to greet me when I returned to Aberdeenshire a few months ago." With their wives and children, no less, the entire lot of them weeping, even the women who'd never laid eyes on him before. "Part of me expected them to have remained as I left them. I've the prettiest niece..."

All red braids and big green eyes. Fiona had been shy and dear, spying on the grown-ups from the balconies and banisters. She told stories to the stable cats and left cheese out for the pantry mice.

"If you were raised in Canada until you turned eleven, and you've spent much of your adulthood in Canada, do you even know your brothers?"

She'd abandoned her rigid, eyes-front posture to peer at him as they glided along.

"I know them. I'll always be grateful to my father for bringing me to Scotland, because I do know my siblings."

"You had to work to convince yourself of this."

Much more of her perceptivity and he might have to lose his grip on her—momentarily, of course.

"I'm unsure if they feel likewise. We got on well as youngsters." They'd been thick as thieves.

"Must we go so quickly?"

He eased their pace back. "We're positively doddering. I hadn't realized being two years Ian's senior made me nigh doddering to him. We were an odd bunch. None of us spoke English as our first language. I taught them some of my tongue, and they soon had me babbling away in Gaelic. Mary Fran seemed to comprehend it all, though she was barely out of leading strings."

"Children manage to delight in one another's company with little but imagination and idle time to aid them."

Her tone held stark wistfulness.

"Have you had enough, Boston? I don't want to overtax you."

He'd meant it solicitously—mostly—but her chin came up a half inch. "Just a few more times around. Didn't your brothers find you very different?"

"They were… fascinated by me, and I by them. I taught them what I knew of tracking—Connor's a natural at it—and they taught me about family tales and the various clan histories. Ian and I shared a bedroom, and when he saw that I intended to sleep on the floor, he made up his own pallet, as if all boys normally slept on the floor."

He'd forgotten these memories, lost them beneath other memories not as happy but nearer to the present.

"What about your younger brothers? Did they resent you?"

"You don't resent family when you live in the

Highlands. There's precious few people of any stripe, much less people you can call your own."

And for the first time, Asher felt a connection between his two families—the Canadian and the Scottish—that resonated right down to his soul. Whether it was the climate, the infernal superiority of the English, the sheer magnitude of the northern wilderness, or something of all three, both families understood the blood bond and valued it.

As he considered this odd paradox, they glided to a stop.

"Are we done then?" She regarded him out of serious green eyes as they stood on the ice in a near embrace.

"We are. We can come back, if the weather stays cold enough."

"I'd like that."

He assisted her up the bank, both of them clumping the few steps to the bench. *I'd like that.* Her words had been shy, almost bashful. "Your hip has to ache, Hannah. You don't need to stand on ceremony with me."

"It usually aches." She crossed one ankle over the other knee, an unladylike, practical posture that let Asher know he wouldn't be unfastening her skates for her. He busied himself with his own footwear.

"I forget," she said, shifting to remove the second skate. "I forget what it's like to move easily—to move symmetrically. I have strength now, in my crookedness, but it's a backhanded strength."

What was she saying? What was she talking about?

"You move as well as most people, Hannah Cooper. A little hitch in the gait is hardly remarkable."

"Most boys do like to sleep on the floor." She'd gotten that bashful quality to her expression again. Her gaze was fixed on the laces of her skates as she knotted them together. "Most boys like secret languages, and they want to think they could be self-sufficient in the wilderness."

She was telling him something, or trying to. "Give me your skates, madam. We should fix ourselves a tot of grog when we're home, to make sure we don't catch a chill."

Hannah passed over her skates, which Asher looped over one shoulder. He extended his hand down to her, vaguely uneasy about what she might say next.

She put a hand in his and rose. "You love them, your siblings, and they love you. That's why you came home. That's why I'll return to my grandmother. You do understand."

The skates clanked against his chest, rather like his heart hammered against his ribs.

"I came back to Scotland because I owe a duty to a blessed title, and that is a damned sight less pleasant a prospect than your old granny's loving embrace."

She said nothing, but walked along beside him, the hitch in her gait making him want to break something and curse at length.

Dimly, through something Hannah could only characterize as homesickness, she perceived that the Earl of Balfour was in a sulk—the English would call it a taking, and she had no idea what the Scots would call it.

Her hip did not ache, but her heart did. Something about being able to stand straight, about moving so smoothly over the ice in the near-embrace of a man sturdy enough to keep her balanced, had her longing for Boston, though only in a general sense.

Not for her mother, not for her bedroom in her stepfather's house, not even for her grandmother, but for the time before she'd fallen, when balance, grace, and the fearlessness that went with them had been hers.

She had been so innocent.

"You're quiet, Boston. This does not bode well for the peace of the realm."

He strode along beside her, only the tension in his voice attesting to his impatience with her gait.

"I'm thinking of home."

He tossed her an unreadable glance and held open a gate that led to his stables—his mews.

"You're annoyed that I think of my home?" She was not simply willing to pick a fight with him, she was *happy* to.

"If your grandmother loves you the way you say she does, she could not possibly want you to turn your back on the future you could have here." He offered this observation with the banked tolerance of a man who knows he's being logical, reasonable even.

Hannah passed into the alley beside the stables and came to a stop. "If, sir, you refer to my future including a husband and children, we do have single men in Massachusetts—scads of them. They can dance and flirt and spout off about the weather the same as all your London dandies, and they don't all bother themselves about who is supposed to go in to dinner paired with whom, in what order, like some military parade."

He crossed his arms and seemed to grow taller. "You've run circles around the Colonials, Boston. Left them dazed and panting at the altar, and they don't deserve you. You need a man who can look after you, who has your measure and won't try to diminish it. You need a man who can match you, who can call you on your queer starts, and go toe-to-toe with you—"

Hannah stepped right up to the presuming buffoon, almost toe-to-toe, and stuck her face in his—to the extent she could, being so much shorter. "I do not need a man to order me about, steal my money, and expect me to be grateful that he keeps his mistresses in better style than his own family. I do not want a man who—"

She should have taken it as a warning when Balfour uncrossed his arms and leaned down.

"You need a man who can kiss the starch right out of you."

His mouth came down over hers, not roughly, but decisively. Hannah's hands settled on his shoulders—for balance, surely just for balance—as the sheer heat of his body enveloped her.

He broke off, his mouth so close to Hannah's she could feel his breath on her cheek. "You need a man who makes you think of his kisses rather than about getting on that westbound ship."

And then he was back, not plundering, exactly, but purposefully investigating her mouth without her permission… And without any protest from her, either.

"You taste like rum buns," she murmured against his mouth.

"Hush, lass. Kiss me." The burr was more pronounced when he whispered. His voice, his accent, resonated inside Hannah and made her *want* to kiss him. He sealed his mouth to hers, and his tongue moved gently over Hannah's lips. She clutched at his wool coat, parting her lips to breathe him in while the skates went clattering off his shoulder and he shifted his sporran to his hip.

Kiss me.

His mouth was a wonder, hot, sweet, gentle, implacable. He explored her with his tongue then left her bereft as he grazed his lips over her eyebrows and chin, her jaw, her eyes. Lest he meander too far afield, Hannah anchored a hand in his thick, dark hair and tried to guide his mouth back to hers.

"Wee, managing baggage," he muttered, but he was smiling. She could hear it; she could feel it as he brought his mouth back to hers.

But the damned man was possessed of *strategy*, for just as Hannah gathered up her courage to trace Balfour's lips with her tongue, his hands landed on her shoulders, and then… moved. He began by massaging her shoulders gently, little squeezes with his big fingers that urged Hannah closer to the heat of his body. When she was plastered against him, his hands went questing down her back, slow, easy sweeps of his palms making her want to—

She *did* groan, softly, right into his mouth. He hitched her closer by virtue of widening his stance and gripping her derriere in a firm, ye-aren't-going-anywhere hold that felt so blessed good Hannah sighed with her whole body.

When she touched her tongue to the soft, damp recess between his lips and teeth, he went still. She did it again, a little sweep of a hidden part of him, and his stillness became something more, something considering.

"Don't stop now, lass."

She let him support her while she focused on learning more of his hidden places, his hidden tastes. Up close, she could smell not only the wool of his clothing, but also the scent of a clean male still warm from his exertions. His mouth savored of cinnamon and nutmeg, a pleasant exotic taste, while against her belly, Hannah felt the solid, unmistakable evidence of his arousal.

He *wanted* her to feel it, too. Made no move to put a polite distance between them, didn't try to furtively adjust himself in his clothing, didn't shift off to the side in embarrassment.

She paused in her invasion of his mouth to focus more clearly on the feel of him, big, hard, and unapologetically aroused simply from kissing *her.*

"It happens when a man kisses a pretty woman—a woman he could bed." Balfour's chin came to rest on her crown. "This does not disgust you?"

Disgust? Oh, it was wicked of her and shameless, but disgust was the farthest thing from Hannah's mind. Rather than confess that she wanted to see him, to touch him—she barely *knew* Balfour, for pity's sake—she shook her head and rested her forehead against his chest.

He held her for a long moment, a moment during which Hannah expected him to step back, grin at her, and resume his lecture about her needing a man to kiss her out of her foolish loyalty to her grandmother. A moment when she should have been stepping back, informing him that a single kiss proved nothing, and a westbound ship was infinitely preferable to being slobbered over in a London back alley.

Balfour's hand stroked over Hannah's hair, a slow, soft, soothing caress—maybe an apologetic caress—while his arousal became less evident against her belly.

And still, Hannah didn't step back.

Nine

Hannah Cooper was breathing hard simply as a result of kissing *him*... or maybe as a result of being kissed by him.

Asher stole another whiff of the sweet lavender scent of her hair and tried to locate enough sense to make his feet move. Hannah threw her whole self into her kisses. She devoured him with her mouth, took him captive with her questing hands, and used her body to obliterate his reason.

And such a body... She did not indulge in the idiot fashion of cinching her waist to sixteen inches to enhance the appearance of her bust. She didn't need to. Her curves were natural and generous, and she used them to strategic advantage when she undertook her kissing.

Great God in heaven...

"Love, we ought not to linger here." The endearment slipped out, a common form of address between common strangers here in England, but not the speech of a belted earl to a female guest under his protection.

She rubbed her nose against the wool of his jacket. "I

did not mean to kiss you, but if you expect me to apologize, you're going to have a long wait, Asher MacGregor."

She also, apparently, did not intend to turn loose of her prisoner.

His lips wandered to her temple, all without him planning it, stirring memories and heartache. "And if I apologized to you, Hannah?"

"I should have to be offended. My kissing needs work, I'll grant you, but in Boston, the gentlemen don't take liberties that often. My opportunities to practice have been limited."

He gave up trying to follow her logic. That would require ratiocination, of which he was not capable with her plastered so warmly against him.

"I'll not apologize then."

"Thank you."

He *had* to turn loose of her. By now every stable hand in the entire block had probably seen the Earl of Balfour taking liberties with his guest, and had seen that guest returning the favor. The chambermaids were likely gawking from the middens, and the nannies in their nursery aeries were dragging their fascinated young charges away from the windows.

And yet… how long had it been since a woman had remained in his embrace like this? The convenient liaisons he'd allowed himself in the past few years had not been intended to foster tenderness or cuddling. A welling of bodily loneliness obliterated the last of Asher's arousal and made him long for the moors outside Steeth.

"You can let me go, Balfour."

"Of course." He shifted his hold to pick up the discarded skates and lace his arm with Hannah's, pausing only to tuck his sporran around front, where it could prevent gross immodesties from befalling him.

"Am I presentable?"

His Boston, ferocious kisser of presuming earls, sounded shy, while her expression was so resolute it made him want to…

"Ye look damnably composed, Boston. I suppose you've made a squirrel's nest of my hair?" This was intended to force her to look at him. She obligingly eyed him up and down and then went up her on toes.

"You look a fright. The squirrels in Canada must be the size of moose," she said, smoothing her hand over his hair and her thumb over his bedamned *eyebrows*, while treating Asher to a maddening hint of lavender.

"It's more a matter of the squirrels in London being the size of American heiresses."

She dropped back to her heels and took his arm, when he'd been half hoping she'd stomp off in a female taking—for reasons not clear to any man Asher knew, only a female could get into a taking.

"You look presentable now, and I think you're safe from squirrels for the remainder of my stay here in England. Come along, Balfour. The temperature's dropping, and you promised me a tot of grog."

They started back in the direction of the house, arm in arm, though Asher was not sure whose arm was steadying whom.

"Balfour!"

Asher stopped. Beside him, Hannah shook loose of his arm and pivoted to face the stables. An instant of concern for her went through him, lest she lose her balance.

A large kilted fellow was striding from the direction of the stables. "By God, man, it's supposed to be spring this far south, and I'm about to freeze my ba—boots off. Perhaps you'll introduce me to the lady?"

Ian MacGregor stood in the middle of the alley in all his dark-haired, green-eyed glory, grinning like a handsome idiot—grinning like a younger brother who had seen far too much in the past few minutes, and who would remain silent about far too little of it.

The men in Scotland must all be the size of trees. Based on the dimensions of Balfour's siblings and their wives, the women weren't much smaller.

First Ian MacGregor had come laughing and shouting out of the stables, the man nearly as tall as his brother, and while he'd treated Balfour to a back-pounding male embrace, he'd bowed properly over Hannah's hand and subjected her to a smile that would have parted any sighted female from her sanity.

Then the others had arrived in two enormous coaches commandeered at the new King's Cross train station. Gilgallon MacGregor and his wife, Genie; Connor MacGregor and Julia; Matthew Daniels and Mary Fran MacGregor Daniels; and Mary Fran's daughter, a delightful sprite by the name of Fiona. Julia, Genie, and Matthew were of English extraction, but their hearts had clearly been claimed by their Scottish spouses.

"You can relax," Genie said as the men departed for "a wee dram" in the library, and the ladies repaired to the family parlor. "Asher's brothers are here at his invitation, and they'll behave, more or less."

Genie was an English beauty, tall, slim, blond, and reserved, while the brown-haired Julia was shorter, rounder, and a few years Genie's senior. Mary Fran, by contrast, was a red-haired Valkyrie whose voice carried a lilting burr not unlike Asher's.

"You'll scare the girl," Mary Fran said, showing a toothy grin. "The menfolk will all be on their good behavior, at least once Ian has Augusta's assurances the baby is settled in." With a confidence Hannah envied, Mary Fran gave orders to the household staff to produce "decent sustenance and some toddies."

"Ian and Augusta seem like devoted parents," Hannah observed, though the word that first came to mind was *besotted*. As Augusta MacGregor had emerged from the coach, she'd handed her baby off to Ian, and the baby had remained in his father's arms until the infant had been pried loose by the mother for transport to the nursery.

"They are ridiculous," Julia said, flopping onto the settee. "I hope Connor is every bit as bad."

She exchanged a look with Mary Fran, and then with Genie, and abruptly, Hannah became aware that all three of these women were likely in expectation of blessed events. Mary Fran's blessed event looked to be making an appearance sooner rather than later.

Gracious heavens.

"The men will behave," Genie said again, taking a seat beside Julia, "but we are not about to be so polite. Tell us, Miss Cooper, how you're faring in London and what we can do to help you make an enviable match."

The lady's blue eyes shone with sincerity, and the expressions of her companions pilloried Hannah with a similarly earnest complement of good will. They deserved honesty, and for all their smiles were kind, Hannah had the sense Balfour's womenfolk would have honesty from her, will she, nil she.

Hannah perched on the edge of her seat, back straight. "I am not set on making an enviable match. I'd like to make no match at all. What I want is to return to Boston as soon as may be, to eventually take up residence with my grandmother. That's all I've ever wanted."

Another set of glances passed around and across the room, more speculative but no less kind, maybe even concerned.

Mary Fran reached down to pet a black-and-white cat that had apparently made the journey south from Scotland. "You're not looking to snatch a title from under the noses of the English debutantes, then?"

"I want to acquit myself adequately through the social Season, then return home on the fastest ship I can find."

To her own ears, Hannah sounded neither wistful nor resolute. She sounded as if she were reciting a prayer by rote—or a history lesson.

"That's a shame," Julia said as the cat stropped itself against Genie's skirts. "The Highlands in summer are glorious, the society to be had in Edinburgh wonderful, and a shopping trip to Paris not to be missed."

"I loathe shopping." The words were out, clipped, emphatic, and irretrievable.

"Ye loathe shoppin'?" Like her brother, Mary Fran's burr became more in evidence as her sentiments came to the fore. "Now what manner of shops has Asher been taking you to, that you'd say such a thing?"

What followed was nothing less than a conference of generals intent on raiding the best shops from one end of the Strand to the other. The ladies planned forays down in Knightsbridge, sweet shops targeted on the fringes of Mayfair, and a milliner's singled out up in Bloomsbury—because they'd be shopping for books in that general direction anyway.

Midway through the planning, large trays appeared with hot drink, sandwiches, and bowls of something that looked like curdled pudding.

"A toast," Mary Fran said, holding up a mug. "Miss Cooper, you'll join us."

The drink was steaming and smelled of clove, lemon, and cinnamon… also of spirits and black tea.

"To successful shopping," Mary Fran said, smiling broadly. "For the necessities and for the fripperies."

Hannah put her drink to her lips, finding the brew restorative indeed. "That's very… pleasant."

"You call Balfour's best whiskey pleasant?" Genie asked.

"Lord Balfour has taken me to some grog shops, and my head for spirits is improving the longer I visit." The ladies found this amusing, as evidenced by their smiles and the way they peered at their drinks, at the cat, and anywhere but at Hannah.

Hannah finished her drink, not wanting to be rude. The ladies did not finish theirs, which struck her as odd—it was a very fine toddy, and the clove flavor put her in mind of Balfour's kiss earlier in the day.

While the others chatted about finding Hannah a decent mount—decent being British for safe and sane—Hannah's thoughts drifted back to that kiss.

She'd wanted to remain in Balfour's arms forever, feeling safe and cherished and anything but sane.

She'd wanted to ask him if her kisses passed muster.

She'd wanted to tell him that his certainly had.

But mostly, she'd wanted to hold him and be held by him, and to never ever leave his arms.

~

"Do I mistake the matter, or did you invite us to travel the length of the realm—your siblings, our spouses, our children, and Fiona's dratted cat—to join you here in London?"

Ian's voice held patience and a touch of amusement. Asher gave him credit for waiting until Con and Gil had gone to "check on the baggage" before posing it.

"I don't recall summoning the cat," Asher replied. "Another dram?"

Ian didn't immediately answer. He studied his brother with green eyes grown perspicacious with age.

Or marriage, or fatherhood. Perhaps from having been declared the earl for a year or two.

"You are staring at that door as closely as Con and Gill did," Ian said, ambling over to the sideboard and refreshing his drink. "They have the excuse of having been cooped up in the damn train for most of the past two days, breathing soot, listening to Fiona beg for stories, and wishing neither the cat nor the baby enjoyed such relentlessly healthy digestion. Why are you pacing like a caged beast?"

Asher came to a halt before the fireplace, which sported the typical stinking, desultory blaze fed by coal. "I have two female guests, foreigners, one of whom doesn't often leave the house, and the other is determined to be difficult about finding a husband. You'd be pacing too."

Which explanation earned him another quiet perusal from his younger brother before Ian passed his drink to Asher. "Let's nip off to the nursery, shall we? Augusta is tarrying there, I've no doubt of it, and you need a proper introduction to our mutual heir."

Asher would rather be put in a cage in the Menagerie than visit the nursery. "This would be the little fellow with the healthy digestion? We exchanged greetings in the general melee accompanying his arrival. You go hide in the nursery with your wife and son, and I'll ensure the womenfolk aren't devouring Miss Cooper's limited store of genteel manners one dainty, carnivorous bite at a time."

He set the drink down untasted and made for the door, hoping Ian would fall in behind without further interrogation.

"He's just a wee baby, Asher. He'll likely have a deal of siblings to get into trouble with, and I've a suspicion his cousins are already on the way. Mary Fran certainly hasn't wasted any time adding to her collection."

Ian spoke quietly, his burr evident: a wee babbie, siblin's…

Asher paused with his hand on the door, his back to his brother, while something—censure, curiosity, *pity*—wafted thickly on the coal-scented air. "All of which reassures me that should I fail to find a bride this year, the succession will continue to be in good hands."

Ian spun him by the arm. "For God's perishing

sake, mon, will you let it go? You came back when you could, and there's an end to it. We managed, you managed, and now we move on. You're not the first man to wander too far from home for too long, and you willna be the last."

"Home is a relative concept, and for some of us, a vague one. You'd best go see to your son."

He was pulling rank, as an older brother, as the ostensible head of the family, as the host. Ian scrubbed a hand over eyes that conveyed fatigue, exasperation, and… affection.

Affection was better than pity—marginally.

"See to my son, I shall. You go rescue the Yankee rebel, though she seems a steady enough sort of female. It shouldn't be too difficult to get her fired off, with the combined might of all the MacGregor womenfolk to see the thing done." Ian's gaze became speculative. "Squiring her about will keep you nicely occupied should the debutantes take notice of you."

"The debutantes will be too busy admiring my brothers and envying their wives."

Ian smirked and stepped back enough that Asher could open the door and flee—and *leave*.

"You can't hide in here," Balfour said, shoving away from the old wooden counter and stuffing a thick pair of glasses into a vest pocket. "*I'm* hiding here, and you should be upstairs with the rest of them, yodeling their ballads and stomping through their flings."

Himself was in a cranky mood, despite the half

smile on his lips. His vaguely belligerent stance, the way his hair stuck out on one side as if he'd run his hand through it repeatedly—not to mention the absence of a proper coat—all suggested Balfour was Not Receiving, not that Hannah's bedclothes were appropriate to a social call either.

"I'm peckish. You wouldn't deny a guest a snack, would you?" She brushed past him without more than glancing at his exposed knees and went to the tea drawers, measuring out a pot's worth of an Assam blend.

"I would not deny you food. Make enough for two, if you please." He set down a document of some sort and went to the bread box. "Will you join me in a scone?"

Hannah was inclined to refuse his offhand invitation, except… she'd *missed* him. In the days since his family had invaded the house, she'd had no peace, no quiet, and no time spent in Balfour's exclusive company. She'd been dragged from one commercial emporium to another by the laughing, energetic MacGregor ladies; she'd been held captive in the nursery, reading stories to Fiona and trying not to notice how dear and adorable the baby was; she'd sat through endless noisy family meals where argument and teasing shared equal space on the menu with good food and fine drink…

While nobody called her Boston.

Nobody noticed what an ordeal it was to manage Aunt Enid.

Nobody kissed her.

"Half a scone will do for me. What are you reading, sir?"

"It's a treatise written several years ago, 'On the Mode of Communication of Cholera.' Butter or jam?"

"Both, please." She took the kettle off the hob and set the tea to steeping. "Is this your idea of recreational reading?"

He fetched the cream from the window box and arranged a tray with scones in a basket next to a little tub of butter and a jar of raspberry jam—all very orderly. "This city is ripe for another epidemic, and nobody really knows what causes them."

"*Another* epidemic?"

"There was a bad outbreak here of Asian cholera less than twenty years ago. Nearly everybody who contracted the disease died from it. Doctor Snow does not think the thing is conveyed by foul miasmas."

Cholera was not a cheering topic, but it apparently interested the earl. "What do you think?"

"I think, between the open sewers, the overcrowding, and the poor health of much of the populace, nobody in their right mind would call this place home if they could help it."

His tone held despair and old misery. He stared at the full tray and ran his hand back through his hair. The light in the kitchen was dim, but Hannah suspected he'd lost weight since they'd come to London.

"Put me on a ship for Boston, Balfour. You can return to your wintry Highlands and brood about foul miasmas to your heart's content."

The half smile was back, and it was a relief to see it. "You never give up, do you, Hannah Cooper?"

She perched on a stool and pulled up her nightgown far enough to stick out her right foot. "I do not give up, but sometimes I accede to the dictates of common sense." She wiggled her toes for good measure.

The half smile on his face blossomed into the genuine article, even reaching his dark eyes. "Maiden's Blush becomes you. Does the lift make your foot ache?"

Hannah dropped her hem and hoped the shadows were sufficient to conceal her flaming cheeks. "Not my foot, but my hip, so to speak."

"Your bum. I am—I was—a doctor. I've dealt with far less genteel concepts than a lady's derriere."

He was still smiling, at her maiden's blush, no doubt. Hannah checked the tea, and even if it had been nigh transparent, she would have declared it strong enough. "Shall we?" She gestured with her chin toward a small round table by the old-fashioned open hearth.

On the floor above them, some lively, stomping Highland dance came to an end. Augusta, or whoever was at the keyboard, switched to a dreamy triple meter.

"How that infant endures such a racket I do not know," Hannah said. "He seems to take it all in stride—for a fellow who's not quite walking."

A shadow flitted across Balfour's face as he took the chair beside Hannah's. "Babies adjust to their surroundings easily enough, as long as their loved ones are close at hand and minding them."

This was not an entirely medical opinion. "You don't hold with children being tucked away in the nursery until they can spout Latin verbs and recite Bible passages by the score?"

He crossed his feet at the ankles, which caused the drape of his kilt to shift over his thighs. "I don't hold with children being expected to labor like adults from their earliest years. I don't hold with children being turned over to the care of paid strangers, such that their parents are then strangers to them. I don't hold with letting children starve not ten blocks from some of the wealthiest, most wasteful—"

Hannah patted his hand where it rested near his untouched tea. "I am not the only one who has decided opinions in this kitchen. I think your brother Ian shares your views of child-rearing. He cuddles that baby at every opportunity."

Balfour blew out a breath. "You want children, Hannah. I've watched you with Fiona. She adores you already and is trying to mimic your accent when she's having tea with her cat."

And when had his lordship caught his niece entertaining in the nursery?

"We can't always have what we want. Balfour, are you going to leave me even a smidgen of jam?"

On the next floor up, in the music room, three male voices rose in close harmony, the words indistinguishable, the tone tender and lyrical.

"What I want, Hannah Cooper, is to dance with you. May I have that honor?"

He was in an odd, off mood, with each unlikely topic of conversation bearing a peculiar agitation. Cholera, babies, and now a kitchen waltz.

"Here, in this kitchen, you want to dance?"

"A test of the magic Maiden's Blush slippers." He rose and bowed, extending one hand while holding the other behind his back, as if he were in some glittering ballroom, not a deserted, cavernous kitchen.

She had missed him. Hannah put her bare hand in his and let him draw her into waltz position. "Your brothers sing very well."

"We made a solid quartet, though Connor probably can't pull off the impressive counter-tenor he sported as a lad."

Balfour drew Hannah closer while she tried to attune herself to the phrasing of the music. She wore no corset, he was in barely decent attire—no sporran this time—and still, he didn't move off with her. He enfolded her against his body, swaying slightly with the music.

The last time they'd been this close, they'd both been fully clothed and dressed for the out-of-doors. The difference was… astounding. Asher MacGregor gave off heat, and without a brisk wind, the scent of him was a concentrated pleasure for Hannah's nose.

Cloves and ginger, maybe a hint of cinnamon, but also… sadness, a soul weariness that made Hannah lean into him for his comfort as well as her own.

"We'll start slowly," he murmured right near her ear. He tucked their joined hands close, so Hannah's knuckles rested over his heart. Her head rested against his shoulder, their posture becoming so sumptuously intimate, Hannah closed her eyes the better to savor it.

When he shifted his feet, Hannah followed him easily. Behind closed eyes, she entrusted him with her entire balance while she floated, safe and warm in his arms. How long they swayed in the shadows she did not know, but when the melody died away above them and the piano fell silent, she made no move to step back.

"Hannah." He gathered her closer, his cheek resting against her temple. "Boston. This isna wise. You should go, lass."

Soon enough, she would go. She would leave, cross an ocean, and not come back. *Now*, she kissed him, raised her face without opening her eyes, used her fingers on his jaw to orient herself, and pressed her lips to his.

He growled and wrapped both arms around her, turning the kiss from a delicate exploration to a passionate onslaught in an instant. Wanting tore through Hannah, for him, for home, for what she could not have. Wanting and relief to have her hands on him again.

"Balfour—"

"Asher, damn it. Ye kiss a man witless, the least ye can do is use his damned name."

She planted her nose against his open collar and inhaled him. "Asher. I've missed you, missed—"

He hoisted her up onto the counter. "Say my name again."

She was off her feet, nearly at eye level with him. Her fingers went to the buttons of his shirt, her hands hungry for the feel of his skin. "Asher MacGregor. You left me to worry, *for days*. I lost sleep, fretting that my kisses were lacking, that you had been humoring the clumsy efforts of a Colonial bumpkin. You sit at the head of the table as if you're an ocean away and barely say a word..."

She was pulling his shirttails from his waistband when he caught her hands in his. "Does this feel like a man who's humoring ye? Like a man who's an ocean away?"

Through the soft wool of his kilt, he used her fingers to shape the length of his arousal.

That he could behave so indifferently toward her before others was troubling. That she might not have any more such private interludes with him was *unbearable*.

"I want you, Asher MacGregor. Now. I want to touch you."

She heard him swallow. While her hand traced his flesh through his clothes, he stepped closer. "I don't mind that ye beggar my reason, Boston—not nearly as much as I should—but I canna allow ye to beggar my honor."

This was some befuddling male allusion to his duty as her host, or his lordly obligations, or some blighted obstacle Hannah would not tolerate. "I am not a virgin. I am ruined, do you understand me? I have no virginity to protect, and *I want you*."

While he went still in that considering, unfathomable way of his, Hannah found the pins holding the kilt closed and withdrew them. The wool slithered to the floor, leaving the earl covered by the long tails of his shirt and the open plackets of his vest.

"I suppose ye want me naked as a newborn?" He didn't growl the question so much as purr it. Hannah's insides turned over, then over again.

She nodded. He shrugged out of his clothing with a twitch of broad shoulders, leaving him wearing only firelight, shadows… and a smile.

"Look your fill, Hannah Cooper, because your expression tells me whoever the blessed fool was you bestowed your favors on, he didna pleasure you properly."

Hannah could not take her eyes off the abundant masculine pulchritude before her. In the course of her travels around London, she had seen the famous statues at the British Museum. They were puny specimens compared to the Earl of Balfour. Puny, cold, and unimpressive, and they were not standing in this kitchen, naked, aroused, and smiling—at her.

Ten

Hannah Cooper had missed him.

The woman had no idea what a weapon she wielded with those words. *Nobody* missed Asher MacGregor. He'd been declared dead, and after years of silence, even Ian had probably believed it so.

His siblings had picked up their lives and moved on without him, the brother they'd known only lately. The family in Canada who might have missed him was gone, and yet Hannah Cooper, starchy, stubborn, and Boston-bound, announced she'd missed him while sharing his very roof.

Though for a woman who'd missed him, her expression was as wary as it was fascinated.

"Am I to be the only one revealing my treasures, Hannah Cooper?"

She blinked but—may she be blessed for all time—kept her gaze on his erect cock. "Can I—May I touch you?"

A question for a question. He did not believe for a moment she'd parted with her virginity in anything but name, and there would be a limit—an *excruciating* limit—on the extent to which he indulged her curiosity now.

"You may touch me, and I will touch you." He used his hands to gently part her knees and stepped between them. "If kisses don't convince you that you'd enjoy the life of a married woman, perhaps pleasure might."

Her brows drew down. "It's not exactly a pleasure to look on you, Asher MacGregor."

"It's no'?" Before she could stare a hole in his parts, he took her hand and wrapped her fingers around his shaft. "It's terrible hard work, is it?"

She shaped him, slipped her palm along his length, and traced the sensitive rim, slowly, as if she were circling the lip of a delicate wineglass. Asher had to strain over the roaring in his ears to hear what the daft woman was saying. "Seeing you like this makes me upset, inside. Anxious and… witless. You make me stupid and… this part of you is very soft."

Her thumb dallied with the tip. Asher's hips flexed forward, and God bless her and the entire city of Boston, she did not take her hand away. "Are ye tryin' to make me spend, woman?"

"I'm trying to learn how you're put together. Men and women are very different."

Some ruined woman she was, babbling her ignorance of anatomy in awestruck tones for all the pots and pans to hear. The surge of sheer affection he felt for her blended with raging desire and restored his resolve.

"You need to learn how you're put together, Hannah. Let me show you."

He covered her mouth with his, wedging himself

as close to her as the bloody counter would allow. She wrapped his cock in a wonderfully tight grip and held him snugly while he teased at her lips with his tongue. "Kiss me, witch."

For once, Hannah Cooper wasn't arguing. While her tongue came out to play skittles with his sanity, her hand started a slow, sleeving caress of his cock.

"I like how hot you are," she whispered, nuzzling his neck. "You're never cold. Not ever."

He'd been cold—he'd been frozen stone solid, but she was thawing him like a female bonfire.

Which was not at all the point of the gathering.

Asher slid his hand up the silky firmness of her calf, slowly, slowly. She was sturdy and female, and more significantly, she was allowing him to hike up her nightclothes with nary a peep of protest.

"Balfour, what do you think you're doing?"

A question, not a protest, and while she did turn loose of his now-throbbing cock, it was only to run her hands through his hair and rest her elbows on his shoulders.

"You've touched me, now I'm going to touch you. You're going to like it, too, Hannah Cooper."

She wrinkled her nose. "You're not to remove my clothing."

The hell he wasn't. Except her eyes shifted away as she issued that order.

"Hannah?"

"Hmm?"

"I've had my hands all over your delectable bum. I've handled your hips, and I've watched you walk from several interesting angles. With your clothes off, you'll look very like any other healthy young woman your age."

She opened her mouth, probably to castigate him for his freely given medical opinion, so he resumed the kissing. This produced a gratifyingly pliant female, one who sighed into his mouth as his thumb brushed over the curls shielding her sex.

The next bit was delicate, so he brought her hand to his engorged cock again. She obliged by stroking him languidly, the sweetest torture a man had ever endured.

"Am I doing it right?"

"Slower," he managed, gliding his thumb down, down to the… right… *there*.

"*Everlasting powers*… Do that again."

She was slick and hot, but he was determined and had an anatomist's keen sense of what went where. He circled on the bud of flesh God had bestowed on women to compensate them for some of the burden of putting up with men. "Like that, lass?"

His answer was a sound from the back of her throat, a low, sighing moan against his neck. "Asher… Mac… Gregor. What…?"

Her hand on his cock stopped moving, and not an instant too soon. "Let yourself have this, love. Let me give it to you."

He cradled her nape in his palm, to steady himself, to keep her from shifting away, to keep the lavender scent of her spiraling through his senses.

Her breathing changed, becoming deeper and harsher, and yet he didn't shift his attentions. Were they lovers, he'd ease away, get his mouth on her breasts, use the raspberry jam to wonderful advantage on her nipples—

"Asher—?"

He could feel the arousal humming through her, gathering momentum. "I'm here, love. Hold me."

Her hand was fisted in his hair, a little pain that gave him clarity of purpose when his body was clamoring to join with hers. She'd be wet, hot, tight, and willing... Her hips started a minute movement against the stroke of his thumb, a little push and retreat that accentuated the pleasure he was building for her.

She'd be *heaven* to make love with.

She *was* heaven, coming apart in his arms with a soft, sobbing exhale while she pushed hungrily into the pressure he held against her sex. He gave her a moment afterward, to settle, to shift from clutching at his hair to stroking her fingers slowly over his nape. While she calmed and went soft against him, he counted the pulse beats in his stones and matched his breathing to hers.

As distractions went, that was wholly ineffective. When he was sure Hannah would not collapse back onto the counter in a boneless sprawl, he stepped back far enough to get to work on the bows holding her nightclothes closed.

She remained silent as he peeled back soft layers of flannel and silk, his darker fingers moving against her pale flesh.

"Watch me, Hannah. Watch while I find the same pleasure you took from me."

With one hand, he began to stroke himself, but lightly—it would take nothing, nothing at all to bring him off. With the other, he pushed Hannah's nightclothes aside, exposing full pale breasts tipped with rosy, puckered nipples. Her chest was still flushed from her orgasm; her eyes bore the sheen of passion; but she did watch him.

And he watched her. Took in the way her breasts gently rose and fell with her breathing, the way her coppery braid moved with them as it cascaded over her right shoulder. He saw her lips part, watched her take visual inventory of him in all his arousal.

He closed his eyes, trying to make the moment last. At the feel of Hannah's hand brushing over his naked chest—just that, just that soft, wondering stroke of her fingers—he surrendered to a drenching, pulsing pleasure.

When it was over, his forehead was braced against Hannah's shoulder, his belly was a sticky mess, and he was trying to remain upright without getting that mess on Hannah or her clothing.

And yet for a few moments, he stayed where he was, Hannah's hand on his neck, her cheek against his temple, the scent of his spent seed wending through the fragrance of her lavender soap and female heat.

With a mighty gathering of resolve and a little push away from the counter, Asher stood upright, then grabbed a napkin from the table and used it to swab at his belly. Hannah shifted on the counter—her bum had to be uncomfortable—and drew her nightclothes around her.

Rather than mourn what had been taken from his sight, Asher snatched up his kilt and got the thing fastened around his waist. The frown Hannah treated him to suggested she might have regretted her hasty covering up when it resulted in him doing the same.

Her fingers started retying bows, and Asher felt loss slicing keenly.

"Let me do that, Hannah."

He brushed her hands aside and took over the task, lingering over each bow and enjoying thoroughly that she'd allow him to tend her this way.

"Is there a name for what just happened?"

"A name for it?" There were many, many names. Foolishness was one, self-torment another. Over a stout serving of whiskey, he could probably think up dozens, and most of them would involve recrimination and regret.

But not all.

"Inside my body, that… I don't know how to describe it. An earthquake of pleasure."

She would be the death of his self-restraint. "You've weathered earthquakes, that you can command such a term?"

"In Virginia," she said, her tongue slipping over her upper lip. "Only the once. Everything shook and shook. *Everything.*"

"It's called an orgasm, and you can bring it on yourself with a bit of practice. I practice frequently, as do, I'm convinced, most people with any sense."

She wanted to ask him more questions, he could see that, though the moment was delicate, full of potential wrong turns and poorly chosen words for both of them.

He finished with the last bow and allowed himself to pat it where it lay at the juncture of her thighs. When he should have helped her off the counter and made some inane observation about the tea getting cold, he instead stepped back into the haven between her legs and slipped his arms around her.

"What happened to you is simply a woman's pleasure. There are medical terms for it and vulgar terms for it, but if you choose properly, your husband will see to it as often as you ask it of him."

She said nothing for a long moment then drew herself up and way from him.

"Was this simply a demonstration, then, of the wonders I can anticipate on the far side of the altar?"

Her question was chilly, as if she were bracing herself for Asher to admit that was exactly what he'd been up to.

As if she knew he'd tried to serve himself that very ration of twaddle.

He could not be so craven. Not with her.

"I was rather hoping, Hannah Cooper, this was a taste of what *I* might anticipate on the far side of the altar."

"I foresee a problem, Husband."

Ian patted the bed beside him. "Your husband is lonely, Augusta MacGregor. That is a problem, though one easily remedied."

The deceptively prim set of her mouth quirked, and yet, she did not immediately hop onto the mattress. No, she finished tying off the long, dark braid snaking over her shoulder—a braid Ian often had unraveled well before morning—flipped it back over her dressing gown, and turned on her vanity stool to regard him.

"Do you know how distracting it is to be tending to my evening toilette while in the mirror I see I have earned the regard of a handsome man who sprawls on my bed wearing only his spectacles?"

"Our bed." He took off his eyeglasses. "Our lonely bed."

She rose and turned down the sconces on either side of that bed. "Your older brother is lonely, Ian. Perilously lonely."

So Asher was to join them in bed, just as he'd haunted his entire family all the years of his absence.

"He sent for us, and we've presented ourselves accordingly, Wife. I considered dragging him into the parlor to sing with us this evening, but the man honestly isn't used to having family about."

She climbed onto the bed in darkness, a frisson of female fragrance—soap, starch, and summer flowers—accompanying the dipping of the mattress.

"He knows about having family underfoot. He was raised with you from the age of eleven, and from everything you've said, he had loving family in his early childhood."

Ian waited while Augusta extricated herself from the voluminous billows of her nightclothes. Since the child's birth, she'd been more modest than when they'd first married, an endearing contradiction when she'd eschewed a wet nurse for their son.

"I can't gainsay your conclusions, Augusta."

"There are things you aren't telling me. Things about our Asher. I like him, you know, but there's a bleakness..."

Augusta got situated along Ian's side, tucking close under his arm.

Ian's wife on the scent of some topic was a force of nature. He didn't even try to change the subject. "Asher's mother died in his infancy, which has to leave a mark on a boy. That his father remarried almost immediately can't have sat well with him either."

A warm female hand stroked over the planes and muscles of Ian's belly. "I think it's worse than that. I think it has to do with his father being willing to leave his mother, to return to Scotland without her, no matter it wasn't meant as a one-way journey. Could you travel from Canada without me?"

God, no. "If you commanded me to, if you insisted I make peace with my family in Scotland, the question might become very different."

The hand on Ian's belly went still, which was damned frustrating when those warm, knowing fingers had been drifting ever lower.

"Asher's mother was literate, Ian. She could have at least written and let the man know he had a son."

The discussion came very close to violating the confidences Ian had sworn he'd keep, but he hadn't yet crossed the line of fraternal loyalty. "I suspect Asher's mother wanted her husband to make a choice freely, between her and his family in Scotland. She withheld news of her pregnancy because she didn't want to take unfair advantage."

"Or she was being an idiot, or maybe she didn't want her Scottish husband back?"

A prudent husband would make no rejoinder to that comment. "So what is this problem you foresee, Wife? Let's set it aside, because there's another problem arising for which I need your intimate and undivided counsel."

To emphasize his point, he wrapped her hand around his burgeoning shaft. Augusta gave him a wifely squeeze and a pat, but other than that withheld her *counsel.*

"I went down to the kitchen, thinking to warm up a mug of milk before we retired, and I found the room occupied."

"Kitchens are generally warm. I've been known to occupy a few myself." He occupied his hand with a luscious female fundament, which at least earned him a sigh in the darkness.

"Asher and Miss Cooper were engaged in a passionate embrace."

Damn, not again. "How passionate?"

Rather than answer, Augusta shifted beside him so her derriere pressed against his hip. This was the marital signal to spoon himself around her, which Ian was abundantly willing to do.

"Your dear brother wore not a stitch, Ian, and Miss Cooper's night clothing was in considerable disarray. Their embrace was *intimately* passionate. I cannot attest to the full extent of the improprieties they were engaged in, but suffice it to say I retreated without gaining their notice."

With the English—Augusta was English by birth and breeding—a man had to listen not so much to their words as to their inflections, their tone, what they chose to keep unsaid. "You were not shocked."

She took his hand and removed it from the pleasurable exploration of her hip and *derriere* to wrap it around her breast. "I'm married to *you*, Ian MacGregor. Shocking me has become a difficult undertaking. I was taken aback. Your brother's eyes were closed, and the expression on his face—"

Ian let her have her pause, because for Augusta to have seen such a private moment would have been intensely uncomfortable, even if she hadn't been precisely shocked. "Is he smitten, then?"

The selfsame question Ian had been asking since coming upon Asher and Miss Cooper kissing in the mews days ago. Augusta shifted again, nudging at his erect cock with her backside. "I think it's worse than that. I think he's in love with the woman and doesn't even know it."

"And Miss Cooper?"

Augusta rolled her hips, allowing Ian to gain the first increment of penetration into damp female heaven. "I could not see her face, but she is determined to return to her grandmother in Boston without marrying."

"And Asher is smitten with her. This is a problem, but not one we are going to solve tonight."

Perhaps not ever. As Ian eased into his wife's body and tasked himself with seeing to her pleasure, he spared his brother one final thought: if Asher was smitten with a woman, any woman at all, it was a problem—Asher being Asher, and having at least two continents worth of guilt stowed among his personal belongings.

It was also a bloody miracle.

Asher watched as Gilgallon—the Family Charmer, according to Hannah—led her in a promenade around the Moreland ballroom. Their Graces presided over the festivities, the duke by turns a green-eyed aging eagle and, when he beheld his duchess, a doting swain from an earlier time. Despite Moreland's geniality on social occasions, he was rumored to be Victoria's favorite confidante among the old guard now that Wellington had ascended to the rank of angel.

"She'll be fine." Ian handed Asher a cup of something noxious, the English being incapable of enjoying good spirits in mixed company.

"It's not her I'm worried about."

Though Asher was worried, or anxious. Further refining on the roiling sense of doom in Asher's gut was not wise though, not when Ian was regarding him with that pensive frown.

"Shall we be worried about you, Brother?"

When a man left his family to shift for themselves, a younger brother could learn to serve as head of that family, and also, apparently, drop back into the role at will.

"Moreland himself has given me the nod, Ian. I'd say I'm settling in nicely."

"Moreland's duchess has given you the nod. Victoria no doubt put her up to it, or the duchess is scouting you as a prospect for one of her regiment of young, marriageable female relations."

This observation was offered humorously, and yet it rankled. Asher had seen the looks from the mamas and chaperones, and felt more than a stirring of pity for Hannah, who was getting entirely different looks from the same quarters.

"I'll marry eventually."

Ian snorted and took a sip of his drink—or pretended to. "You will not *re*marry until you lay your late wife to rest, and that you have yet to do."

One could not simply cock back his fist and use it on

his brother's handsome face in public. "You agreed not to broach that topic, much less in a venue such as this."

"You are a fool, Asher MacGregor. Not one of your family would censure you for taking a bride of mixed blood. Of course you would take a bride, and of course such a woman would understand you and your circumstances better than most."

Monique hadn't understood him, not any better than any other wife might have, but she'd accepted him.

"And you are a fool if you think Monique's heritage has anything to do with why I grieve for her privately."

Across the ballroom, Connor was introducing Hannah to the duke. His Grace bowed over her hand and kept it in his, while the duchess smiled benignly at Connor. For an instant, Moreland aimed a look straight over the heads of the crowd—His Grace still boasted both height and excellent posture—and *challenged* Asher to something without a word.

"Moreland is old school, isn't he?" Ian remarked. "You'd do well to take a leaf from his book. He's patriarchal as hell and understands the value of family. You have family too, Asher, lots of it. They love you. They would share your burdens."

The words were sincere, also misguided. "Ian, they do not *know* me. One cannot love a stranger."

"One cannot love a ghost either."

Marriage to Augusta had honed Ian's ability to deliver such insights from a taut bow of loyalty and exasperation. Maybe Augusta nocked the arrows, in fact, and Ian only fired them at the target.

"My marriage was brief." Brief and happy.

"And over several years ago."

Asher put aside the drink, resisting the urge to douse his brother's lectures with it. "I suppose I'll have to lead Miss Hannah out for the first set?"

Ian lifted his glass to salute some old marquess twirling a young lady down the room. "Your rank will give her consequence. Your support will give her confidence."

As if she needed either. Hannah had flirted shamelessly with the old duke, and now she was batting her eyes at Cousin Malcolm, sparkling her way around the ballroom in a gown of so many shades of green and gold, it hurt Asher's eyes to behold her.

"The lift in her shoe gives her balance, and that's a greater boon than either my title or my company."

"Augusta says the Scots ought to hire out as professional martyrs, but my theory is that you're letting Miss Hannah have her Season tormenting the bachelors and worrying the debutantes before you put your ring on her finger."

Abruptly, the ballroom was too warm, the hour too late, the scent of wealth, perfumes, and overheated bodies too cloying. All that preliminary skirmishing over Mon—over the past had been merely the opening feint, for Ian had only now laid his true concern at his brother's feet.

"Miss Hannah will return to Boston at the end of the Season, there to set up housekeeping with her aging granny, whom I'm given to believe is frail and much in need of cosseting."

Ian's gaze followed Hannah as she beamed at some relation of the Marquess of Spathfoy. Some wealthy, handsome English relation of marriageable age. Cousin

Malcolm had his toothsome self glued to the side of her Connor did not occupy, and the looks from the chaperones had become venomous.

"No female related to Hannah Cooper could have the least patience for cosseting," Ian replied.

Which had been Asher's initial surmise too. "I've made some inquiries. Hannah's stepfather is known for shrewd business practices, and for ruling his home with an iron hand."

"I'm shrewd." Ian's observation held neither arrogance nor humor. "You're shrewd."

"I was trying to be delicate. My sources indicate the man's commercial behaviors cross the line into sharp practice. He's socially tolerated because of his Old World connections, upon which he trades at every opportunity. He has the sole care of Hannah's paternal grandmother, whom Hannah characterizes as a poor relation."

A poor relation who could manage to send her granddaughter only two brief letters in all the weeks Hannah had been from home.

"You're not poor, Asher, and neither would you take advantage of a woman under your protection." Something in the banked ferocity of Ian's gaze suggested the comment did not allude to Hannah's grandmother.

"Do we need to step outside, Ian?"

"We need to clarify what your intentions are toward Miss Hannah."

Ian was shrewd, but he wasn't prescient, nor could he read Asher's thoughts. That he'd turn up as Hannah's champion was something of a puzzle. "I have proposed marriage to the woman on more than one occasion."

The satisfaction of having surprised his brother was bittersweet and short-lived, because Ian immediately reasoned to the logical conclusion. "She's turned you down. What did you do, Asher? You're passably good-looking, wealthy, you've the damned title, and your land marches with royal holdings. No woman in her right mind would turn down all that."

"And yet... Twice, quite decisively. I didn't get the impression she was dithering for show, either. She lectured me sincerely on my duty lying on this side of the Atlantic and hers on the other, and while a gentleman does not argue with a lady, even when she's in error, in this case, the lady is right." And all the while she'd lectured him, Hannah had fastened his waistcoat buttons and tidied his clothing and then his hair.

She'd smoothed her thumbs over his eyebrows too, which curious caress Asher was coming to crave.

Ian dumped his drink in a potted palm. "You own some of the fastest goddamned ships ever to carry freight. Why can't she nip over to Boston every summer and check in on the granny, if the woman's too frail to brave an ocean crossing?"

Yes, why couldn't she?

Why *wouldn't* she?

"My charms are apparently not sufficient to convince Hannah such an arrangement would serve, any more than I could manage the earldom by popping in for a few weeks every summer."

"Get some more charms, then."

Miss Hannah Cooper had fully inspected all but a few of Asher's limited charms, though Ian hardly needed to be apprised of that. "Ian, Hannah may have the right of it. I do need to be in Scotland, and her grandmother may well need the protection Hannah can offer her."

"Elders don't live forever."

Ian had an answer for everything, but his expression had taken on the same resigned exasperation Asher had felt since leaving Hannah in the kitchen three nights past. "Not forever, but how old is Fenimore?"

The soft swearing that ensued was virtuosic, encompassing English, Gaelic, and even a touch of French. Across the room, Cousin Malcolm had found some bloody polite pretext for kissing Hannah's gloved fingers, while Asher occupied himself with calculating the earliest date he might have more answers to the questions he'd sent to his office in Boston.

Eleven

Malcolm MacAllan was a flirt and a comfort.

The comfort came from his smile, which was sympathetic, conveying to Hannah that with Malcolm, she would never have to use her knee to good advantage in some dark corner. His height was reassuring too—just an inch over six feet, which made him merely tall—as were his sandy hair and blue eyes. Nothing about Malcolm held the sense of banked power and emotion common to his MacGregor relations.

Malcolm's friendly smile was at variance with Asher's version of the same expression, which had had a lot of teeth and more than a little challenge to it. *That* smile had gotten Hannah through the ordeal of her first public waltz.

"Thank you." She accepted a glass of some reddish drink from Malcolm. "I don't know how these ladies dance, their frames are that delicate."

The waistlines in evidence were so tiny as to strike Hannah as… deformed, as discordant as the cheerful greetings offered by one young lady after another, completely contradicting the calculation in their eyes.

"They haven't your presence, Miss Hannah. You must pity them."

They hadn't her fortune was what he meant, but a little dissembling in the name of manners had to be permitted.

"Tell me about Paris. I've wondered if it's as beautiful as one hears."

He obliged her with small talk while they strolled the gallery that ran along one side of the ballroom and opened onto a large brick terrace. The breeze from the out-of-doors was heavenly, a siren call to obscure shadows and fresh air.

"Would you like to sit for a moment, Miss Hannah? Dancing slippers have been known to pinch as the night progresses."

Malcolm offered the same friendly smile, making Hannah realize she'd become overly sensitive. He wasn't alluding to her limp, and he could not possibly know about the lift on her right heel.

"Might we take some air, Mr. Macallan?" The question was half-sincere, manners being even more strict here than in the stuffiest reaches of Boston's version of Polite Society.

"Of course. The terrace will be nearly as crowded as the dance floor."

Another not-quite-truth, because save for two couples conversing at the balustrade, the terrace was blessedly peaceful and quiet. Hannah settled herself on a bench and took the opportunity to taste the libation in her glass.

Gracious heavens, the drink was more honey than anything else. She set the glass aside, vowing to follow the example of the MacGregor ladies and tuck a wee flask into her pocket on the next outing.

Malcolm came down beside her on a whiff of gardenia. The scent was soothing, if a trifle odd on a man. "What would you like to know, Hannah Cooper?"

"I beg your pardon?"

"About my cousins, or third cousins, whatever. In Scotland, anybody with a drop of consanguinity qualifies as family, particularly with the Highland clans."

Rather like Boston. "Why is that?"

He let out a sigh, and with it, a bit of his genial persona slipped away into the shadows. "Because there are so damned few of us left. It's the fault of the sheep, you see."

"Sheep here devour Highlanders?"

This was contrary to the tales Hannah's idiot half brothers told regarding sheep and rural populations, though she knew better than to offer that comment.

"Sheep are profitable. They've been bred to thrive even where winters are harsh and fodder hard to come by. For generations, the landlords have been smitten with the idea that more sheep and fewer crofters means better income. The land can't support both the tenants and the flocks. Ergo, the tenants have been burned out."

Malcolm's tone had lost all bantering and taken on an edge of lament—not anger, but sorrow.

"Surely in these modern times, such a barbarity—"

He shook his head. "In these modern times, there are hardly any crofters to burn out and chase down to the docks of Aberdeen and Edinburgh, there to take ship for the New World—any new world—before they starve trying to live on seaweed and mackerel. And what the Clearances didn't accomplish, the famines did."

"I thought the famine was in Ireland." And she'd thought the terrace would be a pleasant respite, not a place to tell tales of ghosts and feudal destruction.

Malcolm glanced over at her, as if trying to gauge how much honesty she might endure without a fit of the vapors. "There is good land in Scotland, but not enough of it. The potato is a humble crop, needing neither rich land nor much tending. It's the only crop suitable for difficult conditions that produces enough yield per acre to support the most impoverished. Then too, it's a simple crop to plant and harvest—children wielding a shovel can see it done. We grew enough potatoes up north to feel the blight keenly."

We. In this he was like the MacGregors. *We* referred to the family, the clan, the nation.

When was the last time Hannah had used the word in any of those senses?

Malcolm squeezed her gloved hand. "I've lectured you to silence. You must retaliate by interrogating me. Did you know Ian used to be the earl?"

A cheerier topic by far, though Hannah had been apprised of this bit of MacGregor history by Augusta herself.

"While Asher was thought dead," she replied. "I haven't quite figured out what Asher was doing larking around in the north woods in the first place, and one can't exactly quiz him on it, can one?" Though one wanted to. Badly.

"One can quiz me. Asher went back to Canada to

keep an eye on Mary Fran's English husband, or so we were told. I suspect he went to ensure his maternal antecedents were faring adequately, given that most of them were incapable of writing, and word of his relations was scarce indeed. Then too, he was a physician, and perhaps wanted to hone his practice in foreign climes."

Hannah was going to pry. She was going to ring a peal over Malcolm's head if he so much as intimated Asher's mother was deserving of anything less than complete respect, but first she was going to pry. "His maternal relations?"

"His mother was of native extraction." The words were offered with studied neutrality, which was fortunate for Malcolm. "I gather you didn't know, though it's not exactly a secret. Asher's father was off seeking his fortune in trade as a younger son will do, and took a wife in the wilderness, which I understand was not unusual for the times."

Hannah knew enough of the trapping culture herself to understand that many of the men deriving their livelihoods from such trade had *two* families—one in the interior, and one at the trading post, with the twain never intended or likely to meet.

In the New World, Asher's father had had one family, and only one.

"And then he became heir to the earldom?"

Malcolm sat forward, his evening coat pulling across shoulders that sported a complement of muscle. He was an attractive, fit man, and why he wasn't twirling some other lady down the room at that moment was a small puzzle.

"Asher's father married his native wife, and was

careful to do so in a manner that would leave no doubt about the legitimacy of their progeny."

Puzzle pieces started to line up, to form edges to Hannah's image of the present earl. "The marriage took place before Asher's father was in line for the title, and then an older sibling or uncle or cousin died, and the union took on a different and far less convenient significance."

"We can't know that. He returned to Scotland, and she did not. He observed every formality in solemnizing their vows. That is what we know. Lady Mary Fran's first husband parted from her because his regiment posted to Canada, and yet nobody accuses him of deserting his wife."

Malcolm's words defended Asher's father, and yet his tone cast doubt on the man's intentions. But then, in this society thirty years ago, what would have been the requirement of honor for a man in line for an earldom and married to a woman whom most would regard as a savage?

If he cared for the woman, would he have tried to make her over into a countess?

If she cared for him, would she have tried to deny him his earldom? Despite Malcolm's invitation to answer Hannah's questions, she posed the next query reluctantly. "How did it come about that Asher was declared dead?"

Malcolm sat back, as if getting comfortable because this question had been anticipated. "Simply the passage of time, I suppose. I'm told entire settlements disappear on the frontier routinely, and the North American wilderness makes the New Forest look like Green Park."

A tame analogy, at best. "Why are you telling me this, Malcolm? Many would say this history does not flatter the MacGregor family."

Most would. Not Hannah.

"I want you to hear the truth, Hannah Cooper. The fair maids of London Society have no interest in seeing an attachment form between you and the present earl. Their version of the story will flatter no one and nothing, except their own chances to marry Asher MacGregor. I hope this is not news to you."

"It is not, not entirely."

"You can see how, presented in the wrong light, doubt might be cast on Asher's claim to the title, on the family's fitness to belong among the peerage. If there's one thing lower than a dirty Scot, it's a dirty mongrel Scot."

Or a dirty Irishman, or a dirty Chinaman, or a dirty Red Indian… Here at the throbbing epicenter of civilization, the list of humans populating the bottom of Polite Society's scale of worthiness was long, diverse, and included members of Hannah's own antecedents, if not Hannah herself.

"You assured me Asher is legitimate."

Hannah realized she'd used the earl's given name only when Malcolm's gaze narrowed. His scrutiny was fleeting, but hinted for the first time that he, too, could be formidable when crossed.

"The documents were examined by the College of Arms, Miss Cooper. There is no higher authority excepting Almighty God. Victoria herself has taken a hand in the matter. Your host is legitimate and legitimately an earl."

An earl who felt it necessary to attend church each Sunday, when his titled neighbors all over Mayfair couldn't be troubled to stir from their beds. An earl who had called upon each and every duke and marquess to be found within two weeks of returning to London. An earl who… had offered to marry a tarnished American heiress, when he clearly had alternatives better situated to improving his address.

Hannah pushed that realization aside and rose, the twinge in her hip negligible compared to what she might have expected even weeks ago. "I appreciate the family background, Mr. Macallan, but this is a social occasion, and we've had our breath of air."

He was on his feet in an instant, his understanding smile in place, his arm winged at her with friendly courtesy. "I want you to like my cousins as much as I do. I also want you to like me—I hope I haven't offended?"

"Not in the least. Family stories are always fascinating, often more interesting than novels. I do like your cousins."

"And the earl?"

Behind his approachability and good manners, Malcolm Macallan was watching her closely. Her answer mattered to him, and for that, Hannah liked him a little more.

"I respect him, *and* I like him."

This honest if inconvenient reply was apparently the right answer, because Malcolm's smile became a tad roguish. "I'm glad. Now, if I wheedle very prettily, will you give me your supper waltz? You made quite the fetching picture gliding around the dance floor with my lucky cousin. If I didn't know better, I'd say the waltz had been invented in America, you dance it so beautifully."

She gave him her supper waltz, though his importuning left her puzzled. Malcolm Macallan had dissembled a bit regarding her wealth, he'd not quite told the truth regarding how deserted the terrace would be, and now he was engaged in outright mendacity, for Hannah had stumbled twice during her waltz with Asher, and both times, her partner had smoothed her through it without a single comment.

And yet, for all his dissembling, misrepresenting, and lying, Hannah had to like Malcolm Macallan because he'd also armed her with the information she needed to protect Asher's interests among the ladies vying for his hand.

Because a fresh breeze stirred from the west and not from the direction of the Thames, and because a storm had come through the previous evening, watching Hannah pen her biweekly epistles to Boston wasn't a torment to Asher's olfactory senses, only to his heart.

He sat in the shade of a lilac bush coming into its glory thirty feet downwind from the scribe in the gazebo. Alas for him, this put him in full view of any relatives intent on disturbing his reverie.

"Gentlemen usually reserve their doting smiles for when the ladies can see them."

Asher gave up watching Hannah to greet one of the three English sisters-in-law his brothers had acquired for him. "Augusta, good morning. I smile at Miss Cooper all the time."

"In the ballrooms, you grimace." Augusta pulled her lips back in an expression that might have graced the features of a berserker charging into battle.

"That bad?"

Her eyes were sympathetic, while the pat she gave his hand was brisk. "When one thinks one might look but shouldn't touch, it's trying."

Hannah bent over her paper, her pen moving in a steady rhythm across the page, just as her hands had moved—

"We've touched."

The murmured words were not carried away on an obliging zephyr. If anything, the sympathy in Augusta's violet-blue eyes deepened. "You don't mean you've handed her in and out of carriages."

From an Englishwoman, this was an offer to accept confidences, but Asher wasn't about to step into that snare. "I've done plenty of that. Tell me how my other sisters-in-law go on."

"You could ask them. You could even ask your brothers."

Reproof underlay her reply, or perhaps… pity. Augusta was a pretty woman, tall, dark-haired, and dignified with a smile that belied all her primness and English starch—when she aimed that smile at Ian or their infant son.

"I prefer to ask a woman. My guess is, the womenfolk are sparing their fellows all the less delicate aspects of carrying a child, and my brothers, being new husbands, don't know how to ask what needs asking.

Ian stands around pouring the whiskey and looking sympathetic, but he isn't going to stir… the pot."

She subjected him to reciprocal scrutiny, long enough that he knew what she was about; then she patted his hand again. "It's early days for Genie and Julia, and Mary Fran has carried a child before. They seem to be bearing up well. They're loosening their stays and napping when the mood strikes them."

Asher's gaze drifted back to Hannah, who was folding her first missive. She would write a second to one of her brothers, a third to her old governess.

"Tell Genie, Mary Fran, and Julia to consume red meat daily and to drink milk too, if they can. Pregnancy can be hard on a lady's teeth, among other things, and organ meats are of greatest benefit."

He hadn't learned that from the medical college. He'd learned it from Monique, who had learned from her mother.

"Anything else?"

Hannah paused between letters, leaning back in her chair and closing her eyes, probably the better to enjoy the rare fragrant day in Mayfair.

"Augusta, I am not fooled. You are the scout. If I provide you detailed medical information, then Mary Fran will be the next emissary, because she's my baby sister, and I cannot deny her what knowledge I have. My money's on Julia next, because she's a widow, and they develop a certain formidability. When they've both interrogated me to their satisfaction, dear Genie will likely come swanning into the estate office asking all manner of indelicate questions, though she'll manage to ask them delicately."

He fell silent because he was trying to scold his sister-in-law into submission, and it was not working. Her smile, a beaming, toothy, mischievous version of the tenderness she aimed at Ian was turning his scold into a… pout.

"Don't forget your brothers, Balfour. Ian will send them straight to you, claiming his involvement in the baby's arrival was limited to events surrounding conception."

Ian, who held his son every chance he got, confided in the boy about all manner of things, and fretted over the child's every smile and burp.

Asher would have stomped into the house, except that would have meant leaving Hannah alone with her letters. He tried for a smile. "Go away. I will provide the names of competent accoucheurs to any sister-in-law who asks, and I will provide whiskey to brothers showing signs of excessive anxiety. Now if you'll excuse me, I'm going to seek the company of a woman who is not given to ambushing a helpless man in his very own garden." *Though she wasn't above sneak attacks in his kitchen.*

Augusta didn't pat his hand this time; she kissed his cheek, a soft, fragrant buss that mercifully heralded her departure back into the house.

Asher spent another moment drinking in the sight of Hannah Cooper at her leisure, eyes closed, her face turned up to the sun slanting into the gazebo from the east. She *ought* to be worried about getting freckles.

He ought to be worried about finding a woman who didn't regard his marriage proposals as misguided courtesy even as she straightened the folds of his kilt.

Knowing Augusta was probably watching from a convenient window, a sister-in-law stationed at each elbow—and knowing some considerate gardener had planted a thriving trellis of pink roses on the side of the gazebo facing the house—Asher crossed the grass, leaned down, pressed a kiss to Hannah's cheek, and laid a sprig of lilacs by her correspondence.

"I've been keeping you out too late if you must steal a nap here in the garden."

She opened her eyes slowly and smiled at him—for which he might have been grateful had her gaze not been so sad. He appropriated the seat beside her without asking, and cocked his head to study her epistle.

"You never write to your mother, and she has yet to write to you."

Whatever tenderness had lingered in Hannah's gaze guttered and died. "I have little to say that can't be conveyed by my brothers. I am well. I am meeting eligibles. I am coming home in a few weeks."

He might catch her napping in the sun, but he'd never catch her wavering from her self-appointed itinerary. "You could marry Malcolm. He'd be happy for a chance to start over in a new world."

Asher tossed out that bait only because Malcolm's appreciation for the company of women was rumored to stop at the bedroom door, though it was rumor only.

Hannah wiped a spot of ink from her third finger with a linen handkerchief, probably ruining the fabric in the process. "What exactly does Malcolm *do*?"

Because Asher had spent years traveling in the former Colonies, he understood the inquiry for the blunt question it was.

"He is a gentleman at leisure, his welfare sustained by our semi-mutual relation, the Baron Fenimore. Do you like Malcolm?"

Hannah drew the lilacs under her nose, though her expression suggested their fragrance was lacking. "A remittance man, then. Malcolm asked me if I liked you. He wants me to like you."

A pronouncement such as that might presage Hannah's intent to flee the gazebo, so Asher took possession of her bare hand and brushed his thumb across her knuckles. "Did you dissemble prettily and tell him you found me very agreeable?"

She regarded his thumb, the motion of it back and forth across the smooth skin of her hand. He'd touched her for his own pleasure, and because he needed to, but with her acquiescence in the contact, it became something else entirely.

"I told him I both like and respect you. I also desire you. I didn't tell him that."

He dropped her hand then wished he hadn't. "You are going to harangue me now about your lack of virginity, about your need to be thoroughly ruined, et cetera, et cetera. I am not now, nor have I ever been, a man who finds ruining ladies a worthy pursuit."

She sat back, looking like a cat disgruntled to have been removed from the toastiest patch of sunlight. "I don't need a major scandal. A tidy indiscretion would do."

He was disappointed that she'd cling to her scheme with such tenacity, and pleased that he'd divined her plans so easily. "In these surrounds, no scandal is minor, Hannah Cooper. If you are ruined while I am hosting your visit, then my reputation will suffer significantly."

"You're a man." She might have said "You're a toad," for all the *respect* and *liking* in her tone. "I could misstep at some ball, and you could pack me off on the next ship, a host victimized by my colonial vulgarity. You'd earn the sympathy of every mama for ten blocks in any direction."

This was a recitation, not a sudden inspiration. All the evenings Hannah had been smiling and swilling champagne punch, she had been mulling over her tactics. Refining some plan that would end in social disaster, could she but manage it.

"How would this go for your aunt, Hannah? You sail home head held high, triumphant in your disgrace, and she—dependent on her brother's charity—must pay the price for having let your fortune slip away from her brother's control."

"It wouldn't be like that."

"She would fall into a permanent medicinal haze, her hope of any sort of dignity and joy blighted for the rest of her days."

Hannah stared at the correspondence spread on the small table in the center of the gazebo, at the lilacs already beginning to wilt for lack of water. While Asher admired the curve of her jaw and the freckles sprinkled across her cheek, a tear slipped down that cheek.

What in blazes?

"You are not to cry." His handkerchief was out, and he was dabbing at her cheek even as he spoke. "Crying is low and female and it isn't… *please* don't cry, Hannah." He fell silent lest he start begging. To see his Boston adrift like this, cast down by tears…

"Aunt is doing m-much better."

"Hush." He tucked an arm around her and pushed her head to his shoulder. "Of course she's doing better. She's chaperoning the wealthiest heiress to be seen here in five years, my brothers are standing up with her almost every evening, and my sisters are distracting her from her potions by day. *Stop crying.*"

And that campaign had ensued after little more than hints from Asher that it would be appreciated.

Hannah turned her face into his shoulder and nigh broke his heart. She hated to lean, hated to show weakness, and while he relished that she'd allow him to comfort her, he hurt for her, too.

And for himself.

"You are the most stubborn woman I know, Hannah Cooper. Too stubborn—" Insight struck, and relief with it. "Are your monthlies plaguing you?"

A physician might have asked that question—had asked it, fairly often, in fact—and a husband might have asked it, but an earl would not.

She harrumphed against his shoulder. "Damn you, Asher MacGregor. I get the weeps as they approach, and I worry more easily. I doubt—" She pulled back abruptly to regard him with a glittery gaze. "What did Augusta want?"

The female mind was even more complicated and worthy of study than the female body—particularly Hannah's female mind. He palmed the back of her head and drew her back to his shoulder lest she gain insights in her study of him. "I am trained as a physician."

An innocuous place to start. Common knowledge. He fell silent, and Hannah prodded him verbally. "So you have informed me."

On the occasion of taking liberties with her foot. Why hadn't he heeded that warning, and why didn't he wave a servant out from the house to put the poor lilacs in water?

"I have not practiced medicine for several years." Also common knowledge. "I cannot foresee that a belted earl will have need of a profession at which he never particularly excelled."

"You were a good doctor, Asher. You could not be else." She offered this rebuke patiently, even sleepily.

"I was a good student of medicine, but I was not a good doctor. The physicians of the previous age knew something we modern fellows have forgotten: much of effective medicine has to do with interviewing the patient. Not examining him or her like a laboratory specimen, but earning the patient's confidences."

"You pluck confidences from me." Her admission was an unhappy one. He stole a kiss to her temple in reward and left his mouth close enough to her crown to feel the silky pleasure of her hair brushing his lips.

"You toss out the occasional admission as a distraction, Hannah. I do not consider myself in your confidence."

"Confidences are supposed to be shared, not hoarded by one party for use in negotiating with another. Why did you stop practicing medicine?"

"I'm not sure."

Even Hannah, in all her brightness, would not understand that he'd just parted with a confidence, much less one that surprised even him. He'd started turning away from medicine to the more lucrative business of the fur trade even before he'd lost Monique, but her death had also signaled the death of his medical interests.

Or had it?

"That is not a confidence, Asher, and neither is this: I want to go home, but I can't go home until I've accomplished what I set out to accomplish."

He tucked her closer, not having foreseen that homesickness was part of her burden. "It's different here," he conceded. "That's hard. Wearying."

Another damned confidence.

She smoothed a hand over the wool of his kilt, her touch so distracted, it was as if she'd failed to notice that his thigh was one layer of fabric away from her bare hand. "People are polite here, but they aren't nice. People in Boston aren't so polite, but they're genuinely nice."

Well said. "Marry me, Hannah. We'll live in Scotland, where people are both polite and nice, if a bit gruff. You'd love Balfour." And he'd love showing it to her.

"You are a plague, Asher MacGregor. I cannot marry you of all men."

Given the height of the sides of the gazebo, their hands at least had privacy from every direction. When she stroked her hand over his kilt this time, he wrapped his fingers around hers and brought her palm to rest over the growing bulge beneath the wool. "I'll swive you silly if we marry, swive you often and enthusiastically, but only if we marry."

He *felt* her smile. She patted his cock. "I'd swive you silly too."

She said nothing for quite a spell as the morning breeze wafted through the roses, and Asher wondered what it meant, that Hannah would ask him to ruin her publicly, pat his cock in private, and then… fall asleep in his arms.

To distract himself from the pleasure of her bodily trust, Asher turned his mind to her ferocious determination to get back to Boston, and what might be motivating it. His gaze fell on the unfinished letter, this one to Allen, the oldest of the three brothers.

"I shall return in a few weeks, and then things will be better. I promise. Give my love to Mama when you safely can, and watch out for Grandmama."

Give my love to Mama when you safely can.

One line, but enough to convey a disturbing realization to a man reduced to sneaking affection behind garden hedges: Hannah worried for her grandmother, understandably, if excessively. She worried as well for her younger brothers, and for her mother too. The mother he'd thought did not care enough to write even once to her daughter.

Or perhaps, the mother who *could not* write to her daughter.

Asher tightened his embrace, and for a long time, sat in the garden shadows, thinking and holding the woman he could not stop proposing to.

Twelve

Thirty years working for the Baron Fenimore meant Hogarth Evan Cletus Draper—"Howie" to his septuagenarian half brother, though only to him—felt some genuine loyalty to the old lord. Losing his baroness less than five years into the marriage, his one true love, had to be hard on a man who wasn't likely to come across any more loves, true or otherwise, in the course of a long and spectacularly cranky life.

A sense of duty and a desire to visit the fleshpots of London were enough to see Draper eventually journeying south at the baron's request. Duty, prurient inclinations, and an entire armed infantry regiment would not have been enough to inspire Draper to set foot on one of those thunderous, smoke-belching dragons of progress known as locomotives.

"Give me a trusty steed any day," Draper confided to his mount. "You don't leave a fellow covered in soot hours later, half the realm away from where he woke up. Never been inclined to cast up my accounts when on horseback."

Unless of course he'd been overimbibing. For a

mature Scot of Highland extraction, overimbibing took time, effort, and the sort of stupidity generally commandeered only by the younger males.

"Show me the locomotive that will get you home when you're in your cups, take you right to your own stables, peaceable-like, and at a kindly walk that don't alert the neighbors to your lapses, and then wait for you to find the ground and a bush you might avail yourself of before taking his own self off to his stall."

Young people were all in a hurry these days, racketing about, when the tried and true methods of travel might leave them time to think, to plan, to sort out such cryptic guidance as the old baron had imparted.

"'Keep an eye on things and see Balfour wed,' says the laird."

The horse flicked an ear.

"Not very specific, but then, the laird has been friendly with the poppy juice lately. Makes a man forgetful." Though no less cranky.

The Earl of Balfour was a strapping fellow whom the ladies would no doubt mob with their interest, and whose title the parents would eye covetously. "And yet, the laird thought the lad might need some nudging toward the altar."

Nudging MacGregor to the altar would take a team of plow horses, two teams if the fellow were inclined to be stubborn. "Just like the laird."

On that profound bit of irony, Draper took out his flask—he didn't journey so far as the privy without it—and tipped the contents to his lips. "Nigh empty, and us barely halfway to Berwick."

The surrounds were desolate, but only in the way

the lowlands could be, an altogether greener, more rolling desolation than the Highlands boasted. And why the desolation should matter…

Draper roused himself from his itinerant reveries to inventory his situation.

"Horse, you are not going unsound on me, are you? Locomotives don't go unsound, though they explode and crash and whatnot."

The horse lifted its tail and commented at some length on that observation, but Draper's senses had not lied. The beast's gait was getting uneven behind. A stone bruise, a close nail in the shoe, or just damned bad luck.

"Badly done of you, my friend. The nearest inn is five miles back, and…"

Draper's gelding plodded around a sharp curve and through a stand of trees to present his rider with more bleak terrain, but this vista was graced with a tidy smallholding, complete with sheep byre, stock barn, and cottage.

Hospitality would be forthcoming, particularly when Draper got out his wallet or the farmer produced his jug. Draper dismounted, loosened the girth on his ailing beast, and prepared to rely on Scottish good manners for the loan of a mount, or at the very least, a refill for his flask.

"Whatever did the English people have to give up to gain a royal promise of access to all this land?"

Hannah's question was posed to the company at large. Julia, Connor's blond, pretty wife, answered.

"The land was in royal hands from the twelfth century, but Charles I came out here to escape the plague in London. When he decided to enclose the Richmond estate, the locals extracted a promise of access to the land. To appease his subjects, Charles agreed."

Asher watched as Hannah's mental gears spun for the space of a wink.

"He sounds like an agreeable fellow, as monarchs go, though isn't Charles I the king who was put to death by his subjects?"

While his sisters-in-law and his sister debated the niceties of regicide versus tyrannicide, and Malcolm tried to interject a list of Richmond Park's various attractive features, Asher stepped away to check the girth on the bay mare Hannah would be riding.

"Did you invite Malcolm to London knowing he'd appoint himself the Season's master of ceremonies?" Ian asked, patting the mare's glossy quarters.

Asher speared his brother with a look over the mare's fundament. "I didn't invite him at all. I thought you were the one who collected him in the general remove from the North."

"He occasionally bides in Edinburgh, but in recent years he's more often found in Paris or Rome."

As head of the family, laird, earl, whatever Asher's post was called, he ought to have known that. "He's here now, and I for one am grateful for a whiff of fresh air and some greenery, regardless of who organized the outing."

The next few minutes were absorbed with seeing the ladies onto their horses, deciding which party would ride in which direction, and sorting out grooms to accompany the various groupings. Asher was not disappointed to find that Malcolm had assigned him to Hannah's exclusive company.

He boosted her onto the horse, organized her skirts over her boots, and waited while she took up the reins.

"Why are you glowering at me, Balfour?"

She'd taken to using his title when they were in company, a habit he positively loathed.

Asher turned his glower on the groom at the horse's head. The man removed to his own mount with a nod and sat waiting several yards off, as immobile as a garden sculpture.

"If I'm glowering, it's because I am concerned for your welfare on a ride of some duration. Will you be all right?"

"You mean because of my…" She fiddled with the reins. "I'll be fine. Riding doesn't bother my leg, though hacking in the park hasn't done much to challenge my stamina."

"I can't imagine it would, not when every fortune hunter in the city has to lurk on the Ladies' Mile, waiting to tip his hat to you."

She smirked at him, looking both smug and smart atop her horse. Malcolm was fussing at the groom, directing the man to change horses and issuing last-minute instructions to all and sundry.

"And you're off to the woods, correct?" Malcolm asked Hannah.

"I am in Lord Balfour's hands," Hannah replied, though Asher thought her tone ironic. "If he's to show me the woods, then I'm off to the woods."

In the several thousand acres of Richmond Park and its policies, there were a number of woods, at least one of them of significant size. Asher waited for the groom to mount up, then aimed his own horse—at the walk—in the direction of the largest wood.

The rest of the group set off in various directions amid laughter, teasing, and Malcolm's reminders to gather back at the starting point in two hours—not a moment longer—for a picnic meal Mary Fran was already seeing unloaded from the coaches.

"You seem to be enjoying Malcolm's company," Asher observed as his horse ambled along beside Hannah's.

"Malcolm is charming, as are all the MacGregor men."

The comment sounded sincere. He ought to tell her the picture she made in a forest-green habit was charming too, particularly when she'd worn her hair in a fat braid that dangled in a loop over her right shoulder. "You find Connor charming?"

"Of course I find him charming. Charming and full of blather are two different things. Malcolm is charming *and* full of blather."

The groom had dropped back far enough to give them privacy, but something in Hannah's expression suggested the conversation might veer off into areas more personal than Asher was willing to allow.

"Have you come across any eligibles whose suit you'd consider, Hannah?"

She did not so much as turn her head to scowl at him. "I have not, nor will I."

"I've heard from your stepfather."

She petted her horse with a slow stroke of her glove down the beast's neck. "Oh?"

"He presumes on our mutual connection with Fenimore, and asks that I forgive a father's concern for his daughter, but would I please consider allowing my solicitors to act as his factors should settlement negotiations ensue with an eligible *parti*."

Had thunder rumbled in the distance—had cannon fire started booming over the distant hills—he could not have more effectively killed the joie de vivre Hannah had brought to the outing. Her horse gratuitously shied at a puddle, and Asher saw her give the reins forward in a tacit display of self-discipline.

"Have you written back to him, told him I have no intention of marrying and am a burden on the household generally?"

She was braced for him to mock her, to resent her, to treat her as a nuisance because she'd rejected his proposals. Would that he might.

"Hannah, from the number of times your stepfather referred to you as lovely, and the heavy innuendo in his financial references, I got the impression he was trying to pander to my pecuniary interests without outright asking how much it would take to make you my countess. Just how much do you have in trust?"

She named a figure that quite frankly astounded.

"I suppose I should not be shocked," Asher said slowly. "I've traded in the New World for a mere five years and found it quite lucrative. Your father probably had decades to build his fortune."

"He did—he was somewhat older than Mama—and he also said the fur trade used to be a considerably easier business because the game was more abundant and the competition for trappers, pelts, and buyers much less."

Rather than dwell on her stepfather's nasty little

epistle, Asher instead posed question after question to Hannah regarding her father's business. She answered with both knowledge and enthusiasm for her topic, until they were in view of the large woods on the Thames's side of the park.

At Hannah's suggestion, they cantered the distance to the wood, and to the extent Asher could determine from surreptitious glances, Hannah remained comfortable in her saddle.

They'd wandered some distance among stately trees and startled a herd of red deer in a grassy clearing when a shout from behind had Asher drawing his horse up.

"That's the groom," Hannah said, bringing her mare to a halt. "He sounds exasperated."

"Your lordship? Milord? Oi!"

"Over here!" Asher nudged his horse down the path, with Hannah falling in behind.

The groom stood beside his dappled cob, stroking a hand over the beast's shoulder. "Come up lame, 'e 'as. Poor blighter must 'ave picked up a stone."

Except examination of all four hooves showed no stone embedded in the frog of the horse's soles or wedged against its shoes.

"You'll have to walk him back," Asher said. "Can you find the way?"

The groom squinted up through the trees, saying nothing. From his accent, he was a city man, and Richmond was more primeval than much of the shires themselves.

"We rode in with the sun to our right shoulders," Hannah said. "If you keep the sun to your left shoulder, you should find your way back easily enough."

City man he might be, though the groom's smile suggested he understood her reasoning. "Right you be, miss. Come along, 'orse. We've a ways to walk."

With a slight bow in Hannah's direction, the man departed down the track they'd just traveled, the horse stumping along behind him.

Asher wanted to ask if their misadventure in Scotland had motivated her to gauge directions by the sun, but she turned a troubled expression on him. "Shouldn't we accompany him back to the meeting point?"

"He's a grown man, Hannah. Part of the purpose for bringing a groom along is precisely so there's somebody in the party who can take a lame horse in hand—"

He fell silent. Her concern was not for the sturdy groom, but for the appearances.

The proprieties. They were alone, deep in an overgrown woods, not another human being within eyesight or earshot, and both of marriageable age.

Abruptly, the moment became *interesting*.

❧

The longer they were in London, the less Hannah could read Asher's—Lord Balfour's—moods and expressions. Today he was in casual English riding attire, which meant tall field boots, breeches, waistcoat, and riding jacket all done in buff, brown, cream, and green. The ensemble complemented his robust complexion beautifully, and the way he sat a horse…

Some men rode well, and some men rode with such an intuitive feel for the horse as to raise the activity to an effortless dance. Horses responded to that sort of assurance.

Hannah had responded to it.

"Let's water the horses," Asher suggested. "If you want to go back, we can, and we'll overtake the groom easily."

"Provided he doesn't get lost."

He gave her an amused look. "You're concerned for the *groom*, Hannah?" He lent the word a mocking emphasis, alluding subtly to bridegrooms, and somehow to himself as well.

When she didn't answer, he swung off his horse and came around to assist her to dismount. This involved taking her boot from the stirrup, unhooking her knee from the horn, turning her seat perpendicular to the saddle, and… putting her hands on Asher's broad, muscular shoulders.

"Down you go." He did not lift her; he waited until she leaned forward enough to tip her derriere from the saddle. She intended to whisk herself to the ground with no more than an instant or two of proximity to him and his shoulders.

And his smile.

Except her plan backfired as she all but pitched against his chest when her hip protested anything remotely resembling *whisking*.

He caught her snugly against a frame as solid as the granite she'd seen in such abundance in the North. "Careful now. Think of all the fellows who'll be disappointed if you have to sit out your waltzes tomorrow night."

She couldn't think, not of the fortune hunters, not

of waltzing, because his scent was assaulting her reason and his voice was a growling burr right near her ear. He was warm and male, and they were alone in a way all the closed doors in London couldn't emulate.

"Have I kissed you yet out-of-doors?" He addressed himself to the top of her head, where he'd rested his chin. "In the gazebo, but that's not quite like kissing you in what passes for the wild in England. And while I cannot convince you to marry me, I can ask for a kiss from a pretty lady on a pretty day—for only a kiss."

He wasn't *asking* for anything. He was breathing in her scent, his chest expanding with each inhalation while Hannah felt a finger clad in soft, horsy-scented leather touch her chin and an exaltation of larks soar aloft under her breastbone.

"Just a kiss, Hannah. Just one more..." He sounded as if he were promising himself it would be the last "just one more," but Asher MacGregor could interpret "one" to mean a single eternity of delicate invitation from his lips to hers, a possession that yielded as it seduced, and a voluptuous promise of pleasures yet unexplored.

Hannah's senses conspired with him, bringing her the sensation—intimate, masculine—of the contour of his jaw beneath her gloved palm, and awareness, even more intimate and masculine, of his erection rising against her belly.

How long she indulged in Asher's version of "one more kiss," Hannah could not have said. Too long and not nearly long enough.

A horse snorted, and Hannah found herself set back, Asher's hands on her shoulders for long enough that she didn't stumble. He tucked a pair of reins into her grasp and turned his back to her, ostensibly to check the snugness of his horse's girth.

"Good morning, all." Connor MacGregor tipped his hat from the back of a stout gray as the beast ambled into the clearing. "Spathfoy and I saw your groom heading back on foot and decided to seek the shade of the woods."

The Earl of Spathfoy tipped his hat as well, both the gesture and his expression more reserved than Connor's smirk. Spathfoy was married to Genie's younger sister, Hester, and to Hannah's eye, he was the predictable result of a Scottish heiress marrying an English lord. Spathfoy had the English air of hauteur, along with the physique of a dark-haired, robust Viking. Hannah dealt with him warily, for all he seemed unabashedly smitten with his countess.

"You tired of hopping hedges and leaping ditches?" Asher asked, circling around to the front of his gelding and looping the reins over its head. "We were about to water the horses."

"A fine idea." Connor vaulted off his horse in a maneuver that involved neither stirrups nor much decorum. Spathfoy's dismount was a more punctilious affair.

"The ladies suggested we might be more likely to find deer here in the wood," Spathfoy observed. "I don't suppose you've seen any fawns?"

He arched an eyebrow at Asher, and Hannah realized Spathfoy might have made a subtle pun. Fauns? A faun was a variation on the satyr, if she recalled her mythology. Subtle but not humorous, at least not to her.

Another rustling in the bushes from the opposite direction was followed by a cheerful, "Well, there you are!"

Malcolm emerged on horseback from the foliage, followed by two young women Hannah vaguely recognized, and at the back of the party, a groom on a pink-muzzled cob.

"Oh." Malcolm's smile faltered. "And Cousin Con, and Spathfoy. Are you lost?"

Asher took Hannah's reins from her hand. "Connor MacGregor couldn't get lost in the woods if it was darkest night and the middle of a dense fog. It's Miss Pringle and Miss Hargreave, isn't it? Ladies."

Asher bowed at Malcolm's companions. They simpered and tittered, and generally let it be known that finding an earl lurking in the underbrush relieved them of any pretensions toward sense. Of Spathfoy and Connor, they took the barest notice, and of Hannah, no notice beyond the civilities.

The interruptions—plural—were welcome because they gave Hannah a moment to regain her composure. By the time the men had watered eight horses, checked eight girths, and restored three ladies to their saddles, Hannah could pretend she hadn't nearly been caught with her tongue in Asher MacGregor's mouth and her breasts pressed to his chest.

"Fine day for a romp in the woods, isn't it?" Connor asked as he held a branch back for Hannah and her mount to pass under.

Or perhaps she had been caught. "The day is lovely."

Or it had been, for a few forbidden moments.

Connor's horse fell in step beside Hannah's mare,

while ahead of them, Asher kept the ladies company. Malcolm rode at the front of the cavalcade, and Spathfoy, like a disapproving Viking nanny, brought up the rear.

"And you're a lovely lady," Connor said, "but we have lovely ladies aplenty in Scotland, and I will even admit that England boasts a few, seeing as my own darling wife hails from Albion."

For him, this was flowery speech indeed. "Is there something you'd like to ask me, Connor?"

"Ask ye?" Dark brows rose, as if the very notion intrigued. "No, not ask. I do admit to some puzzlement, though."

Hannah waited, for there was nothing idle about Connor's puzzlement.

"I ask myself why, when Balfour has had the pick of the lovely ladies in the United States and Canada, and the lovely ladies in Aberdeenshire and Edinburgh, and the lovely ladies in London—of whom there are entire regiments—why does my brother the earl find it necessary to kiss only your wee self?"

Hannah blotted out the image Connor must be carrying in his mind, of her and the earl, plastered against each other, mouths fused, hands busily—

"I have wondered that very thing myself." It was the best she could do. Connor must have known that, because his smile was both sympathetic and curious, and all the way through the wood, across the fields and down the lanes, he didn't ask her even one more question.

"We're going to have to talk, Hannah Cooper." Asher settled himself beside her on the log she'd chosen for her picnic perch. God help him, he even liked saying her name, though Hannah MacGregor had yet still more appeal.

Her smile was guilelessly friendly as she scooted over a few inches. "What shall we talk about?"

Malcolm had spent the last two hours recruiting half the single women of Polite Society to join their party. They might talk about that. Or not.

"We were nearly compromised today," he said, unwilling to dither. "Had it been Malcolm and his lovelies who came upon us, we'd be arguing over a wedding date while the rest of the assemblage started choosing names for our firstborn."

Hannah paused with a slice of apple partway to her mouth, then set the fruit back on her plate. "Over a kiss?"

"Over *that* kiss."

A beat of quiet went by—not silence, because their group was now well over a dozen, all talking and laughing and enjoying lives that were not complicated by one pretty, stubborn, damnably kissable Yankee.

"Then you should not kiss me ever again, my lord."

He snorted. "My *lord*, my blooming aspidistra more like. You should not have kissed me back." For she had. He wasn't mistaken about that, and would go to his grave not mistaken about that.

She picked up the bite of apple again and stared at it. "I should not have. That was badly done of me. I do apologize."

He did not want her apologizing to him, not for

kissing him, anyway. He plucked the slice of apple from her hand and bit off the end. "Apology rejected. I've made inquiries, you know."

When she turned her head to regard him, he held the remaining bite of apple up to her lips. She took the food from his hand delicately, her gaze on him the entire time. The moment was distractingly erotic, though gratifying.

Across the patch of ground appropriated for their picnic, Spathfoy looked up from flirting with his countess and speared Asher with a glance that was the titled English equivalent of… sticking one's tongue out across the schoolyard.

"Chew, Hannah. The food goes down more easily if you chew it up into little bits before you try to swallow it."

She munched, and all the while, Asher felt her gathering arguments and female logic to bludgeon him with. A contest of wills with her was welcome, though, because a woman couldn't ignore a man and fight him at the same time.

"I like your kisses too much, Balfour."

A woman could, however, drive him mad while she resisted his overtures. "Your flattery will surely cleave all reason from my grasp, Miss Hannah."

"You're supposed to say my kisses would do that."

Asher had said exactly that, as loudly as actions could proclaim any eternal verity.

Hannah picked up another fat red slice of apple and glowered at it. "This conversation has become quite personal. Shall we discuss the weather?"

"The breeze is blowing our words in the direction

of the horses, which is fortunate, because our conversation is going to get more personal still. I wouldn't mind a bite of that apple. Another bite."

The glower became a glare, at him, which was much better. She bit off the end of the apple quarter and held the rest out to him. He took his bite from the same end, leaving her a portion at which to direct her ire.

"You want people to talk, Balfour? You want us compromised? Then why did you turn loose of me so precipitously? I would still be there in that wood, likely in want of all my clothing *and* my reason, had you not—"

He guided her hand, the one holding the bite of apple, to her mouth. "I would not have let that happen. I want us married, not publicly humiliated. Actually, I want us naked in a large, fluffy bed, all the pleasures still to prove, *and* my ring on your dainty finger."

The image had popped into his mind as he spoke, a hallucination of happiness that grew more appealing the longer his imagination stared at it.

"You can have that," she said, "all but the part about your ring, at least not permanently. I've been thinking, you see, and an engagement might suffice. A long, public engagement with all the trimmings, and we'll even hire the church and then—"

The hell they would. "I need a countess, Hannah. You need a husband to supplant your stepfather's authority. My logic is unassailable, and you know it."

"I *need* to turn twenty-six without benefit of matrimony."

When she bit into the remaining apple quarter, her

teeth snapped the fruit in half, and she chewed the thing into bits in short order. Asher waited until she swallowed to make his next point, because he was a gentleman.

A somewhat randy, besotted gentleman.

"Say you reach the age of twenty-six, and your fortune passes into your hands, more or less, and you leave your stepfather's house."

"From your lips to the Almighty's ears…" she murmured.

"Do you think he'll allow you to visit your mother?"

Hannah's hands stopped smoothing the fabric of her habit over her lap. "He can't prevent me from seeing my own family."

"He's already prevented you from corresponding with her. Why is that, Hannah?"

"Because he's a fiend."

Progress.

"And because he's a fiend, do you think he won't move legally to have himself appointed as your guardian? Your grandmother's guardian? The woman has to be ancient, and you, my dear, are a mere girl."

"I'm legally—"

"You're legally female, and he has the requisite biological adornments to qualify as male, though one hesitates to refer to such a creature as a grown man. He'll bribe your servants to spy on you, perhaps foist your aunt onto your charity as his spy, keep rumor circulating about your neglect of your grandmother, your eccentricity, your propensity for hysteria."

Hannah set her plate aside, most of her meal untouched. "Why are you being so mean?"

"I am trying, without much success, to be as

compassionate as I know how to be, Hannah. You need a husband who can make your stepfather look like the grasping, dishonorable, devious cipher he is and keep you safe from him, not only until your twenty-sixth birthday, but for all your days."

Hannah looped her arms around her knees and hunched forward, assuming the self-protective posture of a child. "She won't leave him. Mama, that is. When she was widowed, she was terrified, lost, unable to think what to do, for all we were quite comfortable financially. I was too young, and Grandmother was too old, but Grandmother managed anyway, until *he* slithered into our lives, offering condolences, taking care of this errand and that detail… And now she's his wife, the mother of his sons, and she will not leave him while the boys are still at home."

Maybe this was the real reason Hannah had to return to Boston. A single grandmother in reasonable health was a somewhat portable commodity, but a mother and several half brothers all under the unassailably legal authority of a stepfather…

"I'm sorry, Hannah."

Her smile was a parody of the joy Asher often saw on her face. "You aren't the one who should apologize. A system that means a woman gives up her legal existence as a separate person the day she marries is sorry—and another reason not to marry."

She had a point, but he kept trying anyway. "Reform is coming, at least in Great Britain. Some women even claim ladies should have the vote."

"Some women claim the departed Duke of

Wellington is appearing to them in their dreams and telling them to run off with their lovers."

They fell silent. Hannah picked up her plate and went through the motions of eating, while Asher wished the damned Iron Duke would appear in Hannah's dreams and command her to accept the title Countess of Balfour.

She'd probably argue with Wellington himself—and win—so Asher instead turned his thoughts to the additional inquiries that would go to Boston on the very next clipper.

Thirteen

"I THOUGHT YOU SCOTS WERE BIG ON LIGHTNING RAIDS by the full moon, not wooing your ladies in sun-dappled glades." Tiberius Flynn, Earl of Spathfoy, passed his countess his flask as he spoke. From the next blanket over—an earl in expectation of an English marquessate did not perch on a log like some feckless duck—Connor MacGregor answered.

"We believe in reconnaissance, your royal prigship. Fewer casualties that way. Darlin' wife, save me some of that cake."

Julia passed him a bite of chocolate confection on a fork. Connor trapped her hand in his and took what she offered while Spathfoy studied the passing clouds rather than gratify yon Highland swain by watching his fatuous display.

"If you could leave off flirting with your wife for a moment, we have a serious situation to discuss."

"Tiberius?" Hester, the petite blond Countess of Spathfoy, batted blue eyes at her husband.

"My love?"

"Keep your voice down if this serious situation

involves Miss Hannah Cooper and my brother-in-law disporting in the bushes like Adam and Eve before the Fall. Our party has expanded to include a number of guests who are not family. Then too, the baby just went down for his nap."

Well done of the boy, if Spathfoy said so himself. "Precisely my point. If any one of those guests had—"

"Asher knows that," Connor said softly. "And the lass needs a husband, apparently. He knows that too."

Spathfoy's wife began to unlace her boots, a development a prudent husband took note of. "You're saying Balfour is trying to compromise Miss Cooper?" For appearances lent that theory a deal of credibility.

"Never that. He's trying to convince her. There's a difference between when a man merely desires a woman and when he adores her." Julia offered Connor more cake while Spathfoy nigh goggled at the smile Connor MacGregor bestowed on his wife in a public location. "Though I'll tell you something, Spathfoy."

The earl had to blink, because his countess's naked feet were coming into view. He adored those feet. He liked to get one in his hand, the better to guide the accompanying knee an inch wider as he—

"If you're going to offer some auld Scottish profundity, MacGregor, I suggest you be about it before Julia has decimated the cake."

"Hannah Cooper is no blushing debutante. She knows full well what the consequences might be of kissing stray earls behind the bushes. She wasn't exactly fighting him off."

No, she hadn't been. Upon reflection, Spathfoy allowed that the lady had been devouring the *stray* earl every bit as enthusiastically as Spathfoy himself nibbled on any available part of his countess—usually right before the baby awoke.

Said countess rose to her bare feet. "I'm going wading, Spathfoy. Will you accompany me?"

Spathfoy's countess was not a formal sort of countess unless the situation demanded it. In soft Gaelic, he answered her. "I would follow you anywhere, my dearest love, provided you eventually led me to a secluded part of the nearby woods."

Connor laughed around a mouthful of cake while Julia slipped off her boots.

"A lovely day for travel," Draper informed his mount. The beast sported a reset pair of rear shoes, and an improved gait for having enjoyed a day of leisure in a greening pasture courtesy of Theobald MacDuie and his lovely if taciturn helpmeet, Maud. Draper himself was a touch the worse for the delay, owing mostly to MacDuie's private brew.

"Has cousins in the distillery business over by Glasgow," Draper mused. "Never hurts to have cousins in the distillery business."

Draper did not take out his flask to emphasize the point. He wouldn't be taking out his flask until noon at least, when an enormous breakfast of bannocks, eggs, and ham would have settled, and Draper's thoughts might be settled as well.

Drink loosened a man's tongue, even a man like Theobald MacDuie.

"Farmers are all talkers at heart," Draper observed as

his mount shuffled along. "Some are the coy variety. They take a little coaxing first, but then the floodgates part, and gracious, they can hold forth."

The bedamned Sassenach, the barmy, perpetually breeding Queen and her infernal *mein Herr* of a consort, the sneaking Russians, the bastard thieving Americans, the perennially revolutionary French, who were lousy farmers in a good year… the Venerable MacDuie was poet laureate of the international insult.

He'd liked Hannah Cooper though, the pretty little red-haired lass who'd come through with her great strappin' laddie of a fellow weeks earlier. MacDuie had approved of the way the lady had looked at her man with such besottedness and had given him no trouble—even though Miss Cooper had been an American.

This observation, made through teeth clenched around mine host's pipe, was followed by a pointed look at Mrs. MacDuie at her station by the sink. She had banged a few pots and plates in answer, the Scottish wife's version of a minor scold.

Another pass of the jug, and more of the story had come out, about how a crappin' miserable excuse for an English travelin' coach had gone ass over teakettle in the snowy ditch, and the strappin' laddie and his little American princess—he'd called her that once, "Princess"—had had to cast themselves on guid Scottish hospitality lest they fall further victim to the elements.

The recitation had trailed off into another volley of banging pots and marital glowers. Farmers were talkers at heart, but more often than not, farmers' wives dealt in home truths and plain speaking—even when banging their pots.

"Fenimore will be pleased, you know," Draper reflected. "Proud of the boy's resourcefulness. A Scottish winter night in the countryside isn't to be trifled with." The horse did not seem impressed, but the laird would be, both with Balfour's skills and with what a little gratitude and sympathy directed toward an overworked farmwife had yielded.

"MacDuie did not exactly break any confidences, but he should have spent a bit of the earl's coin on his missus." The selfsame missus who had refilled Draper's flask as the old man had taken himself out to the jakes. In MacDuie's absence, she'd indulged in a bit of righteous Christian muttering.

About American girls being no better than they should be, and leading fine Scotsmen astray at the first opportunity.

About what it took to remain alive through a night on the Scottish moors in winter.

About how the wee "princess" had sported no ring, though she'd surely had every opportunity to enjoy the privileges of holy matrimony with her Scottish escort.

As Draper cast back over MacDuie's recounting, he realized MacDuie had avoided even implying that the couple had sheltered at the croft through the night, while the wife had flatly, albeit quietly and with every concern for the American girl's soul, contradicted her husband's chronology.

And neither husband nor wife had mentioned the delicate auntie tasked with chaperoning the host and his guest.

How… interesting.

As noon approached, Draper took stock of the stretch of road before him. Green rolling hills fell away to the south, the tang of the sea came on a breeze from the east, and the sun shone benevolently from above. Spring was making a good show—at the moment.

Perhaps, just this once, a devoted retainer might be persuaded to board a locomotive in Newcastle for part of a journey that had become a trifling bit urgent. Perhaps.

Draper took a nip of his flask and kicked his mount up to the canter.

The day was bright, an occasion Enid would have taken umbrage at only weeks before.

"Perhaps we should go for a turn in the park," Enid observed between sips of delicate Darjeeling.

Across the table, Hannah pushed eggs and toast around on a blue porcelain plate. "We went for a turn in the park yesterday, Aunt."

A few seats down from Hannah, Gilgallon MacGregor hid behind his newspaper, his hand occasionally emerging from the financial pages to lift a teacup or bite of scone. Enid was convinced the real reason newspapers existed was so men could ignore their families at breakfast and eavesdrop while about it.

"It's a lovely day, and the park is where one sees and is seen," Enid said. "Why did we have such fetching dresses made for you, Hannah, if you never show them off?"

"You and Balfour had such fetching dresses made for me in order that Polite Society might know I have coin to spend and lots of it, the better to foist me off on some impoverished knight."

Gilgallon coughed from behind his newsprint shrubbery, while Enid considered her niece.

Hannah had weathered a winter crossing of the North Atlantic without so much as a queasy moment, but the longer she enjoyed the London social Season, the more peaked and wan the girl looked. The overtures and interest other girls would have basked in left Hannah brittle and nervous.

The situation was quite vexing. Perhaps Hannah needed a nerve tonic.

"I'm finding much to enjoy about our outings," Enid observed, "and you are well received socially. A number of young men have approached me to ask about your situation, you know."

The comment was a test, which Hannah failed spectacularly. Rather than dimple with false modesty—the appropriate reaction—Hannah winced and gulped down half her tea. "What do you tell them?"

"I refer them to the earl, of course. He's in correspondence with your father and the best resource for such discussions."

Hannah set her teacup down with a definite *plink*. "*Step*father, though what you ought to tell them, Aunt, is that I am in no wise looking for a spouse, much less one who would anchor me to Albion's reeking shores for the rest of my days."

"The city itself..." Enid let it go. Twenty-eight days out of thirty, London was a wretchedly odoriferous place. "All the more reason to seek the healthier air of the park."

"Where the Honorable Thaddeus Trundle might be out taking the air as well?"

Well, drat the girl. Enid studied her tea rather than meet the teasing in Hannah's gaze.

"Thad—Mr. Trundle is an old friend, nothing more."

"I don't think he's a day over fifty, myself," Hannah said, all innocence.

"If you ladies will excuse me." Gilgallon rose and bowed to each of them. "I will see how my wife fares. If you need an escort this afternoon, you have only to ask."

He left them to the company of their breakfast fare, and Enid noticed Hannah spared the man no more than a passing glance. Gilgallon was the best-looking of the brothers, being fair complected and graced with a sunny smile to go with his green eyes and dashing height.

"Now that we've lost our referee, Aunt, I have to ask if Mr. Trundle's intentions *are* honorable. You danced with him twice, both times the waltz."

Hannah's concern would be dear if it weren't so irritating. "I am of sufficient age to assess the gentleman's intentions, Hannah Cooper. Look to your own interests before you start meddling in mine."

Rather than put the girl off, this lit a battle light in Hannah's eyes. "You can still marry, Enid Strathorn. You're pretty, and older gentlemen need not be concerned with settlements and heirs and all that whatnot. You don't have to return to Boston, don't have to live the rest of your life pretending your brother treats you decently."

She hadn't said you're *still* pretty, and for that Enid

had to love the girl just a bit. "Hannah, this is not a fit topic."

A younger aunt, an aunt who wasn't staring hard at fifty herself, might have been able to carry off that rebuke in convincing tones.

"Mr. Trundle isn't the only man to leave flowers for you, Aunt, nor the only man to stand up with you more than once. You broke hearts here thirty years ago, and it's your own heart you ought to look after now."

From the doorway, the sound of two hands applauding Hannah's sermon announced Balfour's arrival.

"And there you see, Hannah?" Enid said, setting her cup down with as much ladylike punctilio as she could muster. "Intemperate speech always serves the speaker ill. What is his lordship to think of your lack of manners so early in the day?"

Balfour took his place at the head of the table and picked up the discarded newspaper. "Honesty is refreshing at any hour, Miss Cooper. Trundle is a good sort, and comfortably well off if my inquiries are to be trusted. His taste in dancing partners recommends him as well. Tea, anyone?"

Predictably, Hannah got to her feet. "If you'll both excuse me, I have correspondence to attend to." The earl rose to bow her from the room, then resumed his seat.

Enid eyed the unfinished eggs on Hannah's plate. "I blame that grandmother of hers, you know. My brother has provided Hannah every advantage—tutors, governesses, lessons of every kind—and one can't really blame Hannah's mother. The woman grieved her first spouse terribly."

The earl unfolded his napkin and set the paper aside. "Hannah's grandmother is a poor influence on her?"

In morning attire, he was a good-looking fellow, albeit much too dark for fashion, and Enid would never have labeled Balfour an easy man to be around.

And yet… he was not frivolous, either. His dark eyes had a gravity that promised sensible behavior and even… understanding.

"Hannah's grandmother is a law unto herself, the very worst sort of example, for all she is as old as Methuselah and one ought to make allowances."

Balfour topped up Enid's teacup. "For?"

It all came out, the regular consumption of spirits, the maintenance of business activities no lady ought to concern herself with, the complete lack of deference to the man who provided the roof over their heads, and above all, the refusal to die when the old woman by rights should have shuffled off this mortal coil decades ago. By the time Enid had swilled an entire pot of tea, the earl was looking thoughtful.

"So you see, even though the lady is no bigger than this"—Enid held her hand out at about rib height—"and can barely see, she has exerted enormous sway over Hannah, and all of it bad. The girl would be safely wed, several times over, were it not for that woman's pernicious influence."

When the earl said nothing but stirred his tea in silence, Enid felt compelled to add, "She does love Hannah, though. She loves all the children, but her devotion to Hannah cannot be questioned."

"Nor, apparently, Hannah's to her."

"Lamentably. One can only hope the Lord sees fit

to handle the situation in a just, swift, and compassionate manner before Hannah's last prayer of a decent match is gone. The company of a more frail, wizened, and stubborn woman, I have yet to endure."

Perhaps that was a bit too honest. His lordship swiveled his head to gaze out the window of the breakfast parlor, where sunshine came streaming in from the east. When he once again turned his dark eyes on Enid, she had the sense he'd changed his mental horses, put away one topic and started on another.

"About Trundle, Miss Cooper."

Oh, my. Enid reached for the teapot, then recalled it was empty. "My lord?"

"Shall I make further inquiries on your behalf? He's persistent and has the look of a seasoned soldier not about to give up the campaign."

What a charming—and slightly alarming—image, if it was accurate. "Thaddeus enjoys a full complement of determination."

Enid cast around for something to say that would obscure her use of a gentleman's Christian name over her morning tea. If she'd stayed tucked up in her room, a tot of Dr. Melvin Giles's Root Juice and Tincture of Everlasting Health in her tea, then this entire uncomfortable discussion might not be taking place.

But then, neither would Enid have the image of dear Thaddeus, battling his way across the ballrooms to gain a waltz with her.

Or two waltzes, in one evening. Twice now.

Or perhaps it was three times. All that waltzing made a woman so muddled she couldn't keep her evenings straight.

"I will have my men of business make the usual discreet inquiries and post a suitable endorsement to your brother." His lordship patted Enid's hand, the gesture suggesting a familial interest in her situation.

The earl went back to his toast, as if family confidences over breakfast were nothing unusual, as if he were indeed the MacGregor patriarch, and Enid his honored guest. Such consideration of a mere, retiring maiden aunt could only bode well for Hannah.

"You aren't eating enough."

In response to that observation, Hannah beamed up at her dance partner with what she hoped looked like great good cheer as opposed to an urge to throttle the man.

"I'm trying to fit into the dresses you had me buy in such quantity."

Balfour's answering smile held a daunting quantity of genuine concern for her. "I didn't force you to buy dresses that don't fit, Hannah Cooper. If you think for one moment I endorse the contortion of women's waists into impossibly small dimensions simply to make their bosoms look larger by comparison, you are much mistaken about this too."

About this too?

They were in the middle of a London ballroom, and there were limits to how much trouble Hannah could get into simply by being honest.

"Would you care to elaborate? This is the supper waltz, and we'll have time to go at least another two rounds on the topics of your choice."

This was how she managed now, by dodging him at

meals or dodging meals altogether, needling him when they had to be together, and dropping into bed each night too exhausted to torment herself with wishes that would never come true.

"You need a husband, and if it can't be me, then choose some dim-witted, pretty, biddable boy, Hannah. Malcolm would suit admirably—he's kind-hearted without being ambitious. Take over the remittance, and he'll never trouble you again."

Hannah regarded him more closely, because this approach—tossing other Eligibles at her—was a new tactic. "I could not bind him to a contract to that effect. I've asked my lawyers about a husband of convenience, and they say no such agreement would be enforceable. It thwarts the sacred purposes of marriage, or some such rot."

As they turned a corner of the ballroom, Balfour drew her a bit closer, and Hannah allowed it. Dancing with Asher had become her guilty pleasure, a few minutes of the evening when she could be in his arms, inhale his scent, revel in his strength and nearness, and torment herself thoroughly.

Though that last turn… Hannah felt a wave of dizziness pass over her.

"Are you all right?"

"I'm overpowered by your wit and charm, my lord. Don't worry, the effect is fleeting."

The look he gave her shamed her. It held wry humor, concern, and a hint of sympathy. "I've been thinking I should take you back North."

She tried to draw back, the better to regard him. "Kidnap me?"

"No, take you and the entire family entourage to Edinburgh, which is quite fashionable, especially in the warmer months. A Scottish husband might be up to your mettle."

She could not fathom that he'd marry her off to somebody else, and yet, he honestly believed marriage was in her best interests.

"You're Scottish, and I'm not marrying *you*." Saying it aloud hurt, again. Hannah stumbled a little with the pain of it.

"For God's sake, what's amiss?"

"If you mention female bodily functions, my lord, I will not answer for the—" She tried to draw in a full breath, but her stays prevented it.

"Come with me." He deftly turned her off the dance floor and led her through the milling crowd around the ballroom's edge. Hannah followed blindly, the music sounding as if it were coming from a great distance, the edges of her vision darkening.

"I cannot understand why a woman with as much sense as you possess, as much single-minded determination to attend to her own—"

Asher's words made little sense, but his voice and the grasp of his gloved hand on her wrist kept Hannah moving along behind him, even as she struggled to breathe.

Even as the thought tripped through her mind: *So this is what it's like to faint.*

Fourteen

"We cannot—" Hannah pulled against Asher's grip as she struggled audibly to breathe. "We cannot be private." She sagged against a wall of the corridor, her complexion translucent by the light of the sconces.

Asher had seen many women faint, some of them even honestly, but the sight had never engendered such an upwelling of rage, protectiveness, and exasperation.

"You'd rather swoon on the dance floor as so many fashionable ladies do?" He scooped her up against his chest, which made her ball gown and petticoats billow all the hell over the place.

"I'm not—"

Except she was. As he carried her away from the ballroom, she went pliant and silent against him, not entirely lost to consciousness—not her—but subdued to an alarming extent. Asher pushed open the door to the Alcincoates' library and found the room mercifully unoccupied.

A fireplace at least five feet high and five feet deep sported no blaze whatsoever, suggesting continued privacy, as did the meager light cast from two sconces burning low along the inside wall.

"You, madam, know better than to lace your stays this snugly. Avoiding food compounds your folly, and several glasses of Alcincoate's punch was similarly ill-advised." As he laid her on the velvet sofa, he went on lecturing her, mostly to give her something to focus on.

"We should not be in here."

The very feebleness of Hannah's protest made him furious.

"You should not be in that damned corset." Had he been wearing boots, a knife would have been immediately at hand. He had to rummage in the desk drawer for a penknife, though the one he found was blessedly sharp.

He hauled her to a sitting position. "Hold still, Hannah Cooper, lest I turn you over my knee. You don't need a husband, you need a warden."

He undid a few hooks down the back of her gown, then ripped the damned thing apart, haste his only goal. When he'd tucked her dress aside, he sliced through the lacings of her stays in one careful pass of the knife. They parted on a rush of Hannah's indrawn breath.

"Thank you." She lay back, nearly panting, her chest rising and falling in its newfound liberty. "It's the ball gowns, I think."

"Don't think, just breathe." He sat at her hip and smoothed her hair back from her forehead, then laid the back of his hand against her brow. She was cool rather than warm, and when he tugged her glove off to take her pulse, her fingers were cool as well.

Without bothering to consult his watch, he could tell her heartbeat was rapid and her pulse thready.

"I'm taking you home, Hannah. You've laced yourself into a swoon, and considering you aren't even pretending to look for a husband, all this waltzing and smiling is serving no purpose anyway."

She stopped him from escalating into a tirade by pushing his hair off his forehead with one cool hand. "You're to look for a bride. You promised."

Her reminder was gentle, rueful even. Her fingers slipped around to trace the rim of his ear, and all thought, all sense, and certainly any tirades went flying from Asher's mind. The incongruity of her words—he was to be finding a bride—with her touch, which was intimate, dear, and arousing—brought his thoughts to a grand pause.

"Hannah..." He removed her hand from his person, and instead brought her knuckles to his lips. "We can argue about that later. I'm going to call for the carriage and have Augusta and Ian make your excuses."

"You can't." She was trying to sit up, so Asher did not dare attempt to touch her, not with her bodice gaping open and the imprint of her stays visible on parts of her Asher could not stop staring at. Thank God for her chemise, for it was the only thing between Asher and a complete loss of sanity.

He made himself leave the sofa and located a carafe on a gate-legged table against the wall. For himself, he poured a tot of whatever spirits were in the decanter; for Hannah he poured a glass of water.

Of course, there were some who believed London's water supply was responsible for various deadly epidemics. Asher set the water glass down and poured out another tot of spirits.

"It's whiskey," he said, returning to the couch and passing Hannah the glass. "Sip it slowly. When was the last time you ate?"

She barely wet her lips at the rim of the glass. "I eat. It's the oddest thing. The dresses I've brought with me, like my riding habit, are looser on me, but the dresses I ordered here require me to lace up very tightly. I didn't request that they be made that way."

She looked at him inquiringly.

"For God's sake, I wouldn't meddle with your wardrobe." Except he had, with her dancing slipper, in any case. Hannah's rejoinder was lost when the door was swept open, bringing light, noise, and a knot of people into the room.

"My goodness—!" Lady Alcincoate's gloved hand went to the vast, jiggling expanse above her décolletage. "My lord, whatever—"

Malcolm crowded in at Lady Alcincoate's side, and thank God and all his winged angels, Augusta flanked their hostess on the other side. Augusta's height meant the two women behind her had to crane their necks to peer into the darkened library.

"Miss Cooper fainted," Asher said, and because this pronouncement met with nothing but silence, he added, "I was concerned for her."

Hannah was for once exhibiting some cooperation and remaining tucked out of sight on the sofa, but the silence lengthened. Augusta pushed past the gaping Lady Alcincoate and grabbed an afghan from the back of a reading chair. "Late nights will catch up with us. I suppose you'll be wanting the carriage."

Augusta had the blanket tucked over Hannah

in moments, hiding the damage to her dress. Lady Alcincoate advanced into the room, her acolytes coming with her, and all three women wearing looks of gleeful expectation.

"If the young lady was feeling light-headed, my lord, surely escorting her off the dance floor, finding her a seat and a glass of punch would have sufficed."

We must not be private. "She was not light-headed," Asher said, feeling the beginnings of temper. "She was cool to the touch, short of breath, vertiginous, and unless I miss my guess, suffering diminution of the faculties of hearing and sight."

"Diminution—?" Four syllables didn't stop the lady for long. She planted her hands on her cinched-in waist, making her look like a large, indignant insect. "If there was a diminution of senses going on, as opposed to a diminution of *sense*, my lord, then one calls a physician. One does not escort a young lady to a darkened library and allow her to be found reclining with—unless I miss *my* guess—a glass of strong spirits at hand."

The triumph in her voice was that of a hostess presiding at the birth of a scandal. One of the other ladies spoke up; her tone was sweetly snide. "Perhaps we ought to fetch a physician, now?"

"Oh, for pity's sake." Augusta rose from the sofa to her full height. "Lord Balfour *is* a physician, having gained his credentials at St. Andrews years ago. He was in practice in Canada and is certainly capable of dealing with one young lady's case of the vapors. Further delay while some local fellow is roused from his slumbers is hardly in order. If Lord Balfour, who is charged with Miss Cooper's well-being, says she needs to be taken home now, surely a gracious hostess would be calling for her guest's carriage?"

Asher had never been more grateful for an English sister-in-law. The look of disdain Augusta cast down the length of her nose at the other three women was worthy of Mrs. Siddons, and Malcolm did not miss his cue.

"I'll have the carriage brought around. If you'll excuse me?"

He bowed crisply at the ladies and disappeared, leaving Asher in a dimly lit library with five women, at least three of whom would have loved to report that Hannah's bodice was drooping, her dress undone, and her laces damaged beyond repair.

"Perhaps you might be good enough to find the baroness's husband," Asher suggested, making pointed use of Augusta's title. "And as a physician, I'm asking you ladies to give Miss Cooper privacy with my sister-in-law and me."

The invocation of the title, or perhaps the promise in Asher's eyes of social murder, had the women withdrawing in a subdued silence. When the door had clicked shut, Augusta let out a breath.

"A near thing, you two." She took the glass Hannah proffered and drained the contents. "We'll need to get Hannah out to the carriage before Lady Alcincoate can send servants spying with offers of hartshorn and burned feathers. You would not be the first young lady compromised by her stays. Can you walk?"

"I'll carry her." Asher shrugged out of his jacket and passed it to Augusta, who assisted Hannah into it. That Hannah made no protest did not bode well. "Augusta, when we get home, will you see to sending regrets to the social obligations remaining for the next two weeks?"

"There is no need for that," Hannah said, "and it will only make people think the worst."

Asher planted his hands on his hips and glowered down at the recumbent, though rapidly rallying, Miss Cooper. "What could be worse than losing consciousness before all of Polite Society? Striking a head as hard as yours, even on a convenient andiron—"

Augusta put a hand on his arm. "Hannah might be right, Balfour. If she withdraws from Society, all will remark the possible explanations for tonight's bout of the vapors."

Augusta stared at him, as if she could will some insight to penetrate his brain.

"Good God." He dropped to the sofa. "They will think you are carrying and sailed to England to snag a wealthy husband before your indiscretion was obvious."

Worse, that was exactly what they were *already* thinking, assuming they'd discarded the notion Asher was ravishing his own guest in other people's libraries. He wanted to howl and destroy things and take Hannah far from a society that was not polite in the least…

Though all he could do for now was take her home.

"Augusta, get us out of here, please." He lifted Hannah against his chest, and at least that much felt good and right, for all she was too light by half. They waited while Augusta got the mass of Hannah's skirts modestly arranged and the excess folded up in the bend of Hannah's body, then waited again until Augusta assured them the corridor was empty.

Augusta went ahead of them, Ian met the party in the mews, and before Asher could even mentally fashion another scold for his patient, he found himself ensconced with Hannah in the smaller of the family's town coaches.

Ian and Augusta went back to the ballroom to collect Malcolm and Enid—and to scotch gossip—while Hannah squirmed against Asher's side.

"I am perfectly capable of sitting unassisted, Lord Balfour."

He looped an arm over her shoulders, the brisk show of resistance in her voice reassuring him almost as much as the feel of her next to him did. "And you could have walked to the coach unassisted too, but you didn't. One has to wonder why."

She sighed a mighty put-upon sigh, turned her face into his shoulder, and remained silent for the entire journey home.

A tape measure proved that Hannah had not been losing her wits. The waists on the dresses most recently made in England were five inches smaller than the waists on the dresses Hannah had brought with her from Boston, and Aunt Enid's quiet direction to the modiste was to blame.

"I wanted to see you successfully settled. A lady must show herself to her best advantage if she's to gain the notice of a worthy gentleman. Stop pacing, you shall make me dizzy." Enid managed to sound put out rather than contrite, which had an entire shouting match boiling up from Hannah's now full stomach.

Hannah came to a halt with her back to the fire in Enid's sitting room. "*You* made me dizzy. You made me think I was putting on weight, made me think I was losing my wits. You made me an object of gossip and speculation. How do you think your brother will react when he learns of this?"

Enid unclipped her earrings and slipped off rings, one, two, three... seven in all. "It isn't as if you wanted to marry the man, Hannah. You've chosen an inconvenient time to turn up sensitive to the requirements of decorum."

A maid would put the rings, the earbobs, the necklaces, and the brooches into their jewelry box, would make order out of Aunt Enid's chaos, and see to it at some point when Enid would not be disturbed by the activity.

"Polite Society found me in dishabille, swilling spirits, in a darkened library, alone with a man to whom I am not related, an eligible, titled, wealthy man whom they would like nothing more than to accuse of wrongdoing. This situation came about because of your meddling."

Enid looked up from unfastening a ruby-red brooch from her bodice. "You are concerned for our host? He's a man, Hannah. Because he is wealthy and titled, no one will attach any shame to him whatsoever. They will say you enticed him into a shadowed corner to work your wiles on him. This blasted brooch is stuck."

The urge to scream like a mountain lion welled

from Hannah's soul. "I haven't any accursed wiles, for God's sake."

Enid assayed her appearance in the mirror, touching the tips of her fourth and fifth fingers to her part. "You needn't state the obvious, Hannah. I will require at least a posset to get to sleep after all this excitement. In fact, you'd best fetch me my Dr. Giles."

Rather than screech that Dr. Giles wasn't going to solve anything, Hannah took a moment to study her aunt. The hour was late, Enid was tired, and the cosmetics she used enhanced rather than hid her advancing years.

Her mouth had a pinched look, not quite bitter, but thoroughly disillusioned. Her eyes were flat, seeing disappointment far more easily than hope. Her hands were no longer young and soft...

"We're going back to Edinburgh," Hannah said, some of the tension leaving her shoulders. "Balfour is declining invitations, and we're to take a repairing lease among a fresh crop of bachelors."

Enid stopped fussing her hair to scowl at Hannah. "That will not do. You cannot be seen to turn tail and run after tonight's debacle. You must be seen out and about."

And Enid must continue her flirtation with the redoubtable Mr. Trundle.

Hannah crossed the room, intent only on leaving. "I will accept Balfour's guidance in this, Aunt, and so will you."

"You must help me with this brooch, Hannah. I swear I shall tear it off if you don't."

The center of the brooch was a cluster of red gemstones, the intent to remind all and sundry of the biblical worth of a good woman, no doubt. "It's paste," Hannah said, hand on the doorknob. "Do with it what you must, but direct your maid to start packing in the morning. We're going back to Scotland."

Asher found his quarry easily enough, accosting her as she left Enid's chambers and moved down the hallway toward her own.

The medical part of his mind noted that her complexion was back to its normal perfection, and her eyes had their customary alert snap. "You've eaten?"

"I had a very satisfying late supper, thank you, complete with cake."

The consonants were bitten off, the vowels compressed with… not anger. Anger was the decoy, the distraction drawing notice from… her bewilderment.

Or her homesickness, possibly both.

"If you have some time, Hannah, I would beg a word with you."

She arched a brow—likely at the word "beg"—then took him by the wrist and led him to her sitting room. Another private situation, but this time with Hannah being the one to determine their direction and destination.

And yet he was a little pleased when she closed the door behind them, sat herself down on the sofa, and crossed her arms. "You may have that word now, my lord."

She'd closed the door, which meant he hadn't had to see to it himself. "How are you?"

Some of the fight went out of her. She uncrossed her arms and picked up a blue satin pillow from a corner of the sofa. "I am so wroth with Enid I could howl. She had the modiste take in my waistlines, and the result… suffice it to say, I will not be wearing my most fashionable attire anytime soon."

Asher ambled across the room and poked up the fire. "She means well. She wants you to make a good impression."

"The better to marry me off to some fellow with a moldering estate in the Lakes, while the hapless Mr. Trundle stumbles about in Aunt's gun sights like some penned hart at a Continental battue."

The Lakes were beautiful. Now was not the time to make that point. Asher appropriated a seat beside the woman whose suffering he would alleviate by any means possible. "We have a greater problem than Enid's just desserts."

Hannah hugged the pillow to her chest. "How much worse can it be? I was found nearly undressed in your exclusive company by two of the biggest gossips in captivity, and all because Malcolm insisted on looking up some word or other at that very moment."

"Quaquaversal. It means from all sides, or all about one."

She closed her eyes and hugged the pillow more tightly. "I know my Latin, Asher MacGregor."

That she was forgetting to my-lord him was a sign of her upset. What had been repugnant to her rebel sensibilities had become a means for her to keep distance from him, and now…

He tugged on the pillow. She didn't give it up, but met his gaze for the first time since they'd closed the door. "We need to discuss tonight's little drama, Hannah."

Ian had certainly discussed it with Asher, at length and in volume, supported by Gil and Connor. At least Spathfoy hadn't been in the room.

"I swear, Asher MacGregor, if you're going to blame me—"

"I blame myself." He tugged on the pillow, and this time, she let it go. "I should have done exactly as Lady Alcincoate said. Planted you in a chair in full view of the ballroom, let you catch your breath, and borrowed somebody's painted fan to revive your flagging energies."

"I fainted, Asher. I was not in need of reviving. I could not breathe."

On that feeble remonstration, she hunched forward and fell silent, not a silence Asher could read. In the interest of not saying the wrong thing—purely in that interest—he used one hand to knead the muscles between her neck and shoulder blade. "I cannot abide that you are so upset."

That hadn't been on his list of things to say—and he did have a list. A well-reasoned, thoroughly rehearsed, intelligently worded list of negotiating points.

She relaxed some under his hand. "You won't easily be able to find a bride after this, though I don't think you've been looking very hard."

"How do you think I could possibly—? Come here." He pulled her back against him, wrapped both arms around her, and rested his cheek against her temple. She hadn't resisted, not in the least.

"My siblings had a very pointed discussion with me." It had come out, "M' siblin's had a verra pointed discussion w'me." Asher heard the burr stealing into his inflection and made another mental grab for those well-articulated reasons.

"Siblings will do this," Hannah said, nuzzling his throat. "Grandmothers know of almost no other kind of discussion."

Her grandmother was the last person Asher wanted on Hannah's mind at present. "I am a physician, Hannah, which is why tonight's situation will not immediately erupt in scandal."

She pulled back to regard him warily. "You're saying it will *eventually* erupt in scandal?"

His list had gone completely out of his mind, leaving him drowning in Hannah's gaze. She expected the truth from him. She deserved the truth, though he hadn't wanted to force her decision on the matter.

He gently pushed her head back to his chest. "When you remain unwed and are not found to be with child, there are those who will speculate that being a physician, I was in a position to relieve you of your burden."

Cut the wee bairn from her verra bodie, was how Ian had put it—shouted it. The most delicate inference in the world couldn't hide the brutality of the idea, and yet, Ian's tirade had been inspired by whispers that had already started around the ballroom.

Hannah drew up into a knot of tension in his arms. He waited, holding her loosely, expecting her to cry, to screech, to cry *and* screech. Instead, her voice was quiet.

"That is the most vile, vulgar, mean, unfair… how could they accuse you of such behavior when you've been nothing but decent, kind, gracious, patient, generous…" She exhaled and went pliant against him for a long, quiet moment. "I cannot abide this. *I give up*, Asher. I surrender. I'm leaving the battlefield to those who find it entertaining to assassinate character and choke the very breath out of women while they do. I don't know how to fight this, this… army of small-minded venality, and my scheming aunt, and my dratted stepfather. You win. I can't do this alone anymore."

You win.

For more than a minute, he said nothing. He stroked his hand over her back, trying to sort out feelings that ought not to be engendered by a woman's acceptance of a marriage proposal.

Sadness was there, for her, because in part her capitulation was caused by her surprising—and gratifying—indignation on his behalf. He hadn't foreseen that, hadn't put it on his list.

He also felt some peace. They were to marry, and that felt right. A rebel countess from the wilds of Boston suited him, a treasure no one else had noticed, a woman who had backed, bullied, and blustered her way into his heart without even meaning to.

And he felt… desire. The lust was leavened with relief, to have the chase over and won—her word—and the certainty of mutual pleasure assured. He savored that feeling even as his awareness of Hannah's body next to his became more acute.

She wore only nightclothes, no stays, no corsetry or bustle. Nothing but cotton, Hannah, and the scent of sweet lavender. When he gathered her closer, she tucked herself against him with every indication of complicity.

"You are falling asleep, my dear. You are worn out."

She muttered something that was not a protest, so Asher scooped her up and rose, crossing the room with her in his arms. Without her evening finery, she was a smaller package, also more…

Simply *more.*

"I hate it here."

"Love, I know that. You'll like Scotland, though." *Love it*, he hoped.

He laid her on her bed, drew the covers up over her, then turned to tend to her fire lest he linger overlong on the sight of her. Her braid was a thick, burnished rope against the pillow, her eyes lambent by firelight. He wanted nothing—nothing—so much as he wanted to get into the bed and simply hold her.

And to hell with the riot starting up in his trousers.

"Asher?"

He made sure the logs and coal were pushed to the back of the andirons and the screen was snug up to the bricks. "Go to sleep, Hannah. We'll talk in the morning."

"Kiss me."

The last of his sadness on her behalf vanished.

She was prepared to immediately enjoy the fruits of her surrender, a notion he wholeheartedly endorsed. This much, he could undertake happily, and so could she. They could bring each other joy and pleasure in abundance, and with marriage looming, they could do so without reservation.

And yet, he hesitated. "You are tired, Hannah, and it's late, and we still have much to discuss."

From drowsing in his arms, she was now quite awake and wrestling off her dressing gown. "I miss your kisses. If I'm to be pilloried for being a wanton, and you accused of worse behavior than that, I will at least have a kiss."

He did not trust himself to stop at a kiss, and like an angelic chorus bursting into song, his male brain produced the thought: *Nor did they have to stop at a kiss*. An engaged couple was permitted all the liberties of their married counterpart, provided they were discreet.

He could be discreet, his cock cheerfully assured him, as discreet as hell.

Fifteen

Hannah assured herself that catching a ship from Edinburgh for Boston would be no effort at all. Asher would take her North, she'd linger long enough to ensure no one could accuse her of carrying his child—Though what would that matter, given the even worse conclusions Polite Society had already drawn?—and she'd leave this godforsaken land with or without Enid's companionship.

That Asher understood how badly she needed to go home—finally, finally, understood—had to be what explained his capitulation to their mutual attraction. Hannah was too pleased at his belated attack of sense to congratulate him on it.

She regarded the man standing beside her bed, the man whose reputation was now at risk because of her. Of all the times they had sinned, an innocent situation would be what had landed them in trouble.

The thought broke her heart in four different pieces, only one of them for him.

"We can discuss anything you want in the morning, Asher. For now, please kiss me." More explicit than that, she could not be, not with words.

When he might have subjected her to another spate of his infernal reasoning—wonder of wonders—he unbuttoned his waistcoat. Anticipation and relief started a duet in Hannah's body in close harmony: a sweet melody and a throbbing rhythm. She shamelessly gawked at him as he hung his waistcoat over a chair then sat to remove his shoes and stockings.

His shirt came next, and because he'd turned back the cuffs, he could undo a few buttons and pull it over his head.

"That's cheating, Asher."

He looked up from undoing his trousers. A slow male smile revealed white teeth and impending trouble. "Shall I put the shirt back on, Hannah? Would you like to undo me buttons, then, unwrap your prize button by button?"

Ah, the burr. She adored the burr. "Now you're stalling."

A man could shuck out of his trousers and underlinen in nothing flat, and then he could stand there, all shadows and strength not three feet away, while a woman ached to touch him.

"I want you, dear heart, verra much." His desire was made evident by the erection arrowing up along his belly. A peculiar male endowment Hannah wanted to study—some other time.

"I want you too." She'd told him she wasn't a virgin, and she had not lied—not in the medical sense—but her prevarication was making her anxious to get matters under way. "Come to bed, Asher, please."

She was using please rather a lot. She'd use it more,

willingly, if it would get him under the covers with her. What followed now, and possibly in the next several weeks, would be hoarded up against the rest of Hannah's life, against all the arguments with her stepfather, all the maneuvering with the lawyers. She could endure those battles if she could have these pleasures with this man for herself *now.*

As he climbed into the bed, dipping the mattress so heavily Hannah rolled to his side, she admitted one serpent to her garden: consummating her dealings with Asher was a two-edged sword. She would have the pleasure and joy of the memory, but she'd have the torment of it too.

"Now, madam"—he slid an arm under her neck and brought her flush against his side—"did you say something about kissing?"

"In a minute." She wrestled free of his embrace. "You distracted me, flaunting your wares. I have a few wares of my own… what?"

He lay on his back, his arms laced behind his head to reveal dark tufts of hair at his armpits. "Slowly, my love."

Comprehension dawned. When Hannah would have drawn her nightgown straight over her head, she instead slipped a button at her throat through its buttonhole. "This nightgown has a lot of buttons, my lord."

"I'm a patient man, though I'll no' tolerate any me-lording nor Balfouring when we're abed, Hannah."

A patient mon. She hoped he'd speak Gaelic to her when their bodies were joined, hoped he'd say naughty things in any language—and mean every word. More buttons came free, and all the while,

Asher watched her. When she would have crossed her arms to lift the nightgown away, he stopped her by using her braid to tug her down to him.

"Kisses, madam?"

The things he knew… How could Hannah have guessed that kissing him with her nightgown half-on, half-falling off her shoulders would be more inflammatory than were she stark naked? Soft, worn cotton took on sensual powers, dragging over Hannah's chest, back, and arms as Asher levered up to set his mouth to hers.

He held back. She'd kissed him enough to know that this delicate tasting of her lips was intended to part her from her reason, and it was working.

"Stop teasing, sir."

He shifted, and in a blink, Hannah was on her back, pinned by a grinning Scottish earl apparently in no mood to take direction. "Stop managing. It's a habit ye'll give up, Hannah, at least when we're abed."

"The day I—"

Now the kissing began in earnest, a wondrous onslaught of male guile intended to convince Hannah she didn't *want* to manage him in bed, not ever. She decided instead that she'd learn to tease him, to enjoy the wares she wasn't quite sure how to flaunt—and to enjoy his wares.

"That's better, love. We'll go slowly, and take our time, and all the pleasures—"

She pinched his derriere, not hard, but enough to take *pleasure* in the resilient abundance of muscle on his backside as her toes stroked along the curve of his calf.

"I've never petted a man with my feet before."

"Blessed saints, I hope not." The humor in his voice sounded strained. "What other wee tricks would you like to try out on my poor, unsuspecting self?"

"I'll give you a list—later." For now, the feel of his erection, warm, smooth, and heavy against her belly, distracted her sorely. She rolled her hips to remind him of the point of the proceedings, though the perverse man raised himself off her and shifted to his side, taking his weight and warmth away.

"Did I do something wrong?"

He kissed her nose. "Between two people sharing a bed like this, Hannah, there's no right and wrong. There is only what pleases us." He drew his callused finger slowly down the midline of her face: forehead, nose, lips, chin, throat, and on down.

"Are you going to draw on me or make love to me, Asher?"

"Draw on you"—he nuzzled her breast—"for now."

He drew on her nipple with the wet warmth of his mouth, and Hannah nearly came off the bed. "That is… that is *wicked*."

She gripped his head, fingers fisted in his hair while heat leapt out from where he touched her. "That is wicked, and lovely. I can't…"

His hand drifted over her chest, tracing the bones of her sternum, covering her other breast, teasing, tormenting… teaching her that whatever she'd envisioned sharing with him, it was going to be much more personal and of much greater impact than she'd imagined.

For a time, they drifted between kisses and caresses. Hannah discovered that her hands pleased him too—on the angles and planes of his face, over the warmth and power of his chest, down the sinewy length of his arms. He sighed, his breathing hitched, he murmured in unintelligible Gaelic, and he made not one peep of protest when Hannah wrapped her fingers around his engorged member.

How long she mapped the feel of him she could not have said. She acquainted herself with downy, masculine hair, the smooth length of his shaft, the curiously silky head of his cock, and all the little twitches and inhalations that went with her touching him.

"You're braced in some regard, Asher MacGregor. You're enduring this."

"I'm wallowing in it. You are very thorough in your explorations, Hannah, and that pleases me. I would not want you to think otherwise."

He was being honest with her, though still… She trusted her sense that he was waiting for her to look her fill, waiting for her to gather her courage.

"I've explored this part enough." She tugged on his cock gently. "*For now.*"

He shifted up again while Hannah, as naturally as dancing, subsided onto her back. "I will be the judge of what's enough, woman, at least this time."

His kiss was different, more uncivilized. Hannah took that as an invitation to reciprocate, to explore his mouth with her tongue, to breathe through him and undulate up into the hand he traced down her ribs. Something inside her was coming undone—wonderfully, completely undone—and she wanted him undone with her.

This time, he did not linger at her breasts or stop his quest at the soft flesh low on her belly. He brushed his fingers through her curls, gently, gently, a caress as maddening as it was arousing.

"Asher, that's all very—*good gracious.*"

She went silent, let her knees fall open, and waited to see what he'd do next. One leisurely pass of his fingers up the crease of her sex, a little pressure on a particular spot, and words deserted her.

"Shall I do that again, love?"

"Mm." She grabbed him by the back of his head and fused her mouth to his. He chuckled—the dratted beast—and repeated that most interesting caress, this time with a hint more pressure.

Hannah pushed into his touch, and Asher smiled against her mouth. "She likes it. She likes it verra much."

She liked it so verra much she caught a rhythm as he explored for them both all the folds and creases of a woman's most intimate parts. She liked it enough to growl into his mouth and to nearly tear his hair from his scalp.

"You're wet for me, Hannah. I adore that you're wet for me. Shall I love you now?"

She couldn't *even* beg. She tried to scoot under him in answer, to wrestle him over her, and he allowed it, covered her with his heat and strength, braced himself up on his forearms, and went still.

He hitched close, brushed her hair back from her forehead, and spoke right near her ear. "There's no undoing this, my love. No turning back or forgetting it. This is forever."

"Please, Asher…" She sought him with her sex, and there he was. Big, blunt, hot, hard, and everything she wanted, forever and in the next instant.

"Please you, I shall." He eased forward, just that. Hannah's body gave easily at first, welcomed him into soft, damp heat. The next part had her opening her eyes.

"Aren't you going to move?"

He sighed and pushed forward a bit more, to the extent that Hannah's grasp of how intimate they would be underwent a transformation.

"Ye must relax, Hannah. I will linger right where I am until ye do."

He could do it. He could stay right where he was, kissing her brow, her temple, bumping his nose along hers while she lost her mind on the battleground between anticipation and anxiety.

"Asher MacGregor, you're killing me."

"We'll die together."

This time, he shifted to brace one hand under her backside while he propped himself on the other forearm. A short, sharp nudge, and Hannah was wonderfully impaled on his fullness.

"That's better," she began, ready to reassure him that things were proceeding in an acceptable direction.

"You approve?" He started to withdraw, of which she did not approve in the least.

"Don't you d—"

"Then this might be to your liking as well." He glided more deeply into her body, retreated, and eased forward, waltzing his way past her wits and even her ability to think.

"Asher MacGregor, I love"—*you*—"it."

His movement picked up intensity without becoming any faster. "I'll tell ye a secret, Hannah."

He *was* telling her secrets. Wonderful secrets about the body she'd inhabited for nearly a quarter century, and secrets about his body too. "Mm?"

"In this, with me, ye can be greedy. Ye can have all ye want and more, as often as ye like, because my desire for ye will have no end." The blessed man dropped into Gaelic, his tone promising wicked bliss, his body turning the promise into a vow.

Hannah clung to him, moved with him, and when her body shook with the fulfillment of Asher's vows, she fell and fell and fell with him too.

He'd loved her right to sleep.

Hannah's passion was a wonderful, generous, unstinting thing, a measure of intimacy Asher lay thinking about as he held his prospective bride and matched his breathing to hers.

She'd been matter of fact about the aftermath—"That's the scent of your seed, isn't it? The scent of copulation?" and "This is not all neat and tidy. I like that it isn't tidy."—which was very different from Monique's shyness and self-consciousness.

Monique had laughed her way through life's difficult moments. Only now, holding a lady for whom humor played a different role, could Asher see that Monique's approach was that of a very young woman, one who'd not strayed from the smile she'd learned to wield early in life, a means of coping she could not put aside in favor of more mature strengths.

Strengths like courage, resilience, honesty, or trust. "*I like that it isn't tidy.*"

A universe of joyful marital potential lay in that confession.

Had Hannah been awake, Asher might have said to her, "I was married before. It was sweet and precious, and when it ended, I thought I'd died. I *wished* I'd died, and I knew I would never love with my whole heart again." He might have added, very softly, "I was wrong."

Instead, he caressed Hannah's hair and kissed her temple, and—because with her sprawled on his chest, the temptation was too great—stroked his hand over the curve of her backside.

Somewhere in the affray, her nightgown had gone missing. This was convenient, because before he left the bed, Asher intended that Hannah's wits go missing again too—even though he'd finally located his own wits for the first time since leaving Scottish shores years ago.

"By what feat of feminine cerebration did you conclude you were unchaste?"

The question was asked with lazy amusement, the same lazy amusement with which the end of Hannah's braid was brushed across her lips. She rolled to her back to find Asher propped on his elbow beside her.

The birds were singing outside her window, while a faint gray light crept around the edges of her curtains.

She and Asher hadn't much time, though she found it impossible to dismiss him from her bed.

"I was not a virgin. I lacked the requisite…" She batted sleep away from her brain, batted his braid-wielding hand from her face. "There's a name for it, for the little scrap of flesh a girl is to guard with her life, and I parted with mine some time ago."

He kissed her nose. "The name for it is invisible, in most cases. A woman as active as you are is unlikely to be sporting much in the way of a maidenhead so late in her life. Hymen, if you want the medical term."

"Are you calling me old?"

He kissed her ear and spoke right next to it, which tickled. "I am calling you adult, also mendacious. Untruthful, but not quite a liar. Tell me, Hannah."

He wrestled her over him, a position in which they'd made love sometime in the night. The memory was luscious and painful. Hannah curled down onto Asher's chest and wished she could hold back the dawn.

"Hymen. I'd forgotten the word. Your medical knowledge has its uses."

His hand on her back paused then resumed the slow stroking across her skin, which would have provoked her to purring were she capable of it.

"You were a virgin, dear heart. I would stake my life on this. Were you misleading me in an effort to hasten your ruin?"

He wasn't going to let this go, but because he was going to let *her* go—in a few minutes in one sense, in a few weeks in another—she tried to find the right words.

"When I jilted Widmore, he did not deal well with it."

"Most fellows would take umbrage at being made a laughingstock at the altar. I certainly would."

Hannah glanced at the window, listened to the caroling of the birds, and kissed her lover's nose. "He went to my stepfather and stated quite baldly that he'd had carnal knowledge of me. If I refused to marry him, in public with full honors, he threatened to bruit it about that I'd enticed him into anticipating the vows."

Asher's languid caresses slid lower. "His name is Adventus Widmore. He resides at 28 East Breitling Place, Boston. He flunked out of Yale and was given work in your stepfather's offices two years ago as a favor to some business crony. Widmore stands about six feet, is blond, blue-eyed, and has a nick in his left earlobe from where his younger sister aimed a rock at him as a lad. Shall I kill him for you, precious heart?"

"Such endearments. You shame the dawn with your efforts to cheer me."

"Perhaps you'd prefer to see him gelded? Or—my medical training again—I could have him relieved of one testicle but not the other. It's messy, there's a lot of blood involved, and it's quite painful, but a man can still—"

Hannah kissed him on the mouth. "You wax enthusiastic on a surgical topic, and I have yet to break my fast. I was never intimate with Widmore, though not for lack of trying on his part. I learned not to be where he could catch me alone. And I think he realized that smearing my reputation would not inure to his advantage."

At some point in Asher's surgical recitation, Hannah had become aware that in addition to the sun, something else, something equally lovely, was rising right there in the bed.

"So were you lying to me, Hannah? Trying to goad me past propriety?"

His thumb feathered over her nipples. Not a goad,

an inspiration. Hannah flexed her hips, caressing his cock with her sex.

"My stepfather had a midwife examine me, but he gave the woman instructions first."

"I am not going to like this midwife much either, am I?"

He'd probably want to disfigure the poor woman, which was unfair, though endearing. "I like that, the way you tease my nipples. Is there a medical term for the nipple?"

He gasped as she sheathed him in one smooth, sweet slide of her body over his. "For God's sake, Hannah, hold still."

Good advice. She was a trifle sore, which was a new sensation, not exactly uncomfortable, and wonderfully intimate. "Am I hurting you?" She snuggled closer. "I'm a bit tender myself."

"I am very tender."

He wasn't joking, though she didn't think he was referring to his cock—she knew that term—but she couldn't be sure. "Shall I—?" What was the word for untangling their bodies without consummating their joining? "There's an entire vocabulary you're going to have to teach me."

"There is, but you're a quick study. The word for nipple is papilla, though the shortened form—pap—can refer to the breast generally."

He'd regained his balance, the wretch, while she... "Can we simply lie here like this, joined but unmoving?"

"There's no law against it, and no word for it either that I know of. Tell me about the midwife."

The birdsong changed, became polyphony instead

of an avian plain chant. Whereas one bird had been fluting along, greeting the sun with a silvery solo, now others joined in while Hannah remained joined to the man in her bed.

"She described for me the nature of the examination, and explained that she'd also been instructed to ensure my wedding night proceeded without discomfort."

Asher's expression grew more fierce. "She was to destroy the evidence of your virginity, if any she found."

Hannah brought his hands to her breasts. "I suppose so."

Male thumbs feathered over her nipples. "And you weren't to know that's what she was about."

"Not at the time. She was honest though, and told me the lack of a maidenhead was likely to be presented to me when I turned up fractious at a later date. That is an interesting… I feel that caress in places you aren't touching me."

He nudged up with his cock. "Here."

Hannah managed a nod, closed her eyes, and let her head fall to his shoulder. "I like it when you do that."

"Why did you let that woman carry out her instructions? And no, you are not to move, Hannah. You'll need a soaking bath as it is. A long, hot, soaking bath to start your day."

Focusing on the question took effort, for pleasure was building in Hannah's body, even as outside her window the sun was rising. "The midwife assured me she found no evidence of unchaste behavior, and she would swear… swear… if you move any more slowly, Asher MacGregor, I shall bite you."

He stopped moving entirely. "She would swear to your chastity?"

"She said as much and explained exactly what you said. Nobody could tell, in any case, but I might be more comfortable on my wedding night if I complied with the scheme she'd been put to."

He started moving again, slow, easy lunges into her body that went wonderfully deep. "While you concluded you'd be conveniently ruined if the need arose. Are ye comfortable, my heart?"

She met his thrust, counterpointed his rhythm. "Not comfortable, exactly. Are you comfortable?"

While the sun crept over the horizon and the birds sang in welcome, Asher levered up, wrapped Hannah close, and laughed.

"It's no use." Enid's tone was bitter enough that Augusta exchanged a look with Genie and Julia. "Word has gone out. Nobody will be calling. Hannah has received no bouquets, no cards, nothing. We might as well decamp for Poland. She has quite ruined herself, and all over a little swoon. You will excuse me if I need a tot of my medicinals."

Enid pushed her chair back with an unladylike scrape, and left the breakfast parlor amid a series of equally indecorous sniffs into her handkerchief.

"Hannah was smart to linger at her bath," Julia observed, reaching for the teapot.

"None for me," Genie said. "Lately, I use the necessary enough as it is in the mornings."

Mary Fran held out her cup. "That passes. I wish

that woman would leave for Poland, though Matthew says it's a beautiful country. I don't suppose the Poles deserve the imposition, either."

Augusta shook her head at the proffer of more tea. "I have learned a few things from my Scottish husband."

Genie's smile was impish. "We're all learning things from our Scottish husbands, and our nurseries will soon bear the proof."

"Not those sorts of things. Well, those things too. I am learning from Ian that anger need not be a corrosive, bitter thing. Anger can be an inspiration."

"Revenge," Mary Fran said, smiling hugely. "We could take in Enid's crinolines until she can neither breathe nor stand up with her Mr. Trucklebed."

"Trundle," Augusta said. "We could lace her patent remedies with a laxative. We could see her compromised, though she'd hardly object to it. She is upset that Hannah is ruined because it reflects poorly on her, not because Hannah will suffer for it."

"Hannah might be married for it," Julia pointed out. "I'm not sure, given that Asher is the prospective groom, suffering is the appropriate term."

Augusta drew her fingernail along an embroidered seam of the tablecloth. The figure was a depiction of pretty bluish flowers—lilacs and columbines amid greenery against a soft gold background. "Neither one of them wants to be married, and if they do marry, it shouldn't be like this."

Like this—a reference to the things Enid had noted. An absence of bouquets, a lack of calling cards, much less cards with a particular corner bent, indicating the visitor waited, *in person*, for a few minutes with the ladies of the household.

Polite Society was nothing if not articulate in its silences.

Genie buttered a slice of toast but didn't eat it. "Con said he, Gil, and Ian asked Asher what he was going to do about Hannah's situation. Asher didn't answer them directly."

"Perhaps he'll give them an answer on their morning ride," Julia observed.

A knock on the door interrupted the conversation.

"Enter," Mary Fran called out.

Two footmen strode in, each obscured by an enormous bouquet. All four ladies sat up.

"Sweet basil is for good wishes," Julia remarked, breaking off a leaf from the nearer bouquet and bringing it to her nose. "Water lily is for purity of heart. Nobody puts water lilies in bouquets. I forget what arborvitae is for."

"Unchanging friendship," Genie said. "The roses are from Spathfoy, white for purity. But this other bouquet, it isn't gaudy, exactly…"

They regarded the larger arrangement, a pretty assortment of both blooms and greens.

"Jasmine is for grace and elegance," Mary Fran murmured. "I know that one only because Matthew has sent it to me, the daft man."

Augusta rose and plucked a single sturdy evergreen stem from the very center of the bouquet. "Juniper is for protection. Who in the world?" She rummaged around among the blossoms, looking for a card. An elegant little note sat near a creamy magnolia blossom. "Magnolia for dignity."

"There's a carriage pulling up. Crested," Julia reported. "I can't quite… God in heaven. We're to have a caller after all."

They went to the window en masse. A liveried footman sprang from the back of an enormous town coach and strode briskly toward the town house door.

"That crest is familiar," Augusta said. "Somebody make sure Hannah is properly turned out before she comes down. These flowers need to go into the front hallway, and have the footmen fill the card bowl with last week's cards. Alert the kitchen we'll need the best service, and send word to the mews when the men come in that Mary Fran will skelp their bums if they set so much as *one* muddy boot on the back steps while we're entertaining. And do not breathe a word of our caller to Miss Enid. The woman needs her rest."

The ladies scurried off in several directions, so that within the five minutes necessary to assure the footman they were at home and happy to receive guests, word had gone upstairs, downstairs, and everywhere in between.

While the kitchen worked furiously to assemble a tea tray fit for royalty and Hannah's maid put the finishing touches on her coiffure, the Moreland ducal coach disgorged no less than a viscountess, two countesses, two marchionesses, and… one dignified, smiling duchess on the arm of her graciously congenial—if leonine—duke.

Sixteen

"He tries so not to glower, but His Grace is the type to fret over his womenfolk." Her Grace, Anna, Duchess of Moreland, did not sound concerned that every half minute or so the Duke of Moreland took note of his duchess's progress around the garden with Hannah.

His Grace was similarly vigilant regarding his various sisters as they minced about with Con, Gil, Ian, and Malcolm, while the smaller of the two marchionesses, the youngest of the lot, sat among the roses with the MacGregor wives and His Grace.

"He seems a very hale gentleman," Hannah said, hoping it wasn't too plebeian to describe a duke as hale.

The duchess approved, if her smile was any indication. "The Windhams are a hardy lot. The former duke and duchess lived well into their eighties and were seldom under the weather. Moreland shows every sign of taking after his father in this regard."

Her Grace blew her husband a kiss. He bowed slightly in her direction, and Hannah wanted to blush for them both.

"We're quite shameless. The younger generation

mutters about former times being more permissive and the elderly needing humoring. We despair of them, of course, being so strict and proper all the time." Her Grace paused and bent to sniff at a white rose. "Did you enjoy the bouquet?"

This, Hannah suspected, was how a duchess got down to business. "I haven't seen it yet. I was still above stairs when the flowers arrived."

With gloved fingers, the duchess snapped off the rose and passed it to Hannah. "Were you still recovering from last night? We're unfashionable, to be calling at such an hour, but I saw you, you know."

"Saw me?"

"Last night." Her Grace was a tall woman. When she slipped her arm through Hannah's, Hannah had no choice but to wander down the white gravel walkway with her guest. "At the ball. Your swain was so concerned for you he did not notice one little old lady on her way to the retiring room. He was carrying you down the corridor, your skirts billowing, and you were so pale…"

Her Grace's gaze strayed to the flower in Hannah's hand. *Little old lady, indeed.* Hannah found the duchess neither little nor old, though she was, unquestionably, a lady.

"I fainted, Your Grace. I don't know what gossip you've heard, but Lord Balfour was concerned for me, nothing more."

"He was beside himself. I wasn't at all sure we should call so soon, but Moreland was of the opinion that it couldn't hurt."

A duke and a duchess had discussed Hannah's

swoon. The notion was unfathomable, and not in a comforting sense. "We're very pleased to have your company, Your Grace. Were Ash—his lordship here, I'm sure he'd agree."

Except Asher hadn't come back from his ride in the park with his brothers. He'd said something to them about business in the City, and now all and sundry were milling about the garden among near royalty without benefit of Lord Balfour's charming presence.

"I have nine children, Miss Cooper, and an embarrassment of grandchildren. Do you know your eyes change when you think of him?"

Hannah did not dare slip her arm free, but she wanted to. She wanted to tear off directly for the docks. It was one thing to be interrogated by a duchess, quite another to be interrogated by a mother of nine, and something else yet again to answer questions put by a seasoned grandmother.

"Lord Balfour is an estimable man and an exemplary host."

"Moreland says the fellow is besotted with you. His Grace has an instinct for these things—much as his father did—though you'd never think it to watch him duking about."

Her Grace gave her husband a little wave.

"I'm sure His Grace is a very good judge of character." Hannah was wearing gloves too, of course, excellent gloves of pale kidskin. As she twirled the rose between her fingers, a thorn managed to prick her even through the leather.

"He is an excellent judge of character, among many other things—he married me, didn't he?" She beamed at her husband like a girl of eighteen. "His reasoning, to which it is my ceaseless privilege to be privy, went thus: if you and your swain needed a little persuading toward the altar, then this minor tempest would see you wed. That's fine, assuming you are equally besotted." The duchess paused and regarded Hannah levelly. "Are you besotted?"

Of course she was. Besotted wasn't merely in love. Besotted was somewhere between passionately fond and enamored nigh to illness. Hannah considered dissembling, considered mentioning the increasingly cloudy sky. Considered tossing the rose at the duchess's dainty feet and bolting for the house.

"I esteem Lord Balfour above all others, Your Grace, but my responsibilities lie in Boston, and his are in Scotland."

They walked on in silence while Hannah tried to swallow past a tightness in her throat.

"It's as well we came to call then. Were you to marry his lordship, we'd be offering felicitations. Since you are not to marry, our call will ensure a peer of the realm and a blameless young lady preserve their spotless reputations. A word of advice, though, before my husband attaches himself to your other arm and begins to dispense same."

"I am much in need of wise counsel, Your Grace."

"Methinks you are in need of a handkerchief more, or perhaps a stout blow to your common sense."

Grandmothers saw too much, regardless of rank, station, or society of origin. The duke was on his feet, bowing over each lady's hand a dozen yards away.

"Do not hare off to the Colonies posthaste, Miss

Cooper. Gad about at the seashore, go walking in the Lakes, enjoy the rest of the Season, flirt with the young men, make the young ladies jealous. If you make a hasty departure for America now, my efforts will mean nothing. There will be speculation, and that can be as damaging as outright accusations. And, Miss Cooper?"

Would this walk about the garden never end? "Yes, Your Grace?"

"Rare blooms are sometimes surprisingly hardy. They don't merely survive transplanting. Sometimes they thrive all the better for new conditions."

Her Grace patted Hannah's cheek with the exact same blend of affection and warning Hannah's own grandmother would have applied, then turned and called out to the duke. Five minutes later, amid much fluttering and smiling, the ducal conveyance rumbled off, though somehow, despite all the kind wishes and good cheer, the bloom in Hannah's grasp had been torn to shreds.

"Letter for you." Malcolm bounced into the parlor and handed the little epistle to Hannah. "It's from Boston. I peeked. Shameless of me, but there you have it."

"My thanks. If it's for me, then it's likely from Boston, isn't it?"

Malcolm seated himself to Hannah's left, studying his American soon-to-be-cousin. "Earlier today you were officially blessed by more venerable titles than London is likely to see outside of a royal christening, and yet, you look downcast. The Marchioness of

Deene herself *winked* at me, Hannah, and I'm thinking of posting a notice in *The Times* to this effect. What can possibly be amiss?"

He did not add that Hannah was soon to be laughing in the faces of all who'd smirked behind their fans the previous evening. One ducal bouquet would quiet the tabbies utterly, and a visit all but assured Hannah the wedding of the Season. He'd felt bad about the smirking, of course, but inspiration had struck when he'd seen Hannah and Asher skulking out of the ballroom hand in hand.

A man with creditors and mouths to feed did not argue with inspiration, and it had all turned out for the best anyway.

Hannah studied her unopened letter, a single folded page, the handwriting blocky, like a child's. And then, as Malcolm considered Hannah, the bluebirds of much deserved triumph fluttering around in his chest plummeted to his vitals.

"The duchess's visit has not set you to rights, Hannah Cooper. What's amiss?"

She blinked at the letter, a sign of impending disaster if Malcolm had ever seen one. "The duchess's visit has unruined me, and that puts certain other matters in a different, more complicated light."

"Are those other matters related to last night's indiscretion?"

The question was exceedingly uncomfortable. Malcolm had consoled himself that Asher and Hannah belonged together, and his efforts were in the way of nudging two stubborn, independent people in the direction of their best interests. Doubt assailed him, aiming a loaded blunderbuss at the few bluebirds still on the wing.

"Not the indiscretion you're accusing me of. I honestly did faint, you know. Have you any idea where Asher has gone off to?"

He knew exactly where Asher had gone off to, because he'd bribed a street Arab to follow the man. Given how crowded Fleet Street and The Strand were, the job had been easy. "Asher had some business in the City."

"That's the financial district?"

"The business district. The courts, lawyers, and bankers tend to be over that way." Doctor's Commons was in the same direction, of course.

"He's transacting business today?"

Americans had the most persistent sense of curiosity. "Nothing that will take long. Aren't you pleased to have the blessing of the Duchess of Moreland, Hannah?"

For the first time, Hannah shifted her gaze to regard him. "Was there something you wanted, Malcolm?"

He wanted her to be happy. He wanted Asher to be happy. He wanted *himself* to be happy, though he was willing to settle for being solvent and in good health.

"Let's go for an ice." He made a grab for her hand, but she snatched it away.

"It's going to rain, Malcolm, and I do not want an ice. Last night, I was a pariah, a fallen woman, a social failure despite my wealth and despite not having done one thing wrong. Today I'm bosom bows with a lot of sweet-smelling, titled beldames. Did you know, when I arrived here I'd made an objective out of being ruined?"

He had not known that, but she was American. He was coming to believe that was synonymous with unhinged. "Why?"

"I wanted the freedom to tend to my responsibilities. I wanted to be with people who loved me even when they didn't approve of me. I wanted… I wanted to *go home*."

Freedom? Why were Americans always prosing on about their bloody *freedom*? "Scotland has freedom and is home to many, even the Queen and her prince consort sometimes. They're wonderful neighbors. Lots of kiddies underfoot, and Albert is a great sportsman."

She glared at him as if he'd just farted at high tea. "Yesterday, I was a scandal. Today I am the darling of a duchess and her titled relations. I'm getting floral panegyrics from a rascally old duke, and the invitations, as of an hour ago, have filled three baskets."

Moreland would like being called rascally. Malcolm tried a smile, though the conversation was leaving him utterly flummoxed. "It's like that bit with the loaves and fishes, you see. One duchess can work miracles with the calls and invitations."

"I didn't want a miracle. I never wanted a miracle."

She sounded not angry, but bewildered—forlorn. He didn't dare pat her hand. "I take it you aren't going to be cheered to learn that Asher has gone to purchase a special license?"

"A license for what?"

"Holy matrimony, presumably to you."

And then she did cry, not loudly, not untidily, but she broke Malcolm's heart all the same.

"Why is that sitting out here?" Asher asked the question casually, though a sizable trunk in the middle of the barn aisle, where it might get kicked or worse, was not an everyday sight.

The groom who'd taken Asher's horse paused to regard the trunk, a nondescript sturdy piece of gray-green luggage that would hold a fair amount. "Headed for the docks, guv. Young Miss had it out here before her came downstairs."

Young Miss, as distinguished from Miss Enid, though the help had all manner of names for the older houseguest, none of them flattering.

Asher's first reaction was pleasure that Hannah should be so eager to depart for points north. "Don't you mean it's headed for the train station?" King's Cross was the usual point of departure for the north-bound express trains—and they would be taking an express to Edinburgh, of course. Likely hiring private cars, making a family party out of the journey.

"Not the train station." The old groom regarded the trunk again, his expression sad, as if the thing were a casket, not a mere repository for clothes and books.

Asher leaned over to read the address carefully lettered onto the side. "Boston?"

"And she said she'll have several more down here by the end of the week, though she isn't sure t'other lady will be joining her for the return journey. I'da rather kept Young Miss and sent t'other 'un back. Come along, horse."

With a sense of cold foreboding, Asher waited until the clip-clop of the horse's hoofbeats had faded, then took out a knife and slit the twine fastening the trunk.

Hannah's clothing, some everyday, some newly purchased, lay carefully wrapped in thin paper and folded around sachets of lavender and sage. A volume of Walter Scott occupied pride of place on the top of the heap, the edition Asher had last seen at the inn in Steeth.

A set of nightclothes was among the garments Hannah was sending back to Boston—a night-gown and peignoir of green silk bordered in satin, the embroidery a blue, green, and purple riot of peacock feathers and flowers. Beaded slippers completed the ensemble, though there was no lift on the right heel.

He refolded her clothes, the silk cool and soft in his hands.

Fiona's cat came strutting by, standing on its back legs to peer into the trunk. Asher lifted the cat aside, wanting instead to either throw the beast a good distance or pick it up and cuddle it.

"She's sending part of her trousseau back to Boston."

He closed the trunk and sat on it for a long time, stroking the purring cat. Hannah had no sisters. Her granny wasn't going to be wearing such finery, and neither was her uncommunicative mother.

While the black-and-white cat kneaded Asher's riding breeches with needle-sharp claws, Asher mentally revisited his conversations with Hannah the previous evening.

I can't do this alone anymore. He'd seized on those words as an acceptance of a proposal, while Hannah had intended them as an announcement of her departure. And off he'd charged—after swiving her repeatedly—to fetch the special license.

"What are you doing pampering that great hairy beast when he ought by rights to be stuffing his maw with some fat English mousie?"

Ian stood in the doorway in plain shirt, simple black vest, and a black work kilt, hands on hips, regarding the cat.

"I'm exchanging confidences, one peer of the realm to another."

Ian scratched the cat's head. "We've had a surfeit of titles on hand lately. You missed all the excitement."

Asher set the cat aside, though the animal bounded right back onto Hannah's trunk and commenced to wash its paws. "We've had callers?"

Vultures, no doubt. Circling the remains of Hannah's reputation.

"Old Moreland came by with the reigning dowagers. His duchess *and* his sisters. Malcolm didn't know which one to flirt with first. Even Connor was strolling about the gardens like a besotted spaniel."

Not vultures. Not anything Asher could have predicted, though for Hannah, he was glad. "I see."

Ian pushed the cat off the trunk and settled beside Asher.

"You stink of the stables, Ian."

Ian passed him a silver flask. "You stink of the City." The cat popped onto Ian's lap, already purring, while Ian mildly cursed the beast in Gaelic.

Asher took a bracing swallow of fine whiskey. "We're leaving at week's end." He passed the flask back.

Ian tipped it up, offered it to the cat, then put the cap back on and tucked it into his sporran. "And where are we off to, now that our resident rebel has become the darling of Polite Society—despite an unfortunate tendency to lace her stays a bit too tightly?"

"Edinburgh. Home eventually." Where a man could drink himself into oblivion if need be.

"Thank God."

"You don't like showing your ladies off, strutting about in your kilt, and flirting with duchesses?"

Ian smacked him on the arm hard enough to hurt, and that felt—good. "I don't like watching you torture yourself with what you cannot have, and your wee rebel isn't looking any too pleased with life these days either."

"She's not my rebel."

"You missed your moment, then. Before the angels of social redemption came fluttering around, you could have snatched your lady up and made mad, passionate love to her. She'd be sporting your ring and a smile this morning."

A smile perhaps, for a time. That was something. Maybe it could be enough. "She would not be sporting my ring."

Ian paused in mid-scratch, his fingers buried in the cat's fur. "Do you at least have a plan, Asher?"

"Yes, I have a plan." He stood and yelled for a groom to get the bloody trunk back to the house, there to await its eventual removal to King's Cross and a private railcar. "When she's ready to sail for Boston, I plan to let her go."

Evan Draper attributed his eventual arrival in the great metropolis of London to Saint Louis IX. That holy fellow had sired eleven children, gone on two crusades, and was considered a patron of everything from button makers, to prisoners, to some city in northern Africa, and difficult marriages. This last accounted for Draper's acquaintance with Louis, a function of Granny Draper's closet papism and poor luck in husbands.

Louis was also, however, the patron saint of distillers, and indirectly, that lot was responsible for Draper's peregrinations about the realm by train.

Or perhaps St. Matthias—patron saint of gamblers—had taken a hand in things. Thanks to her second husband, Granny had been on good terms with St. Matthias too.

"Why, Mr. Draper, a pleasure to see you." The Countess of Spathfoy was short, blond, achingly young, and possessed of very pretty blue eyes, and yet Draper was sure those eyes missed nothing.

"Your ladyship." He did not dare take her hand. His every pair of gloves had suffered *mal du train*, with soot embedded beyond what any mere rinsing would get out.

"His lordship ought to be home momentarily, Mr. Draper. Shall I ring for some sustenance?"

Draper's hand went to his middle, as if he'd shield his stomach from even the mention of words relating to food.

"No, thank you, your ladyship. All that time aboard the trains has played havoc with my digestion, and I wouldn't want to trouble you unnecessarily. If Lord Spathfoy is from home, perhaps you'd send a note around to MacGregor House on my behalf?"

Her smile didn't falter, but she was without doubt

noting Draper's pallor, the wrinkled state of his suit, and perhaps even his bloodshot eyes. Maybe she also saw how grateful he was that Spathfoy's London residence wasn't so very far from the train station after all.

"The MacGregors all speak very highly of you, Mr. Draper. Are you sure you wouldn't like to tarry for just a bit?"

He was muzzy-headed, not only with overimbibing, but also fatigue. More to the point, he lacked fare for a cab clear to the MacGregor town house. "Perhaps a cup of tea."

"Of course. We'll avail ourselves of his lordship's study."

She meant to *take* tea with him? Was there a saint for dealing with overly gracious, well-intended, wee countesses?

Like a prisoner approaching the dock for sentencing, Draper followed her through a spotless, well-appointed town house. The windows were sparkling even on this dreary day, the floors seemed to give off light so highly were they polished, and the entire house bore a slight scent of cedar.

The effect of all this domestic industry—even of the relatively fresh air—was that Draper's eyeballs started pounding in counterpoint to his throbbing head. And of course, he had to use the necessary. How did one ask a countess for the use of the privy?

"Tell me, Mr. Draper, how does Baron Fenimore go on? I'm given to understand his health may still be troubling him?"

The baron was happily anticipating his own demise, though it didn't seem to be *troubling* him. Perhaps the thought of rejoining his baroness consoled him. "He's as well as may be, your ladyship. I bring his felicitations to the household, of course."

Though if Fenimore knew Draper was reduced to calling on in-laws due to a lack of even cab fare, Fenimore would not be pleased.

"Make yourself comfortable, Mr. Draper. I'll be but a moment."

She left him alone in a room for which many trees had given their lives. Paneling covered every surface, a warm blond oak that rose up the walls and erupted into ornate molding. The desk was of the same wood, as was the mantel over the fireplace. Compared to Fenimore's cramped, camphor-scented office, this room was celestially airy, organized, and attractive.

A man could nap here in one of the big, well-padded chairs flanking the desk.

Because Draper had closed his eyes to contemplate such a possibility, the bang of the door startled him.

"Chamber pot's under the sideboard. Her ladyship will be fussing the kitchen for a moment, if you've a need of privacy."

The footman busied himself closing the curtains, shutting out a view of the back gardens and dimming the room somewhat. The fellow was sandy-haired, freckled, and spoke with a slight burr.

"You're sure?"

"She said you looked like travel hadn't agreed with you, and I wasn't to slam the door for my own entertainment." The fellow smiled and winked, for which Fenimore would likely have fired him.

Fenimore, who welcomed death.

When the countess reappeared some minutes later, the same footman was in tow, no smile in evidence. He set an enormous tea tray down on a table before the hearth. Draper looked away from all that gleaming silver and the sandwiches and fruit sitting upon it.

When the footman had withdrawn, the countess turned a dazzling smile on her guest. "Now, Mr. Draper, my every instinct tells me you've had an adventure. I shall be desolated if you don't share it with me down to the last detail."

Unlike the sunshine, the glaring floors, or the gleaming silver, the countess's smile did not hurt Draper's eyes. Her smile, so full of benevolence and good cheer, beckoned to him and offered a promise of comfort and consolation. She was the sister of two MacGregor spouses, after all, and cousin to Augusta, Baroness of Gribboney, who was married to a third MacGregor.

The countess's smile was the smile of a family member welcoming a prodigal home. Draper glanced up at a corner of the room, where a fat cherub swaddled in oaken clouds was wielding a wooden bow aimed directly at the tea set.

St. Louis had not deserted the weary traveler after all.

"Well, your ladyship, there was a card game, you see. On the train. In the convivial spirit of the impromptu gathering, my flask made its usual appearance."

Her gaze filled with commiseration. She poured a steaming cup of tea, added a dash of sugar and a dollop of cream. "Do go on, Mr. Draper."

By the time he'd downed three cups of very fine oolong, and even managed a nibble of buttered scone, he reached the part about arriving in Manchester, of all the godforsaken destinations, without the very flask given to him by his own dear granny, and without his wallet either.

"The flask, of course, was the greater loss," he observed.

"Of course it was, you poor man."

Whereupon the Earl of Spathfoy joined them, forcing Draper to start the whole miserable tale all over again, though this time he began his story from the point where he'd come upon Theobald MacDuie's smallholding north of Berwick-Upon-Tweed.

Seventeen

The pain was like a brutally laced emotional corset, offering discomfort from every direction, impinging on Hannah's every thought and impulse. While the wheels of the train rumbled rhythmically beneath her feet, Hannah stumbled about mentally, trying to grasp that Asher MacGregor had procured them a license to marry.

Which was the reason—the only reason—he'd gifted her with his intimate favors. She watched him in the close confines of their railcar as he played cribbage with Ian.

Were Hannah to marry Asher, such a sight would become prosaic, commonplace. She would not notice that he looked tired, that with his sleeves cuffed back, his exposed wrists had a particular masculine appeal.

She would not notice that his brothers and sister watched him in stray moments, as if making sure he were still among them.

"You are a thousand miles away, Hannah Cooper." Augusta's voice was kind, offering distraction, only if distraction would be welcome. Her observation was quiet, too, the noise of the train ensuring an odd measure of privacy.

"I'm wondering why my grandmother's letters have grown so sparse. She's a reluctant correspondent, but reliable." If two letters a month could be considered reliable.

"The elderly must be allowed their crotchets. I certainly intend to indulge in them when Ian and I are getting on."

She kissed her baby on his fuzzy head, the infant apparently content to sleep anywhere, provided he was held in loving arms.

Another jab at Hannah's heart: she'd never have children with Asher MacGregor. Never catch him looking at her the way Ian regarded his Augusta when she tended to the child.

"How is it Asher spent years in the Canadian wilderness?"

Augusta's expression didn't change, but her violet eyes filled with sympathy.

"He wasn't in the wilderness for the entire duration. For at least the last few years, he was mostly on the coast, enjoying the blandishments of civilization. I'm told your father was in the fur trade as well."

Hannah managed a nod. She missed her grandmother, she missed her mother. She missed her half brothers, too, with an intensity that was surprising. Lately, though, realizing what she'd leave behind in Scotland, realizing a small part of what her parents had shared and what her mother had grieved, Hannah had also missed her papa.

"Hannah, are you well? You look as if train travel might not agree with you."

No, she was not *well* and never would be again. "I'm fine. When do we arrive to York?"

"Within the hour. This child will wake up just in time to ensure Ian and I have no peace until at least the middle of the night."

"And yet, you want more children exactly like him."

Augusta's smile was soft, female, and a trifle naughty. "Ian says it's our duty to see to the succession, at least until Asher marries and he and his countess can take up the job themselves."

A question hung in the air, like a knife suspended over Hannah's composure. Thank a merciful God, her lapse with Asher had been timed such that conception was unlikely.

"Do you think Asher will ever practice medicine again?" She tossed the question out as a means of changing the topic.

"It isn't likely. Belted earls must tend to other obligations. Would you like to hold the baby? He's ever so dear when he's sleeping."

Hannah reached for the child without thinking. Augusta had never offered before, and Hannah had never presumed to ask. Across the narrow railcar, Ian peered up from his cards and exchanged a glance with Augusta. They communicated much in an instant, about the baby, about train travel, maybe even about plans for later in the evening.

As Hannah hugged the baby gently, she added to the list of jabs and pinches suffered by her heart: she and Asher would not exchange such potent glances while others looked on without being able to translate the nuances.

She and Asher would not spend the shank of an evening murmuring to each other of the day's events in a peaceful darkness.

She and Asher would not use that license, and it was—all of it—her fault.

❧

To cram his entire family together in a few train cars had struck Asher as a brilliant inspiration. With siblings, in-laws, children, and a cat underfoot, there was little likelihood he and Hannah would have to deal with each other directly.

He had forgotten though, or ignored, that such proximity meant they'd all be living on top of each other for two days. Watching Hannah cuddle the sleeping baby had nigh unmanned him, and he had a sense she wasn't faring much better than he.

And now, here she was, standing on the platform between the ladies' sleeping car and the parlor car, wearing her night robe, slippers, and a tentative smile.

Manners. When all else failed, a fellow who'd been stupid enough to dash out and procure a marriage license still had his manners. "I beg your pardon, Hannah. I didn't know you were out here."

"Nor I you."

For an instant, swaying along with the locomotive's rhythm, they said nothing.

Bloody goddamned manners, MacGregor. "Are you looking forward to reaching Edinburgh?"

"Of course. It's said to be a lovely city, though I was in no mood to appreciate it when I first arrived."

"It's an old city, dating back to before the Romans."

He slipped off his coat and draped it around her shoulders. "I'll enjoy showing it off to you."

Assuming she didn't take ship for Boston the very next day. The thought nearly brought him to his knees.

"This coat is marvelously warm. How long will we be staying?"

How long can I get you to stay? "At least a couple of weeks, though I'd like you to see Balfour, too, assuming you're willing to tarry that long?"

She turned so she faced the north country rolling past under the moonlight. "I feel like I'm not going *toward* anything. I feel like I'm racketing about, like one of those round cheeses that's rolled down a steep hill for sport."

A fine analogy. She was leaving, and because she was leaving, she'd permitted him rare and precious liberties.

But she wasn't gone yet. He positioned himself behind her and slipped his arms around her waist. "Do you miss your aunt?"

She relaxed against him, letting him balance for them both. "Miss her? Are you teasing me? When she declared her stomach too delicate to journey north with us, I wanted to dance one of your reels."

"I expect Mr. Trundle did too, discreetly of course. May I kiss you, Hannah?"

If a man was to suffer the torments of the damned, then they ought to at least be the more enjoyable torments. Not the torment of watching her cuddle Ian's dratted infant, or the torment of knowing she was leaving.

Leaving.

Leaving.

She turned in his embrace and propped herself against the railing, wrapping her arms around his waist and resting her forehead on his chest. "We haven't spoken much since leaving London."

The hour being late, he'd discarded his cravat. Hannah's tongue grazed his throat.

"We haven't had any privacy."

"I like your family, Asher. They are very dear, and they are devoted to you and to one another."

Unlike *her* blighted family, all of whom needed Hannah to protect them, or so his informants in Boston implied. He dipped his head to gather her lavender scent. "My family likes you, too. Will you be able to sleep? We'll reach Waverly Station quite early."

She sighed, a weary exhalation that suggested his question was inane, which it was—though bloody polite, too. "I'll not sleep. You'll not sleep either. The baby sleeps, Fiona sleeps, and that infernal cat sleeps. Your brothers are no doubt playing cards and drinking until they can't keep their eyes open, while their wives are 'resting.'"

"You should rest too." And he should go play cards, because if he stood out here with her much longer, he wouldn't answer for the consequences. "The baby is learning the finer points of poker as we speak."

This made her smile, her teeth showing white against the darkness. "Is he taking a wee nip every now and then?"

"No, but I am. Kiss me, Hannah."

She did better than that. She nigh climbed him to fuse her mouth to his, mashing her body against him until his arousal was a throbbing presence between them. It took strength, determination, and cooperation, but within minutes, Asher had her backed against the parlor car, wedged between the wall and the railing, her leg around his hip, and his trousers unfastened.

"We shouldn't, Hannah. There could be a child." Bad things happened when people destined to part procreated. He was the living proof.

She curled her fingers around his shaft. "Stop being reasonable. Whether we suffer one lapse or two makes little difference."

They were up to three lapses, with the fourth impending, when the dratted, blessed woman scooted a little, so that what ought to have been a feat of sexual gymnastics became entirely possible. Asher widened his stance, half-hiked her to a perch on the railing, and probed at her heat, desire clawing its way past reason. "Don't let me drop you."

"Don't let me fall."

They came together in a fit of insanity, as if all the power of the locomotive itself fueled their coupling. He tried to hold back, tried to exercise a little finesse—manners, be damned—but Hannah clutched at him and leveraged herself against the wall to buck into his thrusts.

"Harder, please, Asher. You have to..."

He covered her mouth with his, lest somebody hear her demands. She groaned into the kiss while he got a hand firmly under her backside.

"Better. Hold me tight, Asher."

For an instant he let her balance on sheer strength while he found her hand and used her own fingers to apply pressure to a nipple. The sound she made, low, earthy, and voluptuous, went right to his cock.

He'd seen a meteor once, in the cold, starry depths of the Canadian wilderness. It had streaked into the night sky, growing brighter and brighter as it hurtled across the firmament.

Hannah's pleasure was like that. Glorious, incandescent, a perfect complement to the train rocketing them north at the speed of a horse galloping for its life. He lasted only a half-dozen ferocious thrusts longer than she did, pounding Hannah into the wall before he withdrew and spilled onto their bare bellies.

She recovered first, kissing his jaw. "Put me down. I can feel you shaking."

He didn't want to let her go. He settled for allowing her leg to slide off his hip, while he stood, arm braced above her, panting. That he had her physically cornered was some consolation.

Her fingers winnowed through his hair, trying to put right what she and the train had utterly disordered. "I think I'll sleep now."

"And I'll play cards. Stare at them, in any case."

They both smiled. As long as conversation wasn't expected of them, they were on safe ground.

"You should rest, Asher. I'm going to expect your devoted escort once we get to Edinburgh."

"You'll have it. I'll expect you to be the scintillating American heiress who had old Moreland mustering his troops."

The exchange petered out, and abruptly, Asher was aware of the night wind on his damp, exposed parts. He kissed her again, slowly, a sure way to bring heat back into his system. The words "I love you" began to drum at his brain, but where would that leave them?

Did a man who loved a woman try to hold her against her will with words?

Even honest words?

"Hold still." Hannah fished in his pockets, produced a handkerchief, and dabbed at herself. She folded the thing over to use on his stomach, then arranged his softening cock in his clothes and fastened his trousers.

"You are proficient at that, Hannah Lynn Cooper."

She tossed a look up at him, as if she'd say something, then changed her mind. When she would have ducked around him, left him on the platform without so much as a good-night kiss, he caught her hand.

"What were you about to say?" He could not read her expression, but he could feel her unhappiness with every instinct he possessed. "Tell me, Hannah, because this is as much privacy as we're likely to find, and if you were going to say this mustn't happen again, I agree. It must not. Ever."

What was he saying?

Hannah put her hand to Asher's cheek, as if by touching him she could gain powers of divination to defy the darkness around them. Against her palm, his jaw was rough with the beginnings of a beard, and warm.

She craved that warmth.

He captured her hand in his own and gently removed it from his person. "Shall we sit, Hannah?"

He gestured to a bench fashioned on the side of the platform nearest the ladies' car. A simple, flat surface such as a man might use to enjoy a cigar or to escape from the confines of the train's cramped compartments.

Hannah took a seat, gathering Asher's coat around her. He settled beside her, making no move to put an arm about her shoulders or draw her close.

So that's how it was to be?

"You said this must not happen again, ever. What did you mean, Asher?" Was she to go back to my-lording and Balfouring?

"I want to touch you. It's a distraction not to." He took her hand, though his tone was truculent. "I meant, Hannah Cooper, that after the Alcincoates' ball, we had a discussion, and that discussion led to indiscretions such as we just enjoyed moments ago."

Passionate lovemaking was an indiscretion. He spoke the truth—a truth—but she wanted to pitch him off the train before he could say one more word—or perhaps jump from the train herself.

"My lord—" *Wrong*. For this discussion, all wrong. "Asher, I owe you an apology."

He brought her knuckles to his lips. "You will explain this apology."

The nature of their misunderstanding was apparently clear to him, and yet, she wanted to be the one to acknowledge their mistake. "When we had that discussion, I should have been clearer about my position. I was not accepting your proposal of marriage."

"I know that now. You were announcing your intention to take ship. So why are you still here, holding hands with me?"

And committing further indiscretions? Between

them, that question was fair even if the answer lay beyond Hannah's grasp.

"I learned you had procured that license. Malcolm must have guessed, and he let it slip. I could not find a way to tell you..." That she loved him, that she wanted to spend the rest of her days and nights with him, but that she was leaving him all the same.

"So you're telling me now, after scrambling m' wits in five minutes flat?" That he could manage any pretensions to humor was a testament to the depth of his gallantry.

"My wits were scrambled the moment you stepped onto the platform, sir. They're scrambled still."

His arm came around her shoulders. Her throat began to ache.

"Not scrambled enough, I'll warrant. I'm sorry, Hannah. It's harder when we know what we're giving up."

How could he be so damnably philosophical?

"So we're not engaged? That license doesn't create an engagement?"

His lips grazed her temple. "It's just a piece of paper. You're free to tend to your responsibilities, and I'm free to tend to mine. I'll squire you about Edinburgh for a couple of weeks, maybe show you Balfour if you're interested, and then put you on one of my fastest ships bound for Boston."

A list of tasks to be completed, or a recipe—for heartache.

"Thank you."

"You are not welcome, Hannah Cooper. I have business in Boston, you know. I could visit there from time to time, once I spend a few years playing earl here to everybody's satisfaction."

"You need heirs, Asher. Don't torment me with what-ifs, maybes, and perhapses."

"I'm asking you to plan, Hannah." His voice was very gentle, his grasp of her hand loose. "Plan for that day you're larking around the shops, picking out a book to give a friend or to read to your hundred-year-old granny, and you look up, and there I am, across the street. I might have a touch of gray at my temples, my hair will likely be shorter, and our eyes will meet. Plan for that day, and the regrets and desire that will deluge us both."

And he might be holding the hand of a small boy who resembled him, or have on his arm a pretty, wellborn Scottish countess. She turned her face to his shoulder. "I hate you."

She'd have no husband at her side in that bookshop, though, which was a consolation of sorts.

"Then you also hate the part of you that is responsible, loving, and loyal. I've tried, but I cannot hate these things in you. I can resent them, though, just as you must resent them in me."

His ability to see the situation clearly only made her determination to leave him that much more of a burden. "I want you to rant at me and wave the license in my face and tell me I have no choice."

"We all have choices." More humor, however bleak.

And he was right, blast him to Halifax. Hannah did have choices.

"I choose two weeks in Edinburgh, two weeks at Balfour, and then you will find me that ship."

"A month, then. We'll have one more month."

For him that seemed to settle something. For Hannah, it only raised the question of how she'd endure her life when that month was over.

And then, because he had not and would never take her choices away, she entrusted him with one of her heartaches. "The last letter from my grandmother? She asked when I was coming home. She's never asked that before, and I haven't heard from her since. My brothers have stopped writing."

He remained silent for a time, the sound of the train rolling north reverberating against Hannah's soul. "Tell her you leave in a month. Tell them all you'll be leaving me in one month."

He kissed her, a soft press of lips against her mouth, no insinuation or reproach to it. Just a kiss.

As he offered her an ironic little bow and withdrew to the parlor car, Hannah knew that kiss for what it was: they might kiss again, they might even lapse again if she had the strength to endure such pleasure and passion, but that had been a kiss of parting, a kiss good-bye.

A man wasn't worth the name if he sought to hold a woman by a confluence of desire, misunderstanding, and guilt. For Asher to accept this conclusion required no great love, no feat of sacrifice. Common sense said a female as convinced of her conclusions as Hannah Cooper was would eventually resent any marital choice imposed on her, and resent the man who'd imposed it.

When Asher returned to the parlor car—where else could he go?—his brothers were still in their shirtsleeves, playing cards, drinking just enough to dull the restlessness, and trading desultory insults to pass the time. Their company was at once comforting and oppressive.

"It's Asher's turn to hold the bairn." Connor offered this pronouncement but made no move to pass the infant along.

Asher poured himself a drink and remained standing at the scaled-down version of a sideboard bolted along the wall. "You take turns with him, then? The deal passes to the left, the baby to the right?"

Gil cracked his jaw and tipped his chair back onto two legs. "Bring the whiskey here, why don't you, or at least pour a man a wee dram."

Asher set the decanter in the middle of the table, next to a pile of red, blue, and yellow chips. "Aren't you all up past your bedtimes?"

"Tell it to the lad," Connor grumbled. "Though I've no wish to sleep among the fartin', snorin' lot of you when I ought to be sleepin' wi' me darlin' wife."

"Take the baby," Ian said, speaking up for the first time and spearing Asher with a look. "It's your turn."

"I'm not anybody's nanny, Ian." Asher took a seat next to his brother and heir. "Connor can teach the boy how to fart and snore, assuming the lad doesn't already know. I suspect he does, and his mother thinks him quite the braw fellow for it."

Ian shuffled a deck of cards and let them riffle back into order between his hands. "And you know how to hold a sleeping baby."

God above, not now.

Gil's chair scraped back. "If I join Malcolm in the gents' car, then I have a prayer of getting to sleep before you lot come lumbering to bed. Do your farting out here, if you please. Open a window, and the ladies will pretend not to notice anything come morning."

"We'll be in Edinburgh come morning," Connor observed. "It's always good to get back to Scotland."

He rose and laid the baby against Asher's chest, apparently willing to risk letting the lad tumble to the floor—which, of course, Asher could not allow. He tucked the boy into the crook of his arm while Connor and Gil tossed back whatever remained of their drinks and moved off to find their beds.

"You will admit the earth is not shaking," Ian said, gathering up the chips. "The sky is not falling. Your heart is not ceasing to beat."

Asher used his free hand to reach for his drink. "And I will admit my brother is a bleating fool. Take this baby."

Ian started separating the chips into piles—blue, red, and yellow. "He's happy where he is. Never rile a sleeping baby. I can smell the woman on you."

Which might be why the child was content. Asher sat for a moment, exploring sensations. The baby had the solid feel of a child in good health. He was cozy and warm in his dress and blanket. Every few moments, his little mouth worked in a memory or a dream of suckling.

Beneath all those observations, clinical observations, was an awareness that Asher held life against his body, and not just any life. This child might someday become Earl of Balfour.

"The protectiveness does you no good," Asher said, arranging the blanket more snugly around the sleeping child. "You want to keep them safe, but to keep them safest, you must allow them to suffer. I hate that."

"Is this how you convince yourself that allowing Miss Cooper to return to Boston is the best thing for everybody? You might get a bairn or two or ten on her, and she'd never endure the inconvenience?"

The child made a noise, not a sigh, not quite a sound of sleeping-baby distress. Asher tucked him closer, catching a distinctive and wrenching whiff of clean-baby scent for his trouble.

"You know little, Ian, and you judge much."

The chips stacked higher, as many red as blue and yellow combined.

"I know what it is to be an utter ass where the woman of my heart is concerned. I know what it is to let theories of duty and honor get tangled up with truths fashioned in the soul. I know what it is to be weary and afraid, Asher, and I can promise you this: the only thing that makes the whole burden bearable is to have the love of the woman your heart has chosen."

"My heart has chosen a woman who has other obligations. I suspect Hannah's stepfather is abusive to all in his ambit, and that means she has not only her granny riding her conscience, but also her brothers, her mother, very likely the household help, and the beasts in the stable. She is the Countess of Boston, or her little corner of it."

Ian stared at a blue chip. "A man's home is his castle. The Americans have taken on that much of the common law, so the bastard is free to terrorize all in his personal kingdom. How does Hannah think to stop him?"

"She has money; she has lawyers; she has wits and determination that have likely been beaten out of the others. All she needs is some time to get her hands on the money, and she'll be able to send her brothers off to boarding school, set her granny up in style, and I don't know what for her mother."

Though Hannah likely had a plan of some sort. *Why hadn't he asked her about this?*

"You have money; you have solicitors; you have determination. I'm not sure about the wits."

Asher gave in to temptation—to instinct—and cuddled the child to his chest. "Neither am I."

At that rejoinder, Ian sat back and regarded him out of tired green eyes. "A woman's courage is different from a man's. We pillage and plunder. They endure. I don't pretend to understand it, but I suspect the race would die without their version of courage much sooner than it would without ours."

The lateness of the hour, the topic of the discussion, and the weight on Asher's heart—a month was little more than four weeks—made further thought difficult. "Marriage has turned you up philosophical, or perhaps it's the whiskey."

"Marriage, Asher MacGregor, has made me *happy*. Con, Gil, and Mary Fran would say the same. I bid you good night. Don't let the boy drink too much, or I'll never hear the end of it from his mother."

And just like that, before Asher could protest, whine, or strategize a countermeasure, Ian had disappeared into the gentlemen's sleeping coach, leaving Asher… holding the baby.

The parlor car sported a couch, a well-cushioned, sturdy affair positioned beneath the windows on the far wall. With the one-handed efficiency of a man holding a baby, Asher stashed the decanter back in its bracket, found an afghan in the sideboard, doused the lights, and arranged himself on the couch, the sleeping child swaddled against his chest.

In the darkness, the rhythm of the train brought sleep closer, and memories closer as well.

"Do you know, lad, for a long time I hated my father. He left my mother and went home to Scotland, there to die. Eventually, I understood a man must sometimes make his way, leave his loved ones, and be about his other obligations. I don't like it, but it's the way of the world."

He brushed his lips across the infant's downy crown, the sensation bringing back more memories, memories both sweet and piercingly sad. "I hated my mother next. She let him go—she didn't have to, she might have made the journey with him."

Though for the first time, Asher had to wonder if she'd suspected she was carrying, in which case, thirty years ago, the journey would have loomed as a risky ordeal—to the child at least. The thought made his hand on the child's back go still, and his mind come to rest as well.

"She could have been worried. Afraid for her child, unwilling to see her husband's journey put off for another year." And of course, afraid for her man, assuming she loved him.

"In any case, I hated her for years, for letting him go. And for dying." The hate wasn't in his heart now though. As Asher rummaged through his emotions, the sleeping baby tucked close, he couldn't even find the anger or many traces of bewilderment.

"They did the best they could. You'll find that realization a great comfort at some point. Recall your uncle Asher told it to you first."

And Asher was doing the best he could, too, but that was no comfort—no comfort at all.

Eighteen

Hundreds of miles north of London, the light was different. This was the first thing Hannah noticed as she stepped down from the train. Then too, she had a sense of the train reaching dry land, of endless motion coming to a halt, and the body needing to make an adjustment.

"It's chilly here, for being almost summer."

Asher would not drape his coat around her shoulders in broad daylight, nor did he look chilly in the kilted attire he'd donned for the day. "By local standards, we're in for a sweltering day."

They waited on the platform as the rest of the family debarked, porters dispatched baggage, and the welfare of the baby, the cat, and various expecting women was inventoried.

They'd be dividing up into coaches at any moment, so Hannah slipped her arm through Asher's and led him a few steps away. "I've a question for you."

He patted her hand, not as a lover might, but as a patient host would. "Ask."

"How did you know?"

One swift glance, a perusal that felt to Hannah as if Asher could assess her very memories. "Your trunk was sitting in the mews, labeled for Boston and headed for the docks. It was not laden with mementos and fripperies, so I concluded you intended to follow it to its destination."

Of course. A simple deduction for a man as observant as Asher MacGregor. Fiona's cat started to yowl, an aria of feline discontent that could last indefinitely.

"Where will we be staying?"

Asher turned at an angle that would allow his family to remain in his line of sight. "You will stay with me, Ian, Augusta, and wee John. Mary Fran and Matthew have their own place, as do Con and Julia. I expect Genie and Gil will stay with Con. When they come north, Spathfoy and Hester have the choice of staying at his place or with his mother, though Lady Quinworth positively dotes on my brothers."

When and how these arrangements had been worked out, Hannah did not know. She was simply grateful to Augusta for providing the chaperonage that permitted continued proximity to Asher. "You've never called the baby by name before."

This earned her a twitch of his lips, maybe impatience, maybe humor. "We're drinking companions now. He vows I'm his favorite uncle."

Hannah drew back to study Asher, because the observation wasn't simply self-mocking. Somehow, on this trip, the baby had become not merely an infant, occasionally noisy, often malodorous, but dear enough on general principles. He'd become "wee John," another obligation, another person for the reluctant MacGregor patriarch to love.

Hannah's only warning that the morning was to become livelier was a hint of lilac on the brisk morning air, and then a substantial lady dressed in the height of lavender fashion came swooping along the platform.

"Why, Balfour, you certainly do make a commotion when you arrive to town."

The lady leaned close, as if a kiss to her cheek from any passing earl was only her due. She was a handsome woman of a certain age, red-haired, with a vaguely familiar smile, and the air of a fit and fashionable Amazon.

"If it isn't me favorite marchioness." Connor, for once smiling himself, greeted the woman with an audible smack to both of her cheeks. Two liveried footmen took a nervous step closer, though the lady motioned them back with a wave of her gloved hand.

"And Gilgallon." She accepted a kiss from him. "If my own son can't be bothered to come north yet, I will content myself with what charming company I can find. You must all join me for breakfast. I insist."

"What about me?" Fiona had barged her way between the kilted knees of her uncles, the protesting cat in its hat-box cage still making a racket as she set the thing at her feet. "Am I invited for breakfast too?"

The marchioness dropped to her knees and opened her arms, the gesture at complete variance with her elegant attire, liveried footmen, and the lacy parasol she'd allowed to fall to the ground. "Fee! My darling little Fiona! How much you've grown, and how I have missed you."

The child bundled in for a long tight hug, while Hannah watched and tried not to label the emotions this succession of affectionate greetings had engendered.

Except that envy figured prominently among them, too prominently to ignore.

When the marchioness rose, she had Fiona by the hand. "I feel a kidnapping coming on. These things tend to strike whenever my darling Fiona comes to town." Over the child's head, the lady aimed a look at Mary Fran, who with Matthew had remained on the perimeter of the family circle. "You won't object to a short period of captivity for your daughter, will you, Lady Mary Frances?"

Though this marchioness strolling about the platform in the rays of morning sunshine was clearly a self-possessed woman of both title and means, the smile she beamed at Mary Fran carried a hint of vulnerability, too.

A hint of pleading.

Matthew caught Mary Fran's eye in one of those silent marital dialogues Hannah was also coming to envy.

"A few days of being stuffed with cream cakes never hurt any child," Mary Fran said. "Never hurt a cat either."

The marchioness's smile faltered then blazed anew. "Cats, rabbits, uncles—if Fiona loves them, then they're welcome in my houses. But, Balfour, you are remiss." Still holding Fiona's hand, the marchioness turned her smile on Asher. "Word of your engagement has preceded you. You must introduce me to your fiancée."

Beside Hannah, Asher froze, while the marchioness's smile became bright enough to guide lost ships through dense fog.

He untangled himself from Hannah's arm and

bowed over the marchioness's hand. "I'm afraid your ladyship has mistaken the—"

Hannah spoke right over him. "We're not engaged."

The lady's smile, full of teeth and conviction, was aimed at Hannah. "My dear, I'm very certain—very, very certain—that you and his lordship are quite engaged after all. Not another word now. We'll discuss it *later.* Come along, breakfast en famille is not to be missed."

She swanned off so quickly, Fiona barely had time to snatch up her yowling cat before being towed away toward the waiting coach.

"Spathfoy's mama is a Scotswoman and a damned English marchioness, Boston. You'll not gainsay her in public if you value your life, my life, either of our reputations, or the standing of any of my siblings. The cat alone is safe from her reach, only because he belongs to Fiona."

Hannah was nearly running to keep up with him, and Asher might have slowed down except he was nearly running to keep up with the damned marchioness. When a lady of wealth and title roused herself before dawn, tricked herself out in glorious finery, and met a train in her full regalia, mischief had to be brewing.

Some more mischief, in addition to what he and Hannah had already brewed up.

"Are we engaged, Asher? You said the license was just a piece of paper."

Hannah sounded more bewildered than furious, fortunately. "Her ladyship won't say another word until we're assured of privacy. That was the intent of her ambush, to make sure we couldn't misstep before strangers. Something's afoot."

"Something's *amiss*. Who is she?"

"Fiona's paternal grandmother—another interfering granny. She's Spathfoy's mama, which explains much about them both."

Though as grannies went, Deirdre Flynn, Marchioness of Quinworth, was a force of nature. She looked appreciably younger than her nearly fifty years and wore boldness like an exotic perfume blended exclusively for her.

Asher liked her, though he didn't turn his back on her if he could avoid it. He'd noted that Spathfoy and her husband, the marquess, adopted the same policy while the woman's three daughters emulated her in every particular.

"Into the coach, my dears." Her ladyship's smile still had that compelling quality, like a drill sergeant smiling at newly uniformed recruits before their first forced march. "Fee, you and the beast will join us at the town house. I'll want to hear all about your adventures in London, and so will your grandpapa."

More fussing and organizing took place while ladies were handed into coaches, and Hannah said nothing. At some point, Asher had linked his fingers with hers to make sure she didn't hare off to the docks.

Or perhaps to comfort her.

When Hannah and Lady Quinworth were settled on the forward-facing seat and Asher on the bench across from them, Lady Quinworth gave the roof a smart rap with the handle of her parasol and produced a flask.

"It's the custom in the Western Isles to start the day off with a wee nip. They're hardy people out west."

Hannah accepted the flask and tipped it to her lips. "Thank you, your ladyship. Do I offer it to—?"

"You do not." Her ladyship collected the flask in a purple-gloved hand. "Balfour has his own. Now, imagine my pleasure at being disturbed at my slumbers late last night by a telegram from my darling son. Not a word of greeting, no felicitations—the boy takes after his father—but all dire warnings and bad news. I suspect his dear little wife put him up to it—she's sensible, is our Hester."

Asher did not take out his flask, though the temptation was great. "And the nature of those warnings, my lady?"

The coach lurched off in the direction of the New Town. Hannah wasn't even pretending an interest in the passing sights.

"Forgive me, Miss Cooper, for being blunt. We have little time, because the announcement of your impending nuptials will be in the paper this very morning. I shall be inundated with callers, and we must fashion a proper story, mustn't we?"

Hannah did not answer, but she'd gone pale enough that from across the coach Asher could count the freckles dusting the bridge of her nose.

Asher asked the obvious question, lest Hannah get to contradicting the marchioness again. "Who would announce our engagement, my lady? Miss Cooper and I have not, that I know of, plighted our troth."

Lady Quinworth sniffed. "You've spent the night out on the moors without shelter or chaperone, which comes close enough to a declaration for anybody.

That old fool Fenimore has ferreted out the details. Spathfoy says the baron's man stumbled into their parlor after you'd departed for points north. Quite a tale came spilling forth over tea and crumpets—the entirety of which was dispatched to Fenimore by wire and letter before Draper had even reached London. I can hardly credit it, myself." She shot an appraising look at Asher. "The moors in winter are no place to be caught without food and shelter."

Much less a chaperone.

Hannah raised unhappy eyes to his. "There's to be an announcement?"

Fenimore's doing, no doubt, the rotten, old, conniving sod. "An announcement doesn't make us engaged, Hannah."

"Don't listen to him, Miss Cooper. It's one thing to break an engagement—that merely ruins *you*. It's quite another to make a fool of Fenimore and Balfour both while you do. Balfour is toothsome, well-heeled, and reasonable—as men go—but he has an unfortunate past. I suggest you accommodate the notion that you are to be his countess, lest you create all manner of awkwardness for him and his family."

Hannah looked inclined to argue. She looked, in fact, inclined to toss all twelve stone of the marchioness out of the coach.

"Hannah." He spoke quietly, willing her to understand that they'd talk later, not caring at all that Lady Quinworth had noted his informal address. "We're tired, hungry, and the announcement is apparently already in print. Even an engagement need not necessarily end in marriage."

She sat back, glancing out the window for the first time since they'd crammed themselves into the coach. "Later then, when we are assured of some privacy."

That last was a snub, a blatant, uncompromising snub of the marchioness, whose efforts had been directed at preserving them both from walking straight into complete, unsalvageable folly.

"Of course you'll have some privacy," the marchioness said pleasantly. "Engaged couples are always afforded a great deal of latitude that unattached couples would never be permitted."

Hannah stared resolutely out the window, while Asher fished through his pockets for his flask.

"What would be so awful about being Asher MacGregor's wife?"

Augusta posed the question in the most pleasant tones from her perch on Hannah's settee, while Hannah grabbed for her patience. This was the opening salvo in what would be four weeks of relentless, well-meant cross-examination.

"My brothers have years to go before they reach their majorities," Hannah replied, taking the first pair of slippers—Spanish Bullets, or something metallic—from a trunk and setting them in an enormous wardrobe. "My grandmother, for all her great age, should also have years left, and my mother..."

She trailed off. Mama's circumstances were in some ways the most precarious. No less authority than the Bible, backed up by the law and the good fellows of the American legal system, dictated that Mama remain entirely under her husband's control. In the name of marital discipline, a man could beat his wife, exercise his marital privileges against her will, starve her, and clothe her in rags, and the wife would have no recourse.

"What about your mother?"

"I am all she has, and there's little enough I can do. Sometimes, though, a person will moderate his behavior simply from the knowledge that it is witnessed by others." Hannah paused, her Maiden's Blush dancing slippers in her hands, the right now sporting a discreet lift to the heel. "My stepfather is quite sensitive to public opinion, which is probably why Grandmama continues to live with us."

Augusta fingered the tassel of a bright blue pillow trimmed in gold. "Asher has many business associates on the American seaboard. He could keep an eye on matters in Boston easily enough."

Not only the pink pair, but every pair of Hannah's slippers, shoes, and boots sported a small lift on the heel. When had Asher done this?

Because he'd done it himself. Hannah knew that from the way the edge of each heel had been sanded smooth, the wood matched so the lifts would not be obvious.

"Asher cannot have somebody present at every meal to ensure my mother is permitted to eat. He cannot ensure correspondence is delivered unopened to the intended recipient—or delivered at all. He cannot examine my brothers, mother, or grandmother for bruises in unlikely places. He cannot post a guard who will hear every time somebody in the house is in distress."

Not that her mother screamed. She'd once told Hannah that any show of resistance only made matters worse.

Augusta set the pillow aside, rose, and wandered to a trunk as yet unopened. "Asher can, however, be sure something nasty is slipped into your stepfather's drink when the dratted man is whiling away an evening at his club. I expect a physician has more than a passing acquaintance with poisons."

Hannah started hanging stockings, of which she had acquired an abundance. That such a genteel lady as Augusta MacGregor would leap to ideas Hannah had taken years to approach was reassuring.

"Then I would be as bad as my stepfather, wouldn't I? Worse, in fact, because he only slaps and bullies, while I contemplate murder."

And then Augusta was there, right beside her, without having made a sound. "You have contemplated murder, though, haven't you? Things are that bad."

Such a wealth of compassion communicated itself from Augusta's violet-blue eyes. Hannah tossed the last of the stockings toward a hook. "One grows desperate, and weary, which is why I cannot..."

Augusta was a good six inches taller than Hannah, and she was a mother. When she slipped her arms around Hannah's waist, tears welled from the bottom of Hannah's heart. She leaned into Augusta's support when the weight of impending regrets would have brought her to her knees.

"My youngest brother, we call him Bertie—" Unless the boy's father was in the room, and then, by God, Hannah addressed him as Albert.

"What about him?"

"He was helping me pack, or bothering me while I packed, the night before I took ship. He asked me why I never considered dying my hair. The question struck me as peculiar coming from a schoolboy."

"Boys are odd creatures."

"He said—" Hannah could not explain the dread or the pain of the memory. "He said red hair is wicked, and women with red hair have ungovernable tempers. Just like that. He doesn't even know what 'ungovernable' means, and it came out of his mouth, full of righteousness despite the uncertainty in his eyes."

"He was mimicking his father. Boys do this, and then they rebel, if all goes according to plan."

Augusta was the mother of a son, but that son was still very young. Hannah slipped away and opened the second trunk. "He comes out with pronouncements like that more and more, understanding clearly they are the way to win his papa's approval. I cannot abide the thought that Bertie will end up hating his own sister because she has red hair, feeling superior to her, thinking that if she's beaten frequently enough, the man doing the beating might redress what the Creator Himself put wrong."

The discussion was difficult, but putting Hannah's thoughts into words also helped clarify the answer to Augusta's initial question.

Hannah could find not one thing wrong with being the wife of Asher MacGregor, except that such an honor would require that she abdicate her every responsibility as a daughter, granddaughter, and sister.

And yet, Augusta did not give in. "Asher could—"

Hannah tossed another pair of gossamer stockings toward a hook and missed. "Asher could do nothing. Children are their father's chattel, wives are chattel, and Boston is an ocean away. I will not ask a man I esteem greatly to commit murder for my convenience. Not when I can go home, endure the next little while there, and soon establish my own household."

This earned Hannah a silence while Augusta paced to the window, arms crossed, expression resolute. "How common is it in Boston for a young lady to establish her own household?"

"My grandmother would join me. For a spinster and an elderly relation to live together would not be unusual."

Augusta drew the sash down with a solid *thunk!* and yanked the curtain closed. "And when, as could happen at any moment, your grandmother passes on? Then there you are, twenty-some years old, without male protection, still attempting to battle a man more than twice your age for the safety of people whom you legally cannot touch?"

Hannah picked up the copy of *Waverley* she'd purchased from the inn in Steeth. The book bore a slight lavender fragrance from its prolonged confinement in the trunk, and the peacock feather marking Hannah's place had somehow been lost.

"Augusta, I have to try. I cannot turn my back on my family. Asher understands this."

"And he cannot turn his back on his family. The pair of you will drive me to Bedlam."

Augusta whipped away from the window, swooped down to administer one more tight, fleeting hug, and then left Hannah alone amid clothes and mementos that would be packed up again all too soon.

They were down to twenty-three days, five already having been spent accepting good wishes from a parade of strangers and acquaintances at Lady Quinworth's town house. At some point, Hannah had been whisked away for fittings, though Asher wondered why she allowed such an outing when she never intended to wear the dress.

And now he was supposed to make polite conversation with her, when what he wanted to do…

"How do you like being engaged to an earl, Hannah?"

The weather being fine, they were enjoying the walk up to Arthur's Seat. Or making the walk, regardless. Two footmen struggled along yards behind them, the picnic hamper carried between them.

"You shouldn't joke about such a thing."

He took her hand, ostensibly to assist her up the incline. "I like being engaged to you. I no longer have to guard my besotted gazes, no longer have to hold back every fatuous word that springs to mind."

Though he did. In defense of his heart and hers both, he kept many of the fatuous words behind his teeth.

She smiled. A restrained species of her usual display, but a start. "I have not noticed much in the way of fatuous words from you, Asher MacGregor. Mostly when I see you, you are murmuring civilities at Lady Quinworth's friends, or muttering curse words in Gaelic."

"They sound better in Gaelic. Allow me to demonstrate my most fatuous look." He drew her to a halt on their climb and set both hands on her shoulders. "Look at me, Hannah."

Her smile died. What he saw in her eyes tore at his heart. She was worried, weary, and dreading the next twenty-three days. "I wish I could hold you, right this moment, I wish I could put my arms around you."

She scooted out from under his hands and resumed walking. "If wishes were horses…"

"There wouldn't be a blade of grass left, and we'd have to watch where we stepped much more closely." He took her hand again, feeling the welling helplessness of a man who did not know how to turn love into appropriate action. The feeling was old and immensely frustrating. "My name is being put forth for the Scottish delegation to Parliament."

"That's an honor, isn't it?"

"It… is. I supposedly have a well-rounded view on relations with Canada and the United States. In truth, somebody is thinking I won't know enough of British politics to cause much trouble, possibly Spathfoy's dear papa, the very English Marquess of Quinworth."

They would soon gain the summit, spread their picnic, and have what privacy Asher could manage atop one of the most popular walking destinations in the realm.

"This a positive sign, though, isn't it?" Hannah's gaze flicked over him. "An acknowledgement of your worldly sophistication compared to the insular lords and squires responsible for managing the empire."

"Possibly. More likely it's Victoria meddling in the

neighbors' business. The Lords does little anymore but debate and bluster and rattle sabers."

And yet, Hannah had a point too. Victoria, for reasons of her own, had taken more than a passing interest in the MacGregor family situation. She was also quite fond of Mary Fran's husband, Matthew, though nobody could explain that either. To refuse the opportunity to serve in the parliamentary delegation would not be… prudent.

"You should accept this," Hannah said, pausing as they rounded the bend onto the top of the hill. "You should wade in among the blustering fools and speak your truth, not because you understand the New World better than any of your peers, though you do, but because you understand it might be important that epidemics do not come from foul miasmas."

The view was magnificent, and Asher knew it well. Edinburgh and the sea lay stretched out in one direction; the interior of Scotland lay in the other. Both had beauty and heart, though the fairer view lay to the west.

And yet, what Asher saw was not sweeping vistas and dramatic Scottish skies, but the woman who understood him, who recognized what motivated him, and what would sustain him when parliamentary rules of order were threatening his sanity.

He saw the only woman he would ever propose to. "Let's choose our spot."

She smiled again, the curving of her lips a little softer this time. "You don't want to dwell on the parliamentary honor, but you'll go back and read your monographs, then consider your obligation to your queen with all her little princes and princesses. You'll mention this to your brothers. Then you'll think of little John, thriving in his parents' care now, but so small and help-less, and the decision will already be made."

Yes. Unbidden, the sensation of John, a wee scrap of a lad bundled against Asher's chest, hit him like the slap of the heather-scented wind whipping across the summit.

"I had intended to buy myself a few weeks of dith-ering before committing one way or the other. Where shall we enjoy our meal?"

She brushed another glance his way and hooked an errant strand of hair behind her ear. "A few weeks of dithering won't change the outcome. Let's find a place where we won't be blown into the sea by a strong gust of fresh Scottish air."

They chose a spot well back from the precipice, in the lee of a small, stony black bluff and well away from paths few were treading on a weekday afternoon. When the footmen arrived with the hamper, Asher waved them away to eat their own meals in some other sunny spot.

Hannah dropped to the tartans spread on the sparse grass. "I do like the absence of a chaperone, or the almost-absence. My guess is we're supposed to conclude, given enough latitude, that the blessings of marriage outweigh our misgivings."

He settled himself beside her, prepared to argue with a lady. "They are not *our* misgivings, Boston."

She opened the hamper and peered inside as if a crystal ball or magic carpet might be found therein. "So you'll move to Boston with me, spend the rest of your days as an earl in absentia? Leave wee John to the epidemics, and have the next earl raised in complete ignorance of his birthright? I am vastly relieved to hear this."

Had her voice not held a slight catch, had she not been rummaging blindly in the hamper, Asher might have accused her of meanness.

She hadn't a mean bone in her body, more's the pity. He shifted across the blankets and knelt up so he could wrap his arms around her. "I know, Hannah, in the marrow of my bones and in my soul that you are the woman I should take to wife. I know I am the man whom you should wed. I have no misgivings on that score, and neither do you. We could spend a few years in Boston—"

Hannah shook her head, her suffering palpable even in so simple a gesture. "And what of my mother? When Grandmother dies and the boys grow up, what of my mother? She is far from elderly. Do we send our firstborn son to Ian and Augusta when he's eleven years old, part him from all he knows to live with strangers across the sea?"

He wanted to stop her words, wanted to slip his hand over her mouth, but she would torture herself with these thoughts whether she shared them or not, and if this was all he could bear with her—the doubts and anxieties and regrets—then bear them he would.

"Asher, I'm sorry. Saying these things solves nothing, but I am so very sorry."

Something like anger, though not as corrosive, gave him the strength to turn her loose. "I am *not* sorry. Not sorry we've met, not sorry we've had these few weeks, not sorry for any of it." *Not sorry they'd been lovers.* He kept that last thought to himself, lest it cause her more torment.

She sank back on her heels and studied him. "You mean that."

He did. Realizing this felt like a shift in the wind from one brisk, challenging direction to another, though the second direction bore the faint, welcome scent of home. Rather than let her see that far into his soul, he took his turn sorting through the hamper. "Would you rather I didn't? Would you rather I shrugged and said our dealings were of no moment, Hannah?"

Her brows drew down in the manner that meant she was focusing on a topic inwardly. "No, I would not. You're right—the things I regret are the factors we do not control. Had I not met you..."

Had she not met him, she might have ended up married to one of the Malcolms of the world. A man who would take her coin then leave her to fight her own battles. Or she might have been prey to one of her stepfather's more determined schemes.

Asher shoved that thought off the edge of the precipice some distance up the path. "There's cold chicken, fruit, scones, cheese, and—Cook was feeling generous—apple tarts in this hamper. Also a decent bottle of Riesling. Shall I open it?"

"Please, and let's start with the apple tarts. I'm in the mood to enjoy my sweets first."

The meal marked a turning point, with Asher sensing in Hannah a determination to appreciate the gifts they'd given each other, and to make the best of the time remaining. She had never intended to remain, after all, and he had not seriously intended to marry ever again.

"What do you make of that cloud?" Hannah had

done her part to consume the wine. She lay on her back, Asher's coat bundled under her head and one knee drawn up. Her posture was improper, but he'd paid good coin to ensure the footmen were waving away any who might stumble in this direction.

Asher glanced up from repacking the hamper. "It's white. It's fluffy. When the proper mood comes upon it, it will go carousing with a few of its mates and dump a cold rain on some undeserving village in the mountains."

"Or a deserving village. A village where the gardens are all laid out and the winter stores depend on a good yield." She held out a hand to him, so he arranged himself beside her on the blanket. "I'll miss you, Asher MacGregor. I'll look up at the clouds and wonder if they've blown in from Scotland. I'll think of you."

Ah. He put a name to the shift in their dealings, to what had eased: they were to grieve together for what could not be. Nobody else could grieve with them, and when they parted, they'd have grieving confidences to treasure in memory.

And to torture themselves with in solitude.

He took her hand. "My favorite fruit is a nice crisp, juicy, sweet red apple. What's your favorite fruit?"

The rest of the afternoon went like that, as if they were engaged in truth, sharing secrets, looking forward to a lifetime of intimacy not simply of the body. She favored apples and raspberries; he leaned toward oranges, in addition to apples, provided they were sweet. She much preferred Scott to Dickens, and she did not have a favorite poet, though Tennyson was worth a mention.

Asher had a fondness for the language of the Old

Testament, and as a boy had thought it held some rousing stories. His favorite bird was the hummingbird, for its exotic color, its agility, its ability to draw sweetness from a flower without harming it. Peacocks should be outlawed for the racket they created.

Hannah had watched his mouth as he delivered that last flight of nonsense, and then she had gone quiet for as long as it took for a cloud to drift by. When he was about to suggest they pack up and head down the hill, she curled close, kissed his cheek, and rested her head on his shoulder.

"I will not forget this day, Asher MacGregor, not ever. When I am old and bent and slow, when I neither hear nor see well, I will still recall every detail of this day."

He wrapped an arm around her shoulders and considered burning the city of Boston to the ground. He did not consider telling her that it had been too long since he'd had any word from his scouts in Boston. Any word at all.

Nineteen

In three days, Hannah would have the privilege of once again boarding the trains with Asher, Ian, Augusta, and wee John and heading north. In sixteen days, she would board a ship—Asher's ship—and sail for Boston.

Not for home—which was one of the many insights to befall her in the past ten days.

Another was that when a woman loved a man, intimacy between them could come in many forms. With Asher, all closeness had a sensual thread, though not necessarily erotic. He could touch her with his gaze; he could read her with his body. Even silences across a breakfast table crowded with family could be comforting and speak volumes.

When that breakfast was concluded and Asher had asked her to meet him prepared to go on an outing, Hannah was all too happy to oblige.

"Where are we going, Asher?"

He winged his arm, she curled closer than courtesy required, and they took off across the wide streets of the New Town. "It's a surprise, but I thought we'd wander toward the harbor and stop for some rum buns."

Lovely idea. Lovely day. Lovely man. These few weeks of pleasure were the first superficial, glancing cut of heartbreak, the surprise and instinctive stilling of any response in anticipation of the burn and burden to follow.

She and Asher could remain in this benign state for a few more days, or Hannah could give in to the growing compulsion to hold nothing back, to move closer to the pain that awaited them both.

She walked along beside Asher for several blocks until he spoke again. "Do you realize your gait is no longer irregular?"

Hannah bodily inventoried her movement as they strode along. He was… *right*. "I've lost my limp."

He smiled down at her. "A combination of putting a lift on your heel and walking you from one end of creation to the other. What was wanted was strengthening and straightening, though I'm sure the occasional dash of whiskey wouldn't be ill-prescribed either."

Now she stopped, trying to pinpoint when, where, how…

"Does it hurt, Hannah? Your back, your hip, your knee? Anywhere, does it hurt?"

"No." Those places didn't hurt at all. She resumed movement. "No, it does not. I want to kiss you. It doesn't hurt, and I do not limp."

The moment was a gift, like every moment they'd had together since arriving in Scotland. That she should share this revelation with him, that he should be the one to point it out to her was consolation beyond measure. "I want to skip. I want to ice skate, though it's nearly summer. I want to run and dance in public. Oh, Asher, I want to dance."

He patted her hand; Hannah resented the daylights out of her gloves. "Lady Quinworth's ball is tomorrow night. We'll dance, but for now we've arrived to our destination."

Hannah peered up at the sign hanging over a tidy little shop on a quiet street. The place had a look of age about it, as if its solid granite presence predated the fancy neighborhoods farther back from the water. "This is a jeweler's, Asher."

And abruptly, she no longer wanted to skip and dance or ice skate, though she did still want to run.

A ring was a token of eternal regard, and in that sense, Asher was determined that Hannah should have one from him.

And yet, a ring was risky, and not simply because it announced to the entire world that they intended to marry.

Behind all of Hannah's smiles, behind her affection, behind her comfortable silences and insightful observations, even behind the unfathomable pain of their impending separation lurked *something*, and it tormented Asher with the same sense of frustration as when he'd tried to diagnose a patient whose symptoms did not add up to a known ailment.

Did Hannah battle the identical feeling regarding him?

"If we're to stand up at Lady Quinworth's ball," he said, "then all will be expecting you to wear my ring." Hannah's brows came down, her chin lifted, her expression shifted in a manner that had him adding, "Please let me do this, Hannah. I want to, badly."

The sails of her indignation luffed, then went slack. "An engagement ring, only." She swept past him into the shop.

The shop owner, young, blond, natty, and friendly without being in the least obsequious, was a distant relation, which meant the sign was switched to "closed" when Asher and Hannah were through the door. While Hannah had gone for her fittings, Asher had taken one of her rings and spent a morning sorting through settings, gems, and options.

If all he was permitted to give her was a single piece of jewelry, it had to be right.

"You should not be doing this," she muttered as she stripped off her gloves.

He stuffed her gloves in his pocket as some sort of surety against her departure. "If you raise a fuss before Cousin Alasdair, Lady Quinworth will know of it by luncheon."

"But rings are expensive." She hissed this while Alasdair pretended to root around at the back counters. The shop was small and dark, the better to show off a few gleaming glass-and-brass cases, and a scattering of glittering offerings on jewel-toned velvet cloths. The place was without a discernible scent, as if even smells might dim the brightness of the gems.

"Don't turn up Puritan on me now, Boston. If you won't wear my ring, I'll pierce my ear and display your stubbornness to all who meet me."

He'd do it too, *gladly*.

"I'll wear your ring." She patted his cravat in a manner that said clearly, *for now*.

Alasdair emerged from the back room, bearing a small hinged box of polished maple. He set it on the counter. "If my lord would do the honors?"

A knowing smile accompanied the question, and yet, as if he'd presided over many such moments, his cousin's grin held something of a dare, too. Asher regarded the box then regarded the woman who appeared to be studying a case of silver bracelets.

"Hannah, your hand, if you please." She straightened and faced him, extending her bare hand.

Asher opened the box and beheld his first attempt at designing adornment for a lady. A fat, happy emerald sat amid a Celtic knot of worked gold, winking merrily in all directions. He slid the ring onto the fourth finger of Hannah's left hand, wondering if she heard the same words that rang through his mind: *With this ring, I thee wed…*

"Do you like it?" He would not surrender her hand until he had an answer to his question.

She didn't even look at the ring, but rather, kept her gaze locked with his. "I love it. I love it with all my heart, and I always will."

Damn her, bless her. She was getting even, she was making him want to skip in public, and she was breaking the few pieces of his heart not yet pulverized.

He brought her knuckles to his lips. "That's… good. I love it, too. It's… right, somehow. Perfect. Precious, irreplaceable."

They stood like that, her hand in his, profound sentiments lingering in the air, while Alasdair started chattering about God knew what. No coin was to be exchanged—Asher had made damned sure of that—and Alasdair likely knew better than to try hawking more wares while two hearts broke right before his eyes.

Hannah stepped closer and tucked her arm through Asher's. "Shall we be going? I recall somebody mentioning a rum bun and a tot of grog." She smiled up at him, a credible smile of infatuation, while her eyes held a desperate plea.

Take me away from this place and this moment.

They gained the street, the bright sunshine making Asher blink and hang onto Hannah's arm more tightly. A coach-and-four clip-clopped past, the sound serving as a pretext to put off conversation for a procession of seconds.

"It's a beautiful ring, Asher." Hannah spoke softly. "Should we put it back in its box? My gloves aren't fitted enough that I could wear them and the ring both."

The courage of women, as Ian had said, was different from the courage of men.

"Keep the ring on, Hannah. I'll carry your gloves."

The weather was fine; they were newly engaged. All manner of lapses and indulgences would be tolerated—provided they eventually wed. Asher felt bile rising beneath his heart.

"The grog shop is this way." And when they got to the grog shop, he would pry from her what the something was that lurked behind her smiles, the something that prodded her to make a rash declaration over a simple ring.

Or maybe he'd share with her the news brought by courier two days past, news he'd hoped not to have to burden her with.

"You're very quiet, Asher, and it doesn't strike me as a happy quiet. The ring is spectacular, and you're right: it's perfect."

She was fishing; he wasn't taking the bait. They wandered through the foot traffic of a weekday morning, moving generally in the direction of his town house, until Hannah stopped him.

"Is that the bench we sat on the day I slipped?"

Across the street, on a wider patch of sidewalk, the bench, empty of custom, appeared to enjoy the morning sunshine. Somebody had set a half-barrel of pansies at each end, violet and yellow intermixed. "Shall we sit?"

"Please, let's." They had to wait until a beer wagon rattled past, then ducked across the street, arm in arm.

When she tipped her face up to the sun, eyes closed, Asher wanted to tell her to remain exactly thus until he could memorize the image of her amid the flowers and friendly breezes, his ring winking on her finger in the sunshine.

"What did you bring me here to say, Hannah? I do love you, you know."

She opened her eyes and turned to regard him, probably wondering if he'd left his reason back at the jeweler's shop. "Thank you, though if you're going to inflict such a recitation on me, I'm entitled to reciprocate. I love you, Asher MacGregor. I love you until I'm drunk and sick and crazy with it. Your love makes me wise and foolish and"—she looked him up and down—"and very affectionate. I'll miss that in ways I can't even imagine yet. I already do miss it. I miss you."

She fell silent, allowing him a moment against the emotional ropes to regain his breath. He slipped his fingers through hers where their hands rested on the bench between them. The ring was sharp, warm, and different beneath his hand, a bit loose on her finger. The addition of a wedding ring would steady it.

"What else, love?"

She tipped her face up again, a goddess accepting her due from the elements. "My monthly is late."

Four words that held a universe of conflicting feelings—for them both. There were so many wrong things to say, so many ways a man in all good conscience could blunder past redemption. He closed his fingers more snugly around hers, the emerald cutting into his flesh.

"Then perhaps it's a good thing Fenimore has been having the banns read up in Aberdeenshire."

She gave him a smile that said he hadn't blundered, though possibly *they* had blundered, and she gave him a few more words: "Perhaps it is."

Hannah hadn't known what to expect when she'd confessed to her fiancé that a child might already be growing in her womb.

Would he be pleased, thinking it made marriage a certainty, though it did not?

Would he resent a marriage based on necessity rather than sentiment?

Would he take the child from her to be raised an ocean away from her?

Asher confounded her by simply grasping her hand and keeping it in his. The metaphor extended through the rest of their stay in Edinburgh, as Hannah accumulated the gifts and griefs she'd take with her back to Boston.

She would never learn more than a few words of Gaelic, not until it was too late to understand the language spoken by the man who could turn it into the music of her soul.

She would never learn the reels Lady Quinworth could toss off with such panache, spun from son to cousin to uncle and back into the arms of her adoring marquess.

She would never learn the inner workings of the family distillery or become versed in the whiskey exports laws, much less the many customs surrounding a drink whose subtleties she increasingly appreciated.

She would never see wee John carried on his uncle's shoulders to a favored fishing spot in some high, sunny glen.

Though there were consolations. Wearing MacGregor plaid, she danced the waltz with her beloved while he turned every female head in the room with his formal clan finery.

She clapped and stomped along with the family when Con got out his pipes, the swords were laid down, and in the middle of a crowded ballroom, Asher danced for her alone.

And on the train north, she could lay her head on his shoulder, pretend sleep, and know she could not be censured for her presumption.

"You are not asleep."

She would not be believed in her deception, either, but Hannah made no move to sit up. "I ought to be asleep. I ought to be asleep for a week after dancing with all of your brothers *and* Spathfoy. You Scots take your celebrations seriously."

"We do." He wrapped her hand in his, the gesture having at some point become automatic for them both. "Our betrothal ball was the first time many of the clan have seen me since I was a boy. They grieved when I was declared dead, they rallied to Ian's side, and before they could rally to mine, they needed to see me, to know I would not abandon them again."

"I was hoping you'd come to that conclusion." Hannah certainly had, and while she'd been pleased for him, pleased to see the sheer number and vigor of his extended family, she'd also grieved.

An earl she might have allowed herself to remove to Boston, but not a laird. Not when there were so few left who could live up to the name.

"How are you feeling, Miss Cooper?"

Subject changed. She silently thanked him for it.

"Glad to be on my way to your home. One hears the Highlands are beautiful."

"They're bloody cold is what they are. I think it's one reason the Scots leave home so successfully. Even Canada looks like a fine bargain—the winters are no worse, and there'll be no clearances to part us from our property there. A few bears and wolves are nothing compared to the threats we endure from our neighbors to the south."

He had preferred bears and wolves to home and

family. Hannah took some comfort that his priorities had shifted.

His thumb stroked over her knuckles. "May I ask you some medical questions?"

Ah. *That subject.* "Of course."

"Are you having to use the necessary more often than usual?"

She considered her answer. "I am not."

"Are your breasts tender?"

She might have replied in several ways, some of them flirtatious. "Not particularly."

"And your dresses are still fitting?"

"They are."

"You aren't abruptly sleepy at odd times of the day?"

"I would say I'm tired generally, from touring the city with you or from being up half the night dancing."

He fell silent, though his point was clear: there might be a baby. *There might not.*

In this too, he held her hand. On the strength of that connection and trust, Hannah shared a thought that had plagued her since they'd left London. "I'm told there are herbs, Asher—"

"*No*, my heart. Those herbs are not reliable, and they are not safe, particularly not as a pregnancy advances. I would never ask such a thing of any woman, much less one I cared for deeply."

The immediacy of his reply and the reason for it both warmed her heart. The next words slipped out, no caution or forethought to them at all. "Asher, I don't know what to do."

His lips grazed her temple. "Was that so hard to say?"

He sounded proud of her, but she didn't dare look

into his eyes, not when her uncertainty had been made audible. "I have never voiced such a sentiment to anybody, not even Grandmama."

"Would you like to say it again? In some endeavors, practice is advisable."

"I don't know what to do."

He was quiet, reassuring her with his steady presence and with his warmth rather than with words. "I was married before, you know."

The feeling engendered in Hannah's breast at this confidence—for it was a confidence—was a vast, unconditional protectiveness that chased away her own woes and wobbliness. "You loved her. You still love her."

More silence, while Hannah tucked herself as close as she could without sitting in his lap.

"I loved her as a lonely young man far from home loves a woman given to smiles and laughter. I loved her simply, without reservation, and that was unwise."

"It was not un—"

He pressed two fingers to her lips. "For a physician to watch his family sicken and die is impossible, Hannah. This feeling you have, this great regard for another you admit to me not once but twice, when you are helpless to protect your loved ones, it builds and builds, not knowing what to do, until it becomes a purgatory with no exit."

His family? Not just his wife? No wonder he'd wandered for years in the wilderness. She pressed her cheek to his shoulder and tried not to cry.

"Hannah?" He'd dropped his voice to a whisper.

"I am not in that purgatory any longer. Sometimes there's nothing *to* do but love as best we can."

The griefs in Hannah's heart piled high, like so much snow driven by a harsh, relentless wind into suffocating drifts.

Though the gifts piled higher: because Hannah had come to Scotland and joined her heart to Asher's, there would be an exit from every purgatory; there was a hand to hold, if only in memory.

The train roared northward on the track between the wide, rough sea and the high, cold mountains, and Hannah told herself the memories would be enough.

Asher scowled at the letter before him, a single sheet of crabbed, nigh indecipherable scrawl delivered by messenger right here to the room that served as the Balfour billiards room and armory.

"What does Fenimore have to say?" Across the card table, Ian peered down the barrel of an antique pistol, gun parts scattered before him on a folded Royal Stewart plaid. "Wishing you felicitations on your upcoming nuptials?"

"Hardly." Royal Stewart deserved better treatment than Ian was giving it. "He castigates me for having ruined a good man by allowing him to become distracted by the charms of the weaker sex."

Ian paused in the middle of working a soft, dirty cloth down the gun barrel. His fingers were dirty too. "Which good man?"

Ian would get the letter dirty as well, so Asher didn't pass it to him. "In his peregrinations about the realm on Fenimore's business, Evan Draper made the acquaintance of one Enid Cooper, late of Boston. Draper treated the lady to a recitation of the ills and indignities suffered on his travels, and she was the soul of sympathy and solicitude—had a remedy for all of the man's trials, including his loneliness."

Ian glanced up. "Aunt Enid? *That* Enid Cooper? She's little more than a fading sot herself."

"A fading sot marginally revived by the attention of an old flame from her youth, though Draper appears to have routed the competition."

Which would be downright funny if Asher himself were drunk.

"What else does Fenimore say?"

"He demands we set a date." Nobody else had had the temerity.

"There isn't going to be a wedding, is there?" Ian pulled the cloth through the tube of metal and began reassembling the parts.

Rather than face his brother's questions, Asher folded the letter and set it on the journal that had accompanied it, rose and crossed to the rack of cue sticks on the opposite wall. "Care for a game?"

"Thank ye, no. The baby will going down for his nap soon, and I'll be taking tea with my wife."

Taking tea. Oh, of course. Behind the locked door of their bedroom, Ian and his lady would be taking tea, with his *pinky finger* extended just so. Asher envied his brother and sister-in-law their frequent *cups of tea* almost as much as he envied them the way each knew the other's schedule and whereabouts without even thinking about it.

More, they both knew the child's schedule, and to some extent, organized their lives around it.

Asher racked the balls, broke, and studied the possibilities. "Whether there's a wedding or not hardly matters. Hannah has to leave. I have to stay."

Ian screwed the barrel into its fitting. "You could go with her. I've held the reins here before. I can do it again."

So offhand, and yet the offer was sincere. Asher sank two balls in a single shot, one into each corner pocket. "You have not asked Augusta her thoughts on the matter."

"I have. We do not agree. She thinks Hannah should stay here. I think you should go to Boston."

The next shot wasn't lining up—the price one paid for succumbing to the lure of sinking two balls at once. "I have not been invited to Boston. I have, in fact, been refused entry to the port. Hannah would protect even me."

Ian swore, ostensibly at the gun. "Then I can go to bloody Boston, or Gil or Con can go."

"You all have children to raise, or on the way, and you'd have no more authority in Boston over Hannah's mother or half brothers than I would, and therein lies the difficulty."

Ian threaded screws through the inlays on the gun's handle and tightened them in alternate applications of a small screwdriver. "You can't just reive her family out from under the man's bloody nose? He'd not wrest them away from an earl's keep if you could get them here in one piece."

On the next shot the cue ball rolled slowly, slowly across the table, tipping into a pocket by a whisker, which at least allowed a man to do a little swearing of his own.

"It's good to hear you using the Gaelic," Ian said, finishing with the screwdriver.

"Gaelic is a good language for cursing in. I've considered inviting Hannah's family here, asked my man for his thoughts on the matter, and received no response. Now I doubt my message even got through."

"Inviting. Such an earl you've become." Ian's taunt was without heat, and all the more annoying as a result.

"One doesn't force a woman to marry against her will without becoming the very thing that woman loathes most in the world. Why do you bother cleaning that old pistol when the servants could do it?"

The gun was back in one piece, looking substantial and well cared for in Ian's hand. He wiped it down with the dirty cloth, which somehow did in fact polish the metal. "The woman loves you. A little loathing won't change that, particularly when you've given her a child or two."

"And I love you, Ian, but I would rather not leaven my fraternal affection with loathing. If you can't leave this topic alone, then my preferences will not carry the day."

Ian smiled and sighted down the gun barrel at a portrait of some old fellow in tartan and hunting boots. "You love her too. A sorrier pair I have never seen."

Yes, Asher did love Hannah. The knowledge was unassailable, a fact of Asher's bones and organs and his very mind. "You'd stand up with me, if there were a wedding? Even if there were a wedding merely to give her my name?"

Ian set the gun aside and rose, coming to study the arrangement of balls on the table. "Why'd you set the cue ball down there? It leaves you not one decent shot."

"I'm not playing a game. One needs to practice the impossible shots."

"I'll stand up with you, and so will Gil, Con, Mary Fran, and even that snippy English bastard Spathfoy. If you love Hannah Cooper, then we're standing up with her too." He set the cue ball down two inches from its original location, then scooped up his antique gun and left.

One did need to practice the impossible shots, except, by moving the ball two inches, Ian had changed the entire field of play, such that the impossible had become, in several different ways, the possible.

Twenty

"If grief had a landscape, it would be these Highlands."

Hannah tucked herself more snugly to Asher's side and tried to pretend the sun was not sinking closer to the rugged hills around them. This was no more successful than pretending a week had not already passed since her arrival at Balfour House, a week in which she'd made many such fanciful pronouncements.

Asher shifted, as if eluding a pebble beneath a triple thickness of tartan wool. "Why do you say that?"

"Many reasons. These are not high mountains, not compared to what you've seen in Canada, but they have a forbidding quality. And yet, we've walked them." She shaded her eyes and pointed to the highest summit. "We ate scones and drank whiskey up there, three days ago."

They'd eaten scones and drank whiskey on many a blanket, making more picnic memories in a week than most couples collected in two decades of marriage. They'd ridden out together, fished the River Dee, tramped the woods, and stayed up late playing cards as an excuse to talk far into the night.

Ian and Augusta made no pretense of chaperoning them, which was fortunate. In the wee hours of the morning, and on the high hills and in the forests, Asher had told Hannah of his years in Canada, and he'd told her his family knew little of what had happened there. She'd argued with him over that, until that argument, like so many others, had ended in a spate of kissing.

Lying on the wool blankets under the afternoon sun, he laced their fingers and laid Hannah's palm over his heart. "Your point is that grief can be surmounted."

She'd been trying to say that the sadness she felt when she stared at the calendar had a wildness to it, a passion that had certainly eluded her before her journey across the ocean.

"I don't know if it can be surmounted, but people dwell here, and they love it. You love it, despite the winters, the cold, the loneliness. People have died for this land."

He shifted again, turning her, too, so they were spooned together beneath the wide blue sky, his chest blanketing her back. "There will be no dying of broken hearts, Hannah. You and I are not that kind of people. We will be dignified, like these mountains. We will endure."

They hadn't made love, not since they'd arrived in Edinburgh, and that had broken Hannah's heart more than anything else. And yet, it was good that she could not see his face, or he hers. "I'm not carrying."

He petted her hair and gathered her closer. "You're sure?"

"I'm sure. The day before I start my monthly, I get twinges, warning shots, so to speak, and they've started. I consider it a kindness that my body alerts me this way to impending inconvenience. We'll not be tramping up here again tomorrow."

They wouldn't be tramping much of anywhere for the next several days, which meant they had likely scaled their last peak together.

"I am sorry, my heart. I am sorry we are not to have a child. I sense, though, that a child would have complicated matters for you, not simplified them."

He knew her so well. She could not have loved him more, not if they'd had eighty years together on earth. Hannah turned so she could wrap herself against Asher's body. Their situation was too blessed simple. "Nothing can fix our situation. Nothing."

Nothing made it easier; nothing made it less painful. They would endure, as Asher had said. Dignity was far less certain.

He kissed her, probably for comfort, but Hannah was incapable of being consoled by a mere brush of lips. What raged through her was as implacable as the high barren hills, as deep and unrelenting as the winter that scoured the summits of their trees.

"Asher, I am uncertain of many things. I am uncertain that my decisions have been wise, uncertain of my reception in Boston, uncertain of... much, but I know I want to make love with you right now, right here."

He sighed against her mouth, something about a simple exhalation conveying a stubborn intent to apply reason. "Hannah, there is nothing I would deny you, but you might be mistaken in these twinges and warning shots. You've never carried a child, never conceived before that you—"

"Damn you, Asher MacGregor. I am not asking for your permission, I am asking for your passion."

She pushed him by one meaty shoulder onto his back, and he went. When she straddled him—no dignity there—and unfastened his kilt, he sank his fingers into her hair and extracted one pin after another.

His complicity gradually cleared the fog of desperation choking her, until Hannah could sit back and admire the man whose kilt, waistcoat, and shirt she had nearly torn from his body.

Asher brushed her hair back over her shoulder. "Is it my turn, then? Shall I unwrap m' treasure the way ye've unwrapped yours?"

When a man was blessed with a burr, the inflection in his questions lifted not the end of an inquiry, as was common in Boston, but rather, gave the entire question a lilt.

"Yes. Unwrap your treasure."

He started by framing her jaw in his hands, ensuring that Hannah's gaze collided with his and stayed trapped in what he promised with his eyes. Slowly, slowly, he worked his way down the buttons of her shirtwaist.

Never had a lady's attire had so many buttons. Hannah dragged in one breath after another, while beneath her, Asher's arousal became more and more firm against her sex.

For the last time…

Weeks had gone by while she'd pushed, wrestled, and blasted that sentiment away from her, moment by moment. Through their journey from London, their wandering in Edinburgh, their engagement ball, their travel to Balfour, and every day since.

She let the reality of their parting take over, let the horror and terror of it fill her being, the wrongness of it, the inevitability, and the permanence.

Asher peeled back her blouse but didn't push it off her arms. "Are you sure, Hannah?"

She was ready to deliver a lecture to him that could be heard from one peak to the next until it occurred to her he wasn't doubting her desire for him, but rather, her conclusion regarding conception.

"I am sure. There will be no baby for us." He closed his eyes, as if a great wave of pain had risen up to seize him from within. "I'm sorry, Asher, but there will be no child."

A man who'd buried his family in the Canadian woods would regard their childless state with particular regret, and also with relief. The relief would be trifling compared to the regret.

The need to comfort him flooded past impending loss and tangled with desire, making it nigh impossible for Hannah to hold still while Asher untied her laces.

He patted her bottom. "Your skirts, too, love."

Skirts and petticoats, then drawers and stays, were gathered in a growing pile of clothing at the edge of the blankets, until Hannah lay on her back in nothing but her stockings and garters, and Asher wore not one stitch.

"I'm glad we are not in some darkened bedroom," Hannah said, running a hand down his ribs one by one. "Glad I can see you. See all of you."

The stroke of his hands, warm against her upraised knees, paused. She should have been mortified, but she liked the look of him kneeling naked and aroused between her legs, silhouetted against the white clouds and blue sky.

"You are so fair, and I am so dark. Not every woman would regard the sight of me with welcome."

What would children of such a union look like?

"You will please stop chattering, Asher MacGregor."

He came forward to brace himself above her on his hands. "There's no hurry, Hannah of my heart. The sun will be up for hours yet."

And yet, her skin was already growing chilled, though the sunshine was warm and afternoon wasn't over. At this altitude, at this latitude, nights were short but never quite warm, not like they would be in the middle of a Boston summer. There was every reason to hurry. "Make love to me, Asher. Please."

She reached for him, and he obliged by settling his weight close. "Shall I teach you some Gaelic? Just a few words to pass the time?" He whispered this to her and punctuated his offer by kissing the curve of her jaw.

"I don't want a grammar lesson, you dratted, miserable—"

His arousal, blunt and warm, nudged at her sex.

"That's what you want, isn't it, Hannah? It's what I want, too. What I'll go to my grave wanting. With you."

Hannah closed her eyes, the better to catalogue sensations, to hoard them up against the barren expanse of the rest of her life. At her back was soft wool, three sturdy thicknesses of clan MacGregor tartan. When Asher fell silent, she could hear the wind sighing in the nearby pines on cool, heather-scented breezes. Asher brushed his thumb across her palm, a small touch, and exquisitely tender.

He flexed his hips forward. "*I love you,* Hannah MacGregor." He'd spoken Gaelic, but she recognized her name, the name she might have had if they'd been married.

She arched up to meet him. "*I love you*, Asher MacGregor." The Gaelic was sweet on her tongue, more sincere than anything she'd said in English. "*I love you.*"

He was like the mountains, implacable, incapable of hurry, while Hannah could not govern her desire in the smallest degree. She convulsed around him before he'd even completed their joining.

He nuzzled her ear. "Such a passionate lady. You will not destroy my concentration so easily."

Hannah locked her ankles at the small of his back and tried to still his hips. "For the love of God, let me catch my breath."

"I prefer you breathless." He raised himself up enough to cross his arms under her neck. "I want you panting, in fact. Hot." His lips brushed her mouth then lifted away. "Frantic would be a lovely sight. A sight to remember."

God in heaven. She went on the offensive, seizing him by the hair and fusing her mouth to his, undulating into his movement. "I want *you* frantic, Asher MacGregor. I want you roaring your desire to the hills. I want… I want—"

Oh, gracious heavens, how she wanted.

When she'd come a second time, Asher straightened his arms, letting a cooling draft of air between them. "Ye're all right?"

She brushed his hair back from his brow, needing to imprint the sight of him on her memory forever. The muscles of his chest and arms were exquisite, but the warmth in his gaze—the love and longing, the tenderness—made her turn her head.

"I will be." Sometime, years and years hence, she would be. She would tell her nieces of the great love she'd known in the Highlands—the love she'd lost. "I will be."

His smile was crooked and sad, confirmation that he knew she was lying. He settled closer, bringing Hannah the scent of man and heather. "Ye must not cry, Hannah. Ye'll break my heart all over if ye cry."

Hannah had no argument to such a gentle scold. She wrapped herself around him and let him set an excruciatingly deliberate pace, her hands laced with his, her body moving to his rhythm.

She knew what he was about: he was trying to make it last, holding back time for them for one more moment, then another, until Hannah's passion welled again unstoppably.

"Asher, *please…*" *Come with me, one last time.*

He groaned, softly, raggedly, joining her for a procession of instants in pleasure that obliterated everything else save awareness of each other. Hannah felt him spend, felt the ecstasy and surrender of it, felt the turning point when passion overcame his restraint.

Asher hung over her, breathing like a bellows.

"Come here, Asher. Let me hold you." *One last time.* They would embrace again, they would hold hands, they might even share a bed, but this—to be naked, passionate, wanton—it would not befall them again.

Ever.

He slid his palm under her head and cradled her close. Hannah said nothing, not while his breathing slowed, not while bitter, bitter tears slid from her eyes into her hair. He kissed her tears, wiped them across his cheeks, and let the silence stretch until she had no more tears.

When he had slipped from her body, she still did not let him go. "I never meant to break your heart, Asher MacGregor."

His hand passed over her brow, smoothing her hair back. "You are my heart. You will always be my heart."

The words were meant to comfort, and yet, Hannah hurt. She hurt with an emptiness that resonated in every particle of her soul. When Asher eased away, she let him go, and the pain of that was beyond description.

The mundane business of dressing each other provided the next steps in the direction of their ultimate separation. Asher passed her a handkerchief, and while he pinned and buckled himself into his kilt, Hannah dealt with the less delicate aftereffects of shared passion.

She shook out the little cotton square, intending to refold it into quarters and hand it back. Asher pulled his shirt on and left it unbuttoned, then passed Hannah her drawers, stays, and shirtwaist.

"Shall we go boating on the loch tomorrow?" The burr had been wrestled into submission. The earl was trying to put the lover to rout, an effort Hannah suspected was undertaken for her benefit. Asher was no more interested in boating on the loch than Hannah was.

"That sounds pleasant, if the weather allows."

They'd bring the inevitable picnic, maybe some Walter Scott, and spend another afternoon suffering together. *How lovely.*

He helped her with her stays, though his idea of what constituted a proper fit was much looser than Hannah's. He also laced her boots for her, and when Hannah made no effort to rise from their blankets, he sat beside her, silent and solid.

Only then did she pass him his handkerchief. "It's the same color as my dancing slippers, the first ones you repaired for me."

He took the little cloth, his brows knitting. "The same color?"

Hannah nodded at the handkerchief, which sported three faint pink streaks. "Maiden's blush."

Her next spate of tears was not quiet. Not quiet at all.

Asher had stowed Hannah's bags, inspected her cabin, lectured the maid to within an inch of her life, then conferred with his captain at length, though not one moment of their discussion had been spent on cargo, schedules, or changes made to the ship's crew.

In the morning, Hannah would take ship, and by noon, Asher would be blind drunk. As plans went, it left something to be desired.

"It's when they go quiet you worry the most."

As he offered this observation, Connor took the seat to Asher's left on a comfortable sofa, passing his brother a drink. The inn's appointments were far above reproach, Asher having insisted on the fanciest harborside accommodations Edinburgh had to offer.

He had not wanted Hannah to have to depart for the ship from his town house.

"When who goes quiet?" Asher asked. "Certainly not our brothers."

Con took a considering sip of his whiskey. "The women. I was about eleven when I realized Mary Fran's tantrums weren't the worst havoc she could wreak. She'd go quiet, and it drove me nigh to howlin'. Those big green eyes, the stiff little shoulders. Diabolical, she was. Probably doesn't have to say a word to have Daniels stepping and fetching double-time. Just goes silent, is all. Poor sod's probably on his knees right now, begging her to say something to him."

Asher set his drink aside—time for that later. Less than twenty-four hours later. "Do I have her to thank for everybody's presence here at the inn?"

"We're your family, Asher MacGregor. We've come to see our Hannah off on her journey."

Connor was his baby brother, and yet of all of them, Con was in some ways the most substantial. The man could be as silent as an oak cask, and about as flexible. There would be no running Con off, no intimidating, reasoning, or bullying him into giving Asher privacy.

"When we've seen Hannah off, will you get me home before I start drinking?"

"Aye. And we'll drink with ye, and pour ye into bed, and mind the fires until ye're able to walk again. Ye're neglecting your medicine, Brother."

Con did not neglect his. He downed his whiskey in one swallow, then rose and crossed to the little table where a decanter and glasses sat on a tray. The door to Asher's sitting room opened without a knock.

"And here I thought this was a decent inn." Connor held out a drink to Spathfoy, then poured for Gil. "Asher was just about to get out the cards. Ian, you can get your own drink when you've tossed me wee fartin', stinkin', burpin' nephew into the street for the rag man to pick up."

Wee John liked that idea fine, banging on his father's shoulder with a tiny fist and grinning at his uncles.

"Is he cutting more teeth?" Gil asked.

"He'll be cutting damned teeth until he's in short coats," Ian grumbled. When he took the place on Asher's right, the sofa cushions temporarily heaved up then settled as if on a sigh. "Little man kept his poor mama up half the night, and now he's all smiles."

Asher reached out a hand to the child, knowing his finger would be taken prisoner. "Plotting civil disturbance and insurrection, no doubt. He will be cutting teeth pretty much until he's two, then it comes in spurts."

"Two years." Ian's expression suggested the number was comparable to two thousand. "And we've likely another one just like him coming along behind."

For some reason, Ian's misery was a cheering sight. "Things do improve. They stop cutting teeth, and not long after that, they start to catch on to using the Jordan pot, and what a happy occasion that is."

Spathfoy took a seat at the table uninvited. "Are we going to pick out baby names or take advantage of Balfour's bout of insanity to rob him blind?"

"The bad fairy speaks," Ian muttered. "I'll man the decanters. Spathfoy, why don't you hold the baby?"

"Because you're his papa, and I may be English, but I'm not entirely stupid. What's the game?"

A desultory debate ensued, with the decision being that hearts would make an adequate pastime, though when Asher looked at the clock, the thing seemed to have forgotten how to advance the hour.

He made no effort to toss his brothers out, though he suspected Spathfoy, in a kind of begrudging sympathy, would probably have withdrawn without a fuss. His brothers were holding a wake though, a wake for the dreams Asher had never thought he'd dream again, for the hopes and aspirations of a heart that had sworn off aspiration for all time.

Rest in bloody goddamned peace.

"Your turn to hold the brat." Spathfoy lifted wee John high, high up, brought him down nose to nose, and lifted him up again.

A wet little baby fart resulted, and five grown men went silent. Spathfoy passed the child over to Asher with no further displays of avuncular affection.

"Typical English, handing back the goods when trouble's bound to ensue," Con remarked. He tossed out the two of clubs, and everybody but Spathfoy followed suit.

For Asher to arrange cards with a baby in his arms was not difficult, provided said baby was not in the mood to snatch at the cards with tiny, damp fingers. Asher gave the child a blue poker chip to gnaw on.

"How did you know to do that?" Gil tossed out the ten of diamonds, and everybody followed suit except Spathfoy, who pitched the king of spades onto the table.

Ian was sitting the game out, and true to his word,

topping up drinks between tricks. Asher contributed the king of diamonds, Con the ace. "Do what?"

"Give His Fiendship the chip so he'd stuff it in his maw and leave your cards alone?"

Across the table, Ian pretended to study the whiskey remaining in a simple glass vessel. Loyal of him, more loyal than Asher deserved.

"Must be from being a physician," Con muttered. "Physicians have to deal with bairns and hysterical women and crabbit auld men like Spathfoy."

Spathfoy swirled his drink. "They can also treat conditions of male inability to perform, Connor. You might keep that in mind in case you live long enough to become an auld man."

Con grinned. "Me wife will wear me out long before I'm auld, but I'll die happy and leave a handsome corpse. Unlike some." He led the ten of clubs, tossing the card directly at Spathfoy.

These men are my brothers, and I love them.

The thought bloomed in Asher's heart and in his mind just as the baby pitched a thoroughly gummed chip onto the table. Gil played the eight of clubs, caught the chip as it rolled off the edge of the table, and held it out to Asher.

"Don't give it back to him," Asher said, "or it will soon be raining poker chips in here. The wee ones train us like monkeys, all for their entertainment."

This time, Asher fished in his pocket and passed the boy an empty brass money clip. When he looked up, Gil, Con, and Spathfoy were frowning at him, while Ian's gaze was steady. Just steady.

As wee John brought the money clip to his mouth,

Asher felt a question form over the table. A curiosity coalesced that had probably been building through all the days Asher had ignored John in London, through the morning they'd been found asleep on the train, John clutched to Asher's chest.

"He'll find the taste interesting," Asher said, cradling the boy closer. "It won't hurt him any more than sticking his fingers in his mouth would. Not particularly sanitary..."

Spathfoy set his cards on the table and folded his arms. Con tossed back his drink and set the glass on the table like a judge lowering a gavel. Gil watched the child drooling all over the money clip, and still Ian said nothing—nor did he pour anybody any more whiskey.

Asher brushed a kiss to the baby's downy head as an old pain, one not directly related to Hannah's departure, but one entwined with it, welled from his past.

"Shall I take the bairn?" Ian's voice was soft, carefully neutral, but in that moment, the last thing Asher wanted was to give up the child he held in his arms.

"He's fine."

While five grown men struggled with a taut, aching silence, the baby spluttered happily with his new toy. Asher stroked a hand over the child's head.

He couldn't hurt any worse if he were put to the rack and stretched to the utmost. The thought held a wry kind of grace. Maybe it had helped to rehearse his confession with Hannah, who'd listened and cried and listened some more.

"I had a son."

Con swore softly and nudged Asher's drink closer, not close enough that the baby could knock it over.

"I had a son, and like Ian, I named him for Grandda. I named my boy John."

Ian sighed, not with exasperation. That sigh struck Asher as a sigh of relief, one long overdue.

Gil kept his gaze on the child, his expression unreadable but for the sorrow in his eyes. "Tell us about our nephew, Asher. I wish I could have known him."

The next words were hard, so hard. "He didn't live long, not quite a year, but he was a merry lad."

Spathfoy, to whom Asher was not related, posed the awful question: "Smallpox?"

Asher nodded.

Con swore again and dipped his head, pressing his fingers to his eyes. Gil was blinking rapidly, though Ian found his voice. "Brother, I am sorry for your loss. Your grief is ours."

"No," Asher said, and these words were not so hard to say at all, "it isn't. I haven't let it be. The rest of what I've kept from you is that the boy's mother lasted only a week after she knew our son was gone. I am a physician, schooled by the best, trained for my craft, and for the two people I loved most in the world, there was nothing I could do."

Except love them. He knew that now, like he knew his brothers loved him, and Hannah loved him. The knowledge was all that would get him through the next twenty-four hours and the next twenty-four years.

Spathfoy scowled mightily. "There should be a marker. He lived, he had a name, you loved him, his mother loved him. For the few months of his life, he was in line for an earldom." That would matter to a marquess's heir. The scowl was directed at Asher.

"You loved his mother. There should be a marker. My brother died in the godforsaken Canadian wilderness, but we had a marker made long before we could get him home."

Ian turned a thoughtful expression on Spathfoy. "We forget that you are only half-English, Spathfoy, though it's usually the louder half."

Spathfoy glared at Ian. "The more articulate half."

"Spathfoy is right," Con said. "The wee lad was one of us, his mother too."

That Connor and Spathfoy would agree on anything was extraordinary.

"There will be a marker," Asher said. "A proper memorial in the family plot... and a service." The last felt as important as the marker.

"I'll bring me pipes," Con said. "The ladies will put on a spread, and we'll tell the stories."

The decision was right. It felt right, and as Asher mentally tested around the edges of his various pains and regrets, he found his disclosure had not, in fact, made anything hurt worse. They'd drink and they'd dance, and if they drank enough, maybe even cry—and they'd do it together.

But as for putting Hannah on that ship bound for Boston at dawn tomorrow, that was something Asher had to do alone.

Twenty-one

HANNAH DID NOT BLAME ASHER FOR LETTING HER SLEEP until the last possible moment. She did not blame him for being very much the earl as they left the inn in the predawn chill. She did not blame him for expecting her to take some sustenance with their tea tray.

She drew the line at allowing him to join her in the boat that would row her out to the ship anchored in the middle of the harbor.

"I have this planned," she said. "It's to be like a Viking burial. You watch my ship drift out to sea, and you'll know I've gone. I'll watch the land disappear…"

And die, inside, where a woman loves, she'd die. She didn't tell him that part. Didn't have to.

"Get in the boat, Hannah."

Glowering at him was purely in the interests of bravado. He'd used the same tone of voice in which he'd offered other commands: "Spread your knees, Hannah. Kiss me, Hannah. Hannah, don't cry."

That last one had been honored more in the breach, so to speak. Hannah let him hand her into the boat, and moved over on the little bench amidships so he could sit beside her. Four stout, unsmiling fellows took the oars, and they shoved away from the pier.

"The captain has some things for you, documents and whatnot. He'll give them to you when you reach Boston. Your aunt sends her best wishes, and I had her wedding gift to you stowed on board with your effects. I will explain the situation to Enid when her husband brings her north later this summer."

He went on speaking, the burr ruthlessly suppressed so Hannah had to listen hard for it. She did not attend his words, specifically, but she listened for the music in his speech. The Highlander who crooned in Gaelic and told her he loved her.

"You're to eat, regularly, and not just hardtack. The provisions on this crossing are suitable for the royal barge, Hannah, and I expect you to enjoy them."

Enjoy? She turned her head to peer at him and saw he was in no better shape than she. His eyes were shadowed beneath and within, and for him, he looked pale. Hannah took his hand and brought it to her lips.

"I will contrive, Balfour. You needn't fret. I will eat. I will take air on the deck. I will bathe and dress and comb my hair. I will not plague your captain by falling into hysterics. I will be like those mountains of yours, dignified and serene."

Lies, but they seemed to ease some of the tension about his mouth. "See that you are. And I shall do likewise."

At least they agreed on what they wouldn't be doing.

The ship was before them all too soon, and again, the dear, dratted man would not make his good-byes, but must climb onto the deck immediately after

Hannah's own ascent, leading Hannah up onto the poop deck where the captain was cursing in Gaelic.

She recognized the curses and had practiced them for later use.

Asher commenced exhorting the captain, who was to control the very weather lest any harm come to Hannah. She let the sound wash over her, the sound of a man in love, doing what he could to keep her safe. The little maid stood some distance away, neat, round-eyed, and wise enough to wait until Asher was done blathering.

And then, all too soon, Asher turned to Hannah, took her by the elbow, and led her to the railing.

"I love you. I will always love you. Tend to your family in Boston, Hannah, but know that my heart goes with you."

"Not fair." She swayed into his embrace, and it had nothing to do with the rise and fall of the waves. "You weren't supposed to say it in English."

"I love you. I will always love you. I'm letting you go because I love you, but this is not the end."

He had to say that too, of course, like telling a patient they'd feel only a little burn at the touch of the knife.

"I love you, too." And thank a perverse God, Hannah was beyond tears. "I will always love you."

There was nothing more to say. Nothing more to feel. She went up on her toes and kissed his cheek, which was for once cold from the sea breeze. And because the hardest words always fell to the woman, she said them. "Good-bye, Asher."

He held her impossibly tight, as if he'd hold her

forever if he could just wrap her close enough in his arms, and then he stepped back. "Farewell."

Rather than watch him disappear over the rail, Hannah turned her back to stare at the sea and the ships bobbing and lifting on the water. She had no thoughts. She was one tired, bitter ache, where a woman in love had stood and was still trying to stand.

"Yer ladyship?"

The maid looked resolute, as if she'd borne one of Asher's lectures too. The girl's name was... Ceely, and in her green eyes, Hannah saw some Scottish determination. Probably even MacGregor determination, given the number of second and third cousins in Asher's employ.

"It's Miss Cooper, Ceely. Shall we go below?"

"My very thoughts, milady." The girl marched across the deck, but Hannah didn't make it that far. She stopped at the opposite rail and caught sight of the little boat with its four oarsmen, moving closer and closer to shore. Asher was on the bench in the middle, facing Hannah's ship, bare-headed and immobile.

She blew him a kiss. He returned the gesture, and then she couldn't see him anymore for all the damned tears in her eyes.

~

Ian was waiting when Asher walked up to the inn, sitting outside on a wicker chair facing the harbor, no baby in evidence, no tea and scones, not even a flask.

"You do realize that's your wife you just put on that ship?"

Asher slid into the seat next to him, so he might

torment himself with the sight of Hannah's ship leaving port. "A consummated engagement is a handfast marriage under Scottish law. Of course I realize it. Hannah probably won't until she reads the letter I gave the captain."

"You might have gone with her."

"We've had that discussion. I have no authority over her family, but I can at least give her the protection afforded the Countess of Balfour."

But what if she forgot to read the letter he'd given the captain, didn't collect the money, the ring, the deed to Asher's Boston house? Captain Mills would get them to her… eventually.

Ian scraped his chair back. "Do the Americans recognize handfast marriages? Hannah's not a Scottish citizen. One does wonder."

"You're the bloody lawyer."

"There's still time to catch the ship, Asher. The anchor hasn't been drawn up, the sails aren't lowered. The tide hasn't yet turned."

The tide would turn in less than thirty minutes, and Mills was not one to miss the tide. "Fetch me a drink, why don't you, Ian? Con promised."

Ian rose. "He promised we would not let you start drinking until you were under your own roof. Enjoy the sunrise."

So this wake was to be a solitary one, though Asher's grief was sincere indeed. Sooner or later, when he'd shown the colors long enough as Earl of Balfour and laird of clan MacGregor, he'd travel to Boston and attempt to argue his wife into returning to Scotland. She'd refuse, and because their situation was no kind of marriage for raising children, she'd eventually demand that he return to Scotland.

"It is beautiful here."

An old voice, a very old voice. Asher resigned himself to exchanging civilities and then finding more solitude from which to watch his dreams sail away.

The elderly woman perched three seats over, sitting so straight her back did not touch the chair. She stared out across the harbor like an eagle scanning its territory.

"Good morning, madam, and yes, this is a lovely city."

His unlikely companion was very small, with snow-white hair in a tidy coronet, and clothing in the height of fashion. Her palette ran to magenta, blue, and green, like a peacock. She ought to have a lady's maid fussing about at least, and several shawls. She took out a silver flask. "Today is a beautiful day, a wonderful day."

She offered him the flask. It wouldn't be sociable to refuse. Out on the ship, activity on deck increased and men scrambled aloft.

"My thanks." He passed the flask back, the drink both appreciated and of excellent quality.

"You are welcome." She took a businesslike draught and tucked it away.

"Are you recently arrived to Scotland?" Though what did he care if one old woman was enjoying her travels? What did he care about anything?

"I arrived last night, and today I am to rejoin my granddaughter. She has been very foolish, very stubborn, but she is good-hearted. I have come to talk sense into her."

Would to God that—

In an instant, the entire universe shifted. Hope erupted like a geyser while Asher took the chair beside the old woman. "Your granddaughter is Hannah Cooper. *You came.*"

When she turned her head, it was exactly like a raptor deigning to peer at a scurrying mouse. "Of course I came. You are her Asher? One doesn't ignore letters such as yours. Such detail, even to choosing my inn for me. You must take me to my Hannah immediately. She must not return to Boston when her fool of a stepfather wants to lock her away in one of those awful places. They have pleasant names, but what goes on there is enough to drive any woman to lunacy. Fetch her to me, this moment, please. I am old, and I do not hurry well."

Her accent held French and maybe… *Mohawk?*

Asher shot to his feet. "I can't take you to Hannah just yet, but by God, I can fetch Hannah to you." He paused three paces from the door to the inn. "What of her mother and her brothers? Are they coming?"

One nod. "As you suggested. Hannah's mother announced that she was going to visit her sister in Baltimore, scooped up the boys, and her imbecile of a husband was relieved to see them off on a visit. They will arrive here next week."

Before she finished speaking, Asher had the door to the inn open, while out on the water, the first sail on Hannah's ship had dropped and was flapping madly in a crisp morning breeze.

"'Tis a gift from yer auntie." Ceely pushed the package into Hannah hands. Without thought, Hannah's fingers closed around the parcel. Up on deck, she heard the anchor chain wrapping, wrapping around the capstan as the anchor was drawn up, the sound like a tightening noose around Hannah's heart.

In minutes the ship would turn for the sea, and Hannah's terrible choice would be *fait accompli.*

What have I done?

"Open yer package, mum." Hannah was scaring her maid. Behind stolid Scottish sense, Ceely's voice bore a hint of alarm.

Pretty red ribbon came away easily, revealing a maple wood box with a carved figure of some sprig of foliage on the top. Hannah opened the box, and found in its velvet-lined contents an array of small bottles.

She picked up a bottle at random. "Dr. Melvin Giles's Root Juice and Tincture of Everlasting Health." Dr. Giles shared the box with various remedies and elixirs, most of which, Hannah knew well, would put her to sleep.

It was a solution, of sorts, to the problem of how to endure, how to become like the mountains—though there would be no dignity to it. Hannah took out one small bottle, opened the top, and sniffed. The cloying, seductive aroma of the poppy wafted forth, sickening, but tempting…

"There's a note, mum." Ceely did not approve of this gift—this *wedding* gift that was in truth a parting gift. Censure was manifest in the extra-prim set of her mouth and the narrowing of green eyes.

Hannah picked up the note: "Hannah, if you return to Boston without marrying your earl, you'll need these far more than I ever did. Love, Enid Draper."

No tender sentiments from the new bride, no fond doting from a devoted step-auntie, only oblivion in a bottle. In twenty bottles. Hannah stared at the bottles lined up so neatly in the pretty box. They looked like dead fish, those bottles, salted and packed away for systematic consumption.

This was her future, in one box. This was how the rest of her life would go, one year beside another, salted with regret and packed way with missing Asher MacGregor.

Hannah slammed the lid of the box down. "It isn't ever going to hurt less, is it?"

Ceely took the box without being asked. "Milady?"

"It's going to hurt more and more, because leaving him is *wrong*. I should have trusted him to share my troubles and help me set matters to rights. I should not have abandoned him. I should not—good God, I should not—have left him behind."

"So what will ye do about it?"

The anchor was up, the chain no longer rattling into place. Shouting from above signaled the loosing of the sails, and the ship was riding higher in the waves. "Take me to the captain. We cannot leave port."

But Captain Mills, stout Scottish veteran of the seas, was not about to delay his departure, miss the tide, and violate direct orders from the ship's owner.

The inn's common was empty save for Ian, sitting at the bar, back to the door.

"She's here!"

Ian's head came up. "Who's here? Hannah? I knew she'd come to her senses. You get down on your knees, man, and you promise to goddamn worship her, do you hear me? Augusta said a man on his knees is irresistible, and if Augusta—"

"Not Hannah, ye bletherin' fool. Her grandmother. Her gran came to talk sense into her, but my Hannah's on the goddamn boat, and—" And he was desperate to get to her, but one man would never catch a clipper bent on leaving the harbor.

The right words came to him, from nowhere, from everywhere, from every Scottish laird ever to call for his people.

Asher planted his feet and bellowed, "*To the MacGregor*!"

Ian took up the cry, doors banged upstairs, and in moments, Con, Gil, and Daniels came thundering down the stairs in various states of undress. Spathfoy brought up the rear in full riding attire.

"I need to catch Hannah's ship. Ye"—he speared Daniels with a look—"fetch the auld lady from outside, look after her. Tell her I'll bring Hannah to her if I have to swim the bluidy ocean to do it."

The little ketch was tied up in the same place on the dock. Spathfoy stopped long enough to yank off his boots, while Con, Gil, and Ian each took an oar.

"You man the tiller," Ian barked. "And start yelling for your captain to drop anchor."

The anchor was up, the sails filled, and while his kinsman strained mightily at the oars, Asher started yelling as if his very heart depended on it.

Because it did.

"Now, madam, I have a ship to sail, and Lord Balfour will take it quite amiss if I neglect m' duties for a case of female vapors. Sea travel can be quite pleasant. You must not fret."

Mills, a man of mature years, ruddy complexion, and solid build, exchanged a look with Ceely that said quite clearly: "Drag the daft woman below if you have to, but get her the hell off my deck."

Ceely took a step forward. "Listen to her ladyship, ye auld fool. She's the MacGregor's lady, and if she says to turn the ship around, ye mun listen."

"I *am* the MacGregor's lady," Hannah said, the notion infusing her with renewed determination. "You can catch the tide tomorrow or this evening. There will always be another tide." But there would *never* be another man like Asher MacGregor, not for her. "Drop anchor, Captain, or you'll find yourself relieved of your command."

He rolled his eyes, and Hannah knew the urge to strangle him. "Now you're a pirate, too? And you?" Rheumy blue eyes flicked over Ceely. "A couple of wee Corsairs?" He turned from them, cupped his hands to his mouth, and shouted up to the rigging, "Make sail!"

Hannah planted her fists on her hips and yelled more loudly, "By order of the MacGregor's lady, *drop anchor*!"

The ship was riding the waves, dipping and rising, even turning slightly on the strength of nothing more than the harbor current and morning breeze.

"Captain?" The mate jogged up to his superior's side. "A word with ye, sir?"

"I'm not dropping the damned anchor!" Mills spun away, muttering about daft, bleating women while Hannah directed Ceely to find her knife so she could cut her skirts free and swim to shore.

"Up you go."

"Make fast and come after me," Asher said, leaping onto the rope ladder. "I may need ye to help me kidnap the countess."

The scene on the deck was one to confuse a besotted man on a good day, and this was not a good day. Hannah stood nose to nose with old Mills, the sailors agog from their various posts, while the maid, Cousin Ceely, repelled boarders with a ferocious scowl.

"And furthermore, the MacGregor will not appreciate you arguing with me, Captain! I need a boat and somebody to row it, or I'll row it myself, but let me off this ship this instant!"

What? "Hannah."

She froze as if she'd taken an arrow in the back, then did an about-face and stood her ground, back to Mills. Her boots were beside her on the freshly scrubbed deck, and the sea breeze was making inroads on her tidy bun. The front of her skirt was slashed all to hell, and she wore no gloves.

She could not have looked more beautiful to him.

"Asher MacGregor, please tell this man he cannot take me to Boston. Tell him you will not allow it." She had never sounded more crisp, imperious, or Bostonian.

The temptation to run to her, to snatch her into his arms was overwhelming, but the stakes were far too high for rash behavior. "Why would I not allow it? It's all ye've wanted since ye set foot on Scottish soil, Hannah. It's your duty, your heart's desire. If I love ye, and I do, verra much, why would I come between ye and your heart's desire?"

"Because—" Her hands fisted at her sides. She closed her eyes and turned her face up to the heavens. "Because *you* are my heart's desire. To be your lady is my heart's desire. The rest…" She looked around at the wide sea beyond the harbor, at the shore, and then at him. "The rest will have to sort itself out. I will need your help, but I need you more. The alternative doesn't bear… I can see no alternative."

Behind him, his brothers were clambering over the rail, their boots thumping onto the deck.

"Then come to me, Hannah, and be my lady." He held out his arms, and in her stocking feet, she pelted across the wet deck, as nimble as a goat. Gilgallon swore cheerfully in several languages, and Con and Spathfoy started arguing about who had won the bet.

Hannah held him tight, her arms lashed around his middle. "Don't let me go, Asher."

"You won't fall, Hannah." Though he didn't turn her loose.

"No, don't let me go to Boston. My family has had years to put Step-papa in his place. I can only offer them my home—our home—and hope they'll accept the invitation. I cannot let their lack of sense become my own."

She would have babbled on, would have explained all her reasons and counterarguments and contingency plans to him, but he kissed her, all the argument he needed to make.

The sailors whistled and stomped, Mills barked orders nobody heeded, and Hannah kissed Asher.

And kissed him.

When her enthusiasm for remaining in Scotland was threatening Asher's ability to walk, he broke the kiss. "Madam, we have an audience."

Hannah mashed her nose against his throat. "Good, they can be our witnesses, and your brothers too. The captain can marry us, can't he?"

Ian said something in Gaelic that Asher hoped Hannah couldn't understand.

"The ship's captain cannot marry us, Hannah." He put his lips to her ear. "Under Scottish law, we married the day you had me naked in the hills behind Balfour House. You might want to have a more formal ceremony once your grandmother is done speaking sense to you."

"I liked the informal ceremony." Then her head came up. "My *grandmother*? I'm not waiting weeks, while we beg and plead and bully a stubborn old woman to get on a ship for Scotland, Asher. She can be impossible. She doesn't believe in half measures. I tried to reason with her by correspondence, and she wouldn't even acknowledge my arguments."

Another kiss was necessary to stop this tirade. Why didn't anybody tell schoolboys there was no need to argue with ladies when a more effective tactic lay so close to hand? "Will you wait until we can get you to shore?"

"To shore?"

"I asked your grandmother to come to Scotland, Hannah. I begged, I pleaded, I nigh wept on the pages and told my man in Boston to offer my firstborn and my last groat to get the old woman onto one of our ships. I also offered emphatically to host your mother and your brothers for an indefinite stay, and they've accepted."

Well, in part they had. He could explain the subterfuges necessary to accept his invitation, but Hannah would hardly quibble.

And if she did, he'd kiss her again.

Spathfoy clamped a hand on Asher's shoulder. "So do we stand around in the middle of the harbor all morning, or take turns kissing the bride?"

"Neither. Hannah, into the boat. I'll send a tender out to fetch your things before Mills catches the evening tide."

Now, now that Spathfoy was proposing inappropriate liberties, Hannah stepped away, though she kept her hand in Asher's. "There's something I'd like to do first, Asher. It won't take long."

She said something quietly to Ceely, while Asher withstood his brothers' grins and taunts—in English, lest anybody fail to comprehend that the ship's owner had been one whisker away from ruining the rest of his life.

"You lot get in the damned boat and prepare to man the oars."

Spathfoy bowed, Gil saluted, Ian blew him a kiss, and Con performed the elaborate, wrist-twirling, old-fashioned court bow. Asher understood this display for a version of "I love you even when you're being an ass," known only to him and his brothers.

Ceely appeared from below decks with a wooden box in her hands. "Poison, from her ladyship's auntie. I'm off to pack up that which I spent last night unpacking. Ye'll excuse me."

Hannah accepted the box, which had been tied closed with a red ribbon.

"Enid's gift?"

"Her final lecture. Will you throw it over the side for me?"

The box was gone, heaved many yards from the ship, to disappear into the water with barely a splash. "Now may I take you to greet your grandmother?"

"We're really, truly married, Asher?"

"Yes. Under Scottish law, we're really and truly married. I'm going to suggest we get married under English law as well, and Spathfoy's estate in Northumbria will serve nicely for a quiet family wedding."

Lest she get to planning the ceremony right there on the boat, he kissed her again then sent her down the ladder into the waiting rowboat.

As it turned out, the family wedding in Northumbria was attended by Hannah's grandmother, mother, and half brothers, and several hundred other close family members, all eager to welcome the MacGregor's lady to her rightful place at the laird's side.

And while the earl and his countess did have many children, the first of them, a great, strappin' lad, had the good grace not to arrive until ten entire months after the family wedding.

Read on for excerpts from Grace Burrowes's Scottish Victorian series, and fall in love with the whole MacGregor clan!

The Bridegroom Wore Plaid

Once Upon a Tartan

Mary Fran and Matthew

Now available from Sourcebooks Casablanca

The Bridegroom Wore Plaid

"IT IS A TRUTH UNIVERSALLY ACKNOWLEDGED THAT A single, reasonably good-looking earl not in possession of a fortune must be in want of a wealthy wife."

Ian MacGregor repeated Aunt Eulalie's reasoning under his breath. The words had the ring of old-fashioned common sense, and yet they somehow made a mockery of such an earl as well.

Possibly of the wife too. As Ian surveyed the duo of tittering, simpering, blond females debarking from the train on the arm of their scowling escort, he sent up a silent prayer that his countess would be neither reluctant nor managing, but other than that, he could not afford—in the most literal sense—to be particular.

His wife could be homely, or she could be fair. She could be a recent graduate from the schoolroom, or a lady past the first blush of youth. She could be shy or boisterous, gorgeous or plain. It mattered not which, provided she was unequivocally, absolutely, and most assuredly *rich*.

And if Ian MacGregor's bride was to be well and

truly rich, she was also going to be—God help him and all those who depended on him—*English*.

For the good of his family, his clan, and the lands they held, he'd consider marrying a well-dowered Englishwoman. If that meant his own preferences in a wife—pragmatism, loyalty, kindness, and a sense of humor—went begging, well, such was the laird's lot.

In the privacy of his personal regrets, Ian admitted a lusty nature in a wife and a fondness for a tall, black-haired, green-eyed Scotsman as a husband wouldn't have gone amiss either. As he waited for his brothers Gilgallon and Connor to maneuver through the throng in the Ballater station yard, Ian tucked that regret away in the vast mental storeroom reserved for such dolorous thoughts.

"I'll take the tall blond," Gil muttered with the air of a man choosing which lame horse to ride into battle.

"I'm for the little blond, then," Connor growled, sounding equally resigned.

Ian understood the strategy. His brothers would offer escort to Miss Eugenia Daniels and her younger sister, Hester Daniels, while Ian was to show himself to be the perfect gentleman. His task thus became to offer his arms to the two chaperones who stood quietly off to the side. One was dressed in subdued if fashionable mauve, the other in wrinkled gray with two shawls, one of beige with a black fringe, the other of gray.

Ian moved away from his brothers, pasting a fatuous smile on his face.

"My lord, my ladies, *fáilte*! Welcome to Aberdeenshire!"

An older man detached himself from the blond females. The fellow sported thick muttonchop whiskers, a prosperous paunch, and the latest fashion in daytime attire. "Willard Daniels, Baron of Altsax and Gribbony."

The baron bowed slightly, acknowledging Ian's superior if somewhat tentative rank.

"Balfour, at your service." Ian shook hands with as much hearty bonhomie as he could muster. "Welcome to you and your family, Baron. If you'll introduce me to your womenfolk and your son, I'll make my brothers known to them, and we can be on our way."

The civilities were observed, while Ian tacitly appraised his prospective countess. The taller blond—Eugenia Daniels—was his marital quarry, and she blushed and stammered her greetings with empty-headed good manners. She did not *appear* reluctant, which meant he could well end up married to her, provided he could dredge up sufficient charm to woo her.

And he could. Not ten years after the worst famine known to the British Isles, a strong back and a store of charm were about all that was left to him, so by God, he would use both ruthlessly to his family's advantage.

Connor and Gil comported themselves with similarly counterfeit cheer, though on Con the exercise was not as convincing. Con was happy to go all day without speaking, much less smiling, though Ian knew he, too, understood the desperate nature of their charade.

Daniels made a vague gesture in the direction of the chaperones. "My sister-in-law, Mrs. Julia Redmond. My niece, Augusta Merrick." He turned away as he said the last, his gaze on the men unloading a mountain of trunks from the train.

Thank God Ian had thought to bring the wagon

in addition to the coach. The English did set store by their finery. The baron's son, Colonel Matthew Daniels, late of Her Majesty's cavalry, excused himself from the introductions to oversee the transfer of baggage to the wagon.

"Ladies." Ian winged an arm at each of the older women. "I'll have you on your way in no time."

"This is so kind of you," the shorter woman said, taking his arm. Mrs. Redmond was a pretty thing, petite, with perfect skin, big brown eyes, and rich chestnut curls peeking out from under the brim of a lavender silk cottage bonnet. Ian placed her somewhere just a shade south of thirty. A lovely age on a woman. Con would call it a dally-able age.

Only as Ian offered his other arm to the second woman did he realize she was holding a closed hatbox in one hand and a reticule in the other.

Mrs. Redmond held out a gloved hand for the hatbox. "Oh, Gus, do give me Ulysses."

The hatbox emitted a disgruntled yowl.

Ian felt an abrupt yearning for a not-so-wee dram, for now he'd sunk to hosting not just the wealthy English, but their dyspeptic felines as well.

"I will carry my own pet," the taller lady said—Miss Merrick. A man who was a host for hire had to be good with names. She hunched a little more tightly over her hatbox, as if she feared her cat might be torn from her clutches by force.

"Perhaps you'd allow me to carry your bag, so I might escort you to the coach?" Ian cocked his arm at her again, a slight gesture he'd meant to be gracious.

The lady twisted her head on her neck, not

straightening entirely, and peered up at him out of a pair of violet-gentian eyes. That color was completely at variance with her bent posture, her pinched mouth, the unrelieved black of her hair, the wilted gray silk of her old-fashioned coal scuttle bonnet, and even with the expression of impatience in the eyes themselves.

The Almighty had tossed even this cranky besom a bone, but these beautiful eyes in the context of this woman were as much burden as benefit. They insulted the rest of her somehow, mocked her and threw her numerous shortcomings into higher relief.

The two shawls—worn in public, no less—half slipping off her shoulders.

The hem of her gown two inches farther away from the planks of the platform than was fashionable.

The cat yowling its discontent in the hatbox.

The finger poking surreptitiously from the tip of her right glove.

Gazing at those startling eyes, Ian realized that despite her bearing and her attire, Miss Merrick was probably younger than he was, at least chronologically.

"Come, Gussie," Mrs. Redmond said, reaching around Ian for the reticule. "We'll hold up the coach, which will make Willard difficult, and I am most anxious to see Lord Balfour's home."

"And I am anxious to show it off to you." Ian offered an encouraging smile, noting out of the corner of his eye that Gil and Con were bundling their charges into the waiting coach. The sky was full of bright, puffy little clouds scudding against an azure canvas, but this was Scotland in high summer, and the weather was bound to change at any minute out of sheer contrariness.

Miss Merrick put her gloved hand on his sleeve—the glove with the frayed finger—and lifted her chin toward the coach.

A true lady then, one who could issue commands without a word. Ian began the stately progress toward the coach necessitated by the lady's dignified gait, all the while sympathizing with the cat, whose displeasure with his circumstances was made known to the entire surrounds.

Fortunately, Mrs. Redmond was of a sunnier nature.

"It was so good of you to fetch us from the train yourself, my lord," Mrs. Redmond said. "Eulalie told us you offer the best hospitality in the shire."

"Aunt Eulalie can be given to overstatement, but I hope not in this case. You are our guests, and Highland custom would allow us to treat you as nothing less than family."

"Are we in the Highlands?" Miss Merrick asked. "It's quite chilly."

Ian resisted glancing at the hills all around them.

"There is no strict legal boundary defining the Highlands, Miss Merrick. I was born and brought up in the mountains to the west, though, so my manners are those of a Highlander. And by custom, Ballater is indeed considered Highland territory. We can get at least a dusting of snow any month of the year."

Those incongruous, beautiful eyes flicked over him, up, up, and down—to his shoulders, no lower. He tried to label what he saw in her gaze: contempt, possibly, a little curiosity, some veiled boldness.

Shrewdness, he decided with an inward sigh, though he kept his smile in place. She had the sort of noticing, analyzing shrewdness common to the poor relation managing on family charity—Ian recognized it from long acquaintance.

"How did you come to live in Aberdeenshire?" Mrs. Redmond asked as they approached the coach.

An innocent question bringing to mind images of starvation and despair.

"It's the seat of our earldom. I came of age, and it was time I saw something of the world." *Besides failed potato fields, overgrazed glens, and shabby funerals.* He handed the ladies in, which meant for a moment he held the hatbox. His respect for the cat grew, since from the weight of the hatbox, the beast would barely have room to turn around in its pretty little cage.

Ian knew exactly how that felt.

Once Upon a Tartan

When Tiberius Lamartine Flynn heard the tree singing, his first thought was that he'd parted company with his reason. Then two dusty little boots dangled above his horse's abruptly nervous eyes, and the matter became a great deal simpler.

"Out of the tree, child, lest you spook some unsuspecting traveler's mount."

A pair of slim white calves flashed among the branches, the movement provoking the damned horse to dancing and propping.

"What's his name?"

The question was almost unintelligible, so thick was the burr.

"His name is Flying Rowan," Tye said, stroking a hand down the horse's crest. "And he'd better settle himself down this instant if he knows what's good for him. His efforts in this regard would be greatly facilitated if you'd vacate that damned tree."

"You shouldn't swear at her. She's a wonderful tree."

The horse settled, having had as much frolic as Tye was inclined to permit.

"In the first place, trees do not have gender, in the second, your heathen accent makes your discourse nigh incomprehensible, and in the third, please get the hell out of the tree."

"Introduce yourself. I'm not supposed to talk to strangers."

A heathen child with manners. What else did he expect from the wilds of Aberdeenshire?

"Tiberius Lamartine Flynn, Earl of Spathfoy, at your service. Had we any mutual acquaintances, I'd have them attend to the civilities."

Silence from the tree, while Tye felt the idiot horse tensing for another display of nonsense.

"You're wrong—we have a mutual acquaintance. This is a treaty oak. She's everybody's friend. I'm Fee."

Except in his Englishness, Tye first thought the little scamp had said, "I'm fey," which seemed appropriate.

"Pleased to make your acquaintance, Fee. Now show yourself like a gentleman, or I'll think it's your intent to drop onto hapless travelers and rob them blind."

"Do you think I could?"

Dear God, the child sounded fascinated.

"Down. *Now.*" That tone of voice had worked on Tye's younger brother until Gordie had been almost twelve. The same tone had ever been a source of amusement to his younger sisters. The branches moved, and Rowan tensed again, haunches bunching as if he'd bolt.

A lithe little shape plummeted at least eight feet to the ground and landed with a loud "Ouch!" provoking Rowan to rear in earnest.

From the ground, the horse looked enormous, and the man astride like a giant. Fee caught an impression of darkness—dark horse, dark riding clothes, and a dark scowl as the man tried to control his horse.

"That is quite enough out of you." The man's voice was so stern, Fee suspected the horse understood the words, for two large iron-shod hooves came to a standstill not a foot from her head.

"Child, you will get up slowly and move away from the horse. I cannot guarantee your safety otherwise."

Still stern—maybe this fellow was always stern, in which case he was to be pitied. Fee sat up and tried to creep back on her hands, backside, and feet, but pain shot through her left ankle and up her calf before she'd shifted half her weight.

"I hurt myself."

The horse backed a good ten feet away, though Fee couldn't see how the rider had asked it to do so.

"Where are you hurt?"

"My foot. I think I landed on it wrong. It's because I'm wearing shoes."

"Shoes do not cause injury." He swung off the horse and shook a gloved finger at the animal. "You stand, or you'll be stewed up for the poor of the parish."

"Are you always so mean, mister?"

He loomed above her, hands on his hips, and Fee's Aunt Hester would have said he looked like The Wrath of God. His nose was a Wrath-of-God sort of nose, nothing sweet or humble about it, and his eyes were Wrath-of-God eyes, all dark and glaring.

He was as tall as the Wrath of God, too, maybe even taller than Fee's uncles, who, if not exactly the Wrath of God, could sometimes be the Wrath of Deeside and greater Aberdeenshire.

As could her aunt Hester, which was a sobering thought.

"You think I'm mean, young lady?"

"Yes."

"Then I must answer in the affirmative."

She frowned up at him. From his accent, he was at least a bloody Lowlander, or possibly a damned Sassenach, but even making those very significant allowances, he still talked funny.

"What is a firmative?"

"Yes, I am mean. Can you walk?"

He extended a hand down to her, a very large hand in a black riding glove. Fee had seen some pictures in a book once, of a lot of cupids without nappies bouncing around with harps, and a hand very like that one, sticking out of the clouds, except the hand in the picture was not swathed in black leather.

"Child, I do not have all day to impersonate the Good Samaritan."

"The Good Samaritan was nice. *He* went to heaven."

"While it is *my* sorry fate to be ruralizing in Scotland." He hauled Fee to her feet by virtue of lifting her up under the arms. He did this without effort, as if he hoisted five stone of little girl from the roadside for regular amusement.

"Do you ever smile?"

"When in the presence of silent, well-behaved,

properly scrubbed children, I sometimes consider the notion. Can you put weight on that foot?"

"It hurts. I think it hurts because my shoe is getting too tight."

He muttered something under his breath, which might have had some bad words mixed in with more of his pernickety accent, then lifted Fee to his hip. "I am forced by the requirements of good breeding and honor to endure your company in the saddle for however long it takes to return you to the dubious care of your wardens, and may God pity them that responsibility."

"I get to ride your horse?"

"*We* get to ride my horse. If you were a boy, I'd leave you here to the mercy of passing strangers or allow you to crawl home."

He might have been teasing. The accent made it difficult to tell—as did the scowl. "You thought I was boy?"

"Don't sound so pleased. I thought you were a nuisance, and I still do. Can you balance?"

He deposited her next to the treaty oak, which meant she could stand on one foot and lean on the tree. "I want to take my shoes off." He wrinkled that big nose of his, looking like he smelled something rank. "My feet are clean. Aunt Hester makes me take a bath every night whether I need one or not."

This Abomination Against the Natural Order—another one of Aunt Hester's terms—did not appear to impress the man. Fee wondered if anything impressed him—and what a poverty that would be, as Aunt would say, to go through the whole day without once being impressed.

He hunkered before her, and he was even tall when he knelt. "Put your hand on my shoulder."

Fee complied, finding his shoulder every bit as sturdy as the oak. He unlaced her boot, but when he tried to ease it off her foot, she had to squeal with the pain of it.

"Wrenched it properly, then. Here." He pulled off his gloves and passed them to her. "Bite down on one of those, hard enough to cut right through the leather, and scream if you have to. I have every confidence you can ruin my hearing if you make half an effort."

She took the gloves, which were warm and supple. "Are you an uncle?"

"As it happens, this dolorous fate has befallen me."

"Is that a firmative?"

"It is. Why?"

"Because you're trying to distract me, which is something my uncles do a lot. I won't scream."

He regarded her for a moment, looking almost as if he might say something not quite so fussy, then bent to glare at her boot. "Suit yourself, as it appears you are in the habit of doing."

She braced herself; she even put one of the riding gloves between her teeth, because as badly as her ankle hurt, she expected taking off her boot would cause the kind of pain that made her ears roar and her vision dim around the edges.

She neither screamed nor bit through the glove—which tasted like reins and horse—because before she could even draw in a proper breath, her boot was gently eased off her foot.

"I suppose you want the other one off too?"

"Is my ankle all bruised and horrible?"

"Your ankle is slightly swollen. It will likely be bruised before the day is out, but perhaps not horribly if we can get ice on it."

"Are you a priest?"

"For pity's sake, child. First an uncle, then a priest? What can you be thinking?" He sat her in the grass and started unlacing her second boot.

"You talk like Vicar on Sunday, though on Saturday night, he sounds like everybody else when he's having his pint. If my ankle is awful, Aunt Hester will cry and feed me shortbread with my tea. She might even play cards with me. My uncles taught me how to cheat, but explained I must never cheat unless I'm playing with them."

"Honor among thieves being the invention of the Scots, this does not surprise me." He tied the laces of both boots into a knot and slung them around Fee's neck.

"I'm a Scot."

His lips quirked. Maybe this was what it looked like when the Wrath of God was afraid he might smile.

"My condolences. Except for your unfortunate red hair, execrable accent, and the layer of dirt about your person, I would never have suspected."

Mary Fran and Matthew

One glimpse of Lady Mary Frances MacGregor, and Matthew Daniels forgot all about the breathtaking Highland scenery and the misbegotten purpose for his visit to Aberdeenshire.

"For the duration of your stay, our house is your house," Lady Mary Frances said. She strode along the corridor of her brother's country home with purpose, not with the mincing, corseted gait of a London lady, and she had music in her voice. Her walk held music as well, in the rhythm and sway of her hips, in the rustle of her petticoats and the crisp tattoo of her boots on the polished wood floors.

Though what music had to do with anything, Matthew was at a loss to fathom. "The Spanish have a similar saying, my lady: *mi casa es su casa.*"

"My house is your house." She either guessed or made the translation easily. "You've been to Spain, then?"

"In Her Majesty's Army, one can travel a great deal."

A shadow creased her brow, quickly banished and replaced by a smile. "And now you've traveled to our doorstep. This is your room, Mr. Daniels, though we've others if you'd prefer a different view."

She preceded him into the room, leaving Matthew vaguely disconcerted. A proper young woman would not be alone with a gentleman in his private quarters, and Mary Frances MacGregor, being the daughter of an earl, was a lady even in the sense of having a courtesy title—though Matthew had never before met a *lady* with hair that lustrous shade of dark red, or a figure so perfectly designed to thwart a man's gentlemanly self-restraint.

"The view is quite acceptable."

The view was magnificent, including, as it did, the backside of Lady Mary Frances as she bent to struggle with a window sash. She was a substantial woman, both tall and well formed, and Matthew suspected her arms would be trim with muscle, not the smooth, pale appendages a gentleman might see at a London garden party.

"Allow me." He went to her side and jiggled the sash on its runners, hoisting the thing easily to allow in some fresh air.

"The maids will close it by teatime," Lady Mary Frances said. "The nights can be brisk, even in high summer. Will you be needing a bath before the evening meal?"

She put the question casually—just a hostess inquiring after the welfare of a guest—but her gaze slid over him, a quick, assessing flick of green eyes bearing a hint of speculation. He might not fit in an old-fashioned bathing tub was what the gaze said, nothing more.

Nonetheless, he dearly wanted to get clean after long days of traveling. “If it wouldn’t be too much trouble?”

“No trouble at all. The bathing chamber is just down the hall to the left, the cistern is full, and the boilers have been going since noon.”

She peered into the empty wardrobe, passing close enough to Matthew that he caught a whiff of something female… Flowers. Not roses, which were probably the only flower he knew by scent, but… fresher than roses, less cloying.

“If you need anything to make your visit more enjoyable, Mr. Daniels, you have only to ask, and we’ll see to it. Highland hospitality isn’t just the stuff of legends.”

“My thanks.”

She frowned at the high four-poster and again walked past him, though this time she picked up the tartan draped across the foot of the bed. The daughter of an earl ought not to be fussing the blankets, but Matthew liked the sight of her, snapping out the red, white, and blue woolen blanket and giving it a good shake. Her attitude said that nothing, not dust, not visiting English, not a houseful of her oversized brothers, would daunt this woman.

Without thinking, Matthew picked up the two corners of the blanket that had drifted to the blue-and-red tartan rug.

“Will you be having other guests this summer?” He put the question to her as they stepped toward each other.

“Likely not.” She grasped the corners he’d picked up, their fingers brushing.

Matthew did not step back. Mary Frances MacGregor—*Lady* Mary Frances MacGregor—had *freckles* over the bridge of her nose. They were faint, even delicate, and they made her look younger. She could have powdered them into oblivion, but she hadn't.

"Mr. Daniels?" She gave the blanket a tug.

Matthew moved back a single step. "You typically have only one set of guests each summer?" Whatever her scent, it wasn't only floral, but also held something spicy, fresh like cedar, but not quite cedar.

"No, we usually have as many guests as the brief summers here permit, particularly once Her Majesty and His Royal Highness are ensconced next door. But if your sister becomes engaged to my brother, there will be other matters to see to, won't there?"

This question, alluding to much and saying little, was accompanied by an expression that involved the corners of the lady's lips turning up, and yet it wasn't a smile.

"I suppose there will." Things like settling a portion of the considerable Daniels's wealth into the impoverished Balfour coffers. Things like preparing for the wedding of a lowly English baron's daughter to a Scottish earl.

"We'll gather in the parlor for drinks before the evening meal, Mr. Daniels. The parlor is directly beneath us, one floor down. Any footman can direct you."

She was insulting him. Matthew took a moment to decipher this, and in the next moment, he realized the insult was not intentional. Some of the MacGregor's "guests," wealthy English wanting to boast of a visit to the Queen's own piece of the Highlands, probably spent much of their stay too inebriated to navigate even the corridors of the earl's country house.

"I'll find my way, though at some point, I would also like to be shown where the rest of my family is housed."

"Of course." Another non-smile. She glanced around the room the way Matthew had seen generals look over the troops prior to a parade review, her lips flattening, her gaze seeking any detail out of order. "Until dinner, Mr. Daniels."

She bobbed a curtsy and whirled away before Matthew could even offer her a proper bow.

"Miss MacGregor?"

Mary Fran's insides clenched at the sound of Baron Altsax's voice. She pasted a smile on her face and tried to push aside the need to check on the dining room, the kitchen, and the ladies' guest rooms—and the need to locate Fiona.

The child tended to hide when a new batch of guests came to stay.

"Baron, what may I do for you?"

"I had a few questions, Miss MacGregor, if you wouldn't mind?" He gestured to his bedroom, his smile suggesting he knew damned good and well the insult he did an earl's daughter by referring to her as "Miss" anything. A double insult, in fact.

Mary Fran did not follow the leering old buffoon into his room. Altsax's son, the soft-spoken Mr. Daniels, would reconnoiter before he started bothering the help—though big, blond, good-looking young men seldom needed to bother the help—not so with the skinny, pot-gutted old men. "I'm a bit behindhand, my lord. Was it something I could send a maid to tend to?"

The baron gestured toward the drinking pitcher on the escritoire, while Mary Fran lingered at the threshold. "This water is not chilled, I've yet to see a tea service, and prolonged travel by train can leave a man in need of something to wash the dust from his throat."

He arched one supercilious eyebrow, as if it took some subtle instinct to divine when an Englishman was whining for his whisky.

"The maids will be along shortly with the tea service, my lord. You'll find a decanter with some of our best libation on the nightstand, and I can send up some chilled water." Because they at least had ice to spare in the Highlands.

"See that you do."

Mary Fran tossed him a hint of a curtsy and left before he could make up more excuses to lure her into his room.

The paying guests were a source of much-needed coin, but the summers were too short, and the expenses of running Balfour too great for paying guests alone to reverse the MacGregor family fortunes. The benefit of this situation was that no coin was on hand to dower Mary Fran, should some fool—brother, guest, or distant relation—take a notion she was again in want of a husband.

"Mary Fran, for God's sake, slow down." She'd been so lost in thought she hadn't realized her brother Ian had approached her from the top of the stairs. "Where are you churning off to in such high dudgeon? Con and Gil sent me to fetch you to the family parlor for a wee dram."

Ian's gaze was weary and concerned, the same as Con or Gil's would have been, though Ian, as the oldest, was the weariest and the most concerned—also the one willing to marry Altsax's featherbrained daughter just so Fiona might someday have a decent dowry.

"I have to check on the kitchens, Ian, and make sure that dim-witted Hetta McKinley didn't forget the butter dishes again, and Eustace Miller has been lurking on the maids' stairway so he can make calf eyes at—"

"Come, you." Ian tucked her hand over his arm. "You deserve a few minutes with family more than the maids need to be protected from Eustace Miller's calf eyes. Let the maids have some fun, and let yourself take five minutes to catch your breath. Go change into your finery and meet us in the family parlor. I'll need your feminine perspective if I'm to coax Altsax's daughter up the church aisle."

Ian had typical MacGregor height and green eyes to go with dark hair and a handsome smile—none of which was worth a single groat. In Asher's continued absence, Ian was also the laird, and well on his way to being officially recognized as the earl. While neither honor generated coin, the earldom allowed him the prospect of marrying an heiress with a title-hungry papa.

Mary Fran did not bustle off to change her dress for any of those reasons, or even because she needed to stay abreast of whatever her three brothers were thinking regarding Ian's scheme to marry wealth.

She heeded her brother's direction because she wanted that wee dram—wanted it far too much.

Watch for the first in Grace Burrowes's exciting NEW Captive Hearts Regency trilogy

The Captive

While being held captive and tortured by the French, Christian, Duke of Mercia, lost his wife and son, and very nearly his will to live. He returns to England broken in spirit, until Gillian, Countess of Windmere, shows him that winning her heart is the most important battle of all.

Available July 2014 from Sourcebooks Casablanca

About the Author

New York Times and *USA Today* bestselling author Grace Burrowes's bestsellers include *The Heir*, *The Soldier*, *Lady Maggie's Secret Scandal*, *Lady Sophie's Christmas Wish*, and *Lady Eve's Indiscretion*. *The Heir* was a *Publishers Weekly* Best Book of 2010, *The Soldier* was a *Publishers Weekly* Best Spring Romance of 2011, *Lady Sophie's Christmas Wish* won Best Historical Romance of the Year in 2011 from RT Reviewers' Choice Awards, *Lady Louisa's Christmas Knight* was a *Library Journal* Best Book of 2012, and *The Bridegroom Wore Plaid*—the first in her trilogy of Scotland-set Victorian romances—was a *Publishers Weekly* Best Book of 2012. Her historical romances have received extensive praise, including starred reviews *from Publishers Weekly* and *Booklist*.

Grace is a practicing family law attorney and lives in rural Maryland. She loves to hear from her readers and can be reached through her website at graceburrowes.com.